# A WEEK FROM NEVER

**LOOK FOR THESE EXCITING WESTERN SERIES FROM BESTSELLING AUTHORS WILLIAM W. JOHNSTONE AND J.A. JOHNSTONE**

*The Mountain Man*
*Luke Jensen: Bounty Hunter*
*Brannigan's Land*
*The Jensen Brand*
*Smoke Jensen: The Early Years*
*Preacher and MacCallister*
*Fort Misery*
*The Fighting O'Neils*
*Perley Gates*
*MacCoole and Boone*
*Guns of the Vigilantes*
*Shotgun Johnny*
*The Chuckwagon Trail*
*The Jackals*
*The Slash and Pecos Westerns*
*The Texas Moonshiners*
*Stoneface Finnegan Westerns*
*Ben Savage: Saloon Ranger*
*The Buck Trammel Westerns*
*The Death and Texas Westerns*
*The Hunter Buchanon Westerns*
*Will Tanner: Deputy U.S. Marshal*
*Old Cowboys Never Die*
*Go West, Young Man*

**Published by Kensington Publishing Corp.**

# A WEEK FROM NEVER

WILLIAM W. JOHNSTONE
and J.A. JOHNSTONE

PINNACLE BOOKS
Kensington Publishing Corp.
kensingtonbooks.com

PINNACLE BOOKS are published by

Kensington Publishing Corp.
900 Third Avenue
New York, NY 10022



PUBLISHER'S NOTE: Following the death of William W. Johnstone, the Johnstone family is working with a carefully selected writer to organize and complete Mr. Johnstone's outlines and many unfinished manuscripts to create additional novels in all of his series, like The Last Gunfighter, Mountain Man, and Eagles, among others. This novel was inspired by Mr. Johnstone's superb storytelling.

All Kensington titles, imprints, and distributed lines are available at special quantity discounts for bulk purchases for sales promotion, premiums, fundraising, and educational or institutional use.

Special book excerpts or customized printings can also be created to fit specific needs. For details, write or phone the office of the Kensington Sales Manager: Kensington Publishing Corp., 900 Third Avenue, New York, NY 10022. Attn. Sales Department. Phone: 1-800-221-2647.



Kensington Books Hardcover Edition: April 2026
Pinnacle Books Trade Paperback Edition: July 2026

ISBN: 978-0-7860-5226-4

ISBN-13: 978-1-4967-5743-2

10 9 8 7 6 5 4 3 2 1

Printed in the United States of America

The authorized representative in the EU for product safety and compliance
is eucomply OU, Parnu mnt 139b-14, Apt 123
Tallinn, Berlin 11317, hello@eucompliancepartner.com.

# Chapter 1

"You sure your cousin knows what he's talkin' about?" Cleve Carter asked Beaver Branson as he sat on his horse at the top of a low rise beside the stage road between Waco and Austin. "He mighta got his days mixed up, or they mighta changed their schedule, 'cause that stage ought to be gittin' here by now. It ain't but forty miles back to Waco."

"He knows," Timothy "Beaver" Branson answered. Everybody called him Beaver because of an overbite that made his teeth look like those in a beaver's mouth. "He works in the Waco station and he'da told me if they changed the date they're sendin' that money to Austin. They'll show up here anytime now."

"They better, or I'm liable to have a little talk with your cousin," Carter threatened. The five outlaws were waiting on the south bank of a little river about four miles past a stage station. Cleve Carter, the leader of the gang, planned to strike the stagecoach after it crossed the river and was pulling up on the other bank.

"You want me and Calvin to go on back on the other side of the river and get ready?" Hank Welch asked Carter.

"Yeah, go on back over there and get set up in a good spot. Make sure they ain't gonna spot you before they go into the river," Carter said. "Signal me as soon as you get the first sight of 'em."

"Right," Hank replied, and he and Calvin Darcy crossed back over the little river to conceal themselves in the trees that lined the banks. After another quarter of an hour, however, Hank pulled out of the trees and rode out to the edge of the road to take a look back toward Waco. He jerked his horse to a stop when he spotted the stagecoach in the distance. "Son of a . . ." he started. "They're comin', but it ain't just the stage! There's a couple of guards ridin' ahead of it! I'll tell Cleve. We might wanna back off." He rode back down to the water's edge and called out, "Cleve! The stage is comin', but there's two guards leadin' it! Whaddaya wanna do?"

*Damn!* Cleve thought. *I didn't count on that!* "Just two?" he called back.

"That's all I see," Hank answered, "but I expect they might be US Deputy Marshals."

"Well, what did you expect? That's just good news. Means there's a big payday ridin' in that coach for us. Hell, there's five of us. We need to hit 'em hard before they know they're in trouble. We'll knock those two marshals down and I don't think that feller ridin' shotgun will give us any trouble a'tall after that. He'd have to be crazy to. If there's any passengers inside who wanna give us any trouble, they'll get what they deserve, too. Go on back and get ready. Tell Calvin we'll knock those two deputies down for good, first thing. If they try to get behind the stage for cover, you and Calvin can cut 'em down."

"I'll tell him," Hank replied. He wheeled his horse around and loped back to where Calvin was waiting anxiously to hear whether or not the holdup was still on. "We're going ahead with it," he told Calvin. "There's too much money not to."

"What if there's more marshals ridin' inside that stage?" Calvin responded, not sure it was such a good idea if that was a possibility.

"Then I reckon we'll just shoot it to pieces," Hank answered. "Cleve said we had to hit 'em hard and make sure we knock those two marshals outta the saddle. Then him and Beaver and Ed are gonna stop the stage and take care of the driver and his guard. Me and you'll come up behind 'em and take care of anybody tryin' to jump out the doors."

"I swear, I don't know if we oughta go ahead with this job or not," Calvin said hesitantly. "We'll be wanted all over the country if we kill those marshals."

"That wouldn't be near as bad as if you ran out on this job and had Cleve Carter on your trail. We've got a stagecoach comin' at us carryin' enough money to make us rich. Cleve's right, take the money and kill the witnesses. We'll just make sure those two marshals on horses are took care of and the rest will go all right." He hesitated before saying his last thoughts on the matter. "Let me make one thing clear. If you decide you wanna cut and run when the shootin' starts, that shot you feel in your back will be from my rifle."

"Hell, Hank, whaddaya wanna say a thing like that for?" Calvin responded. "You know I ain't the kind to run out on the gang, right?" Hank didn't answer, his eyes glued on the road and the approaching stagecoach. "You ain't never had no call to say something like that about me."

Ignoring the opportunity to apologize for the remark, Hank said, "Get ready. They're just about here." They both got off their horses and tied them in the trees, then gave their rifles a quick check before moving closer to the road to hide behind a clump of bushes. "Wait here till they ride past us. Then I'll run across the road so I can get a better shot at the one on that side of the coach. If they ain't dead after Cleve and them hit 'em, we'll cut 'em down when they try to get behind the stagecoach." He gave Calvin a hard look. "You ready for it?"

"Hell, I told you I'm ready," Calvin insisted. "Don't worry 'bout me."

"Here they come!" Hank warned. "Get ready!" They hunkered down behind the bushes, gripping their rifles while the two deputy marshals rode past them. A few yards behind them, the horses pulling the stage followed the deputies down into the river and started across. "Don't miss!" Hank whispered, and ran across the road as soon as the coach was in the water.

On the other side of the narrow river, the other three outlaws waited, each man waiting for the right moment when the horses were pulling the stage out of the water. Cleve Carter's shot was the signal to fire. The sound of his Winchester when the bullet struck the guard sitting beside the driver had not faded before Ed Moore and Beaver Branson fired. Both riders were struck and both came off their horses. As Carter had figured, the wounded deputies struggled to take cover behind the stagecoach, where they were met with the rapid fire from Hank and Calvin. The massacre of the guard detail was completed as the deputies were hit time after time until both bodies were floating in the shallow water. Waiting terrified, the stage driver sat paralyzed by the sudden attack.

"Pull that stage up here out of the river," Carter ordered, then stood there until the coach rolled up on the road and stopped beside him. "Halt!" he ordered. Eager to see the treasure he knew was inside, he pulled the door open, only to be met with the point-blank blast of a Colt .45 knocking him backward, causing him to land on his back. Wells Fargo detective James Silverton's last act to serve his employer was to die in a hail of gunfire from Beaver Branson and Ed Moore. The money he was protecting was hidden in a canvas sack behind the backrest of Silverton's seat in the coach.

"Damn!" Beaver exclaimed. "That was a dumb-fool thing to do." He grabbed Silverton's coat and pulled him out of the stagecoach to land on the ground beside Carter.

"I wouldn't say that," Hank said. "Hell, he knew he was a dead man, so he decided he weren't gonna go peaceful. He sure surprised ol' Cleve, though, didn't he?"

“There ain’t no money in here,” Ed declared after looking around on the floor and under the seats.

“The hell there ain’t,” Hank responded. “Get outta the way!” He grabbed Ed by the arm and pulled him out of the coach. Like Ed, he didn’t find anything. “They didn’t send a stagecoach down to Austin, guarded by four men, with nothin’ in it,” he said. Then he took hold of the backrest where Silverton had been sitting and gave it a hard yank. When the seatback gave a good four inches, he was motivated to give it a stronger one. This time, the whole back of the seat gave way to reveal a canvas sack holding five fat packs of twenty-dollar bills. The discovery caused an eruption of cheers and inspired Hank to destroy the remaining seatbacks, but there was no more hidden treasure to be found. He looked over at the stagecoach driver, who was shivering under the watchful eye of Calvin Darcy. “Where’d they hide the rest of the money on the stage?”

“There ain’t no m-more m-money anywhere on the stage,” the driver stuttered. “I swear to you, they was just takin’ whatever’s in that sack to a bank in Austin. I ain’t got nothin’ to do with that money. I’m just a stagecoach driver. How ’bout you just let me drive the coach on back to the station? I can’t identify nobody.”

“I reckon you’re right,” Hank said as he drew his pistol again and shot him twice in the chest. He holstered his pistol and said to Beaver, “Like Cleve said, don’t leave no witnesses.”

“What are we gonna do with the stagecoach and them four horses?” Beaver asked.

“Ain’t gonna do nothin’ about ’em,” Hank replied. “Maybe they’ll run off and start their own stage line somewhere.” He laughed at the thought of it.

“You reckon they’ll pull that stage back to that station back yonder?” Beaver asked, still concerned about the matter.

“I don’t give a nickel’s worth what them horses do,” Hank

told him. "Somebody'll come along and find 'em." He went over to check on Cleve then, who was lying on the ground, mortally wounded, with Ed and Calvin kneeling beside him. "Is he gonna make it?"

"Don't look like it," Ed answered him. "He got two right in the chest. He's tryin' to hang on, but I don't think he's gonna make it."

Hank knelt down beside him and took a look at the blood pumping out of the bullet holes. Then he leaned close over him. "How 'bout it, partner, you gonna make it?"

Cleve's eyes flickered open when he recognized the voice. "Hank," he struggled to speak clearly, "always my right-hand man. Don't let 'em leave me. I'm hurt bad, but I'm gonna make it."

"Don't you worry about it," Hank said. "You know I got your back. You just lay right there for a minute or two while we make sure we've got everything we wanna take with us. Then I'll get you ready to ride." He looked at Ed and Calvin then and shook his head as he got up on his feet again. "Let's see what those bodies have on 'em that we might want and catch up those two horses they was ridin'." Then he walked around behind Cleve, drew his six-gun, and put a bullet hole in Cleve's forehead.

When the other three jumped in reaction to the sudden execution, Hank said, "He weren't gonna make it. Might as well put him out of his misery, right?" When nobody answered, he said, "I reckon that makes me boss now, so let's get the hell outta here. One of ya check that stage to see what kinda food they packed with 'em. Probably a lot better'n what we brought with us." He looked at Beaver and asked, "You still sure you know how to get to that hideout you told us about?"

"Yeah, I'm sure," Beaver answered. "It's almost straight west of where we are right now, over in the hills, about a two and a half days ride from here." He hesitated a few moments before asking, "What about Cleve? We gonna dig him a grave?" It seemed the least they could do would be to bury him.

"Nah," Hank responded, "maybe whoever finds him will think he was riding with the stage or got shot by one of 'em. And they can bury him."

It was the middle of a Saturday morning when the stranger riding the unusual-looking horse turned off the river road onto the main street of the remote settlement called Newtown. Located in the Texas Hill Country, Newtown was not on a popular trail to any major cow town or railhead. In spite of that, it was a town that had continued to grow in size because of the availability of cheap land and dependable water for the small farms and ranches. Like every town in Texas, Newtown had suffered financially since the ending of the war that divided the North and South. But it was finally in the healthy stages of recovery that showed a promise of continuing growth.

The stranger entering the town on this particular chilly morning was accustomed to the stares of the people on the street as he rode the length of Front Street. His horse always caught the casual eye. A white Appaloosa with black dots and solid black shoulders and hindquarters, there were not many like it. While the unusual horse caught the eye first, the rider was also an interesting study. A tall man of slender build, he had a sharp face with a nose similar to a hawk's beak and a thin mustache that drooped to his chin. Dressed in black from his flat crowned hat to his soft leather boots, he had the look of a well-oiled killing machine under his buffalo overcoat.

He walked the Appaloosa slowly up the main street, leading a black packhorse behind him, slowing even more when he came to the jail. He pulled his horse to a stop, looking for a sign that would identify the marshal's office, but there was none. So he figured the marshal's office must be in the jail and guided his horse to the hitching rail, where he dismounted.

Finding the door unlocked, he walked in to discover Marshal Cullen Murphy seated at his desk, cleaning an 1860 Henry rifle.

Murphy looked up when he heard the door open. *Either an undertaker or a gunslinger,* he thought. "Can I help you?"

"Are you the marshal?" the stranger asked.

"That's right, I'm Marshal Murphy. What can I do for you?"

"My name is Spade Atkins." He took a moment's pause to judge if there was a spark of recognition of his name. When there was none obvious, he continued. "I've just rode into town. Never been here before and I always like to check in with the marshal or sheriff whenever I hit a town for the first time."

"Why is that?" Murphy asked.

"Because I'm a professional gambler and I like to let the local law enforcement know I play a straight game. I depend on the luck of the cards and that's all. Sometimes I win, sometimes I lose. I've been winning more times than losing, and as long as that continues, I'll keep doin' what I like to do and that's gamble." He stepped in front of the iron stove heating the small office and opened his heavy buffalo coat to permit some of the heat to get inside it.

"There's no law in Newtown against gamblin'," Murphy said when Spade held his coat open. "There is a law against firin' a firearm inside the town limits, though. I notice you're wearin' a fast-draw holster, most likely totin' a revolver with a five-inch barrel."

Spade smiled. "That's strictly for self-protection. Unfortunately, sometimes the people I'm playin' cards with ain't as honest as I am. There ain't no law against protectin' myself, is there?"

"No, I reckon every man oughta have that right, no matter where he is," Murphy answered. "The place where it makes a difference is when one man pokes at another man to make him mad enough to draw his weapon, knowing all the time he's faster. You look like you're pretty handy with that sidearm you're wearin'. You pretty fast with that gun?"

"I get by, I reckon," Spade replied. "I wear it mostly for show, just to make it look like it might be risky to try me."

"How's that been workin' out?" Murphy asked.

Spade smiled again and answered, "Well, I'm still dealin' the cards."

"Well, Mr. Atkins, like I said, it's against the law to shoot a firearm inside the town limits, except in a situation where somebody attacks you and you have to defend yourself. But if somebody calls you out and you accept the challenge, then the law insists that you take it outta town to settle it. That don't happen very often here, but when it does, they usually take it down by the river."

Spade chuckled. "That's good to know. Since I plan to spend a couple of days in your town, maybe you could tell me where I can find a room to rent. I haven't gone up the whole street yet, but I didn't see a hotel so far."

"We don't have a hotel in town yet, but there are a couple of places to rent a room, depending on which you prefer. A lady named Pearl Johnson runs a rooming house back toward the south end of the street. You passed it if you came up from the river road. You can rent a room there for the night, if you're looking for a nice quiet place. If you wanna stay close to the gamblin', there's a couple of saloons in town that rent rooms upstairs. They're the two biggest. Bradshaw's Saloon is also the best place to eat. They've got a dinin' room built on the back of the saloon called Irene's Café. It's run by a respectable lady named Irene Floyd. You can also rent a room upstairs. The other saloon where you can get a room is Pratt's Saloon. You can pay for the companionship of one of Pratt's saloon girls, if you're of a mind to. Bradshaw's Saloon doesn't offer that."

"That café you said was in the back of the saloon, do they serve three meals a day?"

"That's right," Murphy replied. "It's a regular café. They'll be openin' up for dinner at noon."

"Good, 'cause I didn't have anything left for breakfast this mornin' but a piece of beef jerky. This town is farther from Waco than I thought it was," Spade remarked. "I think you've told me all I need to know, Marshal, and I appreciate it. I can't think of but one more place I need to stop at."

"The stables?" Murphy guessed. When Spade smiled and nodded, Murphy said, "North end of the street." He got up from the desk then. "I'll walk out with you." He walked to the door and held it open for Spade.

*Damn!* Spade thought when Murphy stood up, surprised by the size of the man. *I won't have to worry about taking dead aim. It'd be hard to miss him.* He walked out the door and Murphy followed him, unaware that he was already being sized up by the stranger.

"That's a mighty fine-lookin' horse you're riding, Mr. Atkins." Murphy couldn't help but admire the black-and-white Appaloosa. "That's one of those Palouse horses bred by the Nez Perce Indians, ain't it?"

"That's a fact," Spade answered. "I got him from a man who bought the horse directly from a Nez Perce breeder. I inherited him when that man passed away after a spell of heart trouble." He elected not to go into further detail, but he could have told Murphy the man's heart trouble was brought on by the bullet in his chest. It was a shame. The man had never really been seriously ill a day in his life. That was before the little dispute at the card table that resulted in a face-off between the two former friends.

"Well, you can depend on Paul Mathers to take good care of the horse," Murphy told him. "Paul's the owner of the stable. And you can't see it from here, but it's right at the end of Front Street. If you had come into town from the north, the stable would have been the first thing you saw."

"Much obliged, Marshal, 'preciate the help," Spade said as he stood by his horse, preparing to step up into the saddle. He paused for a short moment to make a quick evaluation of Murphy's potential as a possible opponent in a quick-draw competition. Unlike most of the professional fast guns, himself included, the marshal was not the typical willowy gunslinger whose hand hung naturally to fall on his gun handle. Murphy was tall and brawny, with wide shoulders over a muscular chest. He looked to be more suited to steer wrestling. Spade liked his chances in a face-off against the marshal. He stepped up into the saddle and turned the Appaloosa away from the rail to continue his slow walk up the street to let the people he passed admire his horse. The remote little town may not have heard of Spade Atkins before, but they would be familiar with the name when he left. That much he was sure of.

Cullen Murphy stood outside a few minutes to watch the stranger as he rode up Front Street. He wondered if Spade Atkins was going to cause as much trouble as he looked capable of. This, in spite of his visit to the jail to announce his peaceful intentions. Newtown was not a town big enough to cause a professional gambler to ride all the way from Waco. And it was not on the way to one that was big enough, either.

Murphy had to wonder about the real reason Spade Atkins showed up in Newtown. He turned around and went back into the office to finish cleaning his rifle.

# CHAPTER 2

A little before noon, Murphy locked the office door and walked up to Bradshaw's Saloon. There was a path down the side of Bradshaw's that led to an outside entrance to Irene's Café. It was for those customers who preferred not to go through the saloon. Murphy usually went through the saloon when he went to Irene's. It was a Saturday, but still a little early for the saloon to get really busy. When he walked up to the bar, Pete Brice, the bartender, greeted him. "Cullen, pour you a drink?"

"No, thanks, Pete. I'm just waitin' for the women to open up for dinner," Murphy responded, referring to Irene and her two daughters, who ran the dining room.

"Say, thought you oughta know a feller came in here a little while ago and rented one of the rooms upstairs. Said he was gonna be in town for a couple of days and he likes to play cards. Wanted to know if there was any regular card games here he might could get in on. I told him there was always a few fellers that liked to try their luck, but they weren't usually high-stakes games. He said he didn't care if it was for matchsticks or pennies, he just likes to play cards."

Murphy waited until Pete finished, then said, "He stopped in my office as soon as he hit town this morning to let me know he was a professional gambler—and the only one that was honest."

"Well, what in the world is he doin' in Newtown?" Pete wondered.

"I was askin' myself the same thing," Murphy said. "Might be he's lookin' for somebody. Have you seen any other strangers in the last couple of days?"

Pete shook his head.

"Me neither," Murphy commented. "Can't arrest him for lookin' suspicious. Reckon we're just gonna have to wait and see what he's up to. Might be he's what he says he is, just somebody who likes to play cards." He took out his pocket watch and compared it to the clock on the wall behind the bar. "Wonder what's holdin' up dinner?" He nodded toward the door at the back of the barroom that was the entrance to Irene's Café. Irene's youngest daughter, Bonnie, usually flipped the sign to the OPEN side at noon on the dot. Now, according to his watch and the wall clock, Bonnie was over fifteen minutes late. "Somebody musta dropped a dish and they're havin' to clean it up off the floor before they can put it on anybody's plate," Murphy joked. The smile froze on his face in the next second when he heard the scream.

He didn't take any time to wonder as he rushed to the café entrance. Inside the dining room, he found a stranger holding a gun on another stranger, who was unarmed. Bonnie Floyd, Irene's younger daughter, was standing close by, both hands over her mouth. Her mother and older sister, Ginger, were both standing in the kitchen door, obviously in distress.

Murphy drew his six-gun and commanded, "Holster that weapon unless you want a shot in the back."

The gunman turned halfway around to see who was issuing the demand. Seeing the formidable figure of the town marshal, the gunman decided not to risk it. He wisely holstered his weapon. Since the two men were both strangers to him, Murphy ordered them both to sit down. Then he asked Bonnie to tell him what happened.

She pointed to the gunman and exclaimed, "When I came to the table to ask him what he wanted to drink, he grabbed me and pulled me down on his lap. When I told him to let go of me, he wouldn't do it." She pointed to the young man at the other table and said, "He came to help me get away from him," she referred again to the man who had grabbed her. "But he jumped up and drew his gun and said he was gonna shoot him." She shook her head, still shaken by the sudden turn of events. "I guess that was when I screamed."

Murphy glanced at the unarmed young man, now sitting patiently at his table. Satisfied that he was no threat, the marshal turned his attention to the one who had drawn his gun. "Don't remember ever havin' seen you in town before."

"I ain't ever been in this damn town before," he replied, "and I gotta admit, I wouldn'ta missed much if I'd rode around it."

"Well, I'm right sorry to hear we disappointed you, but you were headin' for a chance to see how you like the inside of our jail and you still might be. Pullin' a gun and threatenin' to shoot somebody will land you in jail in this town. Since you obviously didn't know any better, I'm willin' to cut you some slack. In the first place, you're in the wrong eatin' place. This dinin' room is for respectable folks. You need to go on down to Pratt's Saloon to get something to eat. It ain't as good as what you'd get here, but none of the other saloons serve any food. You can have a saloon gal sit in your lap while you eat at Pratt's, though. So, what's your choice, get on down to Pratt's, or spend the night in the jailhouse?"

"I'll leave," he said, and got to his feet. Under Murphy's watchful eye, he headed for the outside door, pausing only briefly when he walked past the man he pulled his gun on. "You're lucky I didn't put a hole in your head," he murmured low.

Hearing him, Murphy said, "The same gun laws apply in Pratt's and every other saloon in town, so keep that six-gun in the holster till you're outta town." He followed him out the back door and watched him until he got on his horse and rode the path back to the street.

When he went back inside the dining room, he found both of Irene's daughters at the young man's table expressing their thanks for his coming to Bonnie's defense. Murphy paused to take a closer look at the stranger. His dress was that of a typical cowhand and he looked as if he was overwhelmed with the attention he was getting from Ginger and Bonnie.

"Mind if I sit down with you?" Murphy asked.

"No, sir, Marshal Murphy," the young cowhand replied.

Murphy was pretty sure why he had stepped into a confrontation with the man he had just sent on his way, but he wanted to hear him explain. "What's your name?" he asked.

"Will Pickens," the young man replied.

"Who do you ride for?" Murphy asked.

"Well, sir, nobody right now. I hired on to drive a herd up to Abilene in Kansas for the Rocking-J. But I was one of the newer hires, so I wasn't kept on the payroll after we got back. So I've been ridin' the grub line, lookin' for some work, but I ain't had much luck. I decided to spend some of the last of my money on a good meal."

"How'd you happen to get in it with that fellow who just left?" Murphy asked. "You ain't even wearin' a gun."

"I left my gun outside with my horse," Will said. "I figured the folks who own this place would feel better if I left it outside. But it ain't right to treat a lady like he treated that young girl, so I had to try to do something to help her."

"So now you're tryin' to hire on at another ranch," Murphy declared.

"Yes, sir. I'm pretty near broke. But there ain't much chance of hirin' on at any ranch this time of year. I reckon I'm lookin' for any kind of work that'll keep me from starvin' this winter."

"How'd you like to work for me at the jail?" Murphy asked.

Will looked totally surprised, so Murphy quickly explained.

"I'm not talking about law enforcement. I'm lookin' for somebody to take care of the chores in the jailhouse. Cleanin' up the cells, keepin' water buckets filled and chamber pots emptied, just whatever needs takin' care of. I'd pay you thirty dollars a month, same as you'd make herdin' cattle. You get your meals provided right here, three times a day, and you'd have a place to sleep in the back of the jail, and you can keep your horse at the stable. Whaddaya think? Is that too much like a janitor's job for you?"

"No, sir! I'll do most anything, long as it ain't against the law. I appreciate the chance. I'll take the job."

"Well, let's eat some dinner and we'll go over to the jail and you can look it over. And if you still want the job, it's yours," Murphy said. When he took the job as marshal, part of the agreement called for a man to work in the jail. He told the mayor he'd enforce the law and try to protect the citizens, but he wasn't going to take on all the little chores of maintaining a jailhouse. The mayor agreed and assured him that the council had voted to pay for an assistant. Up until now, he hadn't seen any prospects he was sure he could stand for any length of time. But Will Pickens impressed him as the right kind of man when he came to Bonnie's defense, so he decided to give him a chance.

Irene Floyd came from the kitchen with two plates piled high with food and again expressed her appreciation to the young cowhand for coming to her daughter's aid. "And there'll be no charge for your dinner," she said.

"That's mighty kind of you, ma'am," Will replied, "but I've got enough to pay for it."

"I wouldn't think of charging you after you stood ready to protect my daughter," Irene insisted. "I hope you enjoy it."

Calmly watching the incident unfold, another stranger at a table on the other side of the dining room found the altercation interesting. He casually sipped his coffee as he watched the marshal's response to the gunman's attempt to have his way with the young girl. With no regard for the young girl's honor or innocence, he was more interested in observing the marshal's moves. And he had to admit that the marshal showed no signs of the clumsiness oftentimes associated with big, muscular men. It pleased him to notice, however, that the marshal wore his handgun rather high up on the hip, more like a railroad lineman wore his wire cutters. Spade Atkins had seen quite a few fast guns, some he had faced, himself. All of them wore their pistols lower on the hip and in fast-draw holsters. If this small-town marshal actually did have a reputation as a fast gun, it must have been against young losers like the one he just chased out of the dining room with nothing more than a scolding. He smiled to himself and took another sip of coffee. *I think I'm gonna enjoy myself,* he thought.

Murphy nodded to the stranger who had visited the jail that morning and wondered how he happened to be there before Bonnie hung the OPEN sign. *She must have flipped the sign on the outside entrance on time,* he thought.

They finished up their dinner and walked down the street to the jail and took a quick tour of the building. "Where you from, Will?" Murphy asked as he walked him through the cell room to show him where the prisoners were kept.

"Mississippi," Will answered.

"Mississippi?" Murphy repeated. "How'd you end up out here in Texas Hill Country?"

"Tell you the truth, Marshal Murphy, I ain't really sure . . ."

"You don't have to call me Marshal. My name's Cullen Murphy and I ain't quite old enough to be your daddy. All right?"

"Yes, sir, Murphy," Will answered respectfully. "I ain't really sure how I ended up here. I know there wasn't anything working for me in Mississippi, so I reckon I started driftin', tryin' to find something I could make a livin' at. I was in the army for the last two years of the war. A friend I met in the army was from Texas and he talked me into comin' out here to work cattle. We hired on at the Rocking-J, workin' for Mr. Jacobson. That's where my friend worked before he went into the army."

"You said Jacobson cut you loose after the cattle drive. Did he keep your friend on at the ranch?" Murphy asked. He knew Lionel Jacobson to be a fair man, and since Will said his friend rode for the Rocking-J before he went into the army, he figured Jacobson would have kept him.

"No, sir," Will answered, "Fred—that was my friend's name—he bucked off a horse on the drive up to Abilene. He never made it to Kansas. I came back to Texas with 'em, thinkin' I'd stick with 'em, since Fred didn't make it back. But Jim King—the foreman—gave me a month's pay and cut me loose. So I thought that was pretty decent of 'em—the month's pay, I mean."

"Well, you can work with me for a while and see how you like Newtown," Murphy said. "Keepin' the place clean is part of your job. Most of the time, you'll just be keepin' the office open while I'm out walkin' the town. If you're of a mind to, you can take a little time to sharpen up on your shootin' skills, just in case of emergencies." He didn't suggest it, but he was thinking about the future possibilities. He had to admit that one of the reasons he offered him the job was the fact that the young man reminded him of Bert Walker, who was once the marshal of Newtown. "How old are you, Will?"

"I'm nineteen," Will replied.

That was pretty close to what Murphy might have guessed. He was a tall, strong-looking young man and might have the makings of a good deputy sheriff in about a year's time. And Murphy had a feeling Newtown was going to need a deputy.

Thoughts of Bert Walker triggered another reminder, it was time to get new shoes on his horse. Bert had a blacksmith shop before he was talked into the job as marshal. *And that's where he should have stayed,* Murphy thought, always convinced that he was as much to blame for Bert taking the marshal's job as Eliot Baxter and Tyson Bradshaw, the co-leaders of the town council. They offered him the job, but it was Murphy who taught him how to use his sidearm effectively. *Hell, we don't write the book,* he thought. *We just play our parts.*

"Whaddaya think?" Murphy asked. "You wanna give it a try?"

"Yes, sir," Will answered without hesitation. "I'll try it."

"Fair enough," Murphy responded. "You can get your saddlebags and stuff off your horse and put it in that back room where the cot is and I'll walk up to the stable with you to leave your horse."

"Does that come out of my thirty dollars?" Will asked.

"Nope," Murphy assured him. "The city of Newtown pays for your feed and your horse's feed." He waited while Will retrieved his belongings and left them in his room; then he locked the office and they walked up to the stables, leading Will's chestnut gelding.

"Howdy, Cullen," Paul Mathers greeted him when he and Will approached the open barn door. "You lookin' to board that horse?"

"Paul, this is Will Pickens," Murphy answered. "He's gonna be workin' with me at the jail. You'll be takin' care of his horse and just put it on the town's bill. Will, this is Paul Mathers. He'll take good care of your horse for you."

"Pleased to meet you, Mr. Mathers," Will said politely.

"Will," Mathers replied, acknowledging with a nod of his head. "We'll just put your saddle in with Cullen's," he said while Will pulled it off the horse.

"I'm gonna take my horse to the blacksmith," Murphy said to Mathers. "He needs shoeing."

So when they took Will's saddle and tack back to the stall, Murphy picked up his bridle. Nosy came at once to the corral gate when he saw Murphy approaching. Murphy put the bridle on the big bay gelding and led him out the gate. Then they walked next door to the blacksmith shop, where Murphy introduced Will to Joel Trout.

Joel Trout, a large, powerful-looking man with arms the size of hams, wore a heavy black beard that covered his face from his upper lip down to his neck, while not a hair grew above his ears. Relatively new in town himself, Trout stepped away from his forge when he saw the town marshal leading his horse toward him. "Marshal Murphy," he called out, "what can I do for you?"

"I want you to meet Will Pickens," Murphy said. "He'll be working with me in the marshal's office." Looking back at Will, Murphy said, "Joel's almost as new in town as you are. Been about six months, ain't it, Joel?"

"Six and a half months," Trout answered. "Pleased to meet you, Will." He looked back at Murphy and asked, "That's your horse, ain't it?"

"Yep. Have you got time to shoe him this afternoon? If not, I can bring him back in the mornin'."

"No problem a'tall," Trout answered. "Any trouble with the ones he's wearin'?"

"Nope, just general wear," Murphy said. "I'll pick him up before you go to supper. Come on, Will. I expect I better introduce you to the man who okays your hirin'." When they left the blacksmith, Murphy commented that the last time Trout shod his horse, he had to ride twenty miles to get it done. "He had his shop in the little settlement they named San Saba, down the river. But it ain't much of a town. I told him how much Newtown was growin' and that he oughta take a look at it, since there wasn't enough business there in San Saba for his shop. He liked what he saw and moved over here the next week. Took over the old blacksmith shop where Bert Walker started before he went into the law enforcement business."

Leaving the blacksmith shop, they went directly to the Newtown General Store. The owner, Eliot Baxter, was standing by the front door when they walked in the store. "Cullen," Baxter acknowledged.

"Mr. Baxter," Murphy returned. "I finally hired that man we talked about to help me at the jail. So I brought him by to make it official. This is Will Pickens, lately of the Rocking-J Ranch. You can add him to the city payroll today. I've already put him to work."

"Welcome to our little family," Baxter said with an attempt to sound sincerely happy to hear the news. Murphy was sure Baxter was hoping that he would never find a candidate for the job. "I expect the marshal told you the job pays thirty dollars a month."

"Yes, sir, he did," Will answered, "and I appreciate the opportunity."

Baxter was about to say more, but was interrupted by the sound of a gunshot up the street. Murphy went out the door immediately, but there was only the one shot. "Sounded like it might have come from Pratt's," he said. "I'd best check it out."

He didn't wait for Will and headed up the street at a trot. Will followed him, while Baxter stood in the doorway and watched.

# CHAPTER 3

Murphy was halfway to the front door of Pratt's Saloon when the second shot rang out, telling him that the shooting definitely had come from there. He didn't have to guess who was causing the trouble. *I should have thrown him in jail,* he thought as he stopped at the door to take a look inside to see what he might be charging into. He had figured that Francine or Hazel would give the man the attention he had obviously demanded from Bonnie Floyd. *Reckon I was wrong,* he thought, and pushed on through the batwing doors. He found the troublemaker standing in the middle of the barroom, halfway between the bar and the tables along the opposite wall. His six-gun was leveled on Albert Smith, the bartender. Beyond Albert, the large mirror, which ran the length of the bar on the wall behind him, had one section shattered on one side of him and a round hole on the other side. *That accounts for the two gunshots,* Murphy thought.

The stranger turned to the side when he read the reaction in Albert's face when the bartender saw Murphy come in the door. "Well, well," he gloated when he saw Murphy, "I thought you might show up when you heard them shots. That gun ain't much good to you in your holster, is it? How good are you with it? Faster than I can squeeze this trigger? Maybe you'd like it better if I turned my back to you, like you had me in the dinin' room. It's a little different when a man's lookin' right at you, ain't it?" He continued to stand there, his gun cocked and hanging straight down, confident in the knowledge that all he had to do was raise his arm and squeeze the trigger when Murphy reached for his weapon.

*Yeah, I'd like to* know *if you're fast enough, myself,* Spade Atkins thought. He couldn't help but be amused by the coincidence that found him sitting in a card game in Pratt's Saloon when he hadn't found one at Bradshaw's. Now the game was at a temporary halt, due to the antics of a half-drunk fool, as everybody waited to see what was going to happen. Spade thought about calling the fool's hand for interrupting his card game, but he was waiting for bigger game. And he didn't want to demonstrate his lightning speed beforehand. He almost chuckled when one of the card players whispered that the fool was about to get a taste of Murphy's Law.

Murphy, however, gave no response to the man's chiding, made no move toward his gun, and just kept walking slowly toward him. Murphy's eyes were locked onto the smirking man's face, reading his obvious emotions. He was certain the man felt that he had all the advantage he needed with his gun already drawn and cocked. So he stood there, his six-gun hanging by his side, waiting for Murphy to reach for his gun. That way, all witnesses would have to say that Murphy drew his weapon, leaving the stranger no choice but to raise his weapon and fire. A dead quiet fell over the barroom as Murphy approached to within twenty feet of the sneering man, but did not stop walking toward him. At ten feet, the sneer on the stranger's face turned to one of uncertainty and the six-gun began to feel heavy in his hand and he tightened his grip. When it was plain that Murphy was going to walk right over to him, he was forced to take a step backward to still have room to raise his weapon, which he did, now in a panic.

Instead of reaching for his own gun, Murphy caught the stranger's hand and pulled the weapon straight up under the man's chin. With his other hand, the man tried to push Murphy back, but found he was powerfully overmatched as Murphy walked him backward until he was stopped by the bar, where Murphy gave him a choice. "You're so set on killin' somebody, go ahead, pull the trigger." His hand immediately relaxed his grip on the weapon and Murphy snatched it out of his hand. "Let's take a little walk now."

With one hand on the back of his would-be killer's coat collar, Murphy walked him out of the saloon. As he was going out the door, he took his hand off his prisoner's collar and poked him in the back with the captured pistol just long enough to reach into his pocket. He pulled his office key out and tossed it to Will Pickens, who was as amazed as everyone else in the saloon. "Here, Will, unlock the office door for us."

"Yes, sir," Will replied as he caught the key. Then he increased his pace and went ahead to open the door and held it open for Murphy and his prisoner. He held the key out for Murphy when he walked in, but was told to keep it.

"I'll get the other one out of the desk drawer," Murphy said. Then he told his prisoner to take off his gun belt and empty his pockets. "Turn 'em inside out," he directed, and the prisoner did as he was told. "Now, I reckon we're gonna need your name."

"Abraham Lincoln," the prisoner snarled.

"Right," Murphy said patiently. "Good choice, but that name's already taken, so I'll just have to give you another one until I find out the real one. We'll just call you Dung. You like that? Kinda fits, don't it? You got a horse tied up back there at Pratt's, Dung? We'll pick it up and take it to the stable while you're visitin' us."

While the marshal was getting his prisoner settled in the first cell in the cell room, the discussion over Murphy's most recent arrest was lively and noisy back at Pratt's Saloon. "That ol' boy got a quick introduction to Murphy's Law," Elmo Dillon called out to Albert Smith, "didn't he?" The remark brought on a chorus of chuckles.

Murphy's arrest of the drunk impressed Spade Atkins and caused him to wonder. Why the hell didn't Murphy just whip his gun out and shoot the man? That's what he would have done, had he been in Murphy's place. Was it because Murphy wasn't fast enough to accomplish it? To Spade, it was evidence that the brawny lawman wasn't sure if he was or not. And that told him that Murphy was going to be the next notch on his gun butt. His thoughts were interrupted when a man sitting across the table from him asked, "You gonna call or not?"

"Sorry," Spade said, "my mind wandered off for a second. I'll see it and raise it a dollar."

"You musta got somethin' with them two cards you drew," Everett Sims, who was sitting to his immediate left, said.

"Could be," Spade replied. "Just remember, I ain't the one dealin' the cards this hand when you read 'em and weep. But it's gonna cost you a dollar to see this hand you dealt me. So, what are you gonna do?"

"I think you're bluffin', but I ain't got nothin' to call you with," Everett said, and tossed his cards in. The other three players tossed theirs in as well, so Spade tossed his on the pile face down, too, and raked the pot over. "Let's see what you had," Everett said. He reached for the cards, but Spade was quicker and slapped his hand down over his cards.

"Uh-uh," he cautioned. "The price is another dollar if you wanna see my hand."

"Now I know you were bluffin'," Everett said.

"You mean you *think* I was bluffin'," Spade corrected him. "You gotta call to see my hand." He nodded to Elmo, whose turn it was, and said, "Deal 'em and see if you can come up with some better cards for Mr. Sims."

"Mr. Sims has lost enough for one day," Everett said. "I'd

best get back to the post office before my boss finds out what I'm really doing when I take early supper."

"Hell," Elmo said, "Jim Anderson knows where you take early supper. You might as well play a couple more hands."

"I think I've had enough," Everett declared. "We don't usually play a dollar limit on a raise. Fifty cents is our usual limit." He didn't express it, but he had a feeling his bad luck might be a result of playing cards with a professional gambler. And Spade Atkins did not attempt to hide that fact. To the contrary, he announced it when he asked if he could join their poker game, along with a claim that he had checked in with the marshal when he first hit town. Everett took his leave then and met the town marshal looking at the three horses tied in front of the saloon when he walked out. "You lookin' for that fellow's horse?" he asked when he saw what Murphy was doing. "I think it's the gray, 'cause it was the only one tied up at the rail when I came in and that fellow was already in the saloon when I went in."

"I 'preciate it," Murphy said. "I'll go inside and make sure."

He walked inside the saloon to find business as usual once again. The card game was still going and Mack Pratt, the owner, was at one end of the bar talking to Albert. He raised his hand and motioned to Murphy to join them. "Albert and I were just talking about the job that drunk did on the mirror. I appreciate the fact that you took that damn fool outta here without firing any more shots. I'm halfway thinking there ain't no use in replacing those mirrors on that wall back of the bar."

"I doubt it would affect the sale of whiskey one way or the other," Murphy commented.

"That's the same thing Albert said," Pratt replied. "That settles it then. Albert, take the one with the bullet hole in it off the wall, too, and pour Murphy a drink of whiskey."

"Thanks just the same," Murphy said, "but I'll pass on that till after supper. I just came in to check on that fellow's horse and to talk to Hazel or Francine for a minute."

"Francine's upstairs entertaining one of the citizens of our fair city," Pratt said. "But Hazel's over there telling Elmo how to play his hand."

"Is Elmo ahead or behind in the game?" Murphy asked.

"I don't know for sure, but he doesn't act like a winner," Albert answered.

"Then I reckon he won't mind if I borrow her for a couple of minutes," Murphy said. He walked across the room and tapped her on the shoulder. She turned and a genuine smile spread across her wide face when she saw who it was. "Can I talk to you for a second?" he asked.

" 'Course you can, darlin'. I've been wonderin' if you was ever goin' to. A man your age is likely to turn cross-eyed if he don't pay attention to Mother Nature's calls. Then how you gonna aim that Henry rifle you're always totin' around? I'm glad you finally got enough beans in your belly to come talk to me. I know you're mighty friendly with them two little Floyd girls, but by the time they're old enough to be real women, you'll be too old to cut the mustard."

When she paused to take a breath, he said, "I just want to ask you a question. All right?"

"Ask away," she replied. "The answer's yes."

"Did you spend any time entertainin' that drunk I took outta here a little while ago?" he asked.

She looked disappointed by the nature of his question, but answered him honestly. "Yeah, he spent a little time with both of us, Francine and me."

"Did he mention his name?"

She shrugged indifferently, not particularly interested. "He said his name was Ed Moore," she replied.

"Ed Moore," Murphy repeated. "Did he say where he came here from, or where he was headin'?"

"I don't think he knew where he was goin'," she said. "I don't think he really gave a damn where he was goin', either." She shrugged and remarked that he had some cash on him, but he didn't say much about where he had been, or where he was going. Then she remembered something he had asked. "He asked me if a fellow named Beaver Branson had come through Newtown. I remember that name." She cackled in laughter when she repeated it.

"Has he ever come through town?" Murphy asked.

"Not that I know of," she replied. "If he has, he ain't come in here since I started working."

"Beaver Branson," Murphy repeated. "You're right. That's an easy one to remember, all right. I 'preciate the information. I'll let you get back to the poker game now."

"I ain't in no hurry to get back to that game," she declared. "The way he keeps playin' his cards, he ain't gonna have no money left to buy me a drink, let alone go upstairs for a visit."

"You might be right. I'd better let you get back before that gambler cleans him out. Thank you for the information, Hazel. I 'preciate it. I best get back to the jail. I'm breakin' in a new man to help me and he might be a little nervous by himself with a prisoner in the cell room."

"One of these days, you're liable to get an itch somewhere you can't reach. Come on back here and I'll scratch it for you."

"I expect you could, Hazel," he said with a smile. Then he tipped his hat and headed for the door.

Had he chosen to, he might have explained to her his reason for never seeking the services of a prostitute. Being a single man with no known relationship with an unmarried young woman, it would be expected that he might have the need for the compassion of an understanding saloon gal. It never occurred to him why he felt the way he did about the women who chose or were forced into Hazel's line of work. The reason was because his mother was a prostitute and he was raised in her world of saloons and dance halls. He never thought of the women he knew when he was a child as evil or lost women. They were just women doing what they had to do to survive.

When his mother was beaten to death by a drunken cowhand in Fort Worth, Murphy was just ten years old. The owner of the saloon sent for the town marshal when a gunshot was heard in his mother's room. The marshal found the cowhand with a bullet hole in his head, but no sign of the boy. The marshal ruled it a murder-suicide. The ten-year-old boy was unofficially adopted by the other prostitutes and worked for the saloon owner for several years until a cattle rancher named John Tate offered him a job. And that's where he developed a fondness for working with horses.

When he got back to the jailhouse, Murphy found Will sitting on a stool next to the desk, waiting for his return. He got to his feet when Murphy walked into the office. "It's all right if you sit in the desk chair when I'm not here," Murphy told him. "Ain't nothin' formal about our workin' conditions, just as long as you remember you're workin' for me and not the other way around." He dropped the prisoner's saddlebags on the desk.

"Yes, sir, Marshal Murphy," Will replied.

"Cullen," he corrected him.

"Yes, sir, Cullen," Will replied.

Murphy shook his head. "Maybe in time . . ." He grinned. "You have any problems with Mr. Dung while I was gone?"

"No, sir. He was doin' a lot of talkin' to himself, but I just closed the door to the cells."

"Let's take a look at what he's carrying in his saddlebags," Murphy said, and opened one side. "He sure ain't totin' much to live on," he muttered. Then he looked in the other side. "Uh-oh," he muttered. "Maybe he was figurin' on resupplyin' here in Newtown. Here, Will, help me count this." He emptied a canvas sack on the desk and four bundles of twenty-dollar bills fell out. "Wells Fargo," Murphy read out loud from the sack. "He robbed a stagecoach or a train somewhere." He picked up one of the bundles and ran his thumb across the end, fanning the bills. "It don't take but five bills to make a hundred dollars. I'll bet there's five thousand dollars in each one of those bundles. I'd better look through my wanted notices and see if we've got any on a train or stagecoach robbery. Maybe Mr. Dung can help us out."

He took the bundle of bills, which he had been estimating the amount of, and went into the cell room. Will, still in a state of disbelief, followed along. "Are you nice and comfortable, Mr. Dung?" he asked.

"Go to hell," his prisoner replied.

"It's the name you ain't happy with, ain't it?" Murphy replied. "I don't blame you. We'll think of another name for ya. How 'bout Ed Moore? We ain't used that name for a prisoner yet. Does that suit you better? Will, here, thought that one up for you, so we'll stick with that one. We thought about callin' you Beaver Branson, but Will said that don't fit at all."

Will was completely lost, but tried not to show it.

But Ed Moore, on the other hand, became immediately alert.

"We couldn't decide where you got all this money," Murphy continued. "One of us thinks it came from a bank robbery. The other one says it's from a stage holdup. Which one is right?"

"I found that money, hid in an old stump, fair and square," Moore claimed. "I don't know nothin' about no train holdup. Ain't nobody got no claim to it but me."

"Well, now, ain't you the lucky one?" Murphy went on. "What was you fixin' to do next, try to return it to Wells Fargo?"

"Yeah, that's right. That's what I was gonna do," Moore claimed, after a moment of hesitation.

"Well, you sure picked a strange part of the country to look for a Wells Fargo office. There ain't no train tracks in San Saba County anywhere. There ain't but one stagecoach that comes to Newtown to bring the mail and that's just twice a month. But at least you found a safe place to keep the money until we find out where it came from. Is this all the money you found, or does this fellow, Beaver Branson, have the other half?"

"I don't know no Beaver Branson," Moore declared. "That money in my saddlebag is all the money I found. That's all I know about."

"I believe you," Murphy said. "You were lucky to find a place to keep it safe until we can find out where it belongs."

"So now that you know I didn't steal it, you can let me outta here, right?"

"I'm afraid not, Ed." Murphy shook his head sadly. "There's still this little matter of drunk and disorderly conduct, drawin' a firearm and firin' it inside the city limits, and destroyin' two fancy mirrors in Pratt's Saloon. So it looks like you're gonna be a guest of the Newtown City Jail for a spell."

"There's plenty of money you got outta my saddlebags to pay for those two mirrors. Just buy him some new ones."

"You ain't thinkin' straight, Ed," Murphy replied. "Wells Fargo didn't break those mirrors. You broke the mirrors. Wouldn't be right to make them pay for 'em."

"How long are you gonna keep me in here?"

"That's hard to say," Murphy answered him. "We have to wait till a circuit judge can get over here to take you to trial."

"Take me to trial for what?" Moore asked. "I done told you I found the money. There ain't no law against findin' stolen money."

"I understand what you're tryin' to say, but you're leavin' out the one word that makes all the difference—*with*. You were found *with* the stolen money. That makes a difference. Your mistake was not bringin' that money to me as soon as you hit town. You'da most likely gotten a reward for turnin' it in."

Ed thought about that for a moment before proposing a

deal. "You've got the money I found. So, why can't we say I turned it in to you? And we can split the reward. Then I'll get outta town and no harm done. Whaddaya say?"

"That would be one way to handle it, but if I did that, Will would most likely lock me in the cell with you. If we're lucky, we might find out when a judge will be here in the next few days. So make yourself comfortable. It won't be long before suppertime and we'll bring you a nice meal from the café. That'll be your reward for turnin' the money in."

Murphy and Will walked back into the office and closed the cell room door behind them. As soon as they were out of earshot of the prisoner, Will asked a question. "How long do you think he'll be in jail?"

"A lot longer than we wanna fool with him, unless we're lucky," Murphy told him. "The town council won't like feedin' him three meals a day for more than two or three days. So we've gotta come up with some evidence that puts him in on the actual robbery. I haven't even looked at the pack of notices and wanted papers that came in the mail yesterday." He opened the bottom drawer of his desk and pulled out a thick packet of papers and laid it on the desk. Then he took what he estimated to be half of the stack and dropped it on the desk in front of Will. "We might as well look through these notices to see if there's anything about a Wells Fargo holdup." Will pulled the stool up to the desk and the two of them started going through the wanted posters and the robbery notices.

"This might be something," Will remarked. He handed the paper to Murphy. "It came from the US Marshal's Office in Austin."

Murphy read the report, which referred to the ambush of a special Wells Fargo stagecoach between Austin and Waco by a gang of outlaws. The stagecoach was escorted by two US Deputy Marshals and a Wells Fargo detective. All three were killed, as well as the driver and an additional guard riding shotgun. One of the outlaws was killed. The coach was carrying twenty-five thousand dollars to a bank in Austin.

Murphy looked up from the report and said, "Twenty-five thousand, our guest in there has four packs of bills. I'll bet there is five thousand in a pack and they must have divided up one pack so each one of 'em had some money right away, because our prisoner had well over a thousand dollars of pocket money. I reckon they thought it best to hide the rest of it for a while." He chuckled and said, "That didn't work out too well for 'em, did it?"

"I'm wonderin' where the other men who robbed that stagecoach are," Will said.

"I wonder how many there are, and I expect they're wonderin' where Ed Moore is," Murphy replied. "That reminds me, it's gettin' along toward suppertime and we'll have to feed him tonight." He was thinking about the Wells Fargo money he now had possession of and what he should do with it. A good safe would be handy, but he didn't have one. Both Eliot Baxter and Tyson Bradshaw had safes. It might be a good idea to let one of them hold the money, he thought. With no telegraph, it would be quite a while before he could correspond with the US Marshal or Wells Fargo. The closest telegraph was a full day's ride from Newtown. Another thing to think about was the fact that Ed Moore showed up in Newtown. Was that just wild happenstance? Or were the other outlaws close at hand? Maybe like several outlaw gangs before them, they knew about that hideout northwest of town that he had never gotten around to burning down. He had intended to burn it to the ground after he put Rafer Polk's gang out of business. But Baxter and Bradshaw were so against his being out of town long enough to go up in the hills to destroy a cabin and barn that he let it slide.

"Let's lock this place up and go to supper," Murphy said. For want of a better place to keep it, he put the Wells Fargo money in the back cell, under the bunk. Then he locked the cell room door and the office door. "Normally, we might not go at the same time, but as long as the office is closed, I don't worry about it. We'll stop by Baxter's store on the way. I want him and the town council to know we've got a money problem."

# Chapter 4

As Murphy had anticipated, Baxter was not at all comfortable with the idea of keeping that amount of stolen money in his safe. "What if somebody tells this gang of outlaws that their money is in my safe?" The thought of a gang of outlaws riding into town was frightening enough without painting a bull's-eye on his general store.

"Who's gonna tell 'em their money's in your safe, Mr. Mayor?"

"That one you're holding in the jailhouse, maybe," Baxter replied.

"Tell you the truth, I didn't tell him where I hid it just now," Murphy said, "and I wasn't plannin' on telling him where I was gonna hide it."

"I suppose that would be best," Baxter said, aware of a touch of sarcasm in Murphy's response. "I'll talk to Tyson and we'll compare safes to see whose is strongest."

"If you need me, Will and I are going to Irene's for supper."

"You gotta pick up your horse at the blacksmith shop," Will reminded him.

"I swear, I plumb forgot about it," Murphy said. He grinned at Baxter and said, "I must be gettin' old."

"I hope to hell not," Baxter remarked, still thinking about the possibility that a gang of outlaws might have moved into San Saba County.

* * *

Sitting at a table near the inside entrance to Irene's Café, Spade Atkins paused his chewing for a moment when he saw Marshal Cullen Murphy walk into the dining room. The young man who had been involved in the incident in the dining room earlier that day was with him. Spade found it interesting that the young man was now wearing a sidearm and walked behind Murphy. As they passed by his table, Spade made a point of nodding to the marshal, who, in turn, acknowledged, "Mr. Atkins." He continued on to his usual table near the kitchen door, where Ginger Floyd was standing, waiting with the coffeepot.

"I thought maybe you'd forgotten to eat tonight," Ginger greeted them. "We're happy to see you again, Mr. Pickens. Murphy could live on nothing but black coffee. How about you? Would you rather have water?"

"No, ma'am, I expect I might be hooked on coffee just as bad as the marshal is," Will responded.

"We're gonna need to take a plate back tonight," Murphy said. "And the town will be payin' you for Will's meals from now on. He's an official city employee now, working with me."

"I know," Ginger replied. "Mr. Baxter stopped in to tell us that just a little while ago." She gave him a smile. "Welcome to Newtown, Mr. Pickens."

"Thank you, ma'am. I appreciate it, but nobody ever calls me Mister. My name's Will. Mr. Pickens is my daddy's name."

"All right, Will it is, if you'll stop ma'am-ing me. My name's Ginger."

"Now that we're gettin' all the introductions over with, you can call me hungry," Murphy said with a chuckle. "What's for supper?"

"Ham steaks, red beans and rice," Ginger said as she filled their coffee cups, "and here comes Bonnie with yours right now." Bonnie was followed out of the kitchen by her mother, who was carrying a plate of freshly baked biscuits.

"I'm mighty pleased to hear that you've decided to become a member of the Newtown family, Will," Irene said as she placed the plate of fresh biscuits down on the table. Then she looked at Ginger and said, "I expect some of our other customers might like a hot biscuit, too."

"Yes, ma'am," Ginger replied, and went at once to the kitchen. She came back carrying the pan of biscuits her mother just took out of the oven and went to the three other occupied tables and distributed hot biscuits.

When she approached the table where the dark stranger sat alone, he greeted her with a knowing smile. She politely answered it with one of her own. "Would you care for a fresh biscuit, sir?"

"Yes, ma'am, that I would, but I didn't want to disturb what appeared to be a family reunion of sorts," Spade replied.

Ginger smiled and said, "It's more a new addition to the family than a reunion. Marshal Murphy has finally hired someone to help him at the jail. He's been a one-man police force ever since he took the job as marshal, even though the town council told him he could hire somebody to help him. Now he's surprised everybody when he up and hired Will Pickens, who just rode into town this morning. Marshal Murphy hadn't even laid eyes on him until he saw him in here at dinnertime. I think when he came to my sister's defense, he might have gotten the job right away."

"I wouldn't be surprised," Spade remarked. "I was here when it happened. No one else made a move to step in."

"That's right," Ginger said. *Including yourself,* she thought, *and you're the only one dressed up like a gunslinger.* "One enough?" she asked when she placed a biscuit on his plate.

He smiled again while he locked his gaze upon her, as if memorizing every curve of her body. She suddenly felt uncomfortable when he didn't answer her question. "One's plenty," he said when she started to put another biscuit beside the first one. "I never eat more than I need, but it was a fine supper, worth the price."

"Thank you, sir," she replied. "I'll tell my mother you enjoyed it." She hurried back to the kitchen then and was taking the remaining biscuits out of the pan when Irene came in. "I'm putting the rest of these biscuits on a plate in the warmer oven," she informed her mother.

"I saw you talking to that Mr. Atkins," Irene commented. "Was he complaining about anything?"

"No," Ginger answered. "As a matter of fact, he said that it was a fine supper. Said it was worth the price."

"Did he think the price was high?" Irene worried.

"No, Mama, he didn't complain about anything. He talks very politely, but the way he looked at me, I felt like he was undressing me with his eyes. He looks like a hawk, and Cullen said he rides one of those black-and-white spotted horses the Palouse Indians breed."

"What's he doin' here?" Irene asked.

"Cullen said he's a professional gambler, just looking Newtown over. He thinks he won't be here long. There's gambling going on all the time, but it's all small stakes, local men who like to play cards. There isn't any gambling big enough to support the kind of games he's looking for."

"Well, I appreciate the business," Irene remarked, "but he makes our regular customers nervous. He dresses like an undertaker, but he wears that pistol like a gunslinger." She giggled nervously and whispered, "Maybe he shoots 'em, then charges the family to bury 'em."

Ginger giggled with her. "Maybe we should tell him to go to Elmo Dillon's tailor shop to get a new suit of clothes, something cheerful like a clown suit."

Bonnie walked into the kitchen, carrying some dirty dishes. "What are you two giggling about in here?"

"Your sister is quite interested in getting to know Mr. Atkins a little better," Irene japed.

"She better take Cullen Murphy along with her," Bonnie remarked. "That man's dangerous." She went to the stove to fill a plate of food. "Cullen and"—she had to pause to remember the name—"Will . . . are ready to leave, so I'm fixing a plate for their prisoner."

"I notice you've been extra nice to Will," Ginger teased.

"I have to take care of my hero," Bonnie replied. "He came to save me when that man grabbed me." She shrugged and added, "But he is kinda cute. Don't you think?"

When Murphy and Will returned to the jail, Ed Moore greeted them with the relieved look of a pet dog whose master returns after an extended absence. Locked up alone in a jail unlike any he'd ever been in before, he was afraid no one would show up ever again. As promised, they brought him a generous plate of food, which he set upon immediately. When he commented on the unusual construction of the jail cells, Murphy explained that it was originally a café, the very one that was now behind the saloon. So all the walls had to be reinforced and the windows reduced, resulting in a jail that more closely resembled a fort. He didn't offer the information that it was he, himself, who turned the building into a jail and sold it to the town for the total sum of one dollar.

The evening served as a training period for Will, starting with the procedure for passing food and coffee into the cells. There was no opening, so the prisoner was told to sit on his bunk while the door was unlocked and his cup and plate slid inside on the floor. Then the door was locked again before the prisoner was permitted to leave his bunk to get it.

Murphy then explained that he took a walk around the town after supper when most every shop and business was closing for the day. Later on, he said, he took a late walk around when there was usually nothing open but the saloons and they were getting ready to close. "Most of the time when I'm out on the street, you'll be in charge of the office," Murphy said. "So the rule is never open a prisoner's cell for any reason, even if he says he's ailin' and needs some help. If he somehow manages to set himself on fire, you still do not open the cell door." He paused before moving on, then instructed, "In that case, tell the prisoner to stand in front of the steel-screened slots in the door while you throw water through the screens." He paused and asked, "Do you understand what I'm gettin' at?"

"I think so," Will smiled as he answered. "Don't unlock the cell door if you ain't here."

"Good!" Murphy responded. "I believe we're communicatin' right from the start."

There wasn't really much to learn in the running of the marshal's office, so Murphy was confident that Will had a good idea what his responsibilities were, most of them simply housekeeping jobs that Murphy preferred not to do. Will seemed to be content with his responsibilities and was happy to be off the cowhand's winter grub line.

On this, his first night, Will went along with Murphy on his early walk around. They left Ed eating his supper, locked the front office, and walked up one side of the street, then back down the other. They exchanged "good evenings" with those shops still open and checked the locks on the ones that had closed. They checked the activity in the saloons, with special interest for the two busiest ones, Bradshaw's and Pratt's. When they went inside Bradshaw's Saloon, they found that Spade Atkins had managed to find a poker game. He was seated at a table with Elmo Dillon, Joel Trout, and Frank and Robert Jessop. Since Will hadn't met the two Jessop brothers, Murphy stopped at the table to introduce him.

"Say howdy to Will Pickens," Murphy said to Frank Jessop. "He's gonna be workin' with me at the jail." To Will, he said, "Frank Jessop owns the sawmill down the river a ways, and this is his brother, Robert, who does carpentry work. I reckon they've had a hand in most of the buildings in Newtown."

"Including the one where you'll be workin'," Elmo hurried to comment. "Drove half the town crazy wondering what in the world they were making outta that old café building. Turned out it was a jail and Murphy built it because the town didn't have one. And that was before he was the marshal. I reckon he knew he was gonna need someplace to put the slew of riffraff outlaws who thought Newtown was theirs for the taking."

Will didn't expect that. Murphy had failed to mention it. One who was even more impressed, however, was Spade Atkins. Instead of just a hard-bark town marshal, this big cat was a legend in the making. The man who gunned Murphy down might well become a legend, himself. And he had almost decided it was a waste of his time when he arrived in Newtown. Plus it had no potential for big-time gambling. So he gave Murphy a smug grin and a silent promise that their separate trails would eventually meet, but only one would walk away. His thoughts were shattered then by the insistent voice of Elmo Dillon. "It's up to you, Spade. What are you gonna do?"

"I'll call," Spade said, and tossed a dollar in the pot. He looked up at Murphy and said, "I should have brought a new deck of cards with me. This deck the bartender supplied doesn't have much mercy on a stranger."

"Yeah, Newtown is known as a regular snake den for professional gamblers," Murphy said sarcastically. "We're famous for it."

"Read 'em and weep," Elmo said as he spread his hand. "Three beautiful ladies with a king for an escort." He waited a moment for everyone to toss their cards in before raking the pot over to himself. "Thank you, gentlemen."

Spade raked the discarded cards over quickly before anyone turned them over to see what everybody had bet on. He didn't want to take a chance on someone noticing that he had thrown away a jack-high straight. He had brought plenty of money with him to invest in building his "honest" reputation. And he was good enough to do it while still managing to win enough hands to show a small profit.

Murphy could not bring himself to believe the man was strictly honest. It was his belief that any man who was a professional gambler was dishonest. Maybe Spade Atkins would prove him wrong, but he doubted it. He was convinced that the fast-gun holster rig was the real Spade Atkins. And there was no good reason a professional gambler would come to Newtown. If Spade was honest about his passion for gambling, he would likely ride out of town in the morning. *We'll see if he sticks around after tonight,* he thought. "Come on, Will, we'll see what's going on at Pratt's."

The visit at Pratt's was even shorter than the one at Bradshaw's. There were a few unfamiliar faces talking to Hazel and Francine, which was typical for a Saturday night, even this early. Most of them were young cowhands from the small ranches in the area who preferred Pratt's because of the working ladies who were there to separate the cowhands from their meager wages. Will shook hands with the bartender, Albert Smith, and Francine came over to say hello as well.

When they walked out of Pratt's Saloon, they saw Eliot Baxter standing out in front of his store and he called out to them. So they walked back to see what he wanted. Baxter didn't beat around the bush. "Tyson and I talked about that package you asked about," he said. "Take it to him. He's got a heavier safe than I have. Several years newer than my old safe, so we agreed it was better for him to take possession of it."

"All right," Murphy replied, "I'll take it to him as soon as I get back to the jail."

"I don't suppose you've had time to find out where it came from," Baxter said.

"No, not for sure, but we looked through the notices and wanted papers we've received in the mail and we have an idea it's some money stolen in a stagecoach holdup. It belongs to Wells Fargo. I'll send a letter to the US Marshal in Austin tomorrow when the mail stage gets here." He paused, then said, "Unless you want me to take the money to them, myself. It'd take a while to get down there and back."

"In the meantime, we'd be without a marshal again," Baxter muttered, mostly to himself. "No, damn it, it'll just have to take a long time to deal with it."

"And we've got a prisoner in jail that we've got to decide what to do with," Murphy reminded him. "He still claims he found the money in a stump."

"I swear, Murphy," Baxter fumed, exasperated, "I wish to hell you hadn't arrested him and he had just took his money somewhere else."

"I didn't arrest him for having the stolen money," Murphy said. "I arrested him for shootin' off a firearm in Pratt's Saloon. I didn't know about the money until after I emptied his saddlebags." He watched Baxter stew over that for a moment before continuing. "We could send for a circuit judge to try Ed Moore, but it'll take just as long to get one here. And we ain't got any evidence to try him, anyway, on whether he was in on the holdup or not. He might have found the money, for all we know, but I don't think they would wanna leave all that money in a stump." He knew Baxter was mostly upset about the possibility of paying the cost of a prisoner for no telling how long. So he made one more suggestion. "I reckon the citizens of Newtown could appoint their own court and try Ed Moore to determine if he found the money or robbed the stagecoach carryin' it. And we could just keep the money until the US Marshal can get someone over here to take charge of it and let them go after the gang that robbed the stage."

Baxter paused to consider what he suggested. "You may be right. That might be the way for us to go. As long as we inform them we are holding the money, I don't see how we could be in any legal trouble." The more he thought about it, the more it appealed to him. "I'll call a meeting of the town council and we'll decide what to do. I'll want you at that meeting."

"Right," Murphy replied, "just let me know when."

He and Will walked back to the jail then.

As soon as they left the mayor, Will was compelled to ask a question. "Is that legal to do what you and him were talking about? I mean, just makin' your own court and havin' a trial?"

"No, it ain't," Murphy answered simply. "It ain't no different than what happens in a lot of little towns that don't even have a sheriff or a marshal. They form a vigilante committee to capture the outlaw and hang him. It ain't legal, but it's justice served for the good of the town. I expect the law won't be hard on the town, as long as the money is returned."

"What if the court decides Moore is guilty of robbin' that stagecoach and stealin' the money?" Will asked. "They ain't gonna be able to send him to prison. They'll have to hang him, won't they?"

"That's the only choices they'll have," Murphy answered. "Hang him or set him free, 'cause like you said, we don't have any authority to send him to prison. I reckon you have to look at it the way a federal judge would. It wasn't just a robbery. The outlaws killed five men and that's sure as hell a hangin' offense in any court. The only possibility of a miscarriage of justice is if the gunnysack court is wrong and Moore really did find the money, like he claims."

# Chapter 5

It had been a long day for Ed Moore, certainly the longest day in his life. Sitting in his jail cell, he felt trapped, but if he was released, he was a dead man for certain. His whole life had been a parade of poor choices and bad mistakes, but those he'd made this day topped every bad decision he had ever made. He held his breath and listened when he heard a noise coming from the marshal's office, then relaxed when he determined it to be the marshal and his hired man returning from their walk around town.

Once again, he returned his thoughts to how the day had turned out. At first, he thought he was lucky. This hideout that Beaver Branson had told them about was a well-built log cabin with a barn and corral beside a lively spring that flowed down a narrow gulch in the Texas Hill Country. According to Beaver, there were several small cattle ranches and one fairly large one within an easy day's ride. So there would be no shortage of beef to eat while they lay up there for a while. Beaver volunteered to take them to one of the ranches the first morning after they arrived.

The four of them talked it over and decided it was not a good idea to have the Wells Fargo sack of money with them when they went to rustle the cows. Beaver was on the spot again when he showed them a board that could be lifted to reveal a hiding place for the money under the floor of the back room. After more discussion, it was decided that it was too much money to leave unguarded, hidden or not. It was Calvin Darcy's idea to draw straws to see who was to stay there and guard the money. Ed was not particularly happy about drawing the short straw, even though it was better than spending the day driving three or four cows from a ranch some five miles away.

As the morning crept along, he sat around by the fireplace and tried to think of some way to pass the time. It would help, he decided, if he had a drink of whiskey. There were about two shots left in the bottle they had been working on before turning in the night before. So he finished that, but it only served to give him a craving for more. He looked through the belongings of his three partners in case one of them had a hidden bottle, but there was none. Then it occurred to him that they would be gone until suppertime, maybe later, depending on how far the herd they had seen might have moved. Newtown was only a three-mile ride, according to Beaver, and he had a pocketful of money. He could ride into town and eat dinner and have a drink in a saloon. He'd be back in the hideout long before they got back. He had chuckled to think about it. Then he thought about whether or not he should leave the Wells Fargo sack with no guard, even if it was in a hiding place. He formed a picture in his mind of him explaining to the others why he left the money there while he went to a saloon.

He decided he'd better take the money with him. As many times as he had drowned his common sense in alcohol, he should have known when he was headed for trouble. But the more he drank, the more invincible he became, until he found himself sitting in jail, his life not worth a nickel, regardless of what happened next. He would surely hang if a court decided he was guilty of robbing the stage. *If they decide I just found the money, and just run me out of town, I'm dead, too,* he thought. *Ain't no way the boys will believe I wasn't stealing the money.*

It was as much Beaver's fault as his in one respect. Beaver said the town had no law enforcement of any kind. Things had damn sure changed. *If I'd just gone on back to the hideout when that big stud ran me out of that dining room,* he thought. "I swear," he mumbled, "every memory I have is a dang regret."

"What did you say, Ed?" Murphy asked as he walked into the cell room.

"Nothin'," Ed replied, then, "If you'd just let me get outta here, you'd have that money them fellers stole and I'd leave here and never come back again."

"Now, why would I wanna turn you loose, Ed?" Murphy replied.

"I'd be outta your hair and you wouldn't have to feed me for however long it'll take to get a judge over here. It'd save you a whole lotta trouble foolin' with me. I never meant to cause you no trouble. And I give you my word, I found that money, just like I told you."

"In a hollowed-out old tree stump, right, Ed?" Murphy replied, and smiled. "Ain't you the fellow who threatened me with your six-gun already drawn?"

Ed hesitated a moment. "You say stuff when you're likkered up that you don't really mean. I was pretty drunk when I was in Pratt's Saloon."

"You're wasting your breath talkin' to me about settin' you free," Murphy told him. "It's up to the town council to decide what to do with you. They pay my salary and they'll hold the court for you. I expect it would help your case a lot if you would tell me how many there were in that gang that held up the stage."

"How the hell can I tell you that?" Ed responded. "I don't know nothin' about that holdup. I told you, I found that money."

"Right, in a hollow tree stump," Murphy replied caustically, repeating the flimsy excuse again. "You might as well give up on that one, Ed. Nobody's dumb enough to hide a sack full of money in a rotten tree stump and leave it for anybody to find. How many are gonna be comin' after you when they find out you're in this jail? Like it or not, right now I'm the only thing standin' between you and your friends you stole that money from."

"I found that money," Ed insisted.

"Too bad you lost one of your men in the holdup," Murphy said. "The report said one of the outlaws was killed."

"It was his own damn fault," Ed came back. "He shouldn't have pulled . . ." He caught himself before finishing the statement, but it was too late. Murphy's patient smile told him so.

"You saw the report somewhere?" Murphy asked.

"Yeah, I saw the notice at the post office," Ed sputtered immediately. "It said one of the holdup men was killed."

"Was he a close friend of yours?" Murphy pressed. "Wasn't any kin, I hope."

"What—what are you talkin' about?" Ed stammered. "How—how would I know who he was? It didn't say in that notice in the post office."

"What post office was that?" Murphy continued to press.

"Hell, I don't know. Some little town down near Austin, I reckon. I don't remember. It don't matter, anyway. It ain't got nothin' to do with me, and I'm done talkin' about it."

"All right," Murphy said, "let's talk about something else. I expect you and your ex-partners were holed up in that little hideout up on Owl Branch. You can thank me for that. I meant to burn that place to the ground long ago and never got around to doin' it." When he saw the color drain from Ed's face at the mention of Owl Branch, he knew he had guessed right. "Oh, you ain't the first gang of outlaws to camp in that cabin halfway up that gulch. I believe every outlaw in Texas knows about it, and most of 'em ain't ever heard of Newtown, just three miles away. But they always eventually find us and come into town to make trouble, just like you did. But most of 'em ain't like you with their own gang after 'em." He paused for a few seconds to read the expression on Ed's face. Then he said, "You really got yourself in one helluva mess, didn't you, Ed?"

"I reckon there ain't no way around it," Ed decided, totally defeated. "I surely did. But I ain't guilty of stealing that money from my partners. I didn't have no intention of keeping that money. I was gonna go back to the hideout with it, but I drank too much. If you was to let me go, my partners would hunt me down and kill me. You're right, I'm safer in this jail. I'm guilty of robbin' that stagecoach and I shot at two of them deputies—and that's all I'm gonna say about it."

At about the same time Ed Moore blurted his surprise confession, his three partners were approaching the cabin on Owl Branch. They were driving three cows up the backside of the narrow valley and leading a packhorse carrying freshly butchered beef. "I hope Ed's still got a good fire goin," Hank Welch commented. "I wanna cook some more of that meat before I turn in for the night." They had traveled farther than they had expected to before finding a small herd of cattle grazing on the lower edge of the Rocking-J range. They cut three cows out of the herd, as well as a young heifer that chose to follow them. Since it was getting along in the afternoon and they had not eaten since breakfast, they decided to stop and butcher the heifer. After eating what they wanted, they cut the best of the meat into portions to be cooked later, leaving most of the heifer to the buzzards.

"I reckon we're gonna have to build the fire," Calvin Darcy said. " 'Cause we'da seen some smoke by now."

"I don't reckon Ed woulda built a fire outside for just him by hisself," Beaver Branson speculated. "He most likely built a fire in the stove and stayed inside to eat."

"He must be sleepin'," Hank said when they reached the

clearing where the cabin and barn stood. "Somebody could ride in here and carry him and the money off."

"That's why we hid it under the floor," Beaver reminded them.

"Let's wake his butt up," Hank said. He drew his six-gun, fired a couple of shots in the air, and yelled, "Everybody out of the house! You're under arrest!"

"Damn, Hank!" Beaver exclaimed, and pulled his horse to a hard stop. "You're gonna get one of us shot!" They all pulled back then, except the three cows they were driving and they ran on down in the barnyard, frightened by the gunshots.

"Ed!" Calvin yelled. "Hold your fire! It's just us!"

When there was no response from the cabin, they hesitated to follow the cows, so Hank yelled again. "Come on out, Ed. It ain't nobody but me and Calvin and Beaver. We're comin' in." Thinking that Ed might be drunk, they advanced cautiously until they rode past the little barn and Beaver noticed that Ed's horse was not in the corral.

"He ain't here!" Beaver said, and all three pulled up short, came out of the saddle, and stormed into the cabin, guns drawn in case they were needed. No one was inside.

"Light that lantern," Hank said, and as soon as Calvin lit it, they went into the back room to check on the money. The floorboard was in place, with no sign it had been removed recently, but when Hank pulled it up, the lantern revealed an empty space. "He's run off with the money," Hank declared calmly, too shocked to believe it to be true.

Beaver and Calvin were rendered speechless, stunned to believe that they had been so blatantly double-crossed. Both Hank and Beaver directed an accusing gaze at Calvin, as if he might have had some hand in the disappearance of the sack of money. He and Ed had ridden with Cleve Carter long before Hank and Beaver joined them.

"You got no call to look at me like I know somethin' about

it," Calvin declared. "I'm just as surprised as you are. I never woulda thought Ed would do anything like that. Maybe we got tracked here by some marshals or Texas Rangers and they arrested Ed." That prompted all three of them to start looking around in search of any evidence of a fight.

After looking the whole cabin over, they could find no such evidence. "If it was the law that got him, he didn't put up a fight," Hank concluded. "There weren't nobody here but Ed. If it'd been the law, they wouldn'ta put that board back in the floor to hide that place. They wouldn'ta cared who saw it."

Calvin was still finding it hard to believe Ed would risk spending the rest of his life trying to keep the three of them off his trail. "Maybe he just went into town and he didn't wanna leave the money here with nobody guardin' it. Maybe he'll be back tonight."

"He might be layin' up in the bed with one of them saloon ladies," Beaver said, "with his horse tied at the rail with twenty thousand dollars in his saddlebag."

"I wish I knew that was the truth," Hank said. "I'd take great pleasure in draggin' him outta that bed and beatin' him to death." He thought about it for a minute, then said, "If he does show up here tonight with our money, I'm gonna beat him to death, anyway."

It took a while, but finally they had to calm down to the point of deciding what they should do about their situation. One thing they all agreed on was the probability that Ed may or may not have decided to head for parts unknown, but he would most likely make a stop in Newtown to supply himself with whiskey and whatever else he needed for his escape. There was still the hope that Ed would show up at the cabin sometime before morning, having just gone into town to get some whiskey and maybe jump in bed with a working girl. If that was the case, they would handle it appropriately. If he failed to return, they decided to go into town in the morning and see if they could pick up his trail, then follow it until the end, no matter how long it took. So they took care of their horses and drove the cows into the corral so they wouldn't wander. Then Hank built the fire, because he knew he wasn't likely to go to sleep, and when it was going good, he held a slice of beef over it. That prompted Beaver and Calvin to follow suit, and they sat around the fire and ate their fill of fresh beef. Somewhere around three o'clock in the morning, Calvin was the first to surrender to his bedroll. He was only minutes ahead of his partners, however, and soon all three were asleep.

No one stirred until after sunrise when Calvin rolled out of his blanket and sat up. His brain not functioning right away, he just sat there, looking around. Then it finally registered with him and he took a longer look around him. There were still only the three of them. He reached over with his foot and gave Beaver a kick. Beaver grunted, then demanded, "What?"

"He ain't here," Calvin said. "He didn't come back."

Beaver sat up then and looked around the room. "You sure?" he asked hopefully.

"You don't see him nowhere, do you?" Calvin replied. "He woulda woke us up if he came back, anyway."

"He's a dead man," Hank muttered, having wakened in time to hear them talking. "I never had no use for that damn drunk. We shoulda never left him alone with all that money."

"What are we gonna do?" Beaver wondered aloud.

"Ain't nothin' we can do, but go after him," Hank responded.

"We don't even know which way he took off," Beaver said.

"Maybe not," Hank declared, "but we know which way the nearest saloon is and that's bound to be the first place he went to. We'll ride into town and see if we can pick up his trail when he left there. If we're lucky, he mighta got drunk enough to still be there. Let's get saddled up and ride on into that town. We can eat some breakfast there and maybe ol' Ed might still be in bed with some old hooker."

"You may be right," Calvin allowed. "He never could handle his craving for likker. It always got the best of him. But I still think he mighta been intendin' to come back to the hideout last night."

"I reckon we'll find out then, won't we?" Hank said. "I'm still gonna beat him to death."

Since they were not certain what they would find when they got to town, and there was a possibility of picking up Ed's trail out of there, they decided it best to take everything with them. So they loaded up their packhorses and left the corral gate open so the cows could get to the water and graze as well. It was then that they were struck with a fact that had not occurred to any of them before. It was Calvin who announced the obvious. He paused as he was tightening his cinch strap. "Ed's packhorse is still here," he said, "and his packsaddle is layin' in the corner of the shed."

His declaration caused Hank and Beaver to pause to consider the fact. "I swear," Beaver blurted, "that's right. He must notta been running off a'tall. He wouldn'ta left his horse and packs, too."

"He still took all the money with him," Hank reminded them. "Maybe he thought he'd buy himself a whole new outfit." This latest development only served to make him more impatient to find Ed Moore. "Let's get going. Maybe we can catch up with him before he leaves town." They filled the water trough, unloaded their packhorses, and left them in the corral, but left the cows outside. Then in single file, due to the narrow trail that followed the stream down the gulch, they started out for Newtown. Beaver led them, since he was the only one of the three who had been to the town before. He told them the town was not hard to find, if you just remembered it was south of the hideout, and when you came to a junction with another path, to always take the one that took you in a southerly direction. So they came to a crossing path near the bottom of the gulch and switched onto a game trail that led in a more southern direction. They followed that trail and it took them to a wagon road, which Beaver said was the road into Newtown. "Better remember where this little game trail strikes the road," Hank said.

"Simple enough directions to get to town," Beaver said.

"It's a different story goin' from town, back to the hideout," Calvin said. "Maybe Ed got lost on his way back."

Finally they rounded a wide bend in the wagon road and caught their first sight of Newtown, which was Paul Mathers's stable. There was no sign of any activity at the stable, but they caught sight of Joel Trout, the blacksmith, already at work in his shop next to the stables. The huge man paused to give them a look when they passed by, their horses walking three abreast as their riders appraised the town.

"Bigger'n you said it was," Hank commented. "It musta growed a lot since the war." They counted four saloons right away, none of which were open at this early hour. They continued on down Front Street, looking for a hotel or a café where they could get some breakfast. "There's gotta be some place to get some breakfast," Hank said, "one of those saloons maybe."

"There's a place we might could get some grub," Calvin japed, and pointed to a building with a sign that read: NEWTOWN CITY JAIL.

"I thought you said they didn't have no sheriff!" Hank immediately roared. "That might make things a little bit more complicated than we was figurin' on."

"Well, I'll be . . ." Beaver started, every bit as surprised as Hank and Calvin. "They didn't have no sheriff last time I was here. And they sure as hell didn't have no jail. I reckon there's a lot more folks around here now. I wondered about that when we rode by the blacksmith back yonder. Last time I was here, there was a younger feller in that shop, about half the size of that one. Looks like they still ain't got no hotel or eatin' places, though. If I recollect properly, there used to be an eatin' place about where the jail is now, run by a woman and her daughters. They went busted durin' the war and moved their café into that biggest saloon we just passed."

"Bradshaw's?" Hank asked, looking back up the street.

"Yep," Beaver answered. "Maybe they're still there. It was some pretty good cookin'. I remember that. I spent more time down the street at Pratt's Saloon 'cause Bradshaw's didn't have no sportin' women."

"Pratt's Saloon sounds more like the one Ed would pick," Hank said. "But it don't look like either one of 'em is open yet." He was still holding out hope that Ed was asleep upstairs in one of the two saloons.

"If that café is still behind Bradshaw's, they would be open by now and they had an outside entrance," Beaver remembered. He turned to look back at the saloon. "See that path beside it? That leads around to the outside entrance."

"Let's go see if they're still in business," Hank said. "I could damn sure use a cup of coffee right now. We'll get some breakfast and maybe by then the saloon will be open."

"That would sure be to my liking," Calvin said, and Beaver seconded it. So they turned their horses back up the street and rode the path beside the saloon back to the café entrance.

# Chapter 6

"You open for breakfast?" Hank asked when they walked into the dining room.

"Yes, sir," Ginger Floyd answered while wondering how much bigger the OPEN sign on the door had to be. A quick look at the three men caused her to think she might be too critical and possibly they couldn't read. "Good morning. We're open. Just sit yourself down at any table that suits you. Are you all gonna have coffee?"

"Yes'um," Beaver answered at once, and she spun on her heel and went to get the coffeepot. He turned and grinned at Hank and Calvin. "First class, ain't it?"

"I'll tell you after I sample the cookin'," Hank said, finding it hard to rid his mind of the thought that Ed Moore might possibly be getting farther and farther away while he waited for someone to cook his breakfast. Ginger was back in a few seconds with coffee and asked how they wanted their eggs.

"You got eggs?" Beaver asked. "Where do you get eggs out here?"

"From chickens," Ginger answered. "How do you want 'em cooked?"

Beaver chuckled in response, unable to remember the last time he had eaten an egg.

"Any way that ain't runny," Calvin answered for him, "as long as you've got some bacon and potatoes to go with 'em and some biscuits."

"How about scrambled for all three?" Ginger asked.

"That'll do just fine, long as they ain't runny," Calvin said. "How much you charge for breakfast?"

"We'll give you the dollar breakfast," Ginger said, "but we won't charge you but thirty-five cents for it. How's that?"

"That'll do," Hank told her. "I reckon we'll find out for sure after we get a chance to sample the cookin'."

"Fair enough," Ginger said. "I'll get your order in." She went back to the kitchen to get her mother started on the eggs. "Three new customers," she told her mother and her sister. "I wasn't sure when they walked in if they were here to eat breakfast or rob us."

Her comment caused her younger sister to go to the edge of the door and take a peek at them. "They do look like they ain't ever been polished," Bonnie said. "Have they propositioned you yet?"

"Bonnie Floyd!" her mother scolded. "Where is your mind? What a thing to ask."

Both daughters giggled and Bonnie replied, "I'm just saying we seem to be attracting a certain kind of man, like that one Cullen Murphy has in jail now that grabbed me. And those three out there in the dining room look like they went to the same finishing school for gentlemen as he did."

"Where is Cullen, anyway?" Ginger wondered. "It's about his usual time to come to breakfast. To tell you the truth, I'd just as soon have him here right now."

"They haven't said anything to trouble you, have they?" Irene asked.

"No, ma'am, not a thing," Ginger said.

"Then it's a little early to be making judgments," her mother said. "They just might be the most humble, hardworking men who ever came in here." She broke half a dozen eggs into her iron skillet and stirred them in the bacon grease, thinking about the prisoner, Ed Moore, who had grabbed her daughter before. "Here," she said, "come stir these eggs." She handed her spoon to Ginger and quickly walked to the kitchen door to take a look at the three men. "Where is Cullen Murphy?" she muttered. Back at the stove, she took the spoon from Ginger and instructed her. "You watch yourself around that table. I'll help you carry their plates out."

Ginger and Bonnie exchanged glances of amusement before Ginger replied, "I'll be careful." But then she said, "Here comes Cullen and Will, so you don't have to wait on the tables with me." She went out of the kitchen to greet them. "Good morning, Marshal Murphy and Mr. Pickens," she said grandly. "You're running a little later than usual."

"We are?" Murphy responded, surprised. He looked at the clock on the wall, then back at her, puzzled but not enough to pursue it. "Good mornin'," he returned. "We'll be needin' a plate to take back to the jail. Might as well figure on feedin' a prisoner three meals a day for a while, anyway, at least until the town council decides what they're gonna do about him." They proceeded to Murphy's usual table close to the kitchen door, and on the way, he nodded to the three strangers sitting at a table in the center of the room.

All three returned the silent greeting; after he and Will passed by, Hank commented, "Marshal Murphy, she called him. He looks like a stud horse, don't he?"

"Reckon which one's the marshal?" Beaver asked, and received expressions of impatience from both Hank and Calvin.

"That's the dumbest question I ever heard," Hank said. "Who do ya think is the marshal? The big one that talked to the gal about feedin' a prisoner, or the young skinny one walkin' behind him?"

"Well, shoot," Beaver answered, "that young one might be

the fastest gun in the territory. You can't never tell. So they mighta made him the marshal."

"I swear, Beaver, where the hell were you when they was handin' out brains?" Hank asked.

Calvin laughed and said, "Don't be too hard on Beaver. He's still not sure where eggs come from."

Hank didn't laugh with him because another thought struck him at that moment. "Son of a . . ." he started, but paused when Ginger returned to the table carrying a tray with their breakfast. She left the three plates and said she'd be right back with the biscuits. When she left, he expressed his thought to Calvin and Beaver. "The marshal told that gal that he had a prisoner to feed. Whaddaya reckon the chances are that prisoner might be Ed?"

"Ed's got better sense than to get into any trouble here in town when he's carryin' all that money," Calvin said.

"Unless he's been drinkin'," Hank said. "And then he ain't got a lick of sense." Another thought occurred to him then. "We left half a bottle of likker on the table when we left the hideout yesterday, and there weren't no bottle on the table when we got back. We need to find out who they've got in jail. He might not be on the run a'tall. He might be right here, and that means the money is right here, too."

"That's worse than if he was on the run," Calvin said, "unless he had sense enough to hide that money somewhere before he got drunk enough to get himself arrested. We gotta find out if that's Ed they got in jail."

"How are we gonna do that without them wantin' to know who we are?" Beaver asked. "He's got us in a helluva spot!"

"We've gotta play it smart," Hank said. "We gotta find out who that marshal's holdin' in jail. If it's Ed, we gotta know if they've got our money, or if he's got it hid somewhere and they don't know about the money. There's a good chance they're just holdin' him on a charge of drunk and disturbin' the peace, or some such thing." He paused for a few moments, then said, "Eat your breakfast and let me think a minute and I'll tell you what we'll do." They were glad to cooperate, because they were both at a loss when it came to any real planning. By the time Bonnie came around to fill their coffee cups again, Hank had it figured out and he told them what they were going to do.

"What if that marshal wants to know our names?" Calvin asked. "You reckon we oughta make up some names?"

Hank hesitated but a moment to consider that. "No," he decided. "We ain't on no wanted notices in the state of Texas. Better to use your real name, if he asks. That way, you don't have to stop and make sure you remember the name you made up, in case he asks you again later on."

"That's a good idea," Beaver said. "I was already wonderin' if I could make up a good name."

"Hell, you ain't got no need to worry," Calvin joked. "He'll probably take one look at you and call you Beaver."

"You two get all your japin' done 'cause I'm gittin' ready to go talk to him. We don't know if that's Ed he's got in jail or not. And we don't know if Ed gave him his real name or not. We got to get inside that jail and get a look at his prisoner. And you gotta be ready for a shoot-out, if our money's in that jail. You know that? Both of ya, you ready for a shoot-out if our money's in there?" They both nodded, so he said, "Get turned around in your chairs and be ready to use your guns if something goes wrong." He waited until they both moved their chairs slightly to make sure they could get to their pistols quickly.

Hank got to his feet, gulped down the last of his coffee, then casually walked back to the table by the kitchen door. "Beg your pardon, Marshal. I don't want to interrupt your breakfast, but I was wonderin' if I could ask you a question."

*Well, he finally got around to it,* Murphy thought. He had never seen the three men in town before, but he had noticed a distinct reaction of caution in the eyes of all three when Ginger greeted him and Will. "Why, sure," Murphy answered. "What can I do for you?"

"Me and my partners have been hired to chase after a cattle thief who's been rustlin' cows that belong to the Rockin'-J Ranch. And his trail led us right to Newtown." He paused to see if Murphy was buying that, but it was too soon to tell. He continued. "Well, we heard you tell the young lady that you had a prisoner to feed and we wondered if, by any chance, it might be the very man we're chasin'."

"I suppose that's possible," Murphy responded. "I don't think my prisoner is a cattle rustler, although I wouldn't put it past him. Do you know the name of the man you've been chasin'?"

Hank hesitated when he almost said it. "No," he caught himself in time. "We don't know his name, but we got close enough to get a look at him one day before he slipped away from us and headed this way. So I reckon I have to see him to tell if he's our man or not."

Murphy had a suspicious feeling about the stranger's interest in his prisoner, as well as a general feeling of wariness about the looks of the three. "You say this fellow you're trailin' has been stealin' Rockin'-J cattle?"

"That's right," Hank answered.

"Do you and your two friends ride for the Rockin'-J Ranch?" Murphy asked.

"No, we ain't on the payroll," Hank said. "The owner of the Rockin'-J just sends word to me when he needs the help of my boys and me to take care of things like this."

"Well, I'll be . . ." Murphy responded. "I didn't know that. The owner of the Rockin'-J Ranch, Andrew Johnson, just sends for you when he's got some rustlin' goin' on."

"That's a fact," Hank replied. "We've done little jobs like this'un for Mr. Johnson two or three times before. He says it's better than havin' his cowhands searchin' all over the county for this feller."

"I reckon you learn something new every day, if you keep your eyes and ears open," Murphy said. Already this early in the day, he had learned this stranger was a liar. He was well acquainted with Lionel Jacobson, the owner of the Rocking-J Ranch. And even if this stranger was really just bad about remembering names, Murphy knew Jacobson wouldn't hire three saddle tramps like these three to chase down one rustler. He thought there was a definite possibility the three men were in town looking for the stolen money their partner, Ed Moore, had relieved them of. "Well, you're certainly welcome to come in the jail and see if my prisoner is the man you've been chasin'. We're headin' straight back there to take him some breakfast as soon as we finish eating."

"'Preciate it, Marshal," Hank said. "What did you arrest him for?"

"Drunk and disorderly conduct, discharging a firearm in the city limits, destroyin' private property, raisin' a lotta hell," Murphy said.

"I swear, it's a wonder you still wanna feed him," Hank remarked. "Just take your time to eat, though. We don't wanna rush you."

"We're just about done, ain't we, Will? We'll go as soon as Ginger brings the prisoner's plate out." Hank went back and sat down with Beaver and Calvin again. And when they were out of earshot, Murphy said to Will, "When Ginger brings Ed's breakfast out here, you take it." Will nodded, understanding that Murphy wanted to have both his hands free, just in case.

When Hank returned to his table, Calvin and Beaver both pressed him for a report. "Set back in your chairs," Hank barked. "He'll think there's something fishy goin' on. He said we can go in and take a look at his prisoner as soon as he gets done eatin', but I ain't sure it's a good idea for all three of us to go in. He might not be as dumb as he acts. Ed mighta spilled his guts about the whole deal. And if that's the case, it's better if there's just one of us in the jail and the other two can go in and get him out." Both of his partners thought that was a good idea and they were agreed that Hank should be the one to go in.

"Did he tell you the feller's name?" Calvin asked.

"No," Hank replied, "and I didn't ask him. I already told him we didn't know his name, that we just saw him close enough to recognize him. The only thing that's got me worried is what Ed will do when he sees me. If he's got any sense a'tall, he'll keep his mouth shut until he finds out what's goin' on. If we're lucky, he's got the money hid somewhere and we'll just wait around till that marshal lets him outta jail. Then after we get the money, I'm gonna shoot Ed for causin' all this trouble and we'll split the money three ways. Any objections?"

No one had any.

It was just a few minutes later when Ginger came out with Ed's breakfast plate on a small tray and Will immediately reached out to accept it. "Don't dawdle on your way back," she instructed him. "It'll get cold quickly in weather like we're having."

"Right," Will said.

"If any of those three makes a funny move, drop that tray and go for your gun," Murphy said.

"Right," Will said, and followed him to the door, which he held for him to walk through.

They walked briskly down the street to the jail, the three outlaws behind them, leading their horses. When they got to the jail, Murphy unlocked the front door and held it for Will. The three outlaws stood at the rail until Murphy motioned for them to come in. "They're gonna wait out here," Hank said, nodding toward his two partners. "I can tell right away if it's the man we're lookin' for."

"Suit yourself," Murphy told him, and continued to hold

the door after Will went inside and put the breakfast tray on the desk, while he got the cell room key. When Hank walked into the office, Murphy said, "You'll have to leave that sidearm on the desk before you go into the cell room."

Hank expected as much and cooperated, even though extremely uncomfortable to oblige.

"Here's your breakfast, Ed," Murphy said, "so go sit on the bunk while Will puts it inside the door."

Eager to get at the breakfast, Ed went obediently back to the bunk. "You've got a visitor who wants to say good mornin' to ya as well." That sparked Ed's attention, but not as much as the tray of food on the floor, so he came at once to retrieve it. "Will set the coffeepot up with some fresh water before we went to eat," Murphy said. "We'll set that on the stove and you'll have some fresh coffee in a jiffy."

"Obliged," Ed said, and picked up the tray, only to almost drop it when Hank Welch walked into the cell room. Stunned, Ed's mouth dropped open, but he made no sound as he stood frozen in the cell after Hank gestured quickly with a finger to his lips to silence him.

"It's hard to tell for sure," Hank said, "seein' as how we never got a look at him this close, but I do think he favors the cattle rustler who's been after Rockin'-J's cows. Maybe I can talk to him a minute. Would that be all right?"

"It's all right by me," Murphy said, already of the opinion that he was looking at another one of the outlaws who robbed the Wells Fargo stagecoach. "It's up to him. He can talk to you if he wants to. The rule we have here is fifteen minutes' visitin' time with a prisoner. I'll just leave the cell room door open, so we can make sure you don't try to pass anything through those bars." He walked out of the cell room then and went back to his desk and sat down on the corner of it, where he could see them through the open door. He glanced at Will, who was sitting in the one side chair in the office. "We ain't close enough to hear, but we don't really need to hear 'em to know they sure as hell know each other."

Hank moved up close to the cell door and Ed asked, "What the hell are you doin' here?"

"No," Hank responded, "what the hell are *you* doin' here? Where's our money? You didn't get very far with it before you jumped in the whiskey bottle, did you?"

"I know what you're thinkin', but that ain't the story a'tall," Ed pleaded. "I was afraid to leave that money in the cabin with nobody there. I was gonna bring it back, but I had a little bit of bad luck. I weren't gonna turn on you boys, Hank. You know that, don'tcha?"

"Where's the money?" Hank insisted. "Did you hide it somewhere? Me and the boys can go get it. Then we'll see about breakin' you outta here. You did hide it somewhere before you crawled into that likker bottle, didn't you?"

"Like I told you," Ed continued to plead, "I felt like it was my duty to guard that money. I couldn't risk havin' it outta my sight. I owed it to you and the other boys to guard it."

Hank didn't say anything for a long couple of minutes while thoughts of thousands and thousands of dollars blowing away in the wind filled his mind. "The only reason you're alive right now is because that big lawman out there has my gun," he said. "Is the money here, in this jail?"

"I don't know for sure if it is or not," Ed answered. "I swear. Him and that other feller never talked about it when I could hear 'em."

"Does he know you stole it?" Hank asked. He looked back over his shoulder to see Murphy still sitting on the corner of his desk. Hank couldn't help wondering if he was going to have trouble leaving the jail.

"No. I told him I found it," Ed answered.

"You think he believes you?"

"I don't know. I think so. He ain't said he don't believe me."

He shrugged helplessly. "I think he might be smarter than he acts." He couldn't bring himself to confess that he had admitted to having taken part in that holdup.

"Maybe so," Hank concluded. "One thing for sure, we've gotta find out where that money is and that might take some time. So I reckon me and the boys are gonna hang around Newtown for a few days until we figure that out."

"You gonna get me outta here?" Ed asked.

"Now, why would I do that? If we broke you outta here, then all we'd have is your no-good butt and most likely an order to get outta town. How could we find out where that money is if we have to stay outta town? No, you damn drunk, our money's gone because of you, so it's better if you stay locked up to keep one of us from killin' you. If that marshal believes that story you told him about findin' the money, he'll probably let you outta here in a couple of days."

"Maybe," Ed said. He didn't tell Hank about the moment when he went half-crazy and confessed that he had participated in the holdup of the Wells Fargo stagecoach, exchanged shots with the deputy marshals, but didn't murder the driver or his guard. "But you gotta believe me, Hank. I never had no plans to run off with that money. I shoulda left it under the floor, but I was afraid you and Beaver and Calvin would give me hell for leavin' it unguarded."

"You done what you done," Hank said. "Ain't nothin' we can do about it now, but try to find out who's holdin' the money. We find that out and we'll say goodbye to this part of Texas." *And leave you behind in an unmarked grave,* he thought, still determined to punish Ed for all the trouble he had caused. "Well, good luck to ya," he said, loud enough to be heard in the office. "I hope you get your problems straightened out." He walked back into the office.

"Was that the man you and your partners have been trailin'?" Murphy asked.

"No, he wasn't," Hank replied. "He did kind of favor him,

though. The reason I talked to him so long was because he wanted to tell me why he was in jail. He said he found a whole lot of money and you think he robbed a stagecoach to get it."

"Yeah, that's what we think," Murphy remarked. "Did he tell you he didn't?"

"That's what he said," Hank replied, thinking it might be worthwhile to continue the charade on the chance of finding out where the money was being kept. "He thinks you've got it hidden away somewhere here in the jail."

"Ha!" Murphy responded. "This is the last place you'd hide money. We're talkin' well over twenty thousand dollars. I'd be afraid to leave the building if we were trying to hide that much money in here. I wouldn't want to be responsible for guardin' that much money, anyway. No, sir, I just turned that money over to the town council and they found a place to lock it up."

"Is that a fact? Where would that be?" Hank asked.

"Beats me," Murphy replied. "I didn't even want to know where they put it, because then they'd expect me to guard it."

"I see what you mean," Hank said. "I don't blame you. Well, I 'preciate you lettin' me talk to your prisoner, Marshal." He strapped on his six-gun and went out the door.

Calvin and Beaver both looked relieved when he untied his horse from the hitching rail. "Just like we figured," he said. "He had the money in his saddlebags when he was arrested, so they've got it put away somewhere. They think he found it and they don't know anything about us. So we're free to hang around and see if we can find out who's holding our money."

Inside the jail, Murphy and Will watched them as they got on their horses and rode up the street. "Well, there's no doubt about it," Murphy said, "there goes the other three members of the gang that robbed the stage and shot the deputy marshals. And they're gonna be hangin' around town trying to find out where the money is. If we're lucky, we'll have some deputy marshals here to arrest 'em before they quit looking for the money."

# CHAPTER 7

"Good morning, Cullen," Eliot Baxter greeted Murphy when he walked into the Newtown General Store. "What can I do for you?"

"Mornin'," Murphy returned. "I just wanna bring you and the town council up-to-date about that prisoner I'm holdin' in the jailhouse."

"Oh?" Baxter replied. "I thought you sent word to the US Marshal in Austin to come pick him and the money up as soon as possible."

"I did. I sent the letter right away, but I doubt they'll get it before day after tomorrow," Murphy said. "And there's been some more developments I need to tell you about."

Baxter gave him his full attention then, hoping it wasn't something that would cost the town more money. "Are you having some kind of trouble with your prisoner? Or a problem with the assistant you just hired?"

"No, no problem with Will. He's gonna work out fine. It's just that we've got a different situation with the prisoner now."

"Is he still saying he found the money?" Baxter asked.

"No," Murphy said. "As a matter of fact, he admitted that he was one of the four men who held up the stage." He hurried to continue before Baxter could ask another question. "The problem now is that the other three outlaws showed up in town this mornin' looking for Ed Moore and the money."

"Oh, no!" Baxter gasped, and paled visibly.

"Ain't nothin' to worry about yet," Murphy tried to assure him. He told him about Hank Welch's visit with Moore that morning and his pretense that he and his two partners were looking for a cattle rustler. "They don't know that Moore confessed to robbin' that stage, so I expect they'll be hangin' around town trying to find out where the money is. So I don't expect them to cause any trouble a'tall. They'll most likely be on their best behavior until they find out where we're keepin' the money."

"You think we should post a guard at Bradshaw's Saloon?" the mayor asked.

"No, sir, we don't want to tell 'em where the money is," Murphy said. "But I wanted to talk to you and Tyson Bradshaw about the situation to decide what's best for us. I posted another letter to the US Marshal about the three men showing up in town, but they might not get it before they've already sent a couple of deputies on their way up here. And I expect they'll need to send a jail wagon to haul 'em in. Knowin' what we do now about the three outlaws, I would guess the marshal's department would expect me to arrest them right away. Now, I ain't got no problem with that. I can arrest 'em, but I wanted to give you and Mr. Bradshaw some advance notice because my expenses are goin' up when I have to take care of four prisoners. And I don't know for how long. I reckon I just want your approval before I arrest 'em."

"I appreciate you coming to me about this before you made a move," Baxter said. "I suppose it's best to arrest them while they're not wise to the situation. I imagine Tyson Bradshaw would prefer that, since the money's in his safe. Let's, you and I, go tell him what we're dealing with." Murphy nodded his agreement.

"Jeff!" Baxter called to his son. "I'm going to talk to Tyson Bradshaw. I won't be too long. Keep your eye on the register."

They found Bradshaw downstairs in the saloon talking to a couple of his regulars. "We need to talk to you about some town business," Baxter said.

So Bradshaw came to meet him and Murphy at an unoccupied table.

"What's up?" Bradshaw asked as he pulled a chair back. "You need a drink?" Baxter and Murphy both declined the invitation, so he sat down and looked expectantly at both of them. "If you're worried about the money, it's still there," he joked. "But I've thought of a hundred uses for it."

"Had any new customers today?" Baxter asked.

"Yes," Bradshaw answered. "Matter of fact, there's three strangers in the saloon right now, sittin' at that table off to the side near the front door. Pete said they ate breakfast in the café this mornin'. They're a rough-looking bunch, but they ain't hell-raisers." He glanced at Murphy and laughed. "So don't hassle 'em, Marshal. They ain't botherin' nobody and they seem to have plenty of money."

"Well, that's what we're here to talk about," Baxter said. "They may have plenty of money, but they're in town looking for more, about twenty thousand dollars more."

"What are you talking about, Eliot?"

"Tell him, Cullen," Baxter said.

So Murphy explained the situation to him, concluding with the cold fact that the three men sitting in his saloon were actually three merciless killers who had murdered five men and stolen twenty-five thousand dollars. And even now, they were searching for the money that he had in his safe.

"Damn!" Bradshaw swore. "The best place for them is behind bars. That's an easy decision to make. Can you arrest 'em, Cullen? There are three of them. And they look pretty rank."

"I reckon so," Murphy said. "That's what you're payin' me that big salary for, ain't it?"

"Yeah, but there's three of 'em," he repeated. "What if they decide they don't wanna go? It took us a long time to find a good town marshal. I don't want to lose you."

"If I can't arrest three outlaws who show up in town, what good am I as your marshal?" Murphy said. "I should have arrested them this morning." He got up out of his chair, walked up toward the door, and stopped in front of the table. He didn't pull his pistol out of his holster because he wanted to surprise them.

Working on a bottle of whiskey that stood in the middle of the table, they paid him no mind until he stopped and turned to face them. "Marshal Murphy," Hank Welch said, "sit down and we'll buy you a drink."

" 'Preciate the offer, but I'm afraid I'm gonna have to ask the three of you to stand up and hold your hands up in the air," Murphy said.

Completely surprised, all three just sat there for a long moment. "You're makin' one helluva big mistake," Hank said.

"The three of you are under arrest for the holdup of a Wells Fargo stagecoach and the murder of the five people who were with it. Now get on your feet and get your hands in the air. I'm not gonna tell you again."

"I reckon we better do as he says, boys," Hank said. He got to his feet, but kept his hands by his side. Calvin and Beaver followed his lead. "You know, Marshal, I had you figured for better sense than this. You ain't even got your gun outta the holster. So now, all you've got is a quick-draw contest, you against the three of us. And I've gotta be honest with you, we're all pretty fast. So, how do you figure to get all three of us before one of us gets you? I ain't sure there's anybody that fast."

"What you say might be true," Murphy said. "I was hopin' you boys would be willin' to go peacefully. I'm the marshal here, so it's my job to arrest lawbreakers. I reckon we'll find out who's still standin' when this is over. I know that I will get two of you for sure. I'm that fast and I think I've got a good chance to get a bullet in the third one, even if I have to take one to do it. I'm willing to settle for that."

"If you're that crazy, we'll be happy to accommodate you," Hank said.

"He ain't as crazy as he makes out," a voice over to the side called out. "I'm takin' the one on your right, Marshal, and I'll race you to see who gets that second shot in the man in the middle. I'm damn sure I'm that fast." Murphy didn't turn his head to look, but the voice sounded familiar. He had heard it before, but he couldn't place it. He knew, however, that it stopped the quick-draw contest.

Hank threw his hands in the air. "It's a damn trap, boys! Don't fall for it!"

Murphy walked around behind them and collected their weapons. It was then that he saw Spade Atkins, his six-gun still covering the three outlaws. He paused to salute Atkins with a forefinger to the edge of his hat brim. Atkins acknowledged the salute with a grin and gave his six-gun a spin before returning it to his holster. Murphy was very appreciative of the move Atkins made. He may have saved his life, depending on how lucky he was, or how fast Spade was. But he couldn't figure out the reason behind Spade's move.

"That was a neat little setup you fixed back there in the saloon," Hank declared as Murphy marched them back to the jail. "You really had us thinkin' you were gonna face us in a quick-draw contest. Then you and that gunslinger back there would just shoot us in the back and you could tell the judge it was a duel, right?"

"Sounds like a good idea," Murphy said. "It woulda been the best thing for you three, get it over with quick, instead of hanging."

"What's the routine if we take off running. Which one of us will you try to run down?"

"I wouldn't go to the trouble," Murphy said.

"Would you shoot us down?" Calvin asked.

"Why don't you take off and see what happens," Murphy suggested.

"No, thanks, I think I'll pass on that one."

"Well, I'll be . . ." Will Pickens mumbled to himself when he saw Murphy marching the three outlaws down the street. Standing at the window in the jail office, he declared, "Doggone if he didn't arrest the three of 'em." Still too new at his job to know for sure what he should do, he dropped his hand to his six-gun to make sure he had it on. *That's right,* he thought, *I put it on when we went to breakfast.* He tried to think of something he could do to help Murphy with his prisoners and decided to get the keys and unlock the cell room door, as well as the number two cell.

When he went into the cell room, Ed Moore, who had been lying on his bunk, raised up. And when he saw Will go past his cell and unlock the one next to his, he asked, "What's goin' on?"

"You're fixin' to get some company," Will told him. "Your three friends are coming to live with you and I wanna get their cells ready."

When he went into the number two cell and picked up the empty water bucket, Ed said, "You might as well unlock this cell, too. The marshal's probably gonna put one of 'em in here with me."

Will paused. "That's a good idea, but I ain't sure the marshal wants to mess with a jailbreak at the same time he's makin' arrests."

"It was worth a try," Ed commented. *He's young, but he ain't dumb,* he thought.

Will hurried to the pump and filled both buckets with fresh water. He heard Murphy yell for him when he came in the front door. "Back here, Cullen," he answered, "in the cell room."

"Come on up front," Murphy yelled, "we gotta check in some new guests." When Will came out of the cell room, Murphy handed him a double-barreled shotgun. "Keep an eye on 'em while we see what they're totin' in their pockets. And, Will, keep in mind these fellows ambushed a stage and murdered five men that were with it. So one false move on the part of any one of them, empty one barrel on him." Murphy then ordered them to strip down to their long handles and anything that looked as if it might be a useful tool was placed in a bag with their personal belongings.

During the initial process, there was little said by the suspects, and the three new prisoners made no comments to Ed Moore. When Murphy put Hank Welch in one cell by himself, Hank finally said, "I don't know why you think me and my two friends could be involved in some stagecoach robbery. We're chasin' a cattle rustler and you sure didn't find any big amount of money on us, except what we've earned by chasin' rustlers."

"Right," Murphy said, "you're workin' for Mr. Jenkins who owns the Rockin'-J Ranch."

"That's a fact," Hank said, and then hesitated, remembering their conversation before. He smiled confidently. "I believe you're trying to trick me, Marshal. It ain't Jenkins, it's Mr. Johnson."

"You're right, I was testing your story," Murphy confessed. "And just so you can keep your story straight, I'll tell you this. Lionel Jacobson owns the Rockin'-J and he doesn't have to hire outlaws to guard his cattle. You and your friends might as well settle down in our fine jail here until we can try you and hang you."

"You sound awful damn certain for somebody who ain't got no evidence we was anywhere near that holdup, wherever it was."

"See, that's where you're wrong, because there was an eyewitness to the holdup and the murders who can identify every one of you. You're gonna have plenty of time before that jail wagon can get here from Austin. So introduce yourself to the fellow in the first cell. His name is Ed Moore and he's lookin' for a reward for finding twenty thousand of that money in a hollowed-out tree stump. Can you believe that?"

"No, I can't," Hank answered at once. "Is he your eyewitness?"

"No," Murphy said. "I can't tell you his name. They're afraid it might put his life in danger. You'll have to wait for the trial to find that out."

Once they got the three outlaws settled in, Murphy told them to describe their horses and tell him where they left them. "The town will take care of your horses. Will and I will go pick them up and take 'em to the stable. It'll be pretty near time for dinner, so we'll pick that up, too. Just like you was stayin' in a fancy hotel. Talk to Ed, there. He'll tell you it's pretty good eatin'."

"Yeah, we'll talk to him," Hank mumbled low enough not to be heard.

"We'll lock the place up, so nobody oughta bother you," Murphy said, and he and Will left them for their reunion with their old partner.

"You egg-suckin' dog," Hank spat as soon as the cell room door was closed and locked. "We had it made, but you wanted it all. You're the damn eyewitness. You pointed the finger at me and Calvin and Beaver, so you can claim a reward. You're a fool to think they'll give you as much as your share woulda been if you'da kept your hands off the money."

"I swear, I told him I found that money. You gotta listen to me, Hank," Ed begged. "I know I done the wrong thing, but I never had no notion of running off with that money. I told you that. I was afraid you and Beaver and Calvin woulda been mad if I rode into town to get a drink and left the money without nobody to guard it."

"You're one helluva guard," Calvin said. "You mighta just

as well left it for your horse to guard. Oh, I forgot. That's what you did, ain't it?"

"It don't make no difference," Beaver said. "They know he was with us."

"Yeah? How they know that?" Calvin asked.

"Simple," Beaver said. "There was five of us that took that stage and they shot Cleve, so they know there was four of us left. And Ed had the money, so they know he had to be with us, and that makes four."

"I swear, Beaver, you're dumber than a sack of cow patties," Calvin said. "They don't know how many of us there were, five or five hundred. We didn't leave no witnesses."

"Oh," Beaver replied, and paused to think about it. "I didn't think about that." Then another thought occurred to him. "But that marshal said he had an eyewitness to the hold-up, so he would know there was five of us before Cleve got shot."

"Damn it, Beaver," Hank snapped. "There weren't nobody at that river crossin' but them with the stagecoach and us, and we killed every one of them. That marshal's eyewitness is that cowardly double-crosser in the first cell. And he's gonna find out that we've got three eyewitnesses that saw him take part in the robbery and the killin'. I know I can testify that I saw Ed shoot that Wells Fargo agent right after he shot Cleve."

"I never told that marshal anything about you fellers," Ed insisted. "When he found that money in my saddlebags, I told him I found it where somebody hid it in a hollowed-out tree stump. He didn't believe me, but that's the story I stuck with. I figured we had time to look for it before they got a judge over here, and you boys could get me out of here. I never figured he'd go arrest you. He wouldn'ta had no reason to. Beaver, Calvin," he called out, "you know I wouldn't never have told that marshal that you boys robbed that stage. Hell, if I'd told him that, I'da been tellin' him that I was there with you. It just don't make no sense." He went over and sat down on his bunk in total despair, knowing what a stupid mistake he had made when he confessed to the marshal that he had participated in the robbery and the killing. Now here they sat, all four of them in jail, without a shot having been fired. And when his three partners found out the truth of the matter, he was as good as dead.

Ed Moore was not the only one who was amazed by the arrest of the three outlaws without a shot being fired. Cullen Murphy was also mystified by the volunteer involvement in the arrest by Spade Atkins. He was convinced now that Spade might be a professional gambler, but his real talent was in the handling of the .44 Colt he wore. All signs had pointed in that direction. The fact that Spade had decided to back him in the confrontation with the three outlaws was the thing that puzzled Murphy. The gambler had shown no interest in becoming a part of any other situation that didn't involve him personally. The incident that came to mind was the occasion when Ed Moore assaulted Bonnie Floyd in the dining room. And Spade was content to watch, even when Will Pickens came to her defense, unarmed.

As Murphy walked into Bradshaw's Saloon on his way to meet Will for dinner, he saw Spade Atkins standing at the bar talking to Pete Brice. Murphy thought it was due time he thanked him for his part in the arrest of the three outlaws. "Mr. Atkins!" Murphy called out as he approached the bar. "I figure I owe you a drink of whiskey for lending a hand when I came in here to arrest those three holdup men. I'm on my way to meet Will Pickens for dinner. I'll buy you dinner if you want to join us."

"I'll settle for the drink of whiskey, Marshal. I told Elmo

Dillon and Doc Ennis I'd be here to get a little card game started, and I wouldn't want them to think I ain't gonna give 'em a chance to win some of the money back they lost last night."

"I expect Doc already feels like you've cost him some money," Murphy remarked with a chuckle.

"How's that?" Spade asked.

"If you hadn't stepped in to back me up, Doc was sure to have had some business from me, depending on how lucky I was. Those were pretty high odds against me getting a bullet in all three of those boys without taking one, myself. So I owe you."

"You don't owe me anything," Spade said. "Tell you the truth, I didn't think you could do it, and I was tempted to stay out of it and see if you could take all three without takin' a mortal round to yourself."

"I'm just as glad you didn't," Murphy said. He held his glass of whiskey up in a salute to Spade, then tossed it back, slammed the empty glass down on the bar, and paid Pete for the whiskey. He started toward the entry door to Irene's Café, but Spade stopped him.

"Why were you gonna do it, Murphy? Why try it if the odds are so against you pullin' it off?"

Murphy paused and looked at him as if the answer was obvious. "Because I'm the town marshal. I didn't have any other choice. I'm the law in this town. If I back down because the odds are great, then there is no law in Newtown." He smiled at Spade and made one more comment. "Besides, I felt like I could pull it off with no more than a shoulder or arm wound." He headed for the entrance to the dining room and called back behind him, "I'm damn glad you decided to join in, though!"

Spade shook his head in disbelief. He looked at Pete and asked, "Is he always that sure of himself? Or is he just japin' me?"

"I'd have to say I ain't ever met a man as sure of himself as Cullen Murphy is. I've seen him make a few arrests right here in this saloon. And he never does it like you'd expect a lawman to do it. Couple of weeks ago, a young cowhand had more to drink than he could handle and he drew his sidearm on another feller he thought was cheatin' him. I sent for Murphy, and when he got here, he was holding a short coil of rope. That cowhand held his gun on Murphy and dared anybody to try to take it away from him. Murphy told him nobody was gonna try to take his gun away from him. He told him he'd just put it somewhere safe where it couldn't do no real damage while they was talkin' about the problem. Then he grabbed his wrist and shoved that six-gun up under the cowhand's other arm, like this, right up in his armpit." He demonstrated the move Murphy made. "Before that young feller knew what was goin' on, Murphy wrapped his rope around him four or five times. And just like that, that drunk cowhand was wrapped up around his six-gun and Murphy told him, 'Whatever you do, don't pull that trigger, or you'll hurt for a month.'" Pete chuckled away, just from remembering the ridiculous episode.

Spade tried to picture it from the way Pete had described it. "I suspect that's what you folks here are referrin' to when you're talking about Murphy's Law. Right?"

"I reckon," Pete answered. "But only a few of his methods are entertaining like that one. They're just different than what you'd expect from your town marshal. He wears a hard bark, but he's got a sense of humor if you dig deep enough to let it out."

The more he learned about Marshal Murphy, the more Spade Atkins wanted to know, and it seemed the man was equal parts fact and legend. Some of the tales seemed highly unlikely. But the people who told them swore to their accuracy. What made it harder to take was the fact that Murphy never talked about any past confrontations, let alone bragged about actions he had taken to shut a gang down. His thoughts were interrupted by the arrival of Doc Ennis.

"All right, Spade, I'm feeling like today's my day. Where's Elmo and the others?"

"In the dining room, I think," Spade answered. "Let's sit down and play some two-handed Blackjack till they quit wasting their money on food." He wasn't as enthusiastic about playing cards as he tried to let on. He had to remind himself that his whole purpose in Newtown was to engineer an opportunity to face Murphy in a fast-draw contest. So far, nothing was working toward that ever becoming a possibility. One thing for sure, it was going to have to be fair, because a general lynching of the winner would likely result, if it was not.

# CHAPTER 8

Ward Hatcher rode into Newtown one afternoon at exactly half past two o'clock, according to his railroad pocket watch. He wore a US Deputy Marshal's badge on his heavy wool jacket, and a Boss of the Plains hat that made him appear even taller in the saddle. Riding a gray horse named Smokey and leading a dun packhorse, he carried a Winchester 66 repeating rifle in his saddle sling and wore a Colt Army revolver high on his left side for a cross-hand draw with his right hand. He had been to Newtown before, but that had been before the war, so it was like entering a town he had never seen. He recognized a couple of the buildings, Bradshaw's Saloon, Pratt's Saloon, the general store, but that was about the extent of his memory. So he figured he'd best find the town marshal's office to get up-to-date. He didn't see one right away until he noticed an odd building with a JAIL sign on it.

Will Pickens looked up from the desk when the door opened and a stranger nearly as big as Murphy walked into the office. "Can I help you, sir?" Will asked.

Hatcher looked quickly around the small office to see if there was anyone else there. Seeing no one, he announced his business to Will. "I'm US Deputy Marshal Ward Hatcher. I've got a paper here authorizin' me to pick up a prisoner, name of

Ed Moore, as well as a sum of money in the neighborhood of twenty thousand dollars, both of which are to be transported on horseback to the district court in Austin. If you're Marshal Cullen Murphy, I'll need your signature right here and here, showing that you released Moore and the money to me. And I'll sign below there, saying I got both of 'em from you. I'll take a copy and I'll leave you a copy. Then we'll leave everything right where it is and I'll find the hotel and the dinin' room, and I'll pick up the prisoner and be on my way in the mornin'."

In Deputy Hatcher's efficient presentation of his purpose for his visit to the jail of Newtown, designed to answer all questions before they were asked, he left no gaps for queries. So Will was forced to wait for him to finish before he could reply. "I'm not Marshal Murphy, Deputy Hatcher. I'll go find him for you right away. He's out on the street somewhere. I'm guessin' you got Marshal Murphy's first letter to the US Marshals and that's why you ain't got nobody with you. Is that right?"

Not happy with the way this meeting was going, Hatcher said, "That's right. We got your marshal's letter and responded to it immediately. So, what's the problem?" He expected a confession that there was not nearly as much of Wells Fargo's money recovered as was first reported in the letter. It was not an uncommon occurrence. "How much of the money is missing?"

"Oh, there ain't none of the money missing," Will answered. "Now we have every bit of the Wells Fargo money. The problem is, Marshal Murphy arrested the other three men who robbed that stagecoach and killed everyone with the stage."

Hatcher was too amazed to reply right away, so Will answered his question before he asked it. "As soon as Cullen found out the other three were in town, he arrested them and we sent your office another letter to tell you you'd be transportin' four prisoners, instead of one. I reckon it didn't make it to Austin before you left there to come after Ed Moore."

Hatcher was still putting all that together in his mind, so Will continued. "Would you like to take a look at the prisoners?"

"Yeah," Hatcher said at once, trying to decide if he should even consider trying to transport four prisoners all the way to Austin without help. "Yeah," he repeated. "Lemme take a look at 'em."

Will reached into the desk drawer to get the key to the cell room door; then he got up from the chair and led Hatcher into the cell room. A quiet conversation between Calvin Darcy and Beaver Branson, the only sign of life in the cell room, came to a halt when Will and Hatcher walked in. All four prisoners sat up on their bunks when the big man behind Will turned out to be someone other than Murphy. "Stand up beside your bunks for a minute so the marshal, here, can get a look at you," Will said.

"What for?" Hank Welch replied, and lay back again.

"So I can see how many of you will be wantin' coffee to go with your supper tonight," Will answered, already aware of how little respect the outlaws had for him, but rapidly learning how to use what little power he possessed.

Hank took his time in doing it, but he did get up on his feet after his other three partners were already standing beside their bunks. He smirked defiantly at the deputy marshal looking the four of them over before he addressed him. "Deputy US Marshal Ward Hatcher. I thought they retired you boys when you reached your hundred birthday."

"I ain't surprised to find you here in this jail," Hatcher responded. "I heard you was ridin' with Cleve Carter. I saw Cleve's body where you boys left him. He had one helluva surprise on his face. As near as we figured it, he musta opened the stage door and got a big surprise to find that Wells Fargo agent inside. Is that the way it happened?"

Hank responded with a wry smile. "Whaddya askin' me for?

I ain't even heard Cleve was dead until right now. And you're expectin' me to know about some stagecoach holdup that happened way to hell over on the trail between Waco and Austin? I think it's about time you thought about retirin'. They sent you over here to transport the four of us to Austin. Don't they know you must be at least a hundred years old? They can't expect us to take care of your sorry old ass all the way back. This whole thing is all a mistake, anyway. That marshal arrested us without no evidence hookin' us up to that holdup. The only thing we're guilty of is hearin' about that big sack of money that was on that stagecoach and that Ed Moore had found it. We figured there oughta be a reward out for that money, so we was lookin' for Ed, when that wild man they're payin' to keep the law here sprung a big surprise on us. We was just enjoyin' gittin' to know the town a little better when we got a dose of Murphy's Law—that's what these people in this little town call it."

Hatcher was content to let him ramble on while he evaluated the situation he had unsuspectingly walked into. He didn't know anything about Cullen Murphy, so he decided to hold his judgment on the man's idea of running a town until he had the opportunity to meet him. He noticed that Will had written something on a slip of paper when he had called Hank Welch by name. So he figured they might not know any of their names except that one of Ed Moore. He turned to address Will and said, "That little weasel-lookin' one's name is Beaver Branson. I don't know what his first name is, but they call him Beaver because he looks like one. I don't know the other fellow. Let's go find your marshal." He turned around and headed back toward the office.

Will wrote Beaver's name down on his slip of paper, then followed Hatcher out of the cell room. "I don't know the other fellow's name, but I've heard them call him Calvin," Will said. When Murphy had talked to Hazel in Pratt's Saloon and got the first of the four prisoners' name as Ed Moore, she said he had asked her if a man named Beaver Branson had been in town. It was easy to guess that the little man might be Beaver Branson. Now Will knew for sure. "And that story you were just told has changed a lot from the one he gave Marshal Murphy."

Ward Hatcher thoughtfully stroked his chin whiskers while he looked up and down the street as he waited for Will to lock up. When Will stepped down from the office door, Hatcher stated, "I'm lookin' up and down the street, but I ain't seen nothing that looks like a hotel."

"No, sir," Will replied. "We still don't have a hotel in town, but there's a rooming house near the lower end of town, run by a nice lady named Pearl Johnson. You can rent a room in either Pratt's Saloon or Bradshaw's Saloon, but you'll have a much quieter place to sleep at Mrs. Johnson's. Pratt's can offer you female companionship, if that's what you're lookin' for, and they serve some food. Bradshaw's don't deal with female companions, but they serve the best food in town in the café behind the saloon. You can enter it from inside the saloon or at an outside entrance in the rear of the building."

Hatcher continued to wear the same frown of boredom he presented when he first walked into the office until after Will finished talking. Then he smiled and said, "I swear, young fellow, are you a deputy or the official town greeter? I've spent a long couple of days ridin' and I'd just like to find a place where I can get a hot bath and eat a good meal before I go to bed. I'll get a better night's sleep if I go to bed alone, and I may or may not decide I need a drink of likker before I retire for the night. Knowin' all that, young fellow, Will, was it?" Will nodded, so Hatcher continued his comments. "Where would you go to get a room?"

"That's easy," Will replied. "Get you a room at Mrs. Johnson's roomin' house. She's got a nice washroom built on the back of her house. Go to Irene's Café, at the back of Bradshaw's Saloon for supper. That's where Marshal Murphy and I eat all our meals, and they feed our prisoners as well. Then if you decide to have that drink of likker after supper, you can go right into the saloon. It's a pretty good walk from Bradshaw's back to the roomin' house, though," Will thought to point out. "About a hundred and fifty yards, I expect."

Hatcher chuckled. "I'll keep that in mind. I'm gonna need to leave my horses at the stable, too." He looked at Will and remarked, "I expect that's about another hundred and fifty yards, right?"

Will chuckled as well. "Pretty close, I reckon. Paul Mathers's stable's the last place of business at the north end of town. But if you're plannin' to stay over just one night, Mrs. Johnson's got a barn and a corral, and she'll let you keep your horse there for twenty-five cents. Are you gonna take all four of those prisoners back to Austin tomorrow?"

"To be honest with you, I don't know. I ain't made up my mind whether I wanna risk that job or not," Hatcher answered. He had transported two men by himself many times, but it was pretty much common sense not to set out on any trip where you're outnumbered by your prisoners. At any rate, he thought it a good idea to talk to the town marshal, who had taken all three men into custody all by himself. He wasn't that familiar with three of the men in that jailhouse, but he was familiar with Hank Welch, if only by reputation. Welch had been arrested before. The last time was on a murder charge, but he had escaped in a general prison break three days before his hanging date.

Hatcher had worn the badge of a US Deputy Marshal for more than fifteen years. He was the oldest man in his company, and he could testify that you didn't make it that long in this business if you thought you could single-handedly take on a job that required backup. He found himself leaning toward riding out of town in the morning, escorting the one man he had been sent to transport, Ed Moore. He might possibly meet a detail of several marshals coming to get the other three. At that time, he might decide to join forces with them and return to Newtown to get the other three prisoners. That would at least guard against his boss ordering him to risk his neck to transport four dangerous killers back by himself. It would require at least two sleepless nights.

"Yonder's Marshal Murphy," Will declared, "talkin' to Elmo Dillon in front of the tailor shop. You can leave your horses tied up where they are. Won't nobody bother 'em in front of the jail."

"Tell me Murphy's the one who makes about two Elmo Dillons," Hatcher responded as they crossed the street behind a four-horse team pulling a freight wagon toward Eliot Baxter's store.

Will laughed. "Yes, sir, Murphy's the big one."

Murphy and Elmo halted their conversation when they caught sight of Will and the big stranger approaching them. "Who's that with Will?" Elmo asked.

"Beats me," Murphy replied. "Looks like he means business, don't he? Don't let me hold you up, though, if you need to get on down to Pratt's for that poker game." He couldn't resist japing Elmo, knowing his addiction to gossip.

"No, that's all right," Elmo assured him. "I've got plenty of time yet."

"You sure you aren't gonna lose a little bit of your time to visit with Francine?" Murphy teased. "You know, to get your mind right for that poker game?"

"I swear, Cullen, ain't you ever gonna forget that one time when I bumped into you coming outta her room? It ain't like I hang out upstairs all the time. It was just that one time and I explained that I was going through a bad time."

"I don't know why you worry about it, Elmo. Hell, you know you're the only person I ever mention it to. I just thought, since it was just that one time in your life, that you'd like to think about it sometimes."

"Doggone it, Cullen, I've got a reputation as a businessman and a member of the town council to keep clean. I'm afraid you're gonna slip one day and say something you didn't mean to say."

"Don't worry about it, Elmo, I won't ever do that to ya. What's up, Will?" he asked, turning his attention to his employee and the perfect embodiment of a veteran law officer walking beside him.

"This is US Deputy Marshal Ward Hatcher, Cullen," Will announced. "He just rode in with papers for him to transport Ed Moore to Austin. I already told him about the extra prisoners."

Hatcher stepped forward and extended his hand, which Murphy accepted. "Marshal Cullen Murphy," he said. "Sorry for the big surprise, Deputy Hatcher. I expect you mighta brought a jail wagon with you if you had known you had four of that gang waitin' for you."

"That's a fact," Hatcher replied. "It's a sight bigger job than I figured on. Will told me you folks didn't know anything about the Wells Fargo stage holdup when you arrested Ed Moore."

"That's right," Murphy said. "I arrested Moore for gettin' drunk and shootin' his firearm in Pratt's Saloon. It wasn't until we found all that money he was carryin' in his saddlebags that we started lookin' back through all our notices and wanted papers. As soon as we hit on something, I woulda wired your office, but since we don't have the telegraph, all I could do was send you a letter. Will probably told you that the other three members of that gang showed up here the next day." Hatcher said he had, so Murphy brought him up-to-date on the whole issue, concluding with another apology for the lack of a telegraph wire.

"I'm just surprised that a town this size can't be reached by telegraph," Hatcher remarked.

"It just ain't on the way to anywhere that everybody's trying to get to," Elmo spoke up then. "I'm Elmo Dillon. I own a shop here and I serve on the town council. I gather from the conversation that you rode to Newtown from Austin. That's a long ride of three and a half days or so. If you had come here from Waco, it would have been a little longer trip. If you remember those little trails and wagon roads you followed, there wasn't anything worth building a railroad to get to. Newtown's big enough to attract the goods and services the folks who live around here need. But I reckon we're gonna have to strike gold before the railroad comes here."

Murphy studied Hatcher's face as the deputy marshal listened to Elmo's rant about the absence of a telegraph. It was a tired face, but not one without a definite trace of determination and self-confidence. When Elmo concluded his statement, he turned and followed a customer into his shop. "Good to meet ya, Deputy Hatcher," Elmo said.

"And you, too, Elmo," Hatcher replied.

"Now that you know the situation, Deputy Hatcher, what do you plan to do?" Murphy asked. "Are you gonna head back to Austin tomorrow with one prisoner? Or are you gonna stay a couple of days here and wait to see if your boss sent you some help to transport all four of 'em?" When Hatcher didn't answer right away, Murphy offered one more option. "Of course, you could string four horses together and lead a mule train of prisoners back to Austin."

"That wouldn't be a very smart thing to do, would it, Marshal Murphy?" Hatcher responded. "Three and a half days, maybe more, back over those same deserted trails Elmo was talking about, with four cold-blooded killers and twenty-five thousand dollars in cash. Four men with nothing to lose, already condemned to death, constantly watching you and waiting for you to make the first careless move. No, Marshal Murphy, I ain't worn this badge fifteen years without learnin' when the fight ain't yours to win. So to answer your question, I'll be hangin' around your little town for a few days to see if they sent a jail wagon, along with three more guards."

"Well, that sounds like a sensible idea to me," Murphy said. "Feel free to visit us at the jail anytime and join us for supper in the back of Bradshaw's Saloon. Irene opens for supper at five o'clock every evenin', and we ain't usually much later than that. Are we, Will?"

Will just grinned and shook his head.

"I 'preciate your hospitality, Marshal," Hatcher said. "I reckon I'll see if Johnson's Rooming House has a room I can rent, but I think I'll take my horses to the stable, since I'll most likely be here for a bit after today. I'll see you at supper." He turned to face Will then and said, "Thank you, Will."

"You're welcome," Will replied, and walked back to the jail with him to get his horses.

"I'll be back at the jail in a few minutes," Murphy called after Will. "I'd best go by and let Mayor Baxter know what's goin' on, so he doesn't get his bowels in an uproar."

"Howdy, Jeff," Murphy greeted Baxter's son when he walked into the general store. "Is your pa around?"

"Howdy, Marshal," Jeff responded. "He's in the back checking in some merchandise we ordered."

Murphy nodded and walked on back through the door to the warehouse.

He found Eliot Baxter inspecting some sacks of flour the driver was unloading off the wagon. He was complaining about some sacks that had evidently gotten wet from a leak in the tarp they had been covered with. It had only spoiled one corner of the fifty-pound bag, but Baxter told the driver, "I can't sell flour like that to my customers. They won't even take it for pig feed. Throw it over there with those other three and I'll get rid of it for you." Murphy knew that Baxter would dump most of the flour into smaller bags and sell it at regular price and sell the most spoiled to the farmers for pig feed. When he saw Murphy approaching, Baxter told the driver of the freight wagon to continue unloading. "Just throw any more damaged ones over with the others and I'll take a look at them," he said. Then he walked back toward the door to meet Murphy. "Is there a problem?" he asked.

"No, no problem," Murphy answered. "I just want to let you know when something happens that concerns the four prisoners in the jail." He knew how anxious Baxter was to get the four killers out of Newtown.

And as he expected, the mayor was interested at once. "Did they send a jail wagon up here to pick them up?" Baxter asked.

"No, sir, but they responded right away to our first letter. A deputy marshal just arrived in town with orders to pick up Ed Moore and over twenty thousand dollars. He left Austin before they got our second letter."

"Damn," Baxter swore. "Is he going to take all four prisoners with him?"

"No, sir," Murphy said. "That would be a little too dangerous, especially with men like those four. He's gonna wait here for a couple of days to see what kind of help they send him, then decide what to do."

A frown of disappointment spread across Baxter's face as he considered that possibility. "Then, if they don't send a jail wagon in a couple of days, I suppose he'll just transport two of the prisoners and come back here later on to get the other two, right?"

"I suppose so," Murphy replied.

"And you don't suppose this deputy marshal might decide to go ahead and take all four of them in one trip?" Baxter asked.

Murphy maintained his calm with the mayor's impatience to rid the town of all unnecessary expenses. "No, sir. I think the deputy has more sense than that. He's worn the badge for quite a few years. He strikes me as a man fully aware of what he can and can't do."

"All right. Well, thanks for keeping me posted, Murphy. I reckon we should have given some thought toward a vigilante trial and hanging, but we've already involved the US Marshal Service now."

"And there's also the issue of the money that belongs to Wells Fargo," Murphy said. "I expect the US Marshal mighta showed up here, looking for that."

# Chapter 9

Seated at his table of preference, close to the saloon entrance of Irene's Café, Spade Atkins paused to take a second look at the big stranger coming into the dining room from the outside entrance. He was intercepted by Ginger Floyd, and after they talked briefly, Ginger led him to Marshal Murphy's usual table near the kitchen door. As was his habit, Spade studied the stranger's movements as he thanked Ginger and removed his heavy coat to reveal the star he wore on his wool jacket. That was never usually a welcome sign in Spade's life, but at this particular time there was nothing the lawman could be interested in him for.

As a matter of fact, the only notable incident he had been involved in since arriving in Newtown was assisting the marshal in the arrest of three wanted gunmen. He had to admit that he had felt a certain amount of enjoyment as a result of his actions when the marshal faced up to three armed men in the saloon with no backup. He had suddenly gained some respect from the customers in Bradshaw's for having stepped in to back up their marshal, possibly saving Murphy's life. It was a far reach from his original purpose in coming to Newtown, and that was to cause a possible showdown between himself and Murphy after hearing about a fast-gun marshal who ruled a town under what the people called Murphy's Law. Then it occurred to him that the US deputy marshal was here to transport the four men in Murphy's jail to trial.

Like every other sensible person, Spade wondered where the rest of the deputy's party was. How long was he going to have to wait for a jail wagon to arrive? He had intended to stage a cheating situation, but things had not been going to plan. The card games had been too friendly and far too honest. In fact, he was the only one cheating and that was often necessary to avoid showing too many winning hands. Finally he became so frustrated that he quit throwing in winning hands and started winning pots, using tricks and sleight of hand that he had practiced for years.

*Might as well clean this little hayseed town out of the little money there is and get back to greener pastures,* he decided. *And to hell with Cullen Murphy,* he thought, *I've already got bigger names notched on my gun butt.* With that thought in his head, he frowned when Murphy and Will Pickens walked into the dining room, only to be intercepted by Ginger Floyd and hustled to the table where the deputy marshal waited.

"Spade," Murphy acknowledged with a nod when they passed by on their way back to Murphy' s usual table.

"Marshal," Spade responded bluntly while thinking, *I just saved your butt from getting shot full of holes. That ain't enough to be invited to sit at the table with you?* It had conveniently slipped his mind that it was he who had purposely declined an invitation to share a table with the marshal.

"Deputy Hatcher," Murphy greeted the serious-looking lawman as he and Will each pulled a chair back.

"Ward, please," the deputy insisted.

"Right, Ward," Murphy responded. "Call me Cullen and him Mr. Pickens," he said, nodding in Will's direction. It brought a chuckle out of the deputy marshal that served to cause a deep scowl on the face of the customer sitting alone at the table near the saloon entrance.

Young Bonnie Floyd came to the table then with two cups for Murphy and Will and said that Ginger would be right out with three plates of supper. Will reminded her that he also needed four plates for the prisoners.

"Have you decided what you're gonna do?" Murphy asked Hatcher.

"Yeah," Hatcher answered. "I'm gonna give 'em two days, startin' tomorrow to get some more deputies out here to help me transport those four men. Then if I still ain't got no help, I'll take 'em myself, two at a time. Two I can handle, but four's too many for one guard. I know you'd like to get rid of them as soon as you can, but I ain't gonna try to transport four like that four all by myself."

"Sounds like a smart man talkin'," Murphy remarked. "Frankly, I'da thought you were crazy if you started out from here with all four men. They're all four headed to the gallows, so they've got nothin' to lose. If they decided to just lay down and not move, it'd be a helluva job for one man to make 'em go. I expect you might end up shootin' two or three of 'em before you got to Austin."

"It'd save a lot of trouble to shoot all of 'em before I start back," Hatcher said. "Then I could load each one on his horse and lead 'em back in a pack train."

"It's hard to beat that method, if it turns out they don't send anybody to help you. But if you have to change your mind and transport all four of 'em by yourself, I know how I'd do it," Murphy said.

"How would that be?" Hatcher asked, interested.

"Make your own jail wagon," Murphy answered. "We could get a wagon from Paul Mathers. He's got an old wagon he very seldom uses. He might not even charge you anything to use it, if you brought it back."

"That would be damn good if he didn't," Hatcher remarked, " 'cause I ain't got the money to buy a wagon, and I don't know if I'd ever talk my boss into gettin' me reimbursed for one."

"Paul would probably let us make a few modifications on the wagon, and Joel Trout, he's the blacksmith, could rig a long chain from the axle with bracelets for four prisoners. Then when you're ready to go, the four of them are goin' with you, whether they want to or not."

"That's a helluva idea," Hatcher said. "I'm puttin' that down as plan B. Plan A is if two or three more deputies show up in two days. If they don't, we'll go with plan B. Thanks for invitin' me to join you for supper, men. You mighta come up with the way I'm goin' back to Austin in one trip." His last word was almost unheard due to a loud outburst from the table nearest the saloon entrance.

Everyone in the dining room was startled when Spade Atkins stood up so suddenly that his chair tumbled over behind him. He looked around the room and blurted, "What're you all lookin' at? Mind your own business." He slapped some money down on the table and stormed out through the door into the saloon.

Bonnie Floyd hurried to the kitchen, holding her apron up to catch the tears from her eyes.

"I'll be right back," Murphy said. He got up from the table and went into the kitchen after Bonnie. He found her being consoled by her mother and her sister. "Is there a problem, Irene?" he asked.

"Nothing serious enough to concern the marshal's department," Irene assured him. "The mysterious Mr. Spade Atkins must have had a bad day, and he took a little bit of it out on Bonnie."

"He was never so rude like that before." Bonnie looked up at him while blinking away huge tears still forming in her eyes. "I tried to apologize, but it just seemed to make him mad."

"Apologize for what?" Ginger asked.

"His coffee," Bonnie answered. "He'd already finished his supper when I came back with the coffeepot to see if he wanted any more. He acted crazy. Said he mighta wanted some fifteen minutes before that and maybe he'd have gotten some if he was sitting at the table with the lawmen. I tried to tell him I filled his cup just a couple of minutes before that and he got really mad, jumped up on his feet, and asked me if I was callin' him a liar." She looked up at Irene and said, "I swear, Mama, I didn't do anything to make that man mad."

"I know you didn't, honey," Irene said. "He just got up on the wrong side of the bed this morning, or he hasn't had a winning hand all day. He just took it out on you. He might win a big pot tonight and probably come apologizing to you at breakfast."

"Ginger can wait on him in the morning," Bonnie said. "I don't want to."

"I'll take care of him when he comes back," Ginger told her. "Don't worry about that. I'll take care of his problems."

"Listen, both of you," Irene insisted. "Don't make a big thing out of a customer with a thorn in his foot. It's his problem to get over, not ours, so give him a chance to get over whatever's bothering him." She looked over at Murphy then. "We appreciate you being concerned, Cullen, but it's nothing important. Now go on back to your coffee before you start complaining about it being too cold."

Murphy returned to his table to answer the inquisitive expressions on the faces of Will and Hatcher. "Nothing serious," he explained for Hatcher's benefit. "The two young daughters of the owner have both had some bad experiences with some undesirable customers within the last few days and I just thought I'd make sure everything was all right." He didn't mention it, but Spade's comment about not being invited to join them at their table struck him as especially peculiar. Up until this particular moment, Spade Atkins maintained a strict policy of a professional loner. Even after stepping in to back Murphy's attempt to arrest Hank Welch and his two partners, Spade had refused an invitation to have supper with Murphy and Will and settled for a drink of whiskey, instead. That didn't make any sense, he decided. His thoughts were forced back to the present when Will suggested those fried potatoes on his plate were a lot better if he ate them before they got cold.

They took their time finishing supper until Will decided their prisoners were probably about to starve to death. "So I'm gonna go on ahead and take their plates back to the jail. Then I'll make 'em a pot of coffee."

Hatcher had already announced his intention to have a drink of whiskey after supper and then go to his room at the rooming house. He invited Murphy and Will to have a drink with him. Will declined because he wasn't much of a drinker of alcohol and the prisoners were probably hungry.

Murphy said it would be impolite for them both to refuse, so he said he would have one drink with the deputy. "Be sure you lock that office door after you go in, so you don't have any visitors while you're back there in that cell room," he reminded Will. "And go by the rules. If they don't get all the way in their bunks, you don't open that cell door and they don't eat. I shouldn't be too long in gettin' there, myself." He explained to Hatcher that when the building was converted to a jailhouse, openings for food trays weren't included. At the time, the thinking was that it prevented weapons from getting in. Now it seemed more trouble than it was worth. He didn't mention that he was the person who built the jail.

Hatcher made it a point to compliment the girls on the quality of the food, which pleased them very much; so much so, that they insisted his first meal in the café should be on the house. He, of course, was very appreciative and assured them that every meal after this would be in their establishment as long as he was in town.

"Let's go get that drink of likker now," Murphy said, and pointed to the door back into the saloon. He lingered long enough behind him to lay some money down to cover Hatcher's meal. When Ginger fixed an accusing eye on him with one eyebrow raised, he whispered, “You didn’t make a dime off me or Will or four prisoners in the jail. You oughta get paid for something, even if it ain’t but one supper.”

“You don’t have to do that, Cullen,” Ginger whispered. “The town pays for yours and your prisoner’s meals.”

“I know,” he whispered, “but not at the rate you normally charge.”

He hurried along then to catch up with Hatcher, who had already passed through the door. He was struck at once by a quiet that was not at all typical for Bradshaw’s Saloon at that hour of the evening. He knew something was wrong, but he had to move around Hatcher’s wide body to see for himself. When he did, he was not surprised to see who was the cause of the missing barroom noise. Over in the corner of the room where the card game usually went on, there was one man standing. Spade Atkins stood, leaning against the table, glaring at a man still seated on the other side of the table. Murphy moved quickly through the spectators, who had gathered to witness the confrontation, until he could see the man still seated. William “Doc” Ennis was the unfortunate victim of Spade Atkins’s ire.

“What’s the problem here, Atkins?” Murphy stepped over to stand behind Doc’s chair.

“The problem is, I thought I’d been playin’ cards with an honest group of men. Now I find out they’ve been cheatin’ every game I’ve been in. And this low-down yellow dog is pulling aces out of his sleeve.”

“How’d you find that out?” Murphy calmly asked Spade.

“It’s supposed to be my deal,” Spade said. “I was gathering up the cards, and when he handed me his, this ace of diamonds dropped out of his sleeve. I ain’t the only one who saw it. We all saw it and he’s been havin’ a pretty good winnin’ streak, too, now that I think about it.”

“He’s wrong, Cullen,” Doc pleaded. “I tried to tell him I’m

not a cheat. I don't know where that ace of diamonds came from, but it wasn't from out of my sleeve. I showed him there weren't any cards up my sleeves. I took my coat off and there weren't any cards anywhere on me. I haven't ever cheated in a card game with anyone since I've lived here in Newtown. May God strike me dead if I'm lying."

"If you believe what you just said, then we can settle that right quick," Spade smirked. "You're wearin' a gun, so get on your feet and get ready to use it. And I reckon we'll see whether you're lyin' or not."

"Whaddaya say to that, Doc?" Murphy asked. "You wanna shoot it out with Spade to see who's right?"

"Hell no, I don't want to shoot it out with him. I know who's right. I'm right. I don't cheat at cards. And I don't practice shooting a gun, either, and one look at him and you know that's all he does, play cards and practice shooting that gun."

"Well, there you go, Spade," Murphy announced. "Doc don't wanna shoot it out with you, and that's a good thing for both of you because dueling in the city limits is against the law. I'da had to lock you both up. If you both wanna duel in the mornin', you have to take it out of town, down beside the river. Doc, you wanna shoot it out with Spade in the mornin'?"

"Hell no, Cullen, I'm not gonna shoot it out with him," Doc insisted. "I don't cheat at cards, either. Anybody here at the table can tell you that."

"Okay, it's settled," Murphy declared. "There'll be no shootout here in town tonight or out of town tomorrow mornin'. Spade, you're new in town, so it's only fair to tell you something you had no way of knowing. It's like this, everybody in Newtown knows that Doc Ennis is an honest man. So we know that Doc Ennis doesn't cheat at cards. And the town can't afford to lose Doc because he owns the drugstore, he's the town doctor and the town undertaker, too. So you were not aware of the fact that it's against the law for Doc to fight a duel."

A long moment of silence followed Murphy's declaration; then a single cheer from the bar was followed by an outburst of cheering for Doc Ennis. It lasted for several more minutes before the crowd calmed down once more to find Spade Atkins, his long coat pulled back away from his holster, standing now to face Murphy. "How about you, big mouth? Is it against the law in this town to call out the marshal? Can you do anything besides runnin' your mouth all night?"

"All right, Atkins, you made your play for a killin' and it didn't pan out. Don't push your luck. I don't know why you showed up in Newtown in the first place, but it's pretty obvious that you ain't found whatever you were looking for. So I expect it'd be a good idea for you to move on to another town. Maybe you can find one where the gambling is worth your interests."

"Nobody runs me outta town," Spade growled. "I'll leave when I damn well please." He continued to watch Murphy, his body poised to react to any sudden move the marshal made.

"How 'bout if we just ask you politely to leave then, and wish you better luck at your next stop? No? I didn't think so," Murphy said when Spade didn't respond verbally. "You don't really give a damn about Doc, do ya? It's me you want." Spade's only response to Murphy's question was the curling of his upper lip from a snarl to a crooked smile. "You know, I thought that was a helluva thing you did when you stepped in to back me up when I arrested those three killers. It's downright disappointin' to find out now that you were just savin' me for yourself. Well, I'm sorry, Spade, but I don't do fast-draw shoot-outs. Like I said, it's against the law in Newtown, so it's best you leave our town now."

"Against the law, is it?" Spade replied. "I reckon that's the Murphy's Law everybody here talks about, ain't it? Well, Murphy's Law don't apply to me, and this town ain't big enough for both of us. So one of us has to leave, and the only way you're gonna walk outta here is to turn around and walk out that door. I'll count to three, and when this dog comes out, it bites. One . . . two . . ."

"Three!" Murphy declared when the .44 round from his Colt struck Spade Atkins in the chest, the hammer on Spade's six-gun having yet to be cocked. The disbelief reflected in his eyes registered the shock to his brain as he staggered backward and fell across his overturned chair. There was not a sound in the room for a brief few seconds before the eruption of everyone reacting at once. When everyone calmed down, Murphy apologized for the disturbance. "I'm sorry to have to disrupt your card game, but the man was determined to shoot somebody. It is against the law to call a man out in the town limits, but I couldn't convince him of that. At least we won't have to send for Doc Ennis to take care of the body."

"I'll be more than happy to take care of his worthless body," Doc declared, "at no charge to the city for the burial."

"What are we gonna do about Doc's cheating habits, though?" Elmo Dillon japed. "We had a cure there for a few minutes until you walked in."

When the laughter died down, Murphy said, "I think you oughta go through Spade's pockets and divide up what money you find. I expect if there was any real cheating goin' on, it most likely came from him." His suggestion was well received and a couple of them began a search of the body.

"I hope you didn't go to all that trouble to impress me," Ward Hatcher said when Murphy walked back over to the bar to stand beside him. "I got the impression that fellow wasn't a regular card player here."

"No, he showed up here a few days ago, on his way to nowhere in particular, and stopped in my office to tell me he was a professional gambler." He went on to relate the story behind Spade's appearance in town and the sudden change in his personality. "I think he had a definite reason for coming here, but I can't figure out what it was."

"Not knowing any more than what I've just witnessed," Hatcher said, "I'd assume you were the reason for him showin' up here in Newtown. He didn't care anything about settlin' anything with that other fellow, Doc. He was just using him to get to you."

"Tell you the truth, it kinda looked that way to me, too," Murphy admitted. "He was obviously a fast gun, but if he came all the way out here to Newtown to add to his reputation, he couldn't have been comin' after me. I don't have any reputation with a handgun. I figure I musta had a run-in with a friend or family member of his."

"Well, you impressed the hell outta me," Hatcher said. "I sure thought for a minute there that I might have to arrest that fellow."

"Like I told you," Murphy insisted, "quick-draw justice ain't my thing. I'll admit to you that I cheated a little bit on that face-off. I was afraid I might be forced into some fool thing like that. So when I walked over behind Doc's chair, I reached down and cocked my .44 while it was still in my holster. The hammer had been restin' on an empty cylinder, so when I cocked the hammer back, it rotated a loaded cylinder under a cocked hammer. So I had to worry about shootin' myself in the leg, if I was too careless. It was damn near a draw and I was lucky not to squeeze that trigger too soon."

"What is it, Cullen? What's goin' on?" Tyson Bradshaw hurried down the stairs, having heard the single gunshot and then waiting to make sure there were no more before investigating.

"Nothing to worry about, Mr. Bradshaw," Murphy answered. "The boys just put on a little demonstration to show Deputy Marshal Hatcher what life's like in the Texas Hill Country. Ward, this is Tyson Bradshaw. He's the owner of the saloon." While they shook hands, Murphy told Bradshaw that Hatcher was in town to transport the four prisoners in the jail to trial, as well as take that sack of money out of his safe.

"Not too loud," Bradshaw cautioned Murphy. "I heard that gunshot and I thought they were comin' after it then."

"Pleased to meetcha, Mr. Bradshaw," Ward Hatcher said. "I'm with you on that subject. I'd just as soon keep it quiet. I ain't too happy about those four we'll be transportin' knowin' we'll also be carryin' that money."

"Are you taking it and all four of the outlaws by yourself?" Bradshaw asked.

"No, sir, I'm not," Hatcher answered. "I'm waiting here for some help to show up."

"That's what I was fixin' to come and tell you and Mr. Baxter," Murphy said. "I just had to wait until I knew for sure what Ward's plans were. I reckon our plan right now is to have that one drink of likker we came in here for, before Spade Atkins put on his little show. Doc's gone to get his handcart. I'll tote Spade's body out the front door for him to pick up. I found his room key in his coat pocket. Room 4, it says. Is that right?"

"That's right," Bradshaw said. "It's the last room before my office at the end of the hall."

"I wonder what ol' Spade woulda done, if he'da known he was sleepin' that close to twenty-five thousand dollars." Murphy couldn't help but mention that; Bradshaw just shook his head. "Anyway," Murphy continued, "after I have that drink, I'm gonna go upstairs to Spade's room and pick up his things. I just wanted to let you know."

"That'll be fine," Bradshaw said. "Just leave the key with Pete when you're done. Pete," he said, "pour them a drink of the good stuff, on the house."

# CHAPTER 10

A couple of the card players volunteered to carry Spade Atkins's body out the front door, where they propped him up in a sitting position against a corner of the building. Elmo Dillon brought an empty whiskey bottle from inside and propped it on his thigh to lay across his hand. It looked like he was holding the bottle and that was the pose Doc found him in when he came back with his cart.

After Murphy and Ward finished their drinks, Ward said that was all the activity he could tolerate for the night and headed for his room at the rooming house. Murphy went up to Spade's room and looked around. Most of his things were in his saddlebags, so Murphy took them with him. He left the room key with Pete and walked up to the stable to check on Spade's two horses and anything else that belonged to him. Paul Mathers was more than a little interested in what was to happen to the Appaloosa. He usually ended up with the unclaimed horses, but he feared it might be a different situation with an Appaloosa.

He had left the stable and was performing his usual early-evening check on the town when it occurred to him that he had left Will to take care of the feeding of four of the most desperate men he had ever encountered. Will was only nineteen years old, and sometimes he seemed younger than that. The more he thought about it, the more he had the feeling something could easily go wrong. Thoughts of another young man he had trained to be a lawman, Bert Walker, and the hanging death he suffered came back to haunt him. "To hell with the town," he blurted, and went straight to the jail.

He found the front door locked as he had instructed Will to do. As he hurriedly turned his key in the lock, he thought he heard a sound from inside the jail, probably the cell room. Inside, he dropped Spade's saddlebags on the floor, drew his six-gun, and headed for the cell room door. He didn't call out for Will, thinking it wiser not to announce his presence, and he inserted the cell room key slowly and deliberately in an effort to quiet the sound of the lock turning. The bolt had almost drawn open when he heard the sudden plea: "Stop!" It didn't sound like Will's voice.

He didn't hold back any longer, turned the bolt hard, and pushed through the doorway to find a startled Will sitting on the floor outside the second cell. All the prisoners were sitting on their bunks, drinking coffee, except for Beaver, who was on the floor close to the barred cell door. Immediately relieved, Murphy dropped his six-gun back into the holster and asked, "What's the trouble, Will?"

"He won't give me my coffee!" Beaver blurted before Will could answer. "He gave coffee to everybody else, but he won't give it to me."

"I told you what to do to get your coffee," Will told him. "But you won't do like I told you. Your three friends all got their coffee 'cause they followed the rules. They can do it and you can do it, or you don't get no coffee, and I'll drink it, myself."

"Why can't he do like you tell him?" Murphy asked.

"Oh, he's got this idea that he can trick me," Will said. "He's trying to get me to open the cell door just enough to slide the cup in, instead of him going back and sittin' on his bunk while I slide it in the door. He thinks I didn't see him sneak a fork off his supper plate and he thinks he can grab me when I slide the cup inside. Then I don't know what he thinks he can do, stick me with his fork or something, I reckon. He's crazy as a bedbug."

"To hell with him," Murphy said. "He must not want it all that much, anyway. Drink it yourself or throw it out. Let's lock this room up for the night."

Will picked up what dishes he had already taken out of the cell when the others had finished eating and they turned the wicks down on the two lamps outside the cells.

"I heard a gunshot after I left you and Deputy Hatcher back at Bradshaw's," Will said. "I was afraid you mighta run into some trouble and I didn't know if you needed help or not. But I was carryin' all four of the prisoners' dinners, so I waited for a little while. I didn't hear another shot, so I figured that you and Deputy Hatcher must have took care of it."

"That shot you heard was the end of Spade Atkins," Murphy said. "Those are his saddlebags layin' in the floor in the office. He turned plumb loco during the card game and it ended up in a face-off between him and me, causing me to break the law on duels in the town limits. So I came back here to turn myself over to you."

Will chuckled. "Now, tell me what really happened."

When Murphy unlocked the cell room the next morning, he found Beaver still on the floor of the cell beside the bars. Instead of sitting, however, he was lying on his back, sound asleep. His cellmate, Calvin Darcy, was in his bunk, fast asleep, as were Hank Welch and Ed Moore in the other two cells. It was still a little while before the dining room would be open, so Will decided to empty the chamber pots and refill the water buckets before he and Murphy went to breakfast. Rather than wake the prisoner and handcuff him to the bars while this was done, Murphy just stood in the open cell door, covering the sleeping man with the shotgun while Will freshened the pots and buckets. Allowing for the possibility that Beaver might actually be awake and attempting to play possum, they decided to wait and clean his and Calvin's while they were eating their breakfasts.

They found Ward Hatcher waiting for them when they got to the café, seated at Murphy's usual table. "Mornin'," he greeted them. "Miss Bonnie said it was all right if I sat at your regular table."

"I'll have to talk to her about that," Murphy joked. "If I let her get away with a US Deputy Marshal, she's liable to think it's all right to sit a bank robber here, if one walks in."

Waiting beside the table for him and Will to sit down, so she could fill their coffee cups, she responded in kind. "I asked Deputy Hatcher if he wouldn't prefer to sit by himself, but he said he'd try to put up with you and Will." She filled their cups just as Ginger came out of the kitchen carrying three plates.

"I'll tell you one thing," Hatcher commented, "you can't beat the service here and that woman sure knows how to cook."

"I'll have to agree," Murphy said, "and it's always top-notch. How'd you sleep down at Mrs. Johnson's?"

"Like a baby," Hatcher replied. "That bed was like sleeping in a cradle. I swear, I'd think I was on a vacation, if I could forget about those four coyotes waitin' in your jailhouse." He paused to let Ginger serve the plates before continuing. "I've been thinkin' more about building that jail wagon you suggested. I believe it would be the smartest thing for me to do. I could get on back with all four prisoners at once. I wonder how long it would take the blacksmith to fix a wagon up like that. More deputies might show up before he gets it fixed up to go and then I'd have a half-finished wagon on my hands and no reason to complete it."

"Why don't we go talk to Joel Trout after we finish breakfast?" Murphy suggested. "You know, if Austin got that second letter we sent about the other three outlaws, you might have two or three deputies showing up here to help you transport them on horseback, which is a little quicker than a wagon."

"Things sure would be a whole lot simpler if you had a telegraph line run over in this county, wouldn't it?" Hatcher felt compelled to complain.

"Well, it ain't like somebody wants to and we say we don't want the damn wire," Murphy reminded him. "You're just spoiled by workin' in the modern world." Then he thought to ask Will, "You want me to help you take the breakfast plates to the jail first?" Will said no, that he could handle breakfast by himself. Murphy went on to tell Hatcher about the trouble Will had with Beaver and his coffee the night before. "You sure you don't want me to help you with breakfast?" Murphy asked again. Like before, Will insisted he could handle it. "Don't forget to put your pistol on."

"I won't forget," Will insisted.

"'Cause I notice you forgot to wear it right now," Murphy continued.

"I didn't forget," Will said. "I just didn't think I'd need it to get some breakfast."

"Ain't that how we got started?" Murphy japed. "You in here and your gun outside with your horse? And you ended up with all the trouble of feedin' prisoners."

"I didn't think it started any trouble," Will declared. "It got me a job and off the grub line." They both chuckled, and Murphy had to tell Hatcher the story about Will coming to defend Bonnie Floyd when Ed Moore grabbed her.

"Everything happens for a reason, I reckon," Hatcher commented. When they finished eating breakfast, Murphy and Hatcher left the café and walked up to the blacksmith shop to talk to Joel Trout about a jail wagon. Will remained at the table, waiting for the plates to take to the jail.

* * *

"Yeah," Joel Trout responded, "I've got plenty of chain, enough to give you what you're talking about. I'll have to make up some bracelets that you can lock down around your prisoners' wrists. You got the wagon you gonna convert?"

"We figured on usin' Paul Mathers's old wagon," Murphy said. "He don't usually care what you do to it." Joel's sudden change of expression caused Murphy to react. "What?"

"Paul ain't got that wagon no more," Joel said. "He traded it to some farmer about a month ago for a load of hay or something. The rear axle was broke and I rebuilt two of the wheels."

"Damn," Murphy swore. "What was the farmer's name? Maybe he might lend the wagon for some official law business."

"Paul never told me his name," Joel replied. "It was Paul I done the work for."

Murphy was about to suggest they go to the stable to get the farmer's name, but Hatcher interrupted him. "It was a helluva idea, Cullen, but I don't have the time or the money to make it work right now. I'll go back to plan A and wait here for another day. Then if nobody shows up, I'll take 'em back two at a time. It ain't like I never done it that way before. Hell, maybe a couple of the boys will show up here tomorrow with a real jail wagon. And that woulda made a mess of things, if I was in the middle of tryin' to make my own jail wagon."

"I'm sorry it didn't work out," Murphy told him. "I'll still do anything I can to help you out. Although right now I don't know what that might be." He shrugged and added, "Right now, I expect I'd better go back to the jail to see if Will had any trouble feeding our guests."

"I'll go back with you, if I won't be in the way," Hatcher said. "It's either that, go back to the saloon, or go to my room and take a nap."

"You're always welcome to hang out with your friends at the jail, on both sides of the bars. We'll make us a fresh pot of coffee and look through the wanted papers to see if there's anybody we know in 'em." So they left the blacksmith shop and walked back to the jail. Just like the last time Will delivered the prisoners' food, Murphy heard a disturbance just as he approached the front door. This time, however, it was a gunshot from inside the building, which caused both law officers to draw their weapons before charging inside.

There was no one in the office, so Murphy led the way into the cell room, the door of which was locked. He took only a moment to unlock it and flung the door open to startle Will, who was kneeling on one knee outside the second cell, aiming his pistol through the open door. A full plate of food was on the floor, just inside the cell, and Beaver Branson's butt was all you could see of him in his bunk. Calvin Darcy was sitting in the other bunk, eating his breakfast with a wide grin of amusement on his face. Murphy looked quickly at Hank Welch in the third cell and Ed Moore in cell number one. Like Calvin, they were both still eating their breakfast and both seemed highly entertained.

"Will! What the hell!" Murphy blurted.

"It ain't nothin'," Will said. "Just Beaver acting like a horse's ass. He keeps tryin' to get outta that cell. His friends do like I say. They get in their bunks and stay there till I slide their food inside and lock the cell. He won't get in his bunk. So I told him I'd put Calvin's plate inside, but not his until he could go by the rules. When Calvin got out of his bunk to pick up his food, Beaver made a dash to beat him to it. So I put a bullet, which passed pretty close to his head, into the wall. That's why you can't see nothin' but Beaver's butt stickin' up right now. I told Calvin to go ahead and pick up his plate and he took it back to his bunk. I told Beaver he could have his breakfast, but he had to play by the rules or I'd shoot him."

"Beaver Branson!" Murphy yelled. "Do you want your breakfast?"

Beaver stuck his head up and grinned. "Yes, sir, Marshal Murphy, I want my breakfast, but Will won't give it to me."

"You have to go by the rules," Murphy said, "just like Hank and Calvin and Ed did. Do you understand the rules?"

"Yes, I do," Beaver answered.

"What are they, if you want to eat?" Murphy asked.

"Set in the bunk and don't get out of it until Will opens the door and pushes the plate in the cell and locks the door again. Then I can go pick it up."

"Perfect," Murphy said. "Now, do you want to get your breakfast?"

"Yes, sir, Marshal Murphy."

"All right, sit up in your bunk and we'll put your food inside," Murphy told him, and Beaver did as he was told. Murphy unlocked the cell and opened the door. Will put the plate on the floor and carefully slid it inside the cell. Beaver sprang off his bunk immediately and dived for the open door, only to be met with a sharp blow to the side of his head from the barrel of Murphy's six-gun.

"Looks to me like he needs a little quiet time to think about what he's doin'," Murphy said. "A little time in the quiet room will help him think straight." He looked at Calvin and said, "You just set right there and eat your breakfast, Darcy. Will, hold your gun on him and shoot him if he gets out of that bunk." Hatcher trained his sidearm on Calvin as well. Will shifted himself around to take dead aim at Calvin, while Murphy stepped inside the cell and stood a groggy Beaver Branson on his feet. Then he hefted him up to lie across his shoulder and stepped out of the cell. "Lock the cell, then pick up his food and follow me." He walked out of the cell room and went toward the back door of the building. "Fill one of those small buckets with fresh water," Murphy said as he passed through the kitchen and went out the back door.

Murphy could feel the consciousness returning to Beaver's

brain by the slight movements of his body trying to regain his senses as Murphy carried him across the backyard. Finally he came back enough to realize what was happening. "Hey, you big turkey," he slurred, "where we goin'?"

"To the children's quiet room," Murphy answered him, "where nobody can bother you while you're restin'." He stopped in front of a small square building, pulled Beaver off his shoulder, and stood him on his feet facing the door. He removed the latch and opened the door. "Will, put his plate and the bucket of water inside," Murphy directed; then to Beaver, he said, "Now remember which side of the door your food and water are on, 'cause you might have some competition for it."

His senses rapidly returning by now, Beaver protested, "That looks like a damn smokehouse!"

"That's what everybody says," Murphy replied, and with one big boot on the seat of Beaver's pants, he propelled him into the dark abyss and closed the door behind him. He put the padlock back in place, but this time he locked it. "It's been a long time since I've locked this smokehouse. I hope the key is still hangin' on that hook in the kitchen," he muttered as an afterthought.

Ward Hatcher had followed along as a fascinated observer, making no comments, but he could hold his curiosity for only so long. "That really is a smokehouse you threw him in, ain't it?"

"Sure is," Murphy replied. "It's been a lot of years since it was used as a smokehouse, though. Will, you might be interested in this as well. When I came back from the war, I had no interest in being a lawman. I had a little piece of land on the river, and I just wanted to see if I could turn it into anything. Problem was, there was too much lawlessness goin' on in Newtown—and there was absolutely no law. I'll spare you the details, but I got pushed into enforcing the law. And this smokehouse was the only thing I could use for a jail. So Beaver Branson ain't the first to go to solitary confinement in that jail.

One thing for sure, though, good or bad, it damn sure makes an impression on most folks."

They went back inside the jail then and Murphy looked inside the small pantry, first thing. "Yep, there it is." He held the key up for Will to see. "Right here on this little hook. I'm glad I didn't lose it, 'cause I expect Irene would like to have that plate back."

By the time Will checked back in the cell room, the three prisoners there had finished eating and all three had brought their dirty dishes to sit on the floor by the cell door. He had no way of knowing for certain, but Will thought Murphy's handling of Beaver may have been the reason behind the show of peaceful cooperation.

It was not until he had collected the dirty dishes from all three cells in his big dishpan that Hank asked, "Where's Beaver? Is he in some other part of the jailhouse?"

"No, Beaver ain't in the jailhouse no more," Will answered solemnly. "He's somewhere Marshal Murphy has put other prisoners who don't like to follow the rules." He went out of the room then to let their imaginations take over their speculation.

# CHAPTER 11

There was not much for US Deputy Marshal Ward Hatcher to do but wait and hope to spot a brace of deputy marshals riding into town. He passed some of the time cleaning his weapons and a good deal more of it getting to know Paul Mathers at the stable when he visited his gray gelding, Smokey. While at the stable, he checked on the condition of the horses that belonged to the four prisoners in the jail. Most of the rest of the day was spent shadowing Cullen Murphy. It was at dinnertime that an opportunity to vary Hatcher's dull routine presented itself. They were sitting at the table eating their dinner when Hatcher mentioned the fact that the four horses the prisoners were riding were all in good shape and should present no problem for a trip to Austin.

"What kind of shape are their packhorses in?" Murphy asked.

"Paul said they just had the horses they rode in on," Hatcher replied. "He said they didn't have any packhorses with 'em."

"Well, that don't hardly seem right," Murphy said. "You know they had packhorses. As far as they had to travel to wind up here, they had to have some packhorses. And the only reason they wound up here was to use that hideout up on Owl

Branch." He paused while he visualized the cabin near the top of the gulch. "You know, more than likely there are some horses in that little corral up there, maybe without food or water. We better get up there and let those horses out of that corral."

"That's something I can do to make myself useful," Hatcher immediately volunteered.

"I'm afraid you'd never find it," Murphy said. "That's the reason so many gangs have used it. It's hard to tell somebody how to get there. The only reason this gang knew how to get there was because that little dolt locked in the smokehouse had been there with another gang of outlaws."

"Maybe I could do that for you," Will suggested, "since Baxter and Bradshaw are so afraid to have you leave town for any time at all."

"I know you could," Murphy responded, "but you ain't ever been up there before, and I don't think I could ever tell you how to get there. Besides, it's not but three miles from town. I can run up there and be back before anybody knows I'm gone. I won't waste a lot of time tryin' to herd 'em back to town with me, if they don't wanna follow me. I just want to make sure they can get to food and water."

"I'll go with you," Hatcher said, "and maybe I can help herd 'em back this way."

"That might be helpful," Murphy said, "but I wonder if it might be better if you stay here at the jail with Will."

"I can take care of the jail, Cullen," Will declared at once. "You'd best take Deputy Hatcher with you in case there's somebody else in that hideout."

Murphy couldn't suppress a chuckle. "All right," he decided, "Ward and I will ride up there and free the horses. And you'll stay here at the jail. But we'll take all four of the prisoners' dinners to the jail. I'll let Beaver out of the smokehouse and let him eat with the other prisoners. I was gonna keep him in there a little longer, but he's probably had enough by now, anyway." He paused, then added, "If the rats ain't ate him yet."

They didn't linger long after finishing their dinner, and when they left the dining room, Murphy and Will took the four plates back to the jail, while Hatcher went up to the stable to pick up his and Murphy's horses.

When Murphy and Will got back to the jail, they took all four of the meals into the cell room and dispensed with the usual routine, and Murphy opened each cell and stood there with his gun drawn while Will handed the prisoner his plate, then locked the cell and went on to the next one.

When all three were served and eating, Murphy and Will went out to the smokehouse.

There was no sound coming from the smokehouse as they approached the door. "You reckon the rats ate him?" Will wondered aloud.

Hearing the sound of talking, Beaver yelled out, "Let me outta here! I'll be good!" Murphy didn't answer, so he yelled again. "I give you my word! I won't cause you no more trouble!"

Murphy waited a few seconds before he responded, "Your word ain't no good."

"I know, but I swear I'll be good if you let me outta here," he pleaded as he pressed hard up against the door.

Murphy unlocked the padlock and removed it. The door swung open as a result of Beaver's weight behind it, dumping him out on the ground like a newborn, his eyes closed tight against the bright afternoon sunlight.

"I oughta just shoot you and be done with you," Murphy told him.

"No! No more trouble. I swear!" he pleaded, straining to see through eyelids still tightly closed against the light.

"On your feet," Murphy ordered, and grabbed the back of his collar and lifted him up from all fours. He held him until he got his feet planted firmly on the ground; then he marched him into the jailhouse. "I'm gonna let you eat your dinner in your cell, as long as you behave. First sign of trouble outta you and back you go in that smokehouse until you leave this earth. Now march," he ordered, and poked him in the back with the muzzle of his .44.

Inside the cell room, they all got quiet when Beaver was let back in the cell. Will handed him his plate and they locked him in. Not a sound was heard until Murphy and Will closed the cell room door behind them and they heard a small explosion of voices go up.

Ward was waiting in the office. Will assured Murphy that he could handle everything, and Murphy assured Will that he would be back before suppertime. Murphy picked up his rifle and followed Ward out the door. He dropped the Henry rifle in the saddle scabbard, then checked the cinch to make sure it was properly tightened before climbing aboard and leading Ward up the north end of the street.

They did not ride very far past a fork that branched off to the river road that led to several small farms along the San Saba River before Murphy left the wagon road through a small gap in the trees. Ward was surprised to find that the clump of trees hid the beginning of a game trail, leading to the rugged hills farther west. He remembered then that Murphy had said the trail would be difficult to find for anyone who had never been there before. *You would have lost me right there,* he thought. The trail seemed to be generally heading toward a high ridge to the west, but there were a couple more forks to be taken before reaching a trail that appeared to be the main one and it continued for a great distance, crossing several tiny streams before coming to a strong busy branch that Murphy said was Owl Branch. It flowed down through a narrow gulch in the ridge above with considerable force. The main trail continued across the branch, but Murphy pointed to a narrow trail that followed the stream. He turned the bay gelding onto the tiny trail and followed it up through the gulch until the solidly built log cabin came into view. He pulled his rifle out of the scabbard. Seeing him pull it, Ward did the same and they proceeded with caution.

There was no sign of any life around the cabin and no smoke from the chimney. Still cautious, however, they rode around the cabin prepared to return fire. A bullet from a lone drifter was just as deadly as one from an outlaw gang. "Hello the cabin!" he finally called out to no response, so Murphy rode up past the small barn, where he found the four packhorses locked in the corral. They were already looking pretty puny and they crowded together at the gate when he approached it. He reached down, grabbed the latch, and swung the gate open wide. The desperate horses pushed through the gate at once and went down into the stream. He rode Nosy through the gate into the corral. There was nothing there to eat and the watering trough was dry, except for a thin strip of wet mud on the bottom of it.

"I expect they woulda licked that dry before sundown," he said to Ward when the deputy marshal rode up to look in the trough. They both looked at the horses splashing around in the stream.

"Just lookin' at that makes it worthwhile to take this ride up here, don't it?" Ward remarked.

"That's what I was thinkin'," Murphy said. "Let's take a look in that little barn." They dismounted and went into the small building, where they found the packsaddles for the horses. It appeared they were all packed up as if not to return; then for some reason they decided they were coming back. "Somehow, Ed Moore got his hands on all the money 'cause he had it with him when I arrested him. He sure didn't act like a man who was runnin' away with the money, though. He didn't get any farther than Newtown before he stopped to drink all the likker he could hold. His three partners musta figured he was on the run, so they left here, thinkin' they weren't comin' back. But then they took their packs off and threw 'em in the barn, locked their packhorses in the corral, and went to town lookin' for Ed. If he hadn't shot the mirrors in Pratt's Saloon, he mighta come back here with the money and his friends wouldn't be wanting to kill him. You'd almost feel sorry for 'em if it wasn't for the fact they're such a rotten bunch of cold-blooded murderers."

"I wasn't quite to that point yet," Hatcher admitted.

"Let's take a look through these packs to see if there's anything worth saving," Murphy said. "I want to make sure we get back to town before suppertime. I feel bad enough leaving Will to take care of anything that might come up."

"What about the horses?" Hatcher asked. "What do you wanna do with them?"

"Considerin' the fact that I don't have all night to get back to town, I'm inclined to let the horses decide what they wanna do. On the other hand, you might need 'em as packhorses when you take 'em to Austin. They're movin' around pretty good in that water. They look like they're up for a little ol' three-mile trip. I've got plenty of rope and our guests at the jail left their bridles on. Whaddaya say we each lead two horses back to town with us?"

"I think that's a damn good idea," Hatcher replied. "Let's give 'em a little longer to drink enough water, then you can lead us back. I'm pretty sure I can't remember which of those little trails we followed up to this place."

"What's up, Will?" Paul Mathers greeted Marshal Murphy's young assistant when he walked up to his corral.

"Nothin' much," Will replied. "I was just takin' a walk to stretch my legs a little. Thought I'd check with you to see if Cullen was back at the stable yet. He was plannin' on being back here about this time."

Mathers automatically looked at his pocket watch to see

what time it was. "Five minutes to four," he declared. "What time did he say?"

"Oh, no specific time," Will replied, "just about this time." He was thinking that they always went to supper at five o'clock, when Irene's opened. Now he was beginning to worry that he was going to have to go to supper by himself and maybe even feed the prisoners by himself.

"Where was him and that US Deputy Marshal goin'," Mathers asked. "I don't believe he ever said."

"Nowhere," Will answered, knowing Murphy didn't want Eliot Baxter or Tyson Bradshaw to know he was three miles from town. "I mean, nowhere in particular. They was just gonna ride around Newtown." When that was met with a questioning expression on Paul's face, Will hurried to say, "I don't mean ride around in town. Cullen was more interested in showin' Hatcher where the town was most likely to grow. You know, for new businesses comin' to town."

"Really?" Mathers responded. "Was that deputy marshal interested in that kind of thing? I'm surprised to hear Cullen is thinkin' about the best places for the town to expand. 'Course, he kept us all guessin' when he was in the process of building his jailhouse, didn't he?" He chuckled over that. "Maybe he can tell us if he's got any more big plans. Here he comes." He pointed toward the north road out of town.

*Thank goodness!* Will thought when he turned to look in the direction Mathers pointed. Something didn't look right, though, and then he realized Murphy and Hatcher were each leading two horses. *I wish I had said they went to hunt wild horses,* he thought. He considered turning around and withdrawing, but Murphy was bound to have seen him standing there talking to Paul Mathers.

"Everything all right, Will?" Murphy called out as soon as he and Hatcher pulled up in front of the corral. Will nodded rapidly in response, so Murphy turned toward Mathers and said, "We brought four extra horses for you to take care of. They belong to the four prisoners we've got in jail right now. We still don't know how those prisoners are going to be transported yet." He looked back at Will and asked, "Any new law officers show up in town?" Will shook his head. "Any word of any kind come in the mail?" Again his question was met with a slow shaking of Will's head, even though he was anxious to tell him about a letter that came in the mail. "Well, I reckon there's always tomorrow, right?" Murphy said, dismounted, and started taking his saddle off his horse.

"Looks like your plans were interrupted by these horses," Mathers said. "Were you able to check out any of the best areas for expansion?"

"What?" Murphy replied. "What're you talkin' about?"

"You know," Mathers came back, "the best areas around our town for future building."

"Future building?" Murphy repeated. He turned to look at Will, but Will looked the other way. So he looked back at Mathers and asked, "Have you been hittin' the bottle this afternoon?"

"Hittin' the bottle?" Mathers asked. "Why would you ask me a question like that?"

"I reckon we'd best be gettin' ready to eat supper, Cullen," Will said. "I'll help you put these horses away so we won't be late feedin' the prisoners."

"Right," Murphy replied. "How'd our favorite prisoner behave this afternoon?"

"He wasn't any problem at all," Will replied. "Took his plate and his coffee to his bunk and ate his dinner quiet as you please. And when he was through, he put his dirty dishes with everybody else's by the door. And he stayed in his bunk when I pulled the dishes out of the cells."

"Good," Murphy said. "Maybe he'll back off a little bit. I ain't sure he's as crazy as he lets on. I think he just wants us to think he's crazy—this way, maybe, we'll quit watchin' him as close as we do the others. Best you keep that in mind."

"I agree," Hatcher offered. "I ain't lookin' forward to traveling ten miles with that little rat, let alone takin' him all the way to Austin."

Once the horses were taken care of and they left the stable, Will remarked as casually as he could manage, "Oh, yeah, I forgot to tell you, the mail coach made it to town today and there was a letter to you from Austin."

Gaining their complete attention, he paused until Murphy pressed him. "Did you open it?" he asked.

"It was addressed to you," Will said.

"I'm surprised that stopped you," Murphy remarked. "Have you got it with you?"

"I just might happen to have it with me." Will reached in his coat pocket and produced the letter from the office of the US Marshal, Austin, Texas. He held it up and Murphy snatched it out of his hand.

Murphy quickly scanned the letter, then looked at Hatcher, who was equally anxious. "They ain't sendin' a jail wagon, but they've sent one more deputy marshal to help you transport the four of 'em back to Austin. He oughta get here tomorrow. Sez here his name is Frank Foley. I expect you know him."

"Frank Foley," Hatcher repeated, looking very pleased, "I surely do. Frank's an old-timer in the service, like myself. He ain't been with it quite as long as I have, but about nine years, enough time to pretty much ruin a man for doin' anything else in his life. I've rode on many a posse with Frank."

"You don't think you'll have any trouble transportin' those four men with just you two?" Murphy asked.

"Not with Frank to help me," Hatcher answered. "If they didn't send me any help, I was gonna make two trips. I can handle two, but me and Frank together could handle six."

"Glad to hear it," Murphy said. "I know you're anxious to

get started back and I know our mayor will be glad to have those four killers out of Newtown. I think I'll stop by the store and show Eliot Baxter this letter," he said. "You wanna go with me?"

"No, I reckon not," Hatcher responded. "I think I'll go on back to my room so I can wash up a little before I go to supper."

"We'll see you at Irene's then," Murphy said. "Will, I'll meet you back at the jail."

As Murphy expected, Eliot Baxter was more than a little relieved to read the letter. He confessed to having fears that the four outlaws would remain in their midst indefinitely.

"I'll admit that I was concerned that we might have some other lawbreakers that needed arresting and I wouldn't have a place to put 'em. I've only got one empty cell." Murphy shrugged and said, "Maybe we ought to think about buildin' a second floor on the jailhouse."

"Don't even joke about it," Baxter said. "We're already spending more money than we have." He didn't bother to explain how that could occur, and Murphy wasn't interested, anyway.

"Long time, no see, Marshal. Where you been all day?" Hank Welch asked when Murphy came back into the cell room. "We thought maybe you quit."

"Yeah," Calvin Darcy chimed in. "We was bettin' on who would take your place, young Will Pickens or maybe that wore-out old US Deputy Marshal. I don't know who would be worse, a young'un or a grandpa. Whaddaya think, Beaver?"

"I think the old grandpa would be the best," Beaver responded. "We could sit on his knee while he told us stories about how many bad men he's arrested."

Murphy just let them go on with their nonsense until he was ready to go to supper. "You ready to go eat, Will?" he asked.

"Yessir!" Beaver sang out. "I'm ready, if you don't cook him too long. He don't look like he's got much fat on him."

Calvin laughed outright and Murphy couldn't suppress a smile for Beaver's joshing. But neither Hank nor Ed saw the joke in it.

"Come on, Will," Murphy said, "let's go to supper and see if we can't fatten you up a little."

# Chapter 12

It was the middle of the following morning when a rawboned stranger, with a thin mustache that reached his jaw, and stringy black hair that reached his shoulders, walked into the office. "Mornin', are you Marshal Cullen Murphy?"

"I am," Murphy answered.

"I'm US Deputy Marshal Frank Foley," the stranger declared. "I understand you've got some prisoners waitin' to be transported for trial."

"That's a fact, Deputy Foley. Welcome to Newtown. I expect you were expecting to see US Deputy Marshal Ward Hatcher. He just stepped out of here a few minutes ago to go up to the stable to make sure the horses are ready to go. He oughta be back anytime now. This is my deputy, Will Pickens. We just made a pot of coffee. Can I offer you a cup, or do you wanna go look for Ward?"

"As much as I admire Ward Hatcher, a cup of fresh coffee sounds like a better choice right now," he replied with a chuckle.

"I'll go get you a clean cup from the kitchen," Will volunteered, his mind still working on the fact that Murphy had referred to him as his *deputy.*

"You expect to start back today," Murphy asked, "or are you gonna rest your horses up and go back tomorrow?"

"I reckon we'll go back tomorrow mornin'," Foley said. "I know there's some things we're gonna need to take care of the prisoners. Shouldn't be much, though. I expect ol' Ward's pretty much ready to ride." He paused to accept the cup of coffee from Will. "Thank you kindly."

"If you take it with sugar, there's some in that bowl yonder on that little side table," Murphy told him.

"We make coffee for the prisoners," Will volunteered, "but we don't offer any sugar. We tell 'em jailhouse coffee don't have sugar in it."

"When you spend as many days in the saddle as I do, there ain't usually no sugar handy, anyway," Foley remarked. "So you might as well get used to drinking it jailhouse style."

"Ward says that he's rode with you a long time," Murphy said.

"That's a fact," Foley said. "I reckon me and Ward are the two old men in our company. We used to talk about retiring from this business, but the problem is, retire to do *what*?"

Murphy couldn't help asking, "Didn't your boss think it might be a good idea to send another man with you to pick up these four outlaws?"

Foley chuckled. "As a matter of fact, he did wanna send another man with me, a young fellow not much older than your deputy there. But I told him me and Ward Hatcher was plenty enough to handle four killers and I druther not have to keep an eye on his young deputy marshal on top of that—" He was interrupted when Ward Hatcher came in the door.

"I recognized that old flea-bitten gray horse tied at the rail," Hatcher said. "What the hell took you so long to get here? You get lost on the way?"

"I figured you most likely needed a couple of days' rest after that ride all the way from Austin," Foley japed, "so I took my time and enjoyed the ride. Hell, Stephens wanted to send Jack Sawyer with me. I told him we was gonna be too busy to train a new recruit on the job."

"Ain't that the truth!" Hatcher commented. "I just came from the stable and all their horses are in good shape. Marshal Murphy and me took a ride up in the hills yesterday to an old hideout to get four horses these fellers left in a corral up there."

"Let's take my horses to the stable and see what supplies we need to pick up here before we start out tomorrow," Foley said. "Where are you stayin'? I didn't see no hotel when I rode in."

"A roomin' house at the south end of town," Hatcher answered. "A lady name of Johnson runs it. It's furnished with good beds and I know for a fact she's got a couple of empty rooms."

"What about the money?" Murphy reminded him.

"Oh, yeah," Hatcher said. "I swear, I forgot all about the money. We'll have to take possession of that sometime this afternoon. And we'll have to have witnesses sign the forms sayin' how much there was and that we took possession of it."

"You know, that's one thing that surprises me," Murphy commented. "When Wells Fargo sent that stagecoach with the money, there were five men guardin' it, if you count the driver and the man ridin' shotgun. You have to figure Wells Fargo thought it necessary to have one of their special agents *plus* two US Deputy Marshals to protect that amount of money. So I figured the US Marshal Service would send more than two men to bring back the money and the four outlaws that murdered everybody with that stage."

"I can see why anybody would think that same thing," Hatcher said. "But the difference is this. The word leaked out about the twenty-five thousand dollars Wells Fargo was sending to that bank in Austin. A lot of people knew about it and that gang in your jail right now found out when it was goin' to be sent. But now that the money has been recovered, only a handful of people know it and know where it is. And most importantly, only the people in this room know for sure that it's leavin' here in the mornin'." He smiled then. "And to brag about it a little bit, it's also the reason the two oldest and most experienced deputy marshals were sent to do the job."

"When you look at it in that light, I can see what you mean," Murphy said. "Another way to look at it would be to think, if they sent two old worn-out deputies to guard four men, they ain't likely to have anything worth robbing with 'em."

Hatcher and Foley looked at each other in surprise; then looking back at the expression on Murphy's face, they all three burst out laughing.

"I swear," Hatcher said, "he saw right through us. Come on, Frank, let's take your horses to the stable and see what we need for tomorrow. Then we can get you a room." He looked at Murphy then and said, "We'll catch you in the café for dinner."

"Right," Murphy said, "and after dinner we can go transfer that money, if you want to."

"I ain't in no particular hurry to take charge of that money," Ward Hatcher said. "As long as we're still gettin' the horses and supplies ready to travel, I'd just as soon that money stay in that safe. Whaddaya say we pick it up after supper and that way we can sleep with it under the mattress at the roomin' house. Whaddaya think, Frank?"

"It's all right with me," Frank answered. "I'd feel a little more comfortable without that money on me all afternoon."

"I reckon I can't blame you," Murphy said. "I'll tell Tyson Bradshaw we're gonna transfer the money right after supper." He walked to the door with them and watched while Foley untied his flea-bitten gray and led it and his packhorse up the street toward the stable. With Hatcher walking beside him, they were already in heavy conversation.

"I wonder how many miles those two have ridden together," Will wondered aloud.

"Quite a few, I expect," Murphy replied. "Hatcher's been a

deputy marshal for fifteen years or more, and he said Foley's been one for nine years. But I'll bet if you added the two together, it would amount to a lot more than twenty-four years of experience."

"Afternoon, Marshal Murphy," Ginger greeted him. "Afternoon to you, too, Mr. Pickens. Is your guest, Deputy Hatcher, going to be with us today?"

"Yes, he will, Miss Floyd," Murphy answered in the same formal style she had addressed them. "And we'll have another guest who is also a US Deputy Marshal. His name is Frank Foley, and he rode all the way from Austin to eat dinner at Irene's Café."

"The word gets around, doesn't it?" Ginger replied. "Before long, there will be stagecoaches bringing people down from Fort Worth to sample Mama's cooking."

Will looked from one of them to the other, wondering how long the nonsense would continue. Finally he said, "We're gonna need four plates for the prisoners as usual."

Bonnie came out of the kitchen with two cups at that point and Ginger told her she was going to need two more. She went back at once to get two more and placed them at the empty places. "Do you want to wait until the other two arrive?" she asked.

Both Murphy and Will spoke at the same time. Murphy said yes. Will said no. "Which is it?" Bonnie asked. Again they answered at the same time. Murphy said no, but Will said yes. Bonnie shook her head in exasperation.

"Fill Will's cup, please," Murphy said. "I'll wait till they get here. Never mind," he said when he looked up and saw Ginger escorting the two men toward the table. "Here they come now. Fill all four cups."

Bonnie retreated to get the coffeepot, muttering to herself.

Back at the table, Murphy introduced Ginger to Frank Foley.

She welcomed him to the café, then told them what they were serving that day. "Of course, if you don't like meat loaf and mashed potatoes, we can fry a ham steak for you." It was an all-in vote for the meat loaf.

"The prisoners want meat loaf, too," Will said.

"It must be like being on vacation to pull time in that jail of yours," Hatcher said to Murphy. "Three meals a day from this café. It's a wonder you ain't got men lining up to get arrested."

"We did have," Murphy said, "until we made drunkenness and loitering death sentences. And that didn't always work until we changed it to death by starvation."

The joking lasted halfway through the meal before the conversation got around to the reason for the two deputy marshals' presence there in Newtown. Murphy asked if they had everything taken care of and ready to leave in the morning. "I think so," Hatcher allowed, "after we pick up the money tonight. We've been trying to decide if we want to let the prisoners eat breakfast in the jail before we start out or start before breakfast and let that be their first break."

"You didn't even take a look at the prisoners, did you, Frank?" Murphy asked.

"No, they all look pretty much the same after so many years of arrestin' 'em and transportin' 'em. Besides, I'm sure I'll see all of 'em I wanna see before we get where we're going. It's Ward I'll get sick of lookin' at," he japed.

"That's easy enough to fix," Ward said. "I'll just put a gunnysack over your head."

Before they finished dinner, they had decided to eat breakfast there in the café the next morning and feed the prisoners one last meal in the jail. They figured they could saddle all the horses and packhorses while the prisoners ate. Murphy offered his and Will's services to help in any way to make their departure a smooth one. When suppertime came around, they were satisfied that they had covered everything. Will told Irene that he would need one last breakfast for the prisoners and took their supper with him after he ate.

Murphy and the deputies went into the saloon after supper, upstairs to Tyson Bradshaw's office, where Tyson and Eliot Baxter were waiting for them. Both men had met Ward Hatcher, and Frank Foley was introduced at that time. All parties were intent upon making an official transfer of the Wells Fargo money, so as to leave no doubt that the money was all accounted for. To make sure of that, the money was counted again, witnessed, and verified that the four packs of bills added up to twenty thousand dollars. With the pocket money collected from each of the prisoners added, the twenty-five thousand dollar theft was recovered. Deputy Hatcher took the bag with the money, folded it neatly into a package, and tied it with some string on Bradshaw's desk.

Baxter proposed one drink of whiskey to celebrate the transfer of the money, but more importantly, the exit of the four murderers from Newtown. "With all due respect, sir," Hatcher said, "Deputy Foley and I would druther not tote this sack with Wells Fargo on it in the saloon to let anybody start wondering what's in it. You can understand why we'd druther just walk on out the back entrance and go straight back to the roomin' house."

"I see what you mean," Baxter said. "You're right, of course. So we wish you an uneventful trip to Austin, and Tyson and I will drink to those four villains leaving our little town." They all shook hands again and parted company; Baxter and Bradshaw downstairs to the saloon; the two deputies downstairs, but back out through the café; and Murphy and Will carried four plates of food to the jail.

"Lookee here, boys," Hank Welch sang out when the supper dishes finally arrived. "They decided not to starve us to death, after all." Directing his comments to Murphy, he said, "It's a good thing you finally decided to feed us. Beaver was already startin' to gnaw on these blame oak walls, and if you'd been a little bit longer, he mighta gnawed us a hole big enough to get through."

"I declare, Welch," Will bothered to react, "I don't know what it's gonna be like around here when you're gone. Oh, yes, I do . . . Better."

Murphy couldn't help but chuckle in surprise to hear Will make a comment at all. They went through the cumbersome routine necessary to feed the prisoners, then left them to continue talking about their transport to Austin.

As soon as the cell room door was locked again, the four outlaws returned to their discussion of the next day's events. "We couldn't have asked for a better roll of the dice," Hank Welch maintained. "Instead of a jail wagon, they send two deputies to take us all the way to Austin and one of 'em is Ward Hatcher. It's way past time when they shoulda put him out to pasture. Ain't no tellin' who they sent to help him. Likely, some young feller that don't even shave yet."

"I don't know, Hank," Calvin Darcy questioned. "I wouldn't count on Hatcher bein' obsolete yet. He's got a helluva reputation."

"Is that so?" Hank disagreed. "Well, let's you and me have a face-off. I'll take my .44 and you take your reputation and see which one is still standing when the smoke clears. Goin' that distance with four of us to watch, there's bound to be more than one opportunity to make a move," he said. "The main thing is, we have to be ready to make that move. I'm tellin' you, this is an outright gift to us to send us out with just two deputies—and the money, to boot. They'll be lucky to make it a day without givin' us our opportunity."

"How do you reckon they'll take us," Ed Moore asked, "sittin' in the saddle or tied hand and foot and layin' across the saddle?"

"What the hell do you care?" Hank came back at him. "You'll be lucky if we even cut you loose."

"Ah, come on, Hank, you know damn well I weren't runnin'

off with all the money. I admit I shouldn't have done it, but I thought I was protectin' it."

"You low-down dog, you're the only reason we're all settin' here in this blame jailhouse right now. *The only reason!*" he repeated. "Beaver, Calvin, tell me if I'm wrong!" When there was no response from either, he said to Ed, "Now, do you understand why you ain't got a share in that money no more and I ain't decided to cut you free or not? You deserve to stay with the deputies. After all, you are their eyewitness, ain't you?"

"Calvin, you gotta believe me," Ed pleaded. "The only thing I'm guilty of is bein' a drunk and dumb enough to worry about leavin' the money unguarded while I went to get some likker. I was right there with you at the holdup when we killed all five of 'em. I earned my share of that money, same as you did." He turned to plead with Beaver. "You know me, Beaver. I was right there with you when we hit that stagecoach. I ain't no eyewitness. Hell, think about it! The only way I could be an eyewitness is if I was there when it happened. And that would be the same as confessin' that I was part of it. I wouldn't never do somethin' that dumb."

"I don't know," Beaver responded. "It's been hard tryin' to set my mind straight ever since he locked me up in that dark place with all them voices talkin' to me. Most likely, though, you shouldn'ta done what you done and we wouldn't be in this fix." He paused to think about it, then said, "The food's been good since we've been here, though."

Hank shook his head impatiently after hearing Beaver's simpleminded response to Ed's plea for mercy. At least Beaver would do as he was told, so the three of them should be able to take advantage of the two lawmen if given the opportunity. Then he wondered if he was a little overconfident in his assessment of the situation. Maybe he might have made a mistake in his harsh approach to Ed Moore's role in their current predicament. When the opportunity to strike came, it would be better if their advantage was four against two, instead of three against two. He formed a picture in his mind of an incident on the trail when they might be mounting or dismounting and a moment occurred when Ed's hands were free to grab one of the deputies' guns. But Ed made no attempt because they had labeled him a traitor. He made a decision.

"You know what, Ed? What you just told Beaver makes a lot of sense. I believe I came down a little too hard on you and I'm man enough to admit it when I'm wrong. I'll admit I was really sore at you for losing our money, but I reckon I was wrong to think you was thinkin' about stealin' it. So I say we go back to the way it was, the four of us together and the four of us share the money."

Ed could barely believe his ears, and Calvin and Beaver were equally amazed. It wasn't like Hank at all.

"You mean it?" Ed responded.

Hank nodded his head.

"Thank you, Hank. I wouldn't never steal from you fellers and that's the honest truth."

"Let's just all be on our toes in the mornin' and the first slipup those two lawmen make will be their last and we'll be back where we was before this mess." *And then I'll shoot your sorry ass and we'll split the money three ways,* Hank thought.

# CHAPTER 13

It was a nice sunny morning when Ward Hatcher and Frank Foley carried their saddlebags and one Wells Fargo sack, neatly tied up, out the front door of Mrs. Johnson's rooming house. Having paid up for their rooms the night before, they were intent only upon walking out of the house as quietly as possible so as not to waken the other tenants. When they arrived at the outside entrance to the dining room, they found Murphy and Will standing by the door, waiting for Bonnie to open it and turn the OPEN sign around.

Right about six o'clock, Bonnie opened the door wide enough to stick her head out. "We're closed today!" she said, then giggled as she jerked her head back inside and closed the door. They waited a few seconds more and she opened it wide. "Good morning," she greeted them. "It's nice to see so many folks anxious to eat breakfast so they can go to church."

"Maybe that's where we ought to take those four birds before we start out for Austin," Frank Foley commented as they filed into the dining room, "even if it ain't Sunday."

"That might be a helluva test on the church if those four devils and me and you with 'em walked in," Ward Hatcher said. "Might be too much for the building to stand up under."

They enjoyed a big breakfast. Irene made pancakes because it was Ward Hatcher's last chance to enjoy her cooking. Ward complimented her as usual, and this time Frank Foley added his praise as well. "You're surely gettin' us off to a good start," Hatcher told her.

"You're too kind in your praise," Irene told him. "You be careful on that trip back."

"I will," he said. "I promise you that."

They did not linger over breakfast, as there was much to do before they were ready to depart. Bonnie and Ginger both walked them to the door and wished them a safe journey. Frank seemed like a nice man, but Ward had been in town long enough for them to get to know him. According to Bonnie, he was more like a favorite uncle, and she would miss him.

Murphy and Will took four pancake breakfasts back to the jailhouse for their last breakfast before whatever Frank and Ward fed them on their trip. The two deputy marshals went to the stable, where Paul Mathers was waiting to help them with their string of horses. They had opted to take just their own packhorses.

When they were ready to go, Foley produced some extra pairs of handcuffs he had brought with him. The four prisoners had their hands cuffed behind their backs. Then Foley and Hatcher helped them up into the saddle. When they were loaded up and ready to ride, each of the deputy marshals was leading three horses, two carrying prisoners and one packhorse. It looked like an awkward caravan and Murphy commented as much.

"It is a helluva lot more trouble than a jail wagon," Hatcher conceded, "but I've done it before. You just have to keep a constant eye on your prisoners and make sure you tie 'em up good at night."

"Have a good trip back," Murphy said, and he and Will stood in front of the jail and watched the twin columns as they rode out the south end of town, past Mrs. Johnson's rooming house, toward the river road.

"That looks like a dangerous way to transport those four killers," Will commented.

"Yeah," Murphy said, "I'd have to agree with you. How would you have done it?"

"Made 'em ride on their bellies, with their hands and feet tied together," Will answered.

"I'll go along with that," Murphy said. "I reckon they know what they're doin'. As many years as they've been doing that kind of work, they must have done it like that before. I reckon I'd best go back into the office and write a letter to US Marshal Stephens and tell him his four prisoners and the twenty-five thousand dollars are on their way to Austin."

They went back inside the jail where Murphy performed one of his more difficult jobs, writing a letter, and Will went back to start cleaning up the cells.

With Ward Hatcher leading the column of horses, they struck the San Saba River a short mile below Newtown and followed a trail beside the river as it flowed in a northeasterly direction. They rode for a distance of about fifteen miles before deciding it was time to make their first stop, but continued on until finding a place that suited their purpose. It was a small clearing in a wooded area back some distance from the riverbank. *This is as good a spot as any,* Hank Welch thought, and he looked at Calvin Darcy and gave him a solemn nod of his head to remind him to be alert for any opportunity. Understanding, Calvin nodded back at him, figuring one of the lawmen was bound to get careless.

"This'll do to take a little rest," Hatcher announced to the prisoners after he led them into the clearing. "How easy this goes will depend on how much you cooperate."

"Can't you take these cuffs off of us for a little while?" Hank asked. "My arms ain't got no feelin' in 'em."

"Sure," Foley said. "We can do that, but let us get you all off your horses first." He helped Hank off the horse. "There you go. Sit right there and I'll be back to unlock those handcuffs." Then he helped Beaver off his horse and told him to sit there till he took the cuffs off. Hatcher was helping Calvin and Ed off their horses, and he sat them down on the ground.

"Now, then, we'll make you a little more comfortable," Ward said, drawing his .45 and putting a bullet in Ed's forehead. Calvin screamed before Ward casually shot him in the chest. At the same time, Frank executed Hank and Beaver with shots to the chest. Afterward, they added shots to the heads of all three chest wounds to finish them off.

"That was less trouble than I thought it would be," Hatcher remarked. "Let's decide about how much of this stuff we want to mess with."

"I don't think we wanna bother with all these horses," Foley said. "I'd rather keep my own horse and saddle. I don't see anything of theirs that beats my horse, or yours, either. And one packhorse is all I need. What about you?"

"I pretty much agree with you," Hatcher said. "I don't see anything any of them was riding that beats ol' Smokey. One packhorse is all I need, too, so let's take what we wanna mess with and leave the rest for the buzzards and whoever. What about the sack full of money?" he japed. "You wanna bother with that?"

"I forgot we had that with us," Foley joked. "Might as well take it with us." They both enjoyed a good laugh then as they started throwing packs and saddles on the ground to sort through and select whatever items of clothing or cooking utensils appealed to them. When they had made their choices, they stripped the bridles and saddles off the horses that they decided to abandon. Then they got on their horses and went back to continue following the river to leave the scene of the massacre behind them.

"Congratulations on your US Marshal retirement plan,"

Hatcher announced as he pulled his horse to a stop on a rise close beside the river. "This is in appreciation for all the long, hard years you've chased pond scum like the four gentlemen who have provided you these funds for your retirement." He then pulled his badge off his coat and held it up for Foley to see before he threw it as far out in the river as he could.

"I'll be forever grateful for the US Marshal Service for providin' such a generous plan to a couple of its faithful old dogs," Foley declared grandly. Then, following Hatcher's gesture, he pulled his badge off and threw it into the river as well.

With no sense of guilt and a feeling that the service owed them at least that much, they continued to follow the San Saba until it led them to the Colorado River. They would not follow the Colorado very far, a distance of perhaps twenty miles before coming to a trail that led to the northeast. It was an old Indian trail, Hatcher assumed, one he had discovered when following a half-Comanche murderer who led him across Lampasas County.

They decided to camp there beside the Colorado for the night and rest the horses for a long day in the saddle tomorrow. There was plenty of firewood beside the river, so they soon had a fire going and Hatcher sliced some bacon to fry. "This ain't gonna be as tasty as the last supper you had, but maybe we'll run up on something to kill before too long," he said.

"That woman back there at the saloon was one helluva cook, weren't she?" Foley remarked.

"Yes, sir, she was," Hatcher agreed. "That was the best part about havin' to wait back there until you showed up. I gave some thought about kidnappin' her when we left there, but I couldn't figure out how we could work that in the plan."

Foley chuckled. "That might notta been so easy. She was a feisty little woman. She mighta been more trouble than she was worth." He stroked his chin whiskers as he thought about the caper they had just successfully pulled off. He and Hatcher had worked together quite often over the years, and as time passed with no prospects for promotion in the service, they had often talked about what they could do when the day came when they were too old to do the job. It was obvious that there was no decent retirement plan for used-up lawmen. Hatcher had been so bold as to admit he might be tempted to report a recovered sum of money as missing in order to secure his retirement. Foley confessed that he had thought about it as well. And now they had actually done it.

The success of it was due in great part to pure luck. Their boss, Marshal Henry Stephens, was going to send young Jack Sawyer to help Hatcher transport four killers to Austin. Foley and Sawyer were the only deputies in town at the time. The jail wagon with two deputies was in San Antonio. Foley was not thrilled to work with the greenhorn, Sawyer, so he suggested to Stephens that he might want to keep at least one deputy in town, and that his two old dogs had the experience to handle the job. Luckily, Stephens agreed.

Foley had to laugh when he thought about how surprised Ward Hatcher said he was when he heard it would be him helping to transport the four men to Austin. Hatcher had no plans to assassinate the four prisoners and abscond with the money. He needed another man to transport four dangerous men like Hank Welch and his gang, but the other man had to be a partner in the crime. And that would not work with a young deputy like Jack Sawyer. So it was only after Foley arrived that the idea of pulling off the assassination and taking the money was even discussed.

The part of the plan that called for the execution of the four prisoners was not as hard on the conscience as one might expect, especially for dedicated lawmen like Foley and Hatcher. The four outlaws were of the lowest form of humanity, and they were the same as dead, since they were on their way to the gallows. It was the purest form of justice that they should be shot to death, just as they had killed the five men with the stagecoach. It could even be classified as humane, since it was done quickly, without warning, and was certainly preferable to death by hanging.

The only negative point in the plan was the money. It was a goodly sum, but it had to be split between the two of them. Hatcher had hoped for more than twenty-five thousand for himself alone, enough to set him up for the rest of his life. But he reckoned that he would learn to get by with the money, just as he had learned to cope with his limitations all his life. He was not in the habit of spending much money, anyway. He had never been blessed with any particular skills, and he was not a handsome man, so he had never been very lucky with the ladies and not wealthy enough to make up for his plainness with cash. As he got older, he found that he reminded women of their uncles. He had long ago accepted his lot in life, so he figured he'd just accept whatever else was left of it as well.

His thoughts were interrupted then when Foley asked, "You want the last of this coffee in the pot? About a half a cup, 'cause if you don't, I'm gonna dump it out so I can wash the pot."

"Just leave it there," Hatcher said. "I'll drink it and I'll wash the pot. Did you get enough to eat?"

"Yeah, I'm done," Foley replied. "I'm goin' to bed."

"All right, I'll wrap this bacon back up and wash the coffeepot and then I'll be right behind you." Foley stretched out on his bedroll and pushed his hat brim down over his eyes to block the light of a bright new moon. He was snoring by the time Hatcher came back to the fire. Hatcher smiled.

*If that ain't the very image of a man at peace with himself, I don't know what is,* he told himself. *There ain't no guilty conscience there. Makes me feel just a little bit guilty, though,* he thought as the moonlight reflected off the blade of his skinning knife seconds before he drew it across Foley's throat. Foley was a good friend. He would understand that half of twenty-five thousand wouldn't be as much as he needed. In his original plan he was hoping to get an opportunity to ride off with a sum closer to fifty thousand dollars. But he believed the chance would come only once, and if he passed it by, it would never come again.

He cleaned the blood from his knife with Foley's blanket; then he tucked the blanket back up under Foley's chin and closed his eyelids, which had popped open when Hatcher's knife blade traveled from the left ear all the way to the right ear. "Sleep well, friend and I'll dig you a good grave in the mornin'." He crawled into his bedroll then and was soon fast asleep.

He awoke the next morning with the first rays of the sun penetrating the branches of the trees beside the river. He was hungry, but remembering that he had promised Foley he would bury him in the morning, he decided to do that first. *Keep a promise to a friend. Keep a friend,* he thought, having forgotten where he had heard the saying. He took a short shovel from one of the packhorses and selected a spot to leave Foley's remains under the branches of a long oak limb. "This oughta suit you just fine," he said. "That long limb will keep you in the shade when it gets hot weather. And I ought not run into any big roots this far away from the trunk." He was correct in his selection of gravesites, for it turned out to be a fairly easily dug grave. When it was ready, he dragged Foley's body over to the grave and carefully lowered it into the ground.

When he filled the dirt back in, he looked around until he found a couple of limbs he could fashion a cross with and drove the cross in the ground at the head of the grave. "Anybody finds it will know it was a Christian burial," he declared. Thinking then that it would be the right thing to say a few words over the grave, he thought for a couple of minutes before inspiration occurred. "Lord, this is Frank Foley. He was a good deputy marshal and a fine friend. He's comin' to ya a little earlier than he intended to, but through no fault of his own."

With the ceremony for Foley over, Hatcher turned his attention to his earthly needs and brought his fire back to life. When his fire was right, he made half a pot of coffee and sliced some more bacon to fry with some hardtack. After he ate and cleaned up his coffeepot and frying pan, he put his fire out, then selected whatever he wanted to keep out of Foley's packs.

He decided to keep Foley's saddle horse, saddle and all. It was too fine a horse to abandon, so he decided to use it as a second packhorse and freed Foley's packhorse. If he knew there was some place along the trail he was following to sell a horse, he would have kept all four horses. But there was no place. It had been several years, however, since he trailed that half-Comanche. Things might have changed along that trail, but he doubted it and that's the way he preferred it.

Things were back to normal in Newtown since Foley and Hatcher had left the morning before, taking the town's four unwelcome guests with them. At the jail, Will Pickens was on a binge to clean the cell room of every trace of evidence that the four recent occupants had ever been there. Murphy could not help but notice a new eager and willing attitude in Will's general actions.

The mystery was solved at the breakfast table the day after the deputy marshals left town with their prisoners. "Cullen," Will asked, "do you remember when Frank Foley walked in the office and you introduced me to him?"

Puzzled to see where Will was going with this, Murphy said, "Yeah, I guess so."

It was apparent that Will was looking for more of an answer than that. "You remember you introduced me as your *deputy*? Was that just a slip of the lip?"

"Did I do that?" Murphy asked.

Will nodded, disappointed by his reaction.

"Yeah," Murphy stammered, "I—I reckon I was . . . I mean, no—no, it wasn't a slip of the lip. I called you my deputy because I think you have the potential to be one after you grow into the job a little more, and I didn't want him to think you just clean the place up."

Will's face lit up. "You really mean that?"

"Sure, I do," Murphy answered. "You're just nineteen years old. You've still got some growin' to do, but I can see the potential there, if you just give it some time to develop."

"Thanks, Cullen. I'll do my best to learn all I can about bein' a deputy."

"Matter of fact, it's kinda funny you brought this up right now," Murphy said. "Now that the town is back to normal and peaceful as a church, I plan to saddle my horse and give him a little exercise. I was gonna leave you in charge of the jail as a sort of acting deputy. Think you can do that?"

"Yes, sir! I sure can," Will responded. "How long will you be gone?"

"Not long at all. Just three miles down the river road to check on my old place and come right back. Nosy can use the workout."

"That's almost like you're not even out of town," Will said.

"That's right, but you know how the town council thinks. The marshal's gotta be inside the town limits all the time." Murphy made a face and shrugged.

"Don't worry," Will assured him, "I'll make up a story they'll believe."

So Murphy went to the stable and saddled his horse. Then he rode out the south end of town to strike the river road. He wanted to see his property where Brady Creek emptied into the San Saba River. He had given Lionel Jacobson, owner of the Rocking-J Ranch, permission to run cattle on it after he took the job as marshal of Newtown. He broke Nosy into a gentle lope and knew the big bay gelding would hold the pace for most of the way there. As he expected, they covered the short three miles in no time at all. When he arrived, he dismounted and let Nosy go to the river to drink, while he took a quick look at his cabin. It appeared to be in the same shape he had left it. He hadn't gotten far in his renovations after Indians set fire to it. So he figured he could go back to town, but he wanted to rest his horse a little longer before starting, since he held the bay to a faster pace on the way out. So to kill a little time, he walked out to the river road to take a look at the trail left by Hatcher and Foley. He was confused at once. There were no tracks on the road except for those left by a couple of mules and a wagon. There should have been a multitude of fresh tracks left by the two deputy marshals, four prisoners, and a string of packhorses. To go to Austin, this was the road from Newtown and none other. It should have been covered with fresh tracks. He hadn't thought to pay any attention to the road on his way out to his cabin. He had no reason to inspect the road for hoofprints. This didn't make sense at all. He called the bay and the horse came to him at once. He climbed on board but held him to a walk all the way back to the short road to the town, searching for a point where their tracks left the road. But there was no such point. The road was practically devoid of tracks all the way back to the fork that led into town.

He was intent upon at least finding their trail out of town, which he did easily enough. But instead of heading east on the river road, their trail led to the west, toward the Colorado River. He was stunned. Hatcher and Foley had taken their four prisoners in the opposite direction to Austin. There was only one explanation that came to mind, for both lawmen knew the way to Austin. Hank Welch and his three murdering partners somehow managed to overcome their two guards and it appeared they had done it before they left town. For there was no indication of any variation in the trail left by their hooves. When they rode out of town and came to the river road, they turned left instead of right, and that struck a chord of instant alarm for the two deputy marshals. Murphy's first thought was to follow their trail and hope for a miracle. But he was already a full day behind the outlaws. The chance for that miracle was pretty slim, but he had to find out. He had to tell Baxter that he was going to follow the outlaws and he might be gone for a while, so he turned Nosy around and headed back to town.

He rode straight to the stable and told Paul Mathers he needed his packhorse and he didn't have time to check what supplies were left in his packs. But he knew there were always basic supplies, like coffee, flour, beans, and jerky, so he told Paul to put the packsaddle on his packhorse with whatever was in it while he ran to inform the mayor.

On his way to tell Baxter, Will saw Murphy go past the jail, so Will ran out to intercept him. "What is it, Cullen?" Will gasped when he caught up with him. "What's wrong?"

Without stopping, Murphy told Will what he had discovered, and consequently, what he had to do. "Baxter ain't gonna like it, but I can't just ignore it. So here's a chance for you to take on the deputy's job and take care of things while I'm gone. If you need some help with something, talk to Joel Trout, he's offered to help before. Don't you put yourself in danger."

"Don't worry, Cullen, you can count on me," Will told him. "You be careful, though."

"Good man," Murphy said. "Now go on back to the office." He didn't want Will with him when he told the mayor, in case Baxter exploded.

"It's dinnertime," Will said. "Ain't you gonna eat?"

"I reckon not. I'm already a day behind."

# Chapter 14

"Howdy, Cullen, what can I do for you?" Eliot Baxter greeted him when he rushed into the store. "You look like you're in a hurry. Anything wrong?"

"Yes, sir, Mr. Mayor," Murphy answered, "I'm afraid so. I think those two deputy marshals that just left here with our four prisoners might already be dead." He went on to tell the mayor what he had discovered on his little ride—and what looked to be the obvious conclusion.

"Oh, no!" Baxter gasped. "That is a terrible thing. I can't say that I'm surprised. That was a vile gang of outlaws. You can understand why I was so anxious to get them out of our town."

"Yes, sir, I do," Murphy said. "I wanted to come by and let you know I may be gone for a day or two."

"Gone?" Baxter responded. "Where are you going?"

"To track those four outlaws on the chance they didn't kill Hatcher and Foley. There might be time to save them in case they just left them wounded somewhere. Based on the fact that they turned in the wrong direction on the river road, I figure they jumped Hatcher and Foley right after they rode out of town. But I think they wouldn't have dumped their bodies until they got a little farther from town."

"Murphy," Baxter said, "that is a terrible thing to have happened to those two deputy marshals, but that's the risk they take when they volunteer to go into that service. I'm sure they're both dead, just like the guards those four devils killed on the stagecoach. The point is, their latest crimes are out of your jurisdiction and would be the responsibility of the US Marshals, the Texas Rangers, or a county sheriff, if we had one. I can understand how you feel, but it's too late to help those two deputies."

"I understand what you're sayin', Mr. Mayor," Murphy stated calmly. "You're probably right. But I'm afraid my conscience won't let me ignore the possibility that those two men might be lying out there wounded along that trail somewhere, prayin' that some help will come from somebody. And if they are dead, I expect it would be the responsible thing to notify the US Marshal. I'll get back here just as quick as I can. We're in good shape right now. The town seems peaceful enough." He turned around and went back out the door.

Too shocked to react verbally at once, Baxter stood speechless until the door closed behind Murphy. "The outright gall of that man," he finally sputtered. *"The town seems peaceful enough."* He repeated Murphy's words indignantly. "It might be time I called the council together to discuss whether or not he's gotten too big for his britches!"

"He's right, Pop," Jeff Baxter, who had heard the whole conversation, said. "I hope he finds those two men still alive."

Murphy went back to the stable and picked up his horses. When he rode down the street, he realized it was dinnertime and he was hungry. He didn't want to waste another second before going in search of the two deputy marshals, but he rode down beside the saloon to the outside entrance to Irene's Café. He went directly into the kitchen to talk to Irene. "I don't have time to stop to eat. I have to go somewhere. Do you suppose I could take a biscuit or something with me, just anything to put in my stomach?"

"Of course, you can," Irene replied. "Give me just a second or two. Will a couple of ham biscuits do, or do you need more than that?"

"Two ham biscuits will do just fine." He watched as she cut two big slices off a baked ham and put them inside two biscuits just out of the oven. Although the biscuits were large, the ham slices stuck out all around them. "Yes, ma'am," he said, "that'll take me to supper. Thank you, Irene."

She wrapped them in a cloth.

"Bring the cloth back, if you don't lose it," she said.

"Yes, ma'am, thank you, ma'am," he said as he went out the door.

"What was that all about?" Ginger asked her mother when she came in from the dining room just in time to see him go out the back.

"I don't know," her mother replied. "He just walked in and said he didn't have time to eat dinner because he had to go somewhere right away. So I gave him a couple of ham biscuits."

"He didn't say where he had to go to in such a hurry?" Ginger asked. When Irene said he didn't, Ginger said, "Will is in the dining room. I'll ask him."

Holding one of his biscuits in hand, Murphy worked on the ham protruding on all sides of it as he rode out of town. He was working on the biscuit by the time he reached the river road and followed the obvious trail of hoofprints that turned to follow the river northeast. The trail was still rather baffling to him in that there was never any sign in the tracks that would indicate anything had happened during the ride down to the river. He was almost tempted to assume that he was following some other string of horses, instead of those with the deputies.

To cut down on the time, he alternated his horses' gait between a walk and a trot. He had guessed that he would see some variation in the tracks that might indicate a stop within a mile or so of town when they would get rid of the two bodies. But there was no such variation in the tracks. Before he realized it, he had ridden over ten miles with no change in the long trail of hoofprints. He wondered if this ride he was taking was nothing more than a tremendous waste of time, too little and too late. He started to turn around and give up, but decided to push on a little farther. After another couple of miles, he saw what he had been watching for: In the cloudless blue sky up ahead of him, a flock of buzzards circled and made competitive raids toward the ground. He rode on until he came to the center of the buzzards' attraction, which seemed to be over a grove of trees and a clearing in the center of them.

Confident that he had found what he was searching for, he decided to leave his horses in the trees short of the clearing and continue on by foot. So he rode into the trees about twenty yards short of the clearing and dropped his reins on the ground. Then he pulled his Henry rifle out of the saddle scabbard and walked on through the trees until he came to the clearing. Looking for a couple of bodies, he found, instead, four individual carcasses for the buzzards to argue over. He didn't understand what he was seeing at first, but then it struck him. Still, he was not certain. So he approached the closest feasting site and fired a shot into the midst of the arguing birds, then fired another shot before they scattered enough for him to identify the half-exposed skull that resembled that of a beaver. He backed away, his mind turned upside down as he tried to process what he had discovered. *Hatcher and Foley executed their four prisoners!*

It was difficult to accept, so he approached another ravaged body and scattered the buzzards. Most of the flesh was still on the head of this one and he recognized it as Hank Welch. There was no need to identify the remaining two and he could easily form a picture in his mind. They must have ridden this far before stopping, supposedly to eat and rest. They, no doubt, helped them off their horses, then casually shot them.

Murphy turned around and walked back to his horses, still trying to understand how he could misjudge a man as much as he had misjudged Ward Hatcher. The man had seemed to be nothing short of a dedicated lawman. He had not had as much time to form a real opinion about Frank Foley. But it was easy to assume he was much the same kind of man as Hatcher. So the assumption was correct: They were the same kind, just not the right kind. So, what to do now? That was the decision that had to be made. He felt that he had been personally betrayed by the two US Deputy Marshals. They had obviously done this evil deed strictly for the money and were now on their way to distant places and different identities. And they had used him in their pursuit of financial gain, for he had arrested all four of their human sacrifices.

What to do? He had already ridden farther than he had expected, and certainly farther than Eliot Baxter had assumed he would. And Baxter had a valid point, he was hired to protect the town of Newtown and he had no legal jurisdiction outside the town limits. But how could he turn around and let Hatcher and Foley go free without even an attempt to balance the scales of justice? There was a right answer, and he knew it: *He couldn't.*

He went back to his horses, then rode back to the trail by the river, where he picked up their trail leading away from the execution clearing. The horses were four now and he followed their trail for a short distance before they stopped to eat. From there, the trail led a few more miles before the river flowed into what had to be the Colorado River. Their trail was not that difficult to follow, since there was no sign of any recent traffic other than the four horses he followed. It was getting late in the day by then, his horses were tired, and he was hungry, so he began looking for a good spot to camp. He settled for a little grassy knoll that ran down to the river, right after it took a sharp bend. A stand of trees stood in a half circle that formed a nice base for his fire and his bed. He unsaddled his horses and left them free to graze on the knoll and drink from the river.

After he got a fire going, he thought about the second ham biscuit he had in his saddlebag. He sent Irene Floyd a silent thank-you and thought, *That and a cup of coffee is all I need for supper.* So he went to his packsaddle, which Paul Mathers had put on his packhorse for him, to get his coffeepot. It was then he remembered that he was out of the coffee he kept with his packs and had forgotten to buy more. "Damn," he complained, "all I needed was enough to make one cup." *Well, today's the day for it,* he thought, and opened his packs to put his coffeepot away; then he noticed a small package he couldn't identify. He pulled it out to look at it and was amazed to find an unopened one-pound sack of ground coffee. He was baffled, unable to remember buying it, until he realized Paul Mathers must have put it in there. When he put the packsaddle on for him, he must have noticed that empty coffee bag, so he put in a new one. "I'll have to remember that when I get back to town."

The night passed peacefully, with nothing to wake him until the first ribbons of light wove their way through the branches of the trees over his head. He crawled out of his bedroll and took a cautious look around before reviving his fire. He made coffee and cooked some jerky over the fire and decided that was going to have to do for breakfast, because he was anxious to get back on the trail of the two lawmen gone rogue.

Back in the saddle, he started off at a trot, following the trail along the Colorado River. The tracks of the four horses were still easy to follow; and like the day before, he met no one on the trail. He was beginning to believe there was not a soul in the whole county but him and the two he trailed. After a distance of about five miles, he reined Nosy back to a walk. Murphy knew the bay could trot a lot longer than that, but he wanted to make sure his horses stayed fresh enough to gallop, should the need suddenly arrive. By the time he was ready to stop to fix something to eat and give his horses a good rest, he estimated that he had covered about twenty miles. Looking around the riverbank, he noticed the regular pattern of hoofprints he had been following suddenly came apart and wandered in different directions. From years of experience, he recognized it as the sign of the riders coming to a stop. His next thought was that, like him, they decided it was time to stop and rest the horses. He dismounted and started looking for the remains of a campfire. Figuring they would be looking for the same things he would, he picked a couple of spots he would consider. The second one he checked held the remains of a campfire. Looking some more, he found faint impressions left by the bedrolls. They had spent the night here, and by the feel of the ashes, they were still a full day ahead of him. There was nothing he could do but keep going and hope they would stop someplace for a longer stay.

He discovered something he had not noticed at first when he decided that the faint impressions were from their beds. Where one of the bedrolls had lain, it looked like something had been used to sweep some leaves or pieces of bark away, probably a tree branch. Looking at it from the opposite side of the fire, he thought at first they had continued to sweep on up the bank toward a large oak tree. "Or," it suddenly occurred to him, "something was dragged from the bed over to that tree." He hurried over to the tree, where under one extra-long limb, he saw the grave. "Son of a . . ." he started, but was too anxious to finish. *Which one?* he wondered.

He ran back to his packsaddle to get the short shovel he carried, ran back to the grave, and set to work with a vengeance to find out which one of the two men was the more evil. Working hard, he started digging at the end of the grave where the crude cross had been driven; he assumed that should be the head. The body wasn't buried very deep and he soon felt his shovel meeting resistance, so he felt he'd better widen the hole and take more care in removing the dirt from around the head.

Finally he put the shovel aside and started removing the dirt with his hands until he uncovered the face of Frank Foley, an expression of stark panic on his face. Noticing the blood-stained shirt collar, Murphy brushed more dirt away from Foley's neck to reveal the wide gap in his windpipe. Then Murphy sat back on his heels to stare at the grotesque image and create the eerie picture in his mind. "Well, Deputy Marshal Foley, looks like you turned out to be the second worst rat that was ever born."

Thinking he should have some proof of US Deputy Marshal Foley's death, he decided his badge would be proof enough. So he removed more of the dirt away from Foley's chest and shoulders. As he suspected, Foley had not bothered to take his wool jacket off before he lay down to sleep, but the badge was not there. When he looked more closely, he discovered the holes in the coat where the badge had been worn. He assumed that Hatcher had taken the badge for some reason, perhaps to guard against someone finding the body and identifying it. He got up from the grave then and stood looking down at the portion of Foley's body that was uncovered. He tried to decide what he should do about it. Fill the grave back in, or leave him exposed? That was the question. He decided to cover Foley back up again, instead of leaving him for the buzzards to find.

With a temporary loss of appetite, he picked up his saddle and moved his camp a little farther away from the grave, wondering if Foley might still be arguing with the devil that he was in the wrong place. He considered moving on down the river to camp, but he had already stripped Nosy and his packhorse and they were both grazing down beside the river. So he dropped his saddle closer to where they were grazing and went back to get his packsaddle. When he came back with it, he glanced at the other side of the river and it occurred to him that it looked like a trail of some sort entering the river from that side.

When he got back to his new campsite, near the horses, he checked the riverbank more closely and realized that it matched the trail on the opposite side. When he realized that it was actually a trail that crossed the river, he looked back up the bank and he could see where the trail led up through the trees in an easterly direction. Curious as to whether or not it was still used by anyone, he walked up the bank and followed the trail into the trees. The growth of grass and weeds in the middle of the trail was enough indication that the trail was seldom used, if at all. When he looked far out across the rugged terrain, he could make out the trail in the distance, although barely.

His curiosity satisfied, he turned around to return to the river, but something caused him to stop and take another look at a patch of weeds in the middle of the old trail. They were no taller than a foot high, but a clump of them was leaning almost horizontally. He decided to take a closer look. So he knelt down beside the clump to discover it had been flattened by a hoof and not that long ago, because the stalks of the weeds had been cut. His guess was by the edge of a steel horseshoe. Remaining on his hands and knees, he crawled past the weeds, examining the grass until he came to a spot of bare ground with a clear hoofprint in it.

"He left the river," he muttered. "He left the river and took this old trail." Anxious to confirm his discovery, he hurried back to the trail by the river and followed it on past the old crossing trail. The clear tracks of the horses he had been following all day were now gone. For no sensible reason, he walked on for a short distance farther, in case the hoofprints reappeared. Since they did not, he repeated, "He left the river and took that old trail."

Since he was already stopped for the night, he decided to check one more possibility, even though he felt certain it was not likely, considering the disappearance of tracks on the river trail. He called Nosy to come to him and the big bay came at once. Without bothering to saddle him, he climbed up onto the horse's back and rode him across the river in an effort to stay as dry as possible. Fortunately, the river wasn't high enough to force him and the horse to swim. When he got across, he made a close inspection of the old trail until he was satisfied that the tracks on the east side of the river had no matching tracks on the west side of it. So there was no doubt that Hatcher had, in fact, left the river here and followed this old abandoned trail to wherever it could possibly lead. He had to wonder if Hatcher had any idea where it would take him, or if he was just running in hopes of disappearing.

With still no notion if he was making up any ground on Hatcher or not, there was nothing he could do to move any faster. He had to rest his horses and he was rapidly running out of anything to feed himself. There had been very little sign of game since he had left Newtown—deer or small game, either. Thanks to Paul Mathers's thoughtfulness, he had coffee to drink, but little else to go with it. His beef jerky was down to a couple of strips and most of the hardtack he had was pretty moldy. Even if he flushed a deer somewhere along the old trail he was about to set out on in the morning, he wasn't sure he could spare the time to butcher it. These were the thoughts that were worrying his mind as he sat by his fire, barefoot, with his boots and trousers hanging on some limbs he propped up by the fire. The river was low, but it was not low enough to prevent him from getting water up to the saddle. He had moved his camp down closer to the river beside a small stream to make it more convenient to fill his coffeepot and wash his hands.

It was getting close to dark when his horses began to get nervous and Nosy began to make warning noises. "What is it, boy?" Murphy tried to calm him. "Have we got visitors?" He reached over and picked up his rifle. The horses became even more excited, so he knew it was not other horses approaching. It was more of a dangerous situation—two-legged or four-legged threat, he couldn't be sure—so he cranked a live round into the chamber of his rifle and backed away from the fire. Then he spotted them, a pair of wolves stalking his horses. He watched as they split up to come at the packhorse from two directions, inching slowly forward. They must have been really hungry to attack his horses. Nosy reared up on his back legs and warned them. Finally, as if on a signal, they both sprang into action, launching their bodies in an all-out attack on the packhorse. Murphy stopped the first wolf, cranked another round in and stopped the second wolf.

He got up from the kneeling position he had assumed while waiting for the attack and walked forward, looking for signs of the rest of the pack, but there was no sign of any other wolves. He walked over to look at the two wolves, a male and a female. Both were dying, so he decided to end their suffering. He put a bullet in the back of the large male's head, then did the same for the small female. Then he looked all around him again for any sign of the pack, especially since the two wolves had attempted to attack the horses. Large animals were usually hunted by a pack of wolves. Two wolves alone, like these two, would seldom go after the horses. Unlike bears or mountain lions, a wolf, with its long slender snout, was not capable of a lethal bite or powerful bone-breaking blow. Its teeth were designed for pulling and ripping, and a horse was capable of stomping a wolf to death or rendering a back-breaking kick with its hind legs.

"You two must have been as hungry as I am to come after my horses," he said as he stood over the carcass of the male wolf. Then it occurred to him that maybe this wolf and his missus might have been sent there to feed him. "I've never et dog before, but I'll thank whoever's responsible for givin' me a chance to sample his cousin," he offered sincerely. "I'd better hurry, though, 'cause it's gonna be dark pretty quick." He put his boots back on, then took a short piece of rope and hung the female wolf by the neck from the limb of a small tree close to the stream to make it easier to skin her and gut her. Then he made short work of the butchering, taking the best parts of the body with the idea of taking enough meat to give him supper and breakfast, and that was all.

In a short time, he had strips of wolf meat cooking over his fire. As soon as the first slice of meat was done, he took it off the fire and sampled it. As hungry as he was, the meat didn't taste half-bad, so he proceeded to eat his fill. He decided it went very well with fresh coffee. He had heard there were some Indian tribes who thought dog meat was a delicacy. He wondered if you fed those Indians some wolf meat, they might say, "It's pretty good, but it has a kinda wild flavor."

When he was finished with his butchering, he wrapped the portion he had saved to cook for breakfast in the wolf skin, thinking it would still be fine in the morning. He dragged the rest of the female and the body of the male back in the trees, away from his camp, where he didn't think the buzzards would have any trouble finding them. He pulled his still-wet boots off again and set them back close to the fire to finish drying. He crawled into his blankets, thinking that all things considered, it hadn't really been a bad day.

He woke up to the sound of Nosy nibbling grass around his bare toes, which were sticking out of his blanket. "You're right," he told the bay gelding, "it's time to get on the trail." He put his dry socks on, then checked his boots to make sure no predators had moved in during the night while they were drying. Rather than cook his breakfast first thing, he decided to get on the trail and ride until the horses needed a rest, then cook his breakfast. So he cleaned up his camp, covered up his fire with dirt, and saddled the horses. "If you need a good night's sleep," he told Nosy as he was checking his cinch for comfort, "eat some wolf meat for supper." He climbed up into the saddle and turned the bay's nose down the cross trail and said goodbye to the Colorado, unaware that the man he followed was less than twenty miles ahead of him.

# CHAPTER 15

Ward Hatcher sat at the kitchen table in a small log house on Dead Pine Creek, drinking coffee with a Mexican girl sitting on his knee. At the head of the table, the elderly patriarch of the family, Seth Bullock, poked around in the eggs on his plate with his fork before he pushed the plate away in disgust. "That damn Juanita, she can't cook no more. Nothin' tastes like it's supposed to no more."

"Mama cooks better than anybody," the girl on Hatcher's knee spoke up. "You just get too old to know what's good and what's not good."

"I ain't too old to know when a sassy-mouth young'un needs a good hidin' with my razor strop," Seth told her.

"That's right, Papa," Jed Bullock volunteered. "I can do that little chore for ya."

"The day that happens is the day I scratch your eyes out," Maria threatened.

"Uh-oh, little brother," Slim Bullock warned. "You might be better off trying to spank a wildcat. I might have to help you."

"Now watch your mouth, boys," Seth ordered. "You ought not talk about your sister like that."

"She ain't my sister," Jed declared emphatically. "Juanita ain't my mother. She's the damn cook."

"I told you to watch your mouth," the old man said. "When I married Juanita, that made her your mother, and I don't never wanna hear you disrespectin' her."

"Hell, I ain't disrespectin' her," Jed insisted. "She just ain't my mother."

"She's a good cook, though," Tiny said. He was the youngest of Seth Bullock's three sons, and was credited with the death of Ruby Bullock, his mother, when she finally delivered the grossly oversized infant. Ralph Gentry, Ruby's brother and Seth's partner in the cattle-rustling business, claimed that Tiny was bigger than a lot of the calves when they were born. At sixteen years of age, Tiny was already just short of six feet and looked to be almost as heavy as Ward Hatcher.

"You've all got a family you can be proud of," Hatcher said. "I knew I wanted to get by to see you folks before I go north. Don't know how long I'll be up that way. Might be for a long time. But I told you when I left here that I'd see if there was any reward money offered for Sam Black Wolf. 'Course there ain't any reward for a US Deputy Marshal catchin' a wanted man, 'cause that's what I'm paid to do. But I felt like you boys helped me so much in capturin' Black Wolf that you deserved some reward, if there was one offered. Well, I found out that there was one offered by the state of Texas for five hundred dollars. But like I said, a lawman makin' the arrest don't get no reward. So it's took me all this time. What's it been? About three years? I know Tiny weren't half that size. Anyway, I finally got the approval to collect that reward—so I was hopin' you folks were still here—so I could pass it on to you."

"Well, I don't mind tellin' ya, you coulda knocked me over with a feather when you showed up here yesterday and handed me that five hundred dollars," Seth told him. "The whole five hundred, you didn't keep any of it for yourself."

"Like I said, I get paid regular wages to arrest murderers," Hatcher said. "Besides, it was you and Slim, there, that cut that scoundrel down when he was fixin' to bushwhack me." He shook his head slowly as if concerned. "Sam Black Wolf still has friends that try to track me. I just hope I ain't led none of 'em after me on this trail. I don't want to lead any of 'em to your place here on Dead Pine." He couldn't think of anyone who could be on his trail this soon, but it couldn't hurt to have an insurance policy. And he figured he might as well get something for his five hundred dollars, a sum he could now easily afford.

"I wish they would show up here," Seth Bullock said. "Me and the boys would show 'em a good time. Wouldn't we, boys?" All three sons grinned and nodded their heads. "Sorry you're in a hurry to leave. We'd enjoy spendin' a little more time showin' how much we appreciate you rememberin' that reward after all this time. I gotta be honest with you, I didn't really expect you'd go after that money for us. I never counted on it a minute after you left here with that dead half-Comanche hangin' across his saddle."

"I wish I had more time to visit with you," Hatcher said. "I surely didn't expect the royal treatment I received." He sneaked a hand over to pat Maria's bottom and thought, *It usually costs me considerably less than five hundred dollars.* "I expect I'd better get my old bones up from this table and get back in the saddle." He gave Maria an extra pat on her bottom. "Hop up, darlin', Uncle Ward has got to get goin'." He shook Seth's hand and thanked Juanita for her hospitality.

"We hope you come back soon," Juanita said.

"I brought your horses around to the front porch," Slim said. "Looks like you had 'em all packed up and ready to go. So I just led 'em around and tied 'em by the steps."

"Thank you, Slim," Hatcher said, "I 'preciate that." They all walked him out to the front porch and waited while he climbed up into the saddle. "It's been a pleasure spendin' a little time with you folks. I'll stop in again, if I'm back in this part of the country anytime soon." He turned the gray gelding named Smokey down the narrow path that led back to the trail he had been traveling.

Juanita and Maria went back inside the house, while the men stood watching Hatcher ride down the path. "Well, that was a sure-enough unexpected visit," Seth remarked.

"He'll be back," Slim said, "sooner than you think."

"What makes you say that?" Jed asked.

Slim stepped off the side of the porch, bent over, and pulled a sack out from under the porch. He tossed it up on the porch to land at his father's feet. "This!" he answered Jed. They all stared at the sack, with the words *Wells Fargo* printed on it and tied up neatly with a string.

"What the . . . ?" Seth started. He picked up the sack, untied the string, and emptied the contents on the floor. He, Jed, and Tiny all stared in shock at the unbelievable sight.

"Them's thousands and thousands of dollars," Slim said.

"Was it on his horses?" Seth asked, still not willing to believe that what he was seeing was real.

"You saw his horses," Slim said. "He's leadin' one wearin' a saddle and one with a packsaddle. He's using the saddle horse to carry things hanging from the saddle horn and the buckles, but the other horse has a regular packsaddle on it. He had those packs tied up real tight and one side was covered up really tight. It just made me wanna take a look at what he didn't want to get wet. So I took it apart and that's what he was hidin'." He pointed to the sack. "I didn't want him to notice, so I stuffed hay in the hole he had fixed for it and tied it up again."

Jed slapped him on the back and declared, "I swear, little brother, you do beat all. Ain't he gonna swallow his tongue when he opens his packs?"

"What are we gonna do with it, Pa?" Tiny asked. "Are we gonna keep it? He's sure as hell gonna be comin' back here, lookin' for it."

"I expect he will," Seth answered. "Wouldn't you? The question that's tuggin' at my mind right now is, who was ridin' that horse with the saddle on it? He's a lawman, a US Deputy Marshal. If he's an honest lawman, then that other horse could belong to the man who stole that Wells Fargo money. And Hatcher had to shoot him, so now he's takin' the money and the horse back to Austin, where he says his headquarters is."

"If he's headin' to Austin, he's headin' in the wrong direction," Slim said. "It's easier for me to think Hatcher shot the other feller and stole the money. He sure as hell ain't the first lawman to switch sides of the road, and that looks like there's enough money right there to make it easy to hop the fence."

"We could hide the money and play dumb, like we ain't got no idea who coulda done it," Tiny suggested.

"He wouldn't fall for that," Seth said. "He spent the night here, slept in the barn with his horses. You know he woulda checked his packs to make sure his money was there." He paused, trying to think of the best way to handle Hatcher's return. "It galls me to think about him talking about how hard he worked to get us that reward and he just pinched off a little pile of bills from the money he stole. He's a liar and a thief, so we've got every bit as much right to that money as he has. So everybody strap your handguns on and be ready for Deputy Marshal Hatcher's return visit. I'll go in the house and tell the women what's goin' on."

"I don't reckon that coulda gone much better," Ward Hatcher said aloud. "I left there a hero, sure as hell, for gettin' that bunch of morons their reward money." He realized that he could have given them half that much with the same result. But why quibble about it when five hundred dollars seemed so much like a real reward. They were tickled to get it and treated him like he was somebody special, even sent Maria down to the barn to tuck him in for the night. It was a good investment in the form of insurance in case somebody happened to get on his trail. He could count on ol' Seth Bullock to take care of anybody showing up at Dead Pine looking for him. So far, everything he planned had gone according to plan. Consequently, he was in the best of moods when he approached a little creek and decided it was a good place to rest his horses and have some dinner. There was even a lot of deer sign along the creek. If he got lucky, he might have the opportunity to have some fresh meat.

He took the saddles and the packs off his horses and let them go to the creek. It was shady there by the creek, so he gathered enough wood to build a fire. And once he had that going to his satisfaction, he took his coffeepot to the creek for water. When he had that sitting in the edge of the fire, he sliced some bacon to fry.

He untied the canvas where he kept the money, now minus five hundred, because that was where he had packed his sugar. He was confused immediately when little pieces of hay began to fall out of the pack. Moments later, he was stunned when his sack of sugar fell out on the ground in a clump of hay. For long moments then, he stood unable to move over the open pack, as if waiting for it to produce his money. When nothing happened after a couple of minutes, he feared something was wrong with his mind and he attempted to calm himself. *What the hell did I do with the money?* He tried to think back to the time that morning when he was lacing up his packs on the packsaddle. *Where did I put the sack with the money?* He closed his eyes to allow his memory to form a mental picture. All he could see was the money sack next to the sugar sack.

The reality of what had happened to the money was banging away in his brain now, but he still could not accept it. He opened his eyes and frantically searched through all the packs on the saddle. Then he searched through the sacks he had hanging from the saddle on Foley's horse, the saddlebags, then the packsaddle again before he sat down on the ground, exhausted. Those two-faced cattle rustlers had stolen his money.

Even while they entertained him at the kitchen table, one of them went through his packs and found his money. This was a death sentence for the entire family, for they were all in on it, from the daughter to the elderly old man. They all had a part to play.

He haphazardly started throwing his packs back together, dumping the water out of his coffeepot, intending to return immediately to take back that which was his. Then in a lone moment of sanity, he forced himself to reason with the whole situation. In the first place, his horses were tired, and they needed water and grazing. Counting the women, there were six of them, all of whom could fire a gun. He would likely come out on the losing end of any kind of shoot-out with the old man and his three sons, even without the mother and daughter. He had to admit that he didn't know what to do, but he was going to go back for his money. Without it, he had no future.

It was difficult to make himself wait there by the little creek until his horses were ready to travel again, but he knew it might be dangerous for him if they could not perform for him in an emergency. And with what he had in mind to do, there was ample opportunity for an emergency.

He figured he had ridden over fifteen miles from Dead Pine Creek, so after he forced himself to wait long enough for the horses to be ready, he saddled up and started back. When he spotted the big creek a short distance ahead of him, he turned off the trail with the intention of paralleling the creek on the east side, instead of following the small path on the other side that led to the cabin. He felt certain that had he ridden up the path to the cabin, he would have been shot on sight, since there would be no doubt why he had returned. The trees were thick along the sides of the creek, with large bushes between many of them, so he was able to ride pretty close to it.

After a distance of about fifty yards from the old trail, he caught sight of the log cabin on the other side of the creek. So he pulled a little farther away from the creek until he was past the cabin and closer to the barn; then he looked for a good place to tie his horses. During the process, he heard a horse on the other side of the creek whinny a greeting and one of his horses answered it. He stopped dead still and listened, but evidently no one near the cabin heard it, so he continued on until the barn was between him and the cabin. He stopped when he came to a small stream that fed into the creek. He had noticed the stream the night before when he had gone out of the barn to answer nature's call. He tied the horses by the stream so they could drink after their fast trip back.

With what he had to do, he decided his rifle might hamper his actions, so he checked his six-gun to make sure it was fully loaded, then worked his way carefully through the trees to the edge of the creek. Below the short bank, he noticed a log lying on the bottom of the creek and made a mental note that it would tell him where he had tied his horses. It would also give him something to step on to keep the water from getting over the top of his boots. He remained there by the side of the creek to watch the house and the barn for a while to see where everyone was. He looked at his watch and figured they should be getting ready for supper before long.

*I need to find out where they put my money,* he thought, *and maybe I can get to it while they're eating.* In the next moment, the back door of the cabin opened and the daughter, Maria, came out and went into the barn. He didn't hesitate to act, thinking this might be exactly what he needed.

He stepped down into the creek and waded across, scrambled up the other side, and went quickly to the back door of the barn, which was sitting partially open. He peeked inside before going in and saw Maria looking in a line of chicken nests on the other side, her back to him. He didn't hesitate, but slipped inside the door and crept across the barn to grab her with one hand over her mouth, while locking her arms to her sides with his other arm. She went immediately rigid.

"Now you just relax and you ain't gonna get hurt. It's just good ol' Uncle Ward come to get his money. So you be a sweet little honeybee and tell me where they put it." She made an effort to free herself, but she was unable to move against the strength of his arm. "You ain't listening to me, sweetie. You'd best start talkin' when I take my hand off of your mouth, but if you yell out, I'll stick my knife in your belly and walk clean around you. Do you understand?" She nodded her head, terrified when he took his hand away to draw his skinning knife and hold it up in front of her face. "Where is it?" he demanded.

"The kitchen!" Maria gasped. "It's on the kitchen table! I'll go get it for you."

"Oh, I'm sure you would, darlin', but it might be better if you stay out here with me." Still holding her around her arms, he picked her up and carried her over to one of the two stalls in the little barn where he noticed a coil of rope.

Inside the cabin, Juanita waited impatiently for her daughter to return from the barn. "Slim," she finally said, "go out to the barn and see why your sister don't come back. I sent her to find me an egg to go in this corn pudding."

"She ain't my sister," Slim said, "but I'll go see. She probably forgot where she was goin' by the time she went out the door." He got up from the one armchair beside the fireplace and started for the door. As soon as he did, Tiny got up from the floor and sat down in the chair. "You'd best have your big butt outta my chair by the time I get back," Slim warned him.

"Who said it was your chair?" Tiny responded. "It's time somebody else had a turn in the dad-blamed chair."

"It's Pa's chair," Jed told them, "and if he ain't usin' it, it goes by the next oldest, so that would be me, little brother. Now quit makin' so much noise. Pa's takin' a nap."

When Slim reached the barn, "Maria" was the only word he got out of his mouth before Hatcher stepped out from behind the door and laid him out flat with a blow to the back of his head from the barrel of his Colt .45. With plenty of rope to spare, he tied Slim, hand and foot, and stuffed in his mouth a piece of rag, which he had found over by the milking stool.

"How many of you does it take to bring one egg back from the barn?" Juanita complained. "If you want to have your supper tonight, somebody better go find me one egg."

"Something's goin' on," Jed responded. "I'll go find you an egg, Juanita." He walked out the back door. "They musta found something and forgot all about your egg."

"If somebody don't get me an egg, they can forget all about their supper," she threatened again. "You tell them that!" she called after him. "Ever since they all got rich, they can't do a simple chore." She continued her complaining, unaware that Jed had joined the others tied up in the barn.

Hatcher was amazed at how successful his simple plan had been. There were still three people to account for inside the cabin—Juanita, Tiny, and old Seth. He had used up all the rope he had found, but he was confident that he could handle those three in person. In fact, he was eager to settle the score with the old man personally. He had donated a nice sum of five hundred dollars to the old SOB strictly out of the kindness of his heart. And then to have him steal from him outright! He needed to be taught a lesson.

So he took a few moments to check his prisoners he had bound, hand and foot, to be sure they had no prospect of freeing themselves. Satisfied, he walked out of the barn and went to the cabin. After taking a look through the windows to see where the three were, he went back to the kitchen door and kicked it open. Tiny fell face down on the floor when he got tangled up trying to jump up from the armchair. In total confusion, he reached for his gun, which he forgot he hadn't strapped on. Hatcher gave him a shot in the back for his trouble. “Reach for it and you’re dead, boy.”

Hatcher then told Juanita, who made a move toward a shotgun over the fireplace, “You come with me.” She moved in the direction he indicated, and he followed her into the bedroom, where Seth Bullock was clawing his way out of a nap rudely interrupted by the pistol shot.

“What the hell, Juanita?” Seth demanded, still not fully awake.

“It’s Hatcher,” Juanita answered.

“Hatcher?” Seth asked. “What about him?”

“He say he come for his money,” Juanita replied. “He say he think you got his money.”

“No,” Hatcher said, mocking her broken English, “he say he *know* you stole his money.”

“Why do you think I’ve got your money?” Bullock asked, still sitting up on the bed. “I’ve got the money you gave me for the reward. Is that what you’re talkin’ about? You sayin’ you want me to give you the reward money back?”

“Listen, you old coot, I ain’t got time to play games with you. You know what money I’m talkin’ about, and if you don’t come up with it right now, I’m gonna start executin’ one of your worthless sons every five minutes. They’re tied up in the barn waitin’ to see how much you care about them.”

“Now, hold on, Ward,” Seth attempted to calm him down. “Me and my boys don’t know nothin’ about any money you’ve got missin’. Hell, we’ll try to help you find it. It musta fell off one of your horses. Maybe when you crossed the creek or somethin’ like that. I can’t believe you’d accuse us of stealin’ it from you.”

Disgusted with his feeble pleas, Hatcher roared, “Get offa that damn bed and get me my money!” He reached down, grabbed the bed frame, and came straight up with it, dumping Seth on the floor with the bed upside down on top of him.

There, sitting on the floor where the bed had been, was a sack folded into a package with the words *Wells Fargo* printed on the side of it. No one said a word for a long few seconds. Then Seth suddenly made a desperate try to reach for his gun and holster on the table near the bed. Hatcher took great pleasure in putting a bullet in the back of the old man's head. Watching Juanita for her reaction, he saw fear and panic, but no indication of retaliation. He wondered if there was any real affection for the old man, so he picked up the package and unrolled it to make sure the money was all there.

He cocked his six-gun again and casually turned to focus all his gaze on Juanita. She immediately began to cower, bracing for the shot she knew was coming, knowing it was useless to beg for mercy. "Do you know where the five hundred I gave him is?"

She nodded.

"Get it," he ordered, still with the gun aimed at her. He watched her as she went to Seth's coat hanging on a hook behind the bed, reached into an inside pocket, and pulled out a stack of bills. When she extended it out to him, he was struck with a sudden wave of compassion. "You put that away where only you know where it is. I imagine you've sacrificed enough, livin' with that worthless piece of trash. If you decide one day that it's better for you and your daughter to break away from his sons, that'll be enough to give you a start somewhere."

"Thank you," she said softly, blinking away grateful tears.

"I'm done with what I came here to do," he told her. "That boy in the other room, Tiny, he ain't hurt as bad as he thinks. I shot him in the back, but it's more in the shoulder. You need to wrap him up with something to stop his bleedin'; then you can take a look at him to see if you want to get the bullet out or just leave it in. Won't make much difference either way. Everybody else is okay, tied up in the barn, but they ain't hurt none, maybe Slim and Jed a little, but Maria ain't got a scratch on her. I should be gone from here by the time you tend to Tiny and get out to the barn." He paused then to judge her expression.

She nodded, understanding.

"All right, then," he said, "good luck to ya." He turned and left her standing there, staring down at Seth Bullock's body.

When Hatcher walked back through the front room, he found Tiny on his hands and knees, attempting to crawl toward a rolled-up gun and holster on the floor, some six feet in front of him. The wave of compassion having left him, he drew his six-gun and put another bullet in Tiny's back, this one in the center. Then he passed through the kitchen on his way out the back door. He felt no need to check on the other two brothers and the girl, so he walked past the barn and crossed the creek. Taking only a few moments to secure the money on his packhorse, he was soon on his way out of the trees and back to the old Indian trail.

# Chapter 16

When Hatcher approached the trail, he slowed his horses while he took a cautious look in both directions before he once again sought to follow the trail to the east. As before, there was no sign of any travelers east or west. So he set out to ride the fifteen-plus miles he had ridden that morning, planning to stop once again at the shady little creek where he had discovered the loss of his money.

As he rode along at a fast walk, he considered the possibility of pursuit by Jed and Slim Bullock. He really didn't think there was much of a chance for it, based on his opinion that they were trained not to make a move without their father's direction. *Maybe I'm getting too old for this business,* he thought. Maybe he should have shot the rest of them and he wouldn't have even had to give it a thought, plus he would have saved five hundred dollars. He sighed and said, "I must be gettin' soft." But he knew that he never liked to shoot a woman unless she was a real hellcat—and then it was more like putting down a rabid dog. "Nah, they won't come after me," he decided. "Juanita will tell 'em to leave it be. On the other hand, twenty-five thousand dollars might speak louder than Juanita. Well, if they come after me, it's their funeral."

* * *

It was already approaching suppertime when Hatcher was still almost an hour away from the little creek he planned to camp by for the night. It would not be dark for a while yet. He could still see the hoofprints on the trail. There were tracks he had left originally, and now there were tracks going the other way, tracks he had left when he went back for his money. He chuckled when the thought occurred to him that the only traveler he had met, going in the opposite direction, was himself. Finally, when about a mile short of the creek, he heard a rifle shot. He reined Smokey back to a sudden halt. The sound had come from somewhere ahead of him, possibly the creek. He waited, listening, but there was only the one shot. "Damn," he uttered. Having never met a single traveler on the whole trail, it was inconvenient as hell to meet one now, and at this place on the trail. Then he remembered the abundance of deer sign he had seen when he was at the creek before. A hunter, maybe that was what he had heard: one rifle shot, one dead deer. That was a good possibility, he thought. At least the shot was ahead of him. The danger to him was all behind him, so he decided to continue on, but to do it cautiously until he found the source of the rifle shot.

Maintaining a steady walk, he soon saw the light of a campfire in the trees close to the creek, not very far from where he had started to camp before he realized he had been robbed. Then he saw what he was looking for. The form of a man passing by the fire and standing up beside what could be nothing other than a deer carcass, hanging from the limb of a tree. He stopped and watched for a while, but there was no sign of any other form, only the one man butchering a deer. Hatcher smiled. The only thing luckier would have been if someone had shot a deer, gone away, and left the deer hanging there for him. The important thing would be not to frighten the hunter. Like himself, he was probably not expecting to meet anyone on this deserted trail and might be suspicious of anyone traveling it.

When he got within hailing distance, Hatcher called out, "Hello the camp!"

As he expected, the figure jumped away from the firelight and probably reached for a weapon. "Mean you no harm!" Hatcher called out again. "It's just me and my three horses. I was figurin' on campin' here, myself, but I can go on downstream, if it might bother you." There was no reply right away, so Hatcher called out again, "I'm US Deputy Marshal Ward Hatcher." As soon as he said it, he wondered if it was a mistake. He had said it to give the man a sense of safety, but if the man was a fugitive from the law, it might have cost him his life.

There was a short delay before the hunter answered, "You're welcome to come on in and help me get rid of some of this deer I'm butcherin'."

"That sounds to my likin'," Hatcher responded. "That's mighty neighborly of you." He rode on into the camp.

"Find you a spot there, then grab a piece of that deer meat over the fire. I'm fixin' to carve off some more of this backstrap to put on the fire. I like it better than the tenderloin. Most folks think the tenderloin is the best cut, but it's mighty damn hard to get to."

Hatcher didn't need any further invitation to help himself. He took a stick from over the fire with a large slice of backstrap on it and went to work on it with a vengeance. "I swear, that's good meat!" he exclaimed when the hunter stepped away from the hanging carcass and stepped into firelight.

"I'm glad you're enjoyin' it, Ward. You most likely won't have fresh venison in prison before they hang you," Murphy said, no longer trying to disguise his voice.

Hatcher looked up, startled. "Murphy! What the hell are you doin' here?" He stared at the Colt in Murphy's hand, aimed at his nose.

"I've been followin' a string of dead bodies for miles," Murphy answered his question.

"It ain't no business of yours," Hatcher said. "You ain't got no jurisdiction outside the boundaries of Newtown. Them four outlaws we took outta your jail was already sentenced to die. I just made it a little bit easier for 'em. Frank Foley felt the same way and he killed two of 'em. Die by gunshot, die by rope around your neck, all the same. We just carried out the court orders."

"What about Frank Foley? Did the court order him to die?"

"That ain't the same," Hatcher insisted. "That was an accident, Foley come off his horse and broke his neck."

"I think you're mistaken there, Hatcher. I took a look at Foley when I found that grave you dug for him. There wasn't anything wrong with his neck. It was that slice across his throat that went from one ear to the other that did him in. Probably happened while he was takin' a nap."

"Why the hell did you stick your nose in it? You don't have any idea how many of these low-down killers me and Foley have tracked down and put away while you little small-town lawmen are worryin' about some drunk at the saloon takin' a leak on the street."

"I'll tell you why I stuck my nose in it. I don't like you, Hatcher. I can't abide a man who will turn on a friend, like you turned on Foley. And it was all for the money. You sold your soul for twenty-five thousand dollars. What if there wasn't that much money on that stage? Was Foley's life worth ten thousand dollars? How about fifty dollars? Would you have killed him for fifty? I think you would have done it for ten dollars if you needed ten. I'm tempted to empty this .44 in your face right now. But I'd rather take you and that Wells Fargo money back and turn you in; this way, you can enjoy the whole ceremony of your trial and hanging. And all the deputy marshals you've worked with over the years can get to know what a great lawman you were. So let's get one thing straight right now. That's what I intend to do. If you don't cooperate with me, I will shoot you. You can pretend to cooperate, and go along to wait for a chance when I get careless; but when you make your move, I will knock you down. Ward Hatcher, you are officially under arrest. You might as well eat all that venison you want while you've got a chance. If food gets scarce on your trip to the gallows, I'll cut your rations first."

"You're a fine one to be preachin' to me about enforcing the law," Hatcher came back at him. "What is it they talk about in Newtown, Murphy's Law? It ain't the county law or the state law. It's Murphy's Law. Ain't that right?"

"There ain't no difference in Murphy's Law and the county law," Murphy said. "And I ain't gonna debate the question with you. All you need to know about Murphy's Law is that Murphy is holdin' his gun in his hand, while yours is still in the holster. We might as well take care of that right now."

Murphy started to move around Hatcher to pull his gun out of the holster, but Hatcher moved every step with him, keeping his gun out of reach. "Stand still," Murphy ordered, but Hatcher continued to step around in defiance until Murphy fired a round into Hatcher's calf, causing him to yell in pain and drop on one knee. Murphy pulled Hatcher's gun from the holster and stuck it in his belt. "I have to apologize," Murphy said. "I don't have much patience with idiots."

"You shot me, you damn fool!" Hatcher roared.

"I had to get your attention," Murphy said. "I reckon I'm gonna have to take you to the doctor. I don't believe there's one around here, but the next doctor's office we come to, we'll stop in and have him take a look at your leg." He paused, then added, "And any other wounds you pick up on our trip to the gallows. I'm gonna ask you to turn your pockets inside out now."

"What for?" Hatcher asked painfully.

"You still ain't learned yet, have you? I don't give reasons, I give orders." He cocked his .44 and aimed it at Hatcher's other leg.

"All right, all right!" Hatcher fairly screamed. "I'm doin' it!" He emptied his pants pockets out on the ground.

Murphy quickly picked up handcuff keys, a pocketknife, and anything else that looked like it could be used for a tool or a weapon. Then he ordered him to dump his coat and vest pockets out as well. Hatcher protested, but didn't risk another gunshot wound. Once he got Hatcher fed, he forced him to limp over to a small tree and sit down. Then Murphy handcuffed Hatcher's hands around the tree and left him there for the night, while he finished butchering the deer and set his fire to smoke a small amount of it all night. As cool as the weather was for the time of year, Murphy thought the meat would not begin to turn for two days and he planned to reach Austin in two and a half days. He knew the trail that he had turned off of, that followed the Colorado River, would take him to Austin.

When the horses and everything else were taken care of for the night, he offered to take a look at the wound in Hatcher's calf. But Hatcher insisted he didn't want him to touch it. "Well, we'd better take that boot off, because if we don't, your leg might swell up so much that we have to cut the boot off," Murphy said.

"No, it ain't that bad," Hatcher insisted. "It ain't gonna swell up that much."

"I'll take a look at it and pour some whiskey in the wound to keep it from gettin' infected," Murphy said.

"To hell with it," Hatcher insisted. "It don't make a helluva lot of sense to worry about my leg when you're takin' me to be hanged. Besides, it ain't botherin' me none."

"Suit yourself," Murphy said, and shrugged, but he continued to look at the leg. It looked to him like there was a good chance that boot could become uncomfortable during the night. Then another thought struck him; and without warning, he grabbed Hatcher's foot and struggled with the boot until it finally released Hatcher's foot. "Damn," Murphy swore, "it's a good thing we got that boot off. It mighta been really painful in the mornin' with that knife inside it."

"There's a bottle of whiskey in that bag that hangs on my saddle horn," Hatcher said. "You might as well pour a little bit of it on that wound."

Murphy went to fetch the bottle, pulled the sock down, and splashed a generous amount on the wound. After Hatcher yelped with the pain, he asked, "How 'bout if I take a little shot for my insides?"

"Sure," Murphy said, "maybe it'll help you sleep tonight."

Hatcher took a long pull out of the bottle, then offered it to Murphy.

"No, thanks," Murphy said. "One of us better stay sober, so we can find our way home."

"Well, it was worth a try," Hatcher said. "I wouldn't mind having another pull to help me make it through the night wrapped around this tree."

"As many years as you've been in the law business, I know you've handcuffed many an outlaw to a tree for the night," Murphy said. "So you oughta know you can still stretch your body out straight and might even fall asleep."

Morning found the prisoner stretched out asleep, with his arms stretched straight out from the tree that held him. Murphy rolled out of his blanket and started getting the horses saddled and ready to go. When Hatcher showed signs of life, Murphy unlocked one of his cuffs, so he could free his hands from the tree. "You can take a leak before we get on the road," Murphy told him. "Hurry up and get it done, we've got some miles to cover."

"I need a little privacy to do it proper," Hatcher said.

"I don't remember you being that bashful before," Murphy said. "I remember when you rode up to that outlaw hideout and let those horses out of the corral with me, you weren't so bashful. In fact, if I recall correctly, you acted like you wanted to show those horses you were just like them."

"It was different then," Hatcher claimed. "I wasn't a doggone prisoner then."

"Well, just turn your back and walk over there a few steps and get it done. We're gonna ride back to the Colorado and then I'll cook our breakfast while the horses are restin'."

Hatcher limped a few steps while making an obvious show of the pain it caused him. "You made a cripple outta me," he complained. "I need a crutch. If you would give me my rifle, I could use it as a crutch. It ain't loaded."

"That's right," Murphy said. "Everybody knows Winchester makes a dandy crutch. But I'm afraid it might be too much to handle with a gimpy leg, and besides, you wouldn't wanna get the barrel all clogged up with dirt."

"You could wrap a rag around it," Hatcher said.

"Quit wastin' time," Murphy snapped impatiently, and cocked the hammer back on his Colt. "Get your business done or do it in the saddle. I ain't waitin' any longer."

"All right, all right," Hatcher conceded, and limped a few steps farther before answering nature's call. When he was finished, Murphy told him to put his hands behind his back. "Ah, come on," Hatcher complained. "You ain't gonna cuff my hands behind my back, are you? There ain't no sense in makin' me ride that way."

"Did you somehow get the impression that I trust your word?" Murphy asked. "It's either that or put another bullet in you somewhere. Let's get going." He cuffed Hatcher's hands behind his back and helped him climb up into the saddle. He left the camp by the shady creek, with the reins of Hatcher's horse, Smokey, tied to his saddle, as well as the reins of his packhorse. Behind Smokey, he tied Frank Foley's saddle horse and the other packhorse. In his saddlebags he carried the Wells Fargo money. He led them all out on the old Indian trail, back toward the Colorado River, thinking it pure luck that things turned out the way they had. In fact, Murphy had been just as surprised as Hatcher had been when he came upon him butchering the deer.

Murphy had been wondering how he could have possibly gotten ahead of Hatcher. He followed the tracks until they disappeared, going no farther than the little creek. Before reaching the creek, he had begun to notice other tracks, heading back the way he had come, but he had met no one on the trail. After he crossed the creek, he found that the tracks heading in the opposite direction had also disappeared. Then he realized the obvious: Hatcher had turned around when he came to the creek and gone back the way he had come. The mystery still unsolved was why he didn't meet him somewhere on the trail. Thinking there was no other option, he decided to camp there by the little creek, then try to follow the tracks going in the opposite direction in the morning. It was at that point that the deer had come to the creek, giving him an opportunity to get the taste of wolf meat out of his mouth.

It was not the ride that Ward Hatcher had anticipated taking the morning after his parting with the Bullock family. And now, it was a strange turn of events that he saw the Bullocks as his only hope for an escape. This, in spite of the fact that he had killed Seth Bullock and Tiny. He saw a definite possibility that Murphy would stop to rest the horses and cook breakfast when he came to Dead Pine Creek. It was a strong, wide creek, and about fifteen miles from the little creek that they started out from. It would be hard to pass it up. If he was lucky, Murphy wouldn't notice the tracks leaving the trail, short of the creek, to follow it upstream.

Hatcher's plan was a desperate one. He was under no illusion that Jed and Slim Bullock might come to his rescue if they were to discover them camping right below their cabin. His hope was that if they became aware of the camp and saw that he was there, they would realize the opportunity for revenge for their father, as well as another chance to take the Wells Fargo money. Under attack, Murphy might free him to help repel the assault, and when it was done, he might have the chance to kill Murphy before he was handcuffed again. It was a plan based on highly unlikely odds, but it gave him some hope.

So he nodded thoughtfully when Murphy informed him that they would stop at this creek up ahead to cook some breakfast and rest the horses. When they got to the creek, Hatcher was satisfied to see that Murphy seemed not to notice the tracks that led off the trail just before reaching it. He was smug in his guess that Murphy was paying little attention to the trail, since he was no longer tracking.

Murphy picked a spot and handcuffed Hatcher to a tree, while he gathered some wood for a fire. "Build a big one," Hatcher called out. "It gets cold ridin' with your hands pinned down behind your back."

"I'm fixin' to warm you from the belly out with some fresh deer meat," Murphy answered him. "Right after I take care of the horses." He wasted little time in making sure the horses could get to water and some grazing along the creek bank. Then he got his fire going and took some of the cuts of venison from the hide he had wrapped the meat in and started roasting it over the flames.

"Thank you kindly," Hatcher said when Murphy brought him a large slice of venison and a cup of coffee and set them down where he could reach them. "Did you know the name of this creek is Dead Pine Creek?"

"No," Murphy answered, "I did not know that. How did you know it?"

"I've been here before," Hatcher said.

"I figured you musta had some reason for headin' down this way, instead of following on down the Colorado to Austin. To tell you the truth, I was wonderin' if you were goin' back to

Austin when you took the river trail. It made more sense when you turned off on this trail. Where does this trail end up, if I hadn't stopped you?"

"About ten miles past that creek we camped by last night, you'da crossed a wagon road that would take you to Waco. But if you stayed on the trail for about thirty miles farther, you'da struck a trail to Fort Worth. That's where I was headin'."

"Fort Worth and then on up to Indian Territory, huh?" Murphy asked. Hatcher nodded and smiled sadly. For a few moments, Murphy felt a little sorry for him, but then he remembered the reason he had come after him. "How about your partner, Foley? Is that where he was hopin' to go, too?"

Hatcher smiled again, this time deviously. "When you play in a pen of coyotes as long as Foley and I have, it comes natural to turn on your own pack."

"Not in the book I go by," Murphy said. "You want more coffee? I'm fixin' to throw it out." Hatcher held out his cup. Murphy poured the rest of the pot in it and started to the creek to rinse out the pot and put it away.

"How 'bout takin' these cuffs offa me for a couple of minutes," Hatcher called after him. "I can't even scratch my butt."

"Do it like a coyote does it," Murphy replied. "Scrub it up against that tree trunk."

He started to turn toward the creek again, but stopped in his tracks when he heard the sharp crack of a rifle and saw Hatcher slump over and slowly slide down the tree trunk to the ground. He took off at once, running for the creek bank for cover as he felt the snap of a bullet that passed close to his head. The bank was just high enough to permit him to crawl behind it. So he crawled toward his horses, where they were grazing on the bank, with the sound of rifle shots and bullets kicking up dirt above his head. He heard several more shots fired; when he stopped next to a bush to risk a look, he saw a couple of shots cause Hatcher's body to move slightly. He tried to pinpoint the direction the shots were coming from to determine the shooter or shooters' position. Then finally he caught a brief flash of sunlight on a rifle barrel from the trees on the other side of the creek. He continued along the bank toward the horses, which were frightened and moving about nervously. When he got to Nosy, he scrambled up out of the creek and quickly snatched his rifle out of the scabbard and stepped behind a large tree to crank a live round in the chamber.

"Did you hit him?" Slim asked frantically.

"I don't know," Jed replied. "He was movin' pretty fast. We sure as shootin' got Hatcher, though."

"That other feller was a lawman," Slim said. "He had Hatcher handcuffed to that tree, and if we don't kill him, we're gonna be in big trouble."

"We gotta kill him, anyway, because he's got the money now," Jed declared. "He might be a lawman like Hatcher. They're all crooked, so you know he was just after the money, too."

"But if he was just after the money," Slim wondered aloud, "why didn't he just shoot Hatcher? You reckon he was takin' Hatcher to jail?"

"I don't know if he was or not. Maybe he was takin' him to jail. But we already shot Hatcher, so we'd be in trouble with the law for that. The safest thing for us is to find this feller and kill him, so he can't go back and tell no tales. Besides, we need that money. We'll bury him and Hatcher, too, where nobody can find 'em."

"You're right," Slim said, "but first we gotta find him. He crawled down that creek bank and I don't know if he got hit or not. If he didn't get hit, he woulda been shootin' back at us by now. I think one of those shots we fired along that bank musta got him. That bank ain't that high." In agreement on that issue, they very cautiously left the cover of the log they had been firing behind and crept down to the edge of the creek. But there was no body lying below the bank.

"I don't know," Jed considered. "Maybe he was crawlin' in the water."

"Well, we better find out," Slim insisted. "We don't want him poppin' up all of a sudden."

"You mean like now?"

The voice behind them stunned them like the sound of a gun.

They turned to discover an angry demon wielding a Henry rifle, awaiting their pleasure. They both raised their rifles to shoot, with neither man getting off a shot before both were on their backs in the water, bobbing with the current.

Murphy had intended to capture the two stalkers, but they gave him no choice when they chose to shoot. So he was left with questions, for which he had no source for answers. He found it ironic that Hatcher had mentioned that he had been there before, because they obviously knew him. There was no doubt in his mind that Hatcher's killing had been an execution. But why did they mean to kill him, too? It was blatantly obvious that he and Hatcher were not partners, since one of them was handcuffed to a tree. Whatever their history with Hatcher, it must have been bitter.

He started to prop his rifle against a tree, but paused a moment to look around him before doing so. Then he waded out into the creek and pulled the two bodies back to the bank. There was no point in leaving them to contaminate the drinking water. Where had they come from? He decided to scout the woods on that side of the creek to see if he could find their horses.

He felt sure that the two men he dragged out of the creek were the only members of the attacking party. There were no shots from anywhere else, so he walked up the creek to the point where he had seen the sun reflected from a rifle barrel. He discovered a large log and a scattering of empty shells on the ground covered with a thick carpet of dead leaves. That told him right away that he would not likely find many footprints to lead him to their horses. He was reluctant to get out of sight of his own horses as well, especially the bay gelding with a saddlebag containing the money. So he walked a little farther through the trees, his rifle ready and a frequent glance back at his horses, until he reached a point where he could see a path that apparently followed the course of the creek. It occurred to him then that maybe the two snipers were on foot. Maybe there was a camp or a house up that path.

He had a decision to make—get his horses ready to go and leave, or see what was at the end of that path that he might have to deal with ultimately. He had already made up his mind that he was going to carry Hatcher's body back to Austin with the money. He would have settled for the money and the two deputy marshals' badges. Since the badges were missing, however, there wasn't much left as evidence except the body and the money. Time was of the essence, for rigor mortis would set in and Hatcher would start to smell in two or three days at the least.

"I've got to see what my situation is here first," he decided. "I've got to find out where these two came from."

# CHAPTER 17

Before finding out what might lie at the end of that path, Murphy knew he had to be ready to leave this creek. The first thing he did was unlock Hatcher from the tree so that he could pull his arms down to his sides before rigor mortis set in and they got so stiff he couldn't move them. He wrapped the big body in his blanket and loaded him across the saddle of his horse. "Hold still, Smokey," he said when the horse threatened to sidestep away from the body. "It ain't nothin' but your old partner. Don't try to buck him off." Then he saddled and loaded the other horses, so they would be ready to move out when he was.

He checked the two bodies of his snipers and found nothing of value on either one. So he hung their weapons on his saddle and dragged their bodies farther away from the creek to a small clearing in the trees. "Make it a little easier for the buzzards to see you boys," he said. Then he stopped to consider how best to address the next issue, which might turn out to be the most critical. He was reluctant to leave all his horses and supplies there by the creek when he rode to the end of that path. Judging by the fact that the two bodies lying there were the only people he had encountered on that deserted trail, however, he thought the risk was not that great. *At least I'll have the money with me,* he thought, *and that's all they really want back, anyway.*

He climbed up into the saddle and pushed on through the trees to the path. Looking to his left, he saw the trail about twenty yards away. So he turned his horse to the right and followed the path for no more than thirty yards before coming to a cabin. There was a woman and a girl standing on the front porch. With his rifle in hand ready to fire, he quickly scanned the cabin from one side of it to the other. If there were shooters lying in wait, they were well hidden. Over beyond an outhouse, there was what appeared to be a fresh grave, but no sign of anyone else outside the cabin. *What the hell.* He shrugged and, in spite of the fact that he was a sitting target, rode on up to the cabin and pulled up about ten feet short of the steps.

"Mornin'," he offered. "I reckon I'm the cause of all that gunfire you just heard. My name's Cullen Murphy. I'm the town marshal for a little town called Newtown, about a day's ride west of here. My camp was attacked by two men just a little while ago and I have to figure they musta come from here. I'm sorry to have to give you some bad news, but the two men didn't make it back."

"It is just news, not bad news," Juanita said. "Thank you for telling us."

Surprised by the unexpected simple response, Murphy asked, "Did you know the two men?"

*"Sí,"* Juanita answered. "They were Slim Bullock and his brother, Jed Bullock. They see your camp and they go to kill Ward Hatcher."

Still surprised by her frank response, he asked, "Why did they want to kill Ward Hatcher?"

"Because he killed their father, Seth Bullock," she answered.

"Is that Seth Bullock in that grave over there?"

*"Sí,"* she answered, but did not say that Tiny Bullock was

also in the grave. Jed and Slim had thought it was enough work to dig one grave, so why bother to dig a second one for Tiny?

Murphy speculated silently for a moment, then asked, "Was Seth Bullock your husband?"

*"Sí,"* she answered simply.

"Well, I'm real sorry to hear that, ma'am. I'm sorry I didn't get here a little sooner. The reason I'm over this way was to arrest Ward Hatcher and take him to prison."

"Is okay," Juanita responded. "Bad things happen sometimes." She put her arm around the girl's shoulders. "My daughter and me, we'll be okay." Maria smiled and nodded her head.

"Well, I just thought I oughta come tell you what happened down by the creek," he said, and started to wheel his horse away, but stopped when he remembered. "Oh, and I checked the bodies of the two young men who attacked the camp. They didn't have anything of value on 'em, but I brought their weapons. I'll leave 'em with you." He unhooked the rifles and gun belts and Maria came down the steps to take them. "I took care of the bodies," he said, but didn't explain that he served them up for the next buzzard that flew over the creek.

He wheeled Nosy and nudged him into a comfortable lope back down the path, thinking it might be wise to put some distance between them before the young woman went back up the steps with the weapons. *You never can tell,* he thought, *and I'm a lot better at judging outlaws than I am judging women.* Mother and daughter had not appeared to be immersed in a sea of grief over all the killings that just took place. He left with a feeling that the pair might really be floating on a new cloud of freedom. He preferred to go with that feeling.

When he got back to the creek, he realized that the horses had not had as long a rest as he would normally have given them, but it wasn't that far back to the camp beside the Colorado River. He had not had coffee or anything to eat, either.

In fact, he hadn't even built a fire when the shots were fired. But the horses were all packed up and ready to go and Hatcher was ready to ride. So he hitched up his horse train again, rummaged around in his packs until he found a piece of jerky to gnaw on, and started out for the camp on the Colorado.

The distance between Dead Pine Creek and the Colorado River was a little farther than he remembered when he was heading in the other direction. So it was later in the afternoon by the time he pulled up at the campsite he had used before. He apologized to his horses as he relieved them of their saddles and packs and released them to go to the water. Soon he had a fire going and some fresh venison roasting over it. He remembered to give a little prayer of thanks to Paul Mathers when his coffee was ready. Thanks to the visit from Jed and Slim Bullock, he was packing twice as much fresh venison as he could eat by himself, plus a small quantity of smoked venison. So he selected only the choice cuts for his dinner.

When the coffee was ready and the meat was done, he relaxed by the fire and enjoyed the peaceful afternoon beside the river. There was time left for travel on this day, so he did not intend to camp there overnight. He figured ten or maybe twelve more miles before calling it a day, with a thought about the slow-burning fuse in the soon-to-be-rotting dynamite wrapped in a blanket. The trail down the river to Austin was one that Murphy had traveled, but he was not really that familiar with it. For that reason, he wanted to push the horses pretty hard on the first two days of travel. He could imagine that the authorities in the Austin US Marshal's Office were not going to be overjoyed to take possession of the articles of proof he was bringing with him. And they were going to have to take his word for most of it. He could tell them where all the other bodies were buried and give them directions on how to get there.

As he blew on his second cup of coffee, before risking a sip, his mind took him back to Newtown and his last conversation with the mayor. He knew that he was a little abrupt when he told Baxter he was going after Hatcher and Foley. At the time, he mistakenly thought the two deputy marshals were to be the victims when the party turned in the wrong direction upon leaving the town. He had been peeved at the mayor's outright unconcern for the safety of the two law officers. And thinking about it now, he admitted that he must have displayed his disgust. He remembered his parting words to be something in the neighborhood that he'd be back as soon as he was done with what he had to do. Now he was thinking about that. At the time, he had figured one day, maybe two. And now, sitting here probably thirty-five or forty miles away from Newtown, he was having trouble remembering exactly how many days he had actually been gone. And to make matters worse, as soon as his horses were rested, he was going to be even farther away. He shook his head and exhaled. *There is no way in hell that I'll have a job when I finally get back to Newtown!* Even if he turned the horses around and started home that afternoon, he didn't have a prayer that the town council would take him back.

"I hope poor Will hasn't gone insane by now." He pictured the innocent young man who was just now inspired to become a deputy marshal, and he was afraid he had let him down. "But," he said aloud, "you dealt the cards, so you've got no choice but to play the hand." There was no question, the right thing to do was to finish what he had started. Take the perpetrator to the courtroom and return the money to Wells Fargo. It was bad that he left Newtown without a marshal, but it was worse if he had let Hatcher get away with what he had attempted and the people he had murdered. "So I'm goin' to Austin and settle this thing with the US Marshal. Then I'm goin' back to Newtown, because I think they ought to know the true, full story about the men who took the four prisoners out of the jail. Whaddaya think?" The bay gelding nodded his head and whinnied. Murphy asked again, "Whaddaya think?" and the horse nodded his head and whinnied again, because that's what Murphy taught the horse to do every time he asked him that. To be truthful, Nosy would bob his head up and down every time, but sometimes he didn't whinny.

After the horses were rested enough, Murphy packed everything up, including Hatcher, and started down the Colorado River. Due to the winding course of the river, the trail sometimes lost sight of it for miles at a time until returning to follow close beside the river until the next series of loops and turns. The general result was to continue its primary southeast journey past the city of Austin. He rode for approximately fifteen more miles before stopping for the night to set up his camp just as a light rain began to fall. He carried a canvas sheet on his packhorse to be used as a shelter, so he cut the branches of a clump of berry bushes so he could use the bushes as a base for his shelter to keep reasonably dry during the night.

Everything in the packs looked to be protected enough from the rain, with the exception of Hatcher. The blanket he was wrapped in was no protection from the rain and Murphy was afraid it would soon become a soggy sponge around the body. Like Murphy, Hatcher had a canvas sheet in his packs for the same purpose Murphy had used his for. So he looked through the packs on Hatcher's packhorse until he found the canvas.

He spread the canvas on the ground under a large oak tree in an effort to shield it from the rain as much as possible. He dragged Hatcher over to the canvas and rolled him over onto it, then continued rolling him over and over until he used up the whole sheet. The sheet was much longer than Hatcher, so there was a big empty roll of canvas at the top and bottom. "Perfect," Murphy said. He got some rope from his saddle and proceeded to bend the excess canvas down from the head and up from the foot, then bound the whole result into one big package.

The only problem, Hatcher was already an unusually big

man. With the added weight of the soaked blanket and the large canvas, he was going to be one helluva big load to pick up and put on a horse. "I wish now that Foley had cut your throat," he said to the canvas lump. "Foley was half your size. He'd be a lot easier to pick up." With nothing more he could do to help the situation, he struggled to drag the cumbersome bundle up close to the trunk of the tree and managed to lift it so that it would lean on a lower limb at a slight angle.

"Maybe that'll help drain some of the water out through the cracks," he said. "I'll say good night now. Be ready to ride in the mornin'." He went back to his half tent and began building a fire just inside it. He was anticipating a long day in the saddle tomorrow, but at least he was not expecting any trouble on the trip.

He awakened the next morning to find that the rain had stopped sometime during the night, so already the day was off to a good start. Preferring to get on the trail right away, then cook breakfast when he made a stop to rest the horses, he disassembled his temporary shelter and packed it up. Then he packed the rest of the train, saving Hatcher until last. Maybe it was just his imagination, but he thought that the gray gelding was beginning to show some reluctance to transport the eerie-looking bundle and had a tendency to try to sidestep when approached by it. It was difficult enough for Murphy to carry the bundle without having to chase a skittish horse with it. And to make matters worse, he could tell that rigor mortis had begun to set in by the reluctance of the bundle to bend. He considered making a travois to carry the body on, but he was concerned that it would make it too difficult to lead his train of horses, especially over some of the rugged sections of the trail.

"Now, why didn't I think to bring a wagon along with me?" he japed. He ended up with the body lying across the saddle, tied under the gray's belly as snugly as he could get it, with Hatcher's saddlebags used as wedges to prevent it from wobbling. It was an awkward way to carry a totally erect body, but the bundle failed to tilt to either side and slide off the horse for the first segment of the day's travel. Murphy could see that the blanket and canvas wrapped around the body acted as a cushion to help stabilize it a little in the saddle.

He called a halt for breakfast when he came to a nice little creek that emptied into the river. He guessed the distance to be around eighteen miles from their camp of the night before and it had taken four hours. It was past time to rest the horses and he was ready to eat. He was not sure if the venison he kept had turned or not. He would take a look at it and decide; if there was a chance that it was starting to, he decided not to risk it. He still had the smoked meat to fall back on and some bacon that was in Hatcher's packs. His first thought upon stopping was to unburden the horses. He wished he didn't have to remove the canvas bundle on Hatcher's horse, Smokey. It had taken so much to secure the load. But when he started to work on it, he found that the ropes he had tightened so much to secure the body seemed to have loosened just a little bit. That made him wonder and he counted up the approximate number of hours that had elapsed since Hatcher was killed. He realized that the body might just be starting to come out of rigor mortis. He had heard that it usually happened in as little as four to six hours afterward and the body would gradually become flexible again. Maybe Hatcher would come out of the rigor mortis by the time they reached Austin. The only bad part about that was the body would start to putrefy after that, turn greenish purple, then stink like hell. And he had seen all that he wanted to see of that when he was a sergeant in the late War Between the States.

He made a final decision on the fresh deer meat and cooked a generous serving of it for his breakfast, then dumped the rest of the uncooked venison on the riverbank for any interested scavenger that happened by. In contrast to his travels so far on the San Saba River trail and the old Indian trail, he met an occasional traveler on the Colorado River trail, especially when he got to within a day's travel of the town of Austin. As a rule, the people he met looked to be farmers and gave him a wide berth. They generally nodded in response to his "Howdy," and turned to watch him until he rode out of sight.

When he made his last camp before entering Austin the next morning, almost all the rigid stiffness in Hatcher's body had disappeared. Murphy determined that the body would hang over the saddle like a man just shot. So he decided to untie the bundle and unroll him from his blanket and canvas wrap, and possibly make the deputy marshal a little more presentable for his return to his home base.

He found that there was no possible way to deliver a dignified lawman who had been dead so long that his eyelids were locked open behind his bulging eyeballs, which were resting on his greenish-black skin. But Murphy did what he could. The blanket and the canvas sheet he had been bundled in were beyond saving due to the matter and fluids that had been forced from the body via several exits. Murphy vowed he would never, under any circumstances, repeat a like mission. He discarded the canvas and the blanket behind some bushes away from the trail and carefully transferred the corpse into Hatcher's heavy overcoat. Luckily, he had saved Hatcher's hat, so that helped hide the ghoulish greenish-black face.

# CHAPTER 18

"What is it, Sawyer?" US Marshal Henry Stephens looked up from his desk, obviously irritated to have his morning-coffee ritual interrupted.

"In the street, in front of the courthouse," US Deputy Marshal Jack Sawyer replied. "There's a fellow with a string of horses and what looks like a dead body hanging over one of 'em."

"What're you bothering me for?" Stephens responded. "Go get the sheriff."

"He says he came to see you," Sawyer said. "He sez he's the town marshal in Newtown, over in San Saba County."

"Newtown. That's where I sent Hatcher and Foley to transport four prisoners and that Wells Fargo money shipment back here. Send him in here. No, wait a minute, you say he's got a corpse with him? I'll go out there to talk to him." He took a few quick gulps of his coffee, then followed Sawyer out the door.

Out in front of the courthouse, Stephens saw the string of horses, one with a body draped across the saddle; they had already attracted a little ring of spectators. Standing at the head of the column, he saw a rugged-looking man holding the bridle of his horse. "You wanted to see me?" Stephens asked.

"Yes, sir, my name's Cullen Murphy. I'm the town marshal in Newtown and I brought one of your deputies back to ya."

"You're Murphy?" Stephens asked, remembering the name from the letters he had received.

"Yes, sir," Murphy replied.

"And who's the dead man?" Stephens asked. "Did you say he's a deputy marshal?"

"Yes, sir. He's Deputy Marshal Ward Hatcher and he ain't in the best of shape to be looked at right now. He's been dead for a few days, but he's about all the evidence I've got to back up my report—him and a sack of twenty-five thousand dollars of Wells Fargo money."

Stephens turned at once to look in the direction of the body. "That's Hatcher?" he asked in shocked disbelief. He had expected Hatcher back yesterday, or today at the latest, but not without Frank Foley and the Wells Fargo money. He had also expected four prisoners to stand trial for the Wells Fargo robbery and murders. Turning back to address Murphy, he asked, "Where's Foley and the four prisoners they were transporting?"

"Foley's buried on the bank of the Colorado River, a little over two days' ride from here. The four prisoners' remains are scattered where Hatcher and Foley left 'em, near the San Saba River."

Stephens's mouth dropped open with his confusion. "Who killed the prisoners?" he asked.

"Hatcher and Foley," Murphy answered.

"Who killed Foley?" Stephens asked, even more confused.

"Hatcher," Murphy answered simply. When Stephens still could not believe what he was hearing, Murphy started at the beginning and told him how the story unfolded, and why he went after them.

"I find it hard to believe," Stephens stated frankly; he looked at Sawyer, who was as dumbfounded as he. "Ward Hatcher was a respected deputy marshal with over fifteen years as an officer of the law. I trusted him explicitly."

"Yes, sir," Murphy replied, "I trusted him, too, till his true colors showed up. I reckon the money was too much to pass up." He paused, then added, "And too little to share with Frank Foley."

"So you shot Hatcher?" Stephens asked, still not completely clear on that point.

"No, sir, I arrested Hatcher and I was on my way to bringin' him back here for trial. The two Bullock brothers shot him when I was camped and Hatcher was handcuffed to a tree. I shot the two Bullock brothers."

"And why did the Bullock brothers shoot Hatcher?" Stephens asked. "No, never mind, that's not important, just more confusion."

"Because Hatcher killed their father," Murphy answered, anyway, because he wanted to establish the fact that he did not kill the deputy marshal, although he would have if it had come to that.

"Well, you say you brought the money?" Stephens asked. "I'll take that off your hands. We'll go in the office and take care of that." He paused, then walked over to Hatcher's gray horse to take a look at his former deputy. He reached down and took hold of the collar on Hatcher's overcoat and pulled the coat away from his face. "Damn!" he uttered, and released the collar when he got a whiff of the putrid odor. "He's starting to putrefy already! Sawyer, get the undertaker out here to take that body off the street. Murphy, get the money and follow me into the office."

"I'd like a piece of paper tellin' anyone that I turned that money over to you," Murphy said.

"You'll get one," Stephens replied, "but first we'll have to take a count of exactly how much you turned over."

"I want it understood that I turned over every dollar Hatcher had in his possession when I arrested him. I know how much there was in that sack when I arrested the four men who stole it from the stagecoach. I told you that amount in the letter I sent you. So, whatever the amount is now, that's on Hatcher and Foley. I was gonna bring their badges back as proof they were dead, but they were gone. They musta got rid of 'em when they decided to retire from the US Marshal Service. That's Hatcher's horse and saddle he's ridin' on, and that other saddle horse was Foley's. Hatcher kept it after he done for Foley with a knife across his throat. Sentimental reasons, I reckon," he added. "There was just one packhorse. Don't know what happened to Foley's packhorse, or the prisoners' horses, for that matter."

"Don't worry," Stephens said, "I'm not questioning your account of this disaster, and I want to thank you for the trouble you've gone through to deliver the body and the money. After hearing your testimony, I doubt we would have ever found the money or the accused if you hadn't taken it upon yourself to right a wrong. We were expecting Hatcher and Foley back here with the four perpetrators yesterday. Their trial was set for tomorrow and an attorney for Wells Fargo arrived today to act as prosecutor. I would appreciate it if you would stay in town tonight and attend the trial tomorrow, in case your testimony is needed. We will, of course, pay your expenses for the hotel and dining room."

"Sure, I'll stay over tonight, but who will the attorneys be tryin'?" Murphy asked. "All the people that committed the crimes are already dead. And I'll tell you the truth, if I took a notion to take some of that money for all the trouble I went through to bring it to you, there would be a helluva lot more of it missing."

Stephens had to chuckle in response to that. "I didn't really consider putting you on trial. I should have said that now, the way things turned out, there won't be a trial. We'll just have a hearing, I guess you'd call it, so that Wells Fargo can learn all the facts. And nobody's got more of the facts than you. So I'm inviting you to be a guest of the US Marshal Service tonight and tomorrow."

"In that case, thank you kindly," Murphy said, "and here's your money." He reached into his saddlebags and pulled out the Wells Fargo sack. "I'll be glad to get rid of it."

"I'll take it inside and put it in the safe," Stephens said. "Here comes Sawyer with the undertaker. If you'll wait right here for me, I'll put this away; then I'll go with you to get you a room at the hotel." He went back to his office.

Murphy untied Smokey's reins from the back of his saddle, since the man walking toward him beside Sawyer didn't bring any kind of conveyance to carry a body with him. "Marshal Murphy," Sawyer called out, "this is Harry Morgan. He'll take over the body now."

Murphy nodded and acknowledged the man. "Mr. Morgan. He's pretty far along. You might just wanna lead his horse back to your place."

Morgan walked over to Smokey and lifted Hatcher's coat collar, just as Stephens had done, but he didn't drop it right away. "He is far along, three or four days, at least. It's hard to recognize Ward Hatcher, but blamed if that ain't who it is. I better get him right back to my place." He looked at Murphy and asked, "Anything you need out of the saddlebags?"

"Nope," Murphy answered as he untied the packhorse behind Smokey. "He's all yours. He's gonna need some water before long." He paused a second, then said, "The horse, not Hatcher." Sawyer laughed, then said he'd better go to the office because Stephens would want him there while he went to the hotel with Murphy, especially since the Wells Fargo money was there now.

When Stephens came out again, Murphy told him that he would like to take care of his horses pretty soon, as it was past time for water and feed. "I only expect to take my horses when I leave here tomorrow. So that's just this horse and that packhorse. The rest of them belonged to Hatcher and Foley."

"After we get your hotel room, just take the horses to the stable and tell Steve Dawkins the US Marshal's Office will pay the bill for all the horses, and tell him which ones you're taking with you. Steve's a good man. He'll take good care of your horses."

"Much obliged," Murphy said.

They went to the hotel then and Stephens told the desk clerk to charge Murphy's room to the US Marshal Service.

"I've got to get back to the office now," Stephens said. "Why don't I meet you back at the hotel dining room at noon and I'll see if Robert Stone can join us for dinner?"

"Sounds fine to me," Murphy said. "I'm looking forward to a good meal after several days without one." He was thinking mostly about the wolf meat he had eaten.

Stephens went back to his office, and Murphy got his saddlebags and his rifle and went upstairs to see his room. He would leave the rifle in his room. He just preferred not to leave it in the stable while he was in town. Too many people walked around unobserved in most stables and it would be too easy to pull a Henry rifle out of a saddle scabbard and walk out the back door with it. He left the hotel and took the horses to the stable, which was only a block from the hotel.

"You're the fellow who brought Ward Hatcher back to town, ain't you?" Steve Dawkins asked. Murphy said that he was. "Who shot him?"

"A couple of outlaws named Bullock," Murphy replied.

"I swear that's a real shame," Dawkins said. "Ward Hatcher was a decent man. That's his gray there, Smokey, Ward called him." He walked up to the horse and gave it a gentle scratching around his ears and neck. "Yeah, you remember me, don't you, Smokey?" He looked back at Murphy and asked, "What're you gonna do with him now?"

"I'm gonna leave him with you," Murphy said. "I'm just takin' the two that belong to me, this bay and that sorrel packhorse. Henry Stephens said to put 'em all on his bill. I'll be going back home tomorrow. I don't know exactly what time I'll be leavin', whenever Stephens gets through with me."

"Well, don't you worry about your horses," Dawkins said. "I'll take good care of 'em. I'll take extra good care of Ward's horses, too. That's the least I can do to honor a man who spent most of his life goin' after the scum that prey on innocent folks. I reckon he knew that sooner or later he was gonna come out on the losing end when you had to deal with the outlaws he had to deal with."

"I reckon that's so, I expect he fought 'em right up to his last breath," Murphy said as a picture formed in his mind of Hatcher handcuffed to a tree as shot after shot caused his body to twist and turn in a spastic reaction.

He left the stable with enough time to take a little walk around the main street. It reminded him of Newtown in many ways. For a time, Austin had begun to fade with a loss of population when the capital was moved to Houston, only to recover and renew its growth when the capital was returned to Austin. Newtown was in a downward spiral because of a lack of law and order. But now, with an established marshal's office and a city jail, the town was growing with new businesses every year. He didn't stake a claim for sole credit, but he was satisfied that he had helped. Then he looked around him and thought, *But here I am a hundred miles away from Newtown because we don't have telegraph or railroad.*

He took a look at a couple of saloons on the street in case he had an urge for a drink after supper that night. It was early in the day yet, but the two busiest was the Capital City Saloon and another smaller one called Becker's Saloon. The time slipped away from him when he realized it was almost noon. So he cut his tour of the town short and headed for the hotel.

When he walked into the dining room, he found himself in a small reception area, with a young man behind a pulpit-like registration desk. The young man smiled politely and asked, "Can I help you, sir?"

"Yeah," Murphy answered. "I'm supposed to meet a couple of fellows here for dinner."

"Do you have a name, sir?" the young man asked.

"Yeah, I've got a name," he answered. "Everybody's got a name."

The young man's face flushed red. "I mean, do you have the name of the party you are here to meet?"

"Oh, it ain't gonna be a party. We're just gonna eat dinner. I'm supposed to meet Marshal Henry Stephens, but I don't know the other fellow's name, but he's a guest in the hotel, same as me."

"Oh, then you'd be Mr. Murphy," he said.

"I'd be," Murphy responded.

"Marshal Stephens is already here; I'll take you to his table. Since this is your first time eating here, may I ask you to take your gun off and let me put it in the cabinet over there until you leave?"

"You can ask, but I don't know. Will I be the only man in the room without a gun?" Murphy asked.

"No, sir. We ask everyone to remove their firearms while eating in the dining room, for the safety of all our guests."

"Well, that seems fair enough to me," Murphy said. "I'll go along with that." He unbuckled his gun belt and rolled his holster up in it. "Have you got a name?"

"I beg your pardon?"

"Have you got a name?" he repeated. "What's your name?"

"Oh . . ." He hesitated to answer, then said, "My name is Roger."

"Well, Roger, I 'preciate your patience with me. I didn't intend to cause you that much trouble."

Roger gave him a broad smile. "You were no trouble at all. I'll show you to your table and I hope you enjoy your meal."

Roger placed Murphy's gun in the cabinet, then led him into the back part of the dining room, where only a couple of the tables were occupied. Stephens and the Wells Fargo attorney were seated at one in the corner. "Here he is," Stephens announced. "Have a seat, Cullen. You don't mind if I call you by your first name, do you?"

"I wish you would," Murphy replied. "It doesn't sound right when you call me Marshal, when that's your official title." His reply caused both Stephens and the attorney to chuckle.

"Titles aren't good for much, anyway; it's what the man wearing one does that counts," Stephens contended. "And I don't know any other town marshals who put as much on the line as you did in going after Hatcher and Foley. I've been telling Mr. Stone, here, about how you went about going after the men who stole Wells Fargo's money. Say howdy to Mr. Robert Stone, of the Wells Fargo Company."

Stone reached up to offer his hand and Murphy shook it before he sat down at the table. "Sorry if I'm a little late. I was takin' a walk around town."

"Not at all," Stephens said. "Mr. Stone and I just got here, ourselves . . ." He paused when the waiter, an elderly-looking man, came to ask if they were ready to order.

Murphy wasn't expecting to be given a choice between two entrees. He decided on the steak and potatoes, thinking that Irene Floyd should see how fancy this dining room was.

"I guess I should start by thanking you for your efforts in bringing Wells Fargo's money back," Stone said. "And I'm amazed that you would have single-handedly taken on the quest at all, you being responsible for crimes committed inside the town limits only. I have to ask, what made you decide to go after the two deputy marshals? What was your first clue that they might be planning on killing the four prisoners and taking the money?"

"When I decided to go after Hatcher and Foley, it wasn't because I thought they were gonna do what they ended up doin'. I decided to go after them because I thought they were in trouble and I hoped I could catch up to them in time to help. They were transportin' four of the meanest killers I've ever run into, and they were headed for a hangin' for sure after they killed everybody on that stagecoach. And when I saw that they turned in the wrong direction right after they left town, the first thing I thought was that they had somehow overpowered Hatcher and Foley. And maybe if I was lucky, I could catch up before they killed 'em. I didn't know till I came to that open plain near the river that they turned into a buzzard-feedin' ground that it was the other way around. It was the four prisoners who needed my help. I coulda turned around and gone home or decided to go after two low-down murderers who couldn't resist stealin' the money they were entrusted to deliver."

"I'll tell you, it was a hard thing for me to believe that two faithful lawmen like Hatcher and Foley could cross over the line like that," Stephens commented. "I'm still having trouble digesting it."

"Hard to say what a man will do after dealin' with outlaws like Hank Welch and his gang for as long as Hatcher has," Murphy said. "It might be easy to figure the four of 'em were goin' to die for sure. So, what difference does it make if they die from a bullet in the back of their heads or a rope around their necks? I could almost say fair enough for that. But the part about turnin' into a low-down thief and runnin' off with the money, I can't abide that."

"I compliment you for your attitude," Stone remarked.

"Thank you," Murphy replied. "Ward Hatcher's quite a bit

older than I am, and he's been in the business of law and order for a helluva lot longer than I have. So I reckon you never can tell which way a man will go till he's facing that crossroads."

The discussion continued while they ate and Murphy was left to his own devices until nine o'clock the next morning when he was asked to attend a hearing on the matter in the courthouse. He would have preferred to start back to Newtown immediately, since he figured they knew the whole story now, but Robert Stone insisted on a legal hearing to finalize the matter.

# CHAPTER 19

With an afternoon to kill, Murphy was hard put to find some way to entertain himself, so he decided it might be the right thing to do if he made a courtesy call on the sheriff while he was in town. The sheriff's office and jail were a block from the river on a side street. Murphy had discovered it when he had gone for a walk along the Colorado River after dinner. So he returned to the entrance to the office and opened the door to discover a heavyset man, with a close-cropped black beard, seated at a large desk.

"Somethin' I can do for ya?" the sheriff asked.

"I'm just in town for a day or two," Murphy said. "My name's Cullen Murphy. I'm the town marshal in Newtown, over in San Saba County. I thought I'd stop in and say howdy." He reached into his vest pocket and pulled out his badge to show the sheriff. He had decided to take it off while he was in town to avoid any complications it might cause.

The sheriff got up from his chair and offered his hand. "Pleased to meet you, Cullen. I'm Sheriff Hazzard. The US Marshal told me you were in town. Understand you brought Ward Hatcher back to town, along with the missin' Wells Fargo money from that robbery. I went over to Harry Morgan's place to take a look at Hatcher. Boy, he was a sure-enough mess. Is that true, what Henry Stephens says about him killin' Frank Foley?"

"I'm afraid so," Murphy said, and once again found himself telling the story of his chase to arrest Ward Hatcher, a tale he was already sick of retelling. He was glad when a man opened the door, stuck his head inside, and said someone was causing trouble at Becker's Saloon. "Need any help?" Murphy asked Hazzard.

"No, thanks, anyway," Hazzard replied. "It's just ol' Ike Thompkins, one of the town drunks, bothering Becker's regular customers. I expect he needs to take a little nap in one of the cells. I'm sure you know how it is."

"Yessir, I surely do," Murphy replied. "Maybe I'll see you later." He walked out the door with Hazzard, but headed for the hotel, not Becker's. He decided to take advantage of the hotel's bathroom, since the US Marshal was paying all his expenses. He had the attendant pour him a tub of hot water and he took his time soaking and scrubbing, even washing his hair. When he was finished, he had the attendant rinse him off with warm water, then dried himself with a great big towel. He had no clean clothes to change into, but he changed into his cleanest shirt and underwear. When he was ready to leave, he noticed the attendant standing close by, watching him. So he asked him if he was normally paid for his services and he answered that he was tipped anything from twenty-five cents to a dollar. So Murphy gave him a dollar, thinking it would be the only time he felt like a bigwig. He tried to imagine how a bigwig really felt, but gave up on it after a few moments. For lack of anything better to do, he went out to sit on the hotel's front porch for a spell to watch the comings and goings of the people on the street.

He had evidently made a friend when he was in the dining room earlier because when he went there for supper, Roger greeted him graciously and asked him how his day was going.

Murphy said fine so far and volunteered his sidearm. "Are you meeting anyone tonight?" Roger asked. When Murphy said he was not, Roger asked him if he had any preference for a table. Murphy asked if he could have one of those by a window. "Right this way," Roger said, and led him to a small table beside a window. "I hope you enjoy your supper," he said when he left.

"Thank you, Roger," Murphy replied. "If it's as good as dinner was, I'm sure I will." *You'd think I was the governor of Texas,* he thought. *I oughta tell Ginger and Bonnie how I get treated in a fancy dining room.*

Supper was as good as dinner had been; since steak was one of the choices again, he chose another one for supper. When he was finished, he stopped on the way out to tell Roger he enjoyed his supper, then left the hotel for a walk, which took him as far as the Capital City Saloon. He decided the saloon sounded official enough for him to have a drink before retiring to his hotel room for the night. He stepped inside the batwing doors to find the saloon fairly busy for the early-evening hours. There was plenty of room at the long bar, so he walked to the far end of it. When the bartender greeted him, he said he would like a drink of corn whiskey.

"You the fellow that brought Ward Hatcher's body back to town?" the bartender asked.

"Yeah," Murphy replied. "How'd you know that?"

"Word gets around town pretty quick," the bartender said. "There were a couple of fellers in earlier that was out in the street when you led that string of horses into town. They got a look at him when Harry Morgan came to get the body. Said he looked like nothin' they ever saw before. Said you wouldn't know Hatcher from the devil." He poured Murphy's whiskey and slid the glass over to him.

"He'd been dead for more than three days," Murphy said. "That's what they'll look like if there ain't nobody to bury 'em." He was tired of telling people that he just found Hatcher and knew he was from Austin. And he wasn't interested in telling them he tracked the double-crossing murderer down and arrested him. From the short time he had been in Austin, he had learned that Hatcher held a reputation as a fearless, hardworking guardian of the law and a man to be admired. He felt it was better to let them remember him that way and decided to drink to that. He tossed his corn whiskey to the back of his throat and swallowed. The bartender stood ready to refill the glass.

"Hold on a minute," Murphy said when he saw Sheriff Hazzard walk in the door. Easily spotting Murphy standing at the bar, Hazzard walked over to join him. "Howdy, Sheriff," Murphy greeted him. "I'd like to buy you a drink of likker, unless you make it a rule not to drink when you're makin' your rounds."

"I think the occasion calls for it," Hazzard said. "The usual, Eddie." Eddie reached for a bottle of rye whiskey and poured a drink. Then he filled Murphy's glass again. "Here's to everything workin' out right," Hazzard proposed, and held his glass up in a salute. Thinking it an odd toast, Murphy held his glass up, too; then they both tossed the liquid back. Eddie stood ready to pour another round, but Hazzard held his hand up to stop him. "Just the one for me. The night is young and I've gotta finish makin' my rounds. Thank you for the drink, Cullen."

"My pleasure," Murphy said. "We don't want you too drunk to protect the town. Do we, Eddie? And that's enough for me, too. I don't usually take more than two drinks, anyway." He paid Eddie for the three drinks and turned to face Hazzard. "Don't let me hold you up. I'm fixin' on goin' back to the hotel and go to bed early."

"Sounds like a good idea," Hazzard said. "Wish I could do that. I'll see you at the courthouse at nine o'clock in the morning."

"Oh? Are you gonna be at that hearing with the Wells Fargo

fellow in the morning?" Murphy asked, surprised that he would be.

"Yeah," Hazzard replied. "Henry Stephens said he'd like to have me there."

Murphy was surprised to hear that. "Why did he figure he needed you there?"

Hazzard shrugged. "I don't know, he just said he thought it would be a good idea if I sat in on the hearing."

Murphy wasn't comfortable with that news. Why would Stephens want the town sheriff there? You would only want the sheriff there if you anticipated the possibility of some trouble. "Well," Hazzard announced, "I'd better get out there and see what the rest of the town is up to."

"Yeah, I'm ready to go back to the hotel now," Murphy said. "I'll walk out with you." They walked out the front door and parted. "I'll see you in the mornin'."

As he headed toward the hotel, the more he thought about it, the more he began to become concerned. Everybody in the whole town had held the highest opinion of US Deputy Marshal Ward Hatcher. Murphy could not dispute the man's record as having earned that status of respect. The same could be said of Frank Foley. They both could have earned the respect of lawmen and ordinary citizens alike. The fact of the matter was, however, they snapped when confronted with an opportunity to take possession of a sum of money large enough to tempt them to kill four prisoners. Even though the four were going to be executed, anyway, it didn't make their action any less heinous.

The question on Murphy's mind now was if the reputations of these two lawmen were too strong to accept the fact that they might have snapped. If that was the case, then where did that leave him? The stranger who brought the money and the rotting corpse of Ward Hatcher back to Austin with wild tales about mass executions and turncoat lawmen might have the hardest story to prove.

He considered the definite possibility that he had successfully managed to make himself a genuine suspect in the murders of Ward Hatcher and Frank Foley. But what else could he have done? He hadn't thought Hatcher was capable of doing the evil things that he did. He didn't have the time to know Foley as well as he did with Hatcher. But he didn't think that he was of a lower sense of honesty than Hatcher. Because of their reputations, he had to try to save them from execution at the hands of four evil men.

"I made a mistake coming back here," he confessed out loud. When Hatcher was killed by the two Bullock brothers, he should have turned around and gone back to Newtown. He should have sent a letter to Stephens telling him that he had recovered the money and to tell Wells Fargo to send someone to Newtown to take possession of it. "But I didn't," he stated. "So, what do I do now to keep from going to prison for the murders of two US Deputy Marshals?" The fact that he had brought the money back should have the most importance in proving his story. But was it enough? There had been no mention of a reward for the return of the money and he had purposefully never asked about the possibility of one. He just wanted to get on his horse and go home to Newtown.

When he got back to his room, he continued to wrestle with how he could prove his story was true—if, in fact, they chose to disbelieve him in the hearing. The only way he could substantiate his story would be to take someone back over the journey he had taken to bring Hatcher's corpse back to justice. And he knew that would be impossible to expect. The more he tried to come up with proof for his testimony, the more frustrated he became. Until finally it came to two choices based on the one major decision he had made: *I am not going to jail!* Once they put him in jail, he would be helpless from that point on.

Whichever choice he made, he would do the same thing when he got up tomorrow morning. He would take his things from the room and go to the stable and get his horses. He would eat breakfast in the dining room, in case one of the men who was going to be at the hearing was there also. This, in order not to cause suspicion. Then he would get on his horse and ride out of town and go straight back to Newtown. That was choice one.

Choice two was to tie his horses somewhere at the courthouse and attend the hearing. If everything went the way it was supposed to go, and he was not charged with anything, he would wish them all a good day and take his leave. On the other hand, if there would be requests for him to remain in Austin pending any further investigation, he would refuse to cooperate and inform them that he was leaving Austin. If there was any threat of arrest for any reason, he would not go peacefully—and he would guarantee serious consequences.

He awoke early in the morning and got up at once to dress and pick up his belongings. With his rifle and saddlebags in hand, he paused to decide, then left his key on the dresser and closed the door behind him. He thought it better not to check out or let anyone know he was not planning to return. He was not paying for the room, anyway, so it shouldn't make any difference to the hotel staff. Walking as quietly as he could, he walked down the hallway, took the back stairs down to the first floor, and went out the back door by the bathroom. The only activity in the hotel was going on in the kitchen–dining room wing of the building, although they would not be open for another hour yet. The sun was still struggling to make itself seen above the rooftops of the town as he walked the short distance to the stable. He hoped Steve Dawkins was not a late sleeper. In answer to his thought, Dawkins opened the barn door from inside just as he was approaching.

Startled at first, Dawkins recovered quickly enough to say, "Good mornin', Mr. Murphy. You're an early riser. You leaving town this mornin'?"

"Not this early, but I thought I'd go ahead and get my horses ready to go as soon as I've finished with a meeting I've gotta go to this mornin'. I've got a long ride back home and I'd like to get started as soon as I can."

"Let me give you a hand," Dawkins said. "You're just takin' that bay you were ridin' and the one packhorse, right?" Murphy said that was right. "I thought that was what you said," Dawkins continued. "So I put that bay and the sorrel in a stall with your saddle and packsaddle." He led him through the barn and into the stables to a back stall. When they approached the stall, Nosy greeted him with a whinny. Dawkins chuckled. "Reckon he's your horse, all right."

"That he is," Murphy said, then turned to face the bay and asked, "Whaddaya think?" And Nosy bobbed his head up and down and whinnied. He paused there for a few seconds; then he turned toward Dawkins again. "You know what? I think I'll change my mind. That meeting I'm supposed to go to ain't until nine o'clock. I haven't even had my breakfast yet. The dinin' room doesn't even open until six o'clock. It don't make much sense to saddle my horses and let 'em stand around for a couple of hours before I even get started. I think I'll let Marshal Stephens buy them a portion of oats while I go to breakfast. Is that all right with you, Mr. Dawkins?"

"Whatever you say," Dawkins replied.

"Good," Murphy said. "Sorry to trouble you this early for nothing. I'll come get my horses just before I go to the meeting. And I can saddle 'em. No need to bother you with it. I'll just be killin' time, anyway."

"Weren't no trouble a'tall," Dawkins said.

Murphy turned back toward his horse. "Whaddaya think?" Nosy bobbed his head up and down and whinnied. "I thought you'd like that better. I'll see you a little bit later, Mr. Dawkins." He turned and walked out of the stable, leaving Dawkins chuckling.

Just as he went out the door, he heard Dawkins say, "Whaddaya think?" But he didn't hear Nosy whinny.

He went back to his room in the hotel to wait for the dining room to open. And as long as he had decided to change his plans, he put his room key back in his pocket. As he sat there looking out the window at an almost-deserted street below, he wondered if he had made the right decision. If he had decided on choice one, he would have already ridden that deserted street out of town and would be on his way to Newtown. The trouble with that was that it resembled the actions of a guilty man, and all he might have gained was the time it would take to send someone after him. He sat there by the window, checking his watch frequently until it was a quarter after six, preferring to give them time to officially open and prepare to serve breakfast.

"Good morning, Cullen Murphy," Roger greeted him cheerfully. "Do you like pancakes?"

"Good morning, Roger," Murphy returned as he handed his six-gun to him. "Yes, I do. I expect just about everybody likes pancakes, don't they?"

"I expect you're right," Roger agreed, "and I recommend ours with fresh butter and maple syrup. It's a breakfast that'll stay with you till dinnertime."

"I'll take your word for it," Murphy said. "A good pancake breakfast is a good way to start my last day here."

"You're leaving?" Roger asked. "I thought you might be with us for a while. I hope you've enjoyed your visit with us."

"I have," Murphy replied. "I've enjoyed eatin' here. You folks have been mighty nice, especially since you had to teach me how to eat at a fancy dinin' room like this one. I appreciate it." *You showed me how the fancy folks eat,* he thought. *I expect you might starve to death if somebody didn't kill your breakfast for you.*

"You're giving me too much credit," Roger insisted. "I think you were just havin' a little fun with me. I enjoyed it. Come on, I'll show you to a table." *I taught you how to eat in a decent establishment,* Roger thought as he led him to a window table. *You could have, no doubt, taught me how to rip the hide off a live squirrel and eat it raw.*

Murphy took his time eating breakfast and was still there when US Marshal Henry Stephens came into the dining room. Roger showed him to a table in the back of the room. As Stephens followed him, he glanced over and noticed Murphy sitting by a window. He nodded to Murphy, but followed Roger to the table and sat down. He waited until a waiter came to the table to get his drink order; then he got up and came over to Murphy's table.

"Good morning. Hope you had a good night's sleep. I would ask you to join me, but I've got a breakfast meeting about some business I need to clear up before our nine o'clock hearing."

"That's quite all right," Murphy replied. "I've already finished breakfast and I'm just drainin' the rest of my coffee cup before I go to take care of my horses. I'll see you at the hearin'."

Stephens went back to his table and sat down. Within a couple of minutes, Robert Stone, the Wells Fargo attorney, walked in, following Roger back to Stephens's table. Like Stephens, Stone noticed Murphy and nodded, but continued on to his table and sat down. Murphy nodded in return and wondered if his name was going to come up in their little breakfast meeting. *This might be a good time to saddle my horse and ride out of this town,* he thought. *I'm not going to jail,* he repeated to himself. *That's for damn sure.*

He finished his coffee and got up from the table, unable to resist a quick glance at the table near the back wall of the dining room. They both caught his glance and they both gave him a nod. He returned the nod, but hurried out of the dining room with a sudden urge to recover his gun from Roger's cabinet. He had a thought that Sheriff Hazzard might be possibly waiting for him to finish his breakfast. But there was nobody there at the desk but Roger, who went to the cabinet to get his weapon.

"How were the pancakes?" Roger asked as he handed him his Colt .44.

"Best I ever ate," Murphy lied, and strapped on his gun belt.

"Good," Roger replied, and stepped back to let him pass. "Now don't go out and shoot anyone."

"I can't guarantee it," Murphy responded, "but I'll do my best."

There was still plenty of time left before the nine o'clock hearing. It was not yet seven, but he decided to go ahead and get his horses ready to travel. His supplies were getting pretty slim by the time he had arrived in Austin, so he intended to add to them before starting back to Newtown. As long as he had the time, he decided to drop his key off at the hotel registration desk, so he did that when he left the dining room. Then he went to the stable.

"I gave both horses a portion of grain," Steve Dawkins told him when he came back. "You need some help saddling up?"

"No, thanks, though," Murphy answered. "Do I need to pay you for the grain?"

"No," Dawkins said at once, "I'll just put it on the US Marshal Service's bill. Let me know if I can help you with anything. I'll be out in the corral."

"I'm just gonna look through my packs to see what I need to pick up before I leave town. I know I was runnin' out of a lot of things. Where's the best place to buy coffee, flour, bacon, stuff like that?"

"Haddaway's Merchandise," Dawkins said. "Halfway up the

street, past the hotel. He's got the inventory, and he'll treat you right on the price."

"Yeah, I wondered about that store," Murphy remarked. "I noticed it when I took a walk yesterday." He went into his packs and bags on his packsaddle then, to get a good idea of just how short he was on the basics. One thing he knew he needed was extra coffee, because he owed Paul Mathers a sack of coffee. In addition to coffee, he needed flour, sugar, salt, bacon, and beef jerky, plus some hardtack.

Finished with his inventory, he saddled the packhorse and loaded it back up. Then he saddled the bay and led the horses out of the stable and over to speak to Dawkins, who was still in the corral, scrubbing out the water trough. "I swear, Dawkins, I didn't think anybody ever cleaned out a waterin' trough."

"They get gummed up just like anything else," Dawkins responded. "You look like you're ready to leave."

"Yep, I expect so," Murphy said. "I wanna thank you for takin' care of my horses."

"You bet, Cullen. Hope you have a good trip back to Newtown. Stop in to see us, if you're down this way again."

"I'll do that," Murphy said, although he was not sure how welcome he might be in Austin. It might depend on how his departure went this morning.

He wheeled the bay away from the corral and rode past the hotel to Haddaway's Merchandise. Dawkins had been correct in his recommendations for the store. The young man who waited on him said he was Haddaway's son and he had everything Murphy needed and settled for a fair price. With that taken care of, he was ready to start out on the way home. There was now only one last detail to take care of. So he turned Nosy and walked his horses farther up the street toward the courthouse.

The city had plans for a real stone-walled courthouse to be constructed when the money for it was available. In the meantime, the state and county business was conducted out of a rambling two-story structure, one wing of which held a courtroom. This was where Murphy was told this morning's business would be conducted.

"There ain't but one thing you do in a courtroom," he told Nosy, "and that's have a trial."

# Chapter 20

He rode around the courthouse to the courtroom wing, a single-story structure with large windows along the side. The thought that first came to mind was: *If it's necessary to leave through a window, at least it wouldn't be from the second floor.* A quick look at his watch told him he still had ten minutes before nine. There were several large oak trees scattered randomly in the vacant area beside the courtroom, so he picked the closest one to the building and this was where he tied his horses. He noticed that it was not far from a back door to the courtroom, but he went around to the front entrance. When he walked in the door, he was surprised to find the courtroom empty. He quickly looked at his watch again and compared it to the clock on the wall behind the judge's stand. They both agreed. It was nine o'clock.

"What the hell . . ." he started, certain that the hearing was at nine. A door behind the judge's stand opened then and a woman carrying a broom and a dustpan walked in.

Equally surprised to find him in the courtroom, she asked, "Are you looking for the marshal's meeting?" He said he was, so she said, "They're in the meeting room." When he asked where that was, she said, "Out that door I just came in, across the hall to another door. That's the conference room."

"Thank you, ma'am," he said, and hurried past her. When

he went out the door, he came to a narrow hallway and directly across it there was another door and it was open. Through it, he could see a large table, with several people sitting around it. He walked in and stopped just inside the door to look the situation over. He saw the US Marshal and Robert Stone seated at one end of the table across from each other. The young deputy marshal, Sawyer, was in attendance, as was Sheriff Hazzard and the man Murphy recognized as the undertaker who came to take possession of Hatcher's body. There was one person he did not recognize, however—a rather fragile-looking man, who had a large pad and several pens and an inkwell.

"Come in, Marshal Murphy. Take a seat wherever you like," Henry Stephens said. "I believe you've met everybody here with the exception of Milton Kline. He's a court recorder and his job is to write down everything we say here in shorthand and transcribe it to an official accounting of the meeting."

Murphy took a seat that gave him a good view of Sheriff Hazzard, as well as Deputy Marshal Sawyer, the only people other than himself who were armed.

"I'll point out for the record that it is against the law to wear guns in the courthouse," Stephens continued, "unless you are an officer of the law. And the three wearing firearms at this hearing are all officially officers of the law." He glanced at Robert Stone then, as if to placate him.

Murphy speculated then that Hazzard and Sawyer's presence at the hearing was solely for the purpose of having him outgunned.

"This hearing has a look about it that reminds me more of a trial," Murphy spoke out then. "And I feel like I'm the defendant here. I can understand you wantin' to defend the honor of your deputy marshals, but the fact is that they did what they did. The only thing I'm guilty of is being a damn fool. I was convinced that Ward Hatcher and Frank Foley had come to Newtown to do the job they were sent to do. So when I discovered they were heading in the opposite direction when they left town, I thought they had been overcome by their prisoners. And I went after them, hoping to save their lives. I was wrong to do that. I shoulda said to hell with it, it's out of my jurisdiction." He looked directly at Robert Stone then. "And Marshal Stephens wouldn't know what happened to his two veteran deputy marshals, and Wells Fargo wouldn't have gotten their money back or found out if the four men who held up the stage got away with the money, after all. If you wanna see Frank Foley's grave, I can show you where it is. And I can show you where those four murderers' remains are scattered and where Hatcher met the devil—"

Stone interrupted him. "Why did you bring Hatcher's body back?" he asked. "Why not bury him, or just leave him for the buzzards?"

"So you could see how he died," Murphy answered. "His body and the money was all the evidence I could bring back. Ask the undertaker about the body."

Harry Morgan didn't wait to be recognized. "He was shot to death by rifle fire," he volunteered. "I dug nine .45-caliber bullets outta his body and I suspect there were a lot more in his insides that I didn't bother going after, and not a single wound on his face or head anywhere. He had deep wounds on his wrists where I suspect he was pulling against his restraints. His wounds were all typical of a man killed like Murphy says he died, handcuffed to a small tree. The tree must have protected his head, but it wasn't big enough to protect the rest of him. I suspect if you found the tree where he had him handcuffed, the trunk would be full of lead."

No one said anything for a few moments while they pictured Hatcher's brutal death. Then Stone asked, "Why did you bring the money back?"

"What kind of fool question is that?" Murphy answered. "Because the money didn't belong to me, that's why."

"That wouldn't have made any difference to a lot of people," Stone suggested. "Finders keepers, losers weepers."

"Maybe so," Murphy allowed, "but I knew who the money belonged to."

"There is a portion of the original twenty-five thousand dollars that is missing," Stone continued to harp on the money. "After you captured all four outlaws, you notified Marshal Stephens that you recovered twenty-five thousand dollars. What do you suppose happened to five hundred dollars missing from that sum when you brought the money back here?"

"I wouldn't have any idea, Mr. Stone," Murphy replied. "You'd have to ask Deputy Marshal Hatcher about that. If you're thinkin' I took it to cover my expenses, you'd be wrong. I woulda charged you a helluva lot more than five hundred dollars." He let that sink in for a few seconds before continuing. "Now, gentlemen, I've told you the complete story of what actually happened. If you cannot accept my word as the truth, I can guide you over the entire trip from Newtown back to Austin by way of the Colorado River. As I said, I can show you where Hatcher and Foley had the four prisoners dismount, then executed all four of them and left them for the buzzards. Then I can lead you to the bank of the Colorado where Hatcher murdered Foley. You'll have to give Hatcher credit for some compassion for his partner. He buried Foley in a shallow grave. I had to dig part of the grave up to see which one was in it. That's the true story, so I want to know what you intend to do about it. I believe my business is finished here, my horses are saddled, and I plan to ride out of Austin right away. Does anybody object to that? I need to get back to my job as town marshal, if I still have that job after being gone for so long."

"You never asked about a reward," Stone said.

"I didn't do it for a reward," Murphy said.

"Well, this hearing is finished to my satisfaction, Marshal Stephens," Stone said. "I'm convinced that this crime happened exactly the way Marshal Murphy said it did."

"I think we're all agreed then," Stephens said. "The meeting is adjourned. Thank you for your patience, Cullen."

"Yes, Cullen," Robert Stone said, "and I'd like to thank you on behalf of Wells Fargo for your diligence in pursuing this business and bringing the money here to Austin."

"Glad I was able to help," Murphy said, thankful that he didn't have to try to shoot his way out of the courthouse. He got up to leave.

"One more thing before you go," Stone said. "I'm authorized to write you a check for one thousand dollars, which is the reward Wells Fargo has offered."

"W-what?" Murphy stammered "I didn't do it for a reward," he repeated. "I didn't even know there was one."

"That makes it even more a pleasure for me to give it to you." Stone sat back down at the table and pulled a checkbook out of his briefcase, grinning when he saw Murphy's genuine shock.

Murphy was speechless for a moment as he watched Stone write the check. Then it occurred to him. "I can't cash a check. There ain't no bank in Newtown."

Stone chuckled. "Then I guess you're going to have to delay your departure long enough to go to the Bank of Austin to get it cashed. I'll go with you to make sure they know the check is good."

"This sure will come in handy, because I might be out of a job by the time I get back to Newtown. I wasn't even gonna be gone overnight when I left there," Murphy commented.

"Is that a fact?" Henry Stephens responded. "Well, if you're out of a job when you get back, turn around and come back to Austin. I can put you to work as a US Deputy Marshal. I just lost two that I thought were good ones. Sounds to me like you ain't supposed to be stuck in that town, anyway."

"I 'preciate the offer, Marshal," Murphy said. "But Newtown and I have a lot of history together. They didn't even have a sheriff or a marshal when I got back from the war and I sorta had to fill the role. The trouble right now is, I don't really have a deputy. He's young and he wants to be a deputy, but I'm afraid he ain't up to handling the job. And to tell you the truth, I'm kinda worried about him tryin' to watch the town while I'm ridin' all over hell and back."

"I just want you to know I'm making you a serious offer," Stephens said. "I know more about you than you know." He grinned and said, "I heard tales about Murphy's Law that turned that little town right side up. So if you find out this little trip has cost you a job, you know where you've got another one."

"Thanks, Marshal Stephens, I 'preciate it."

"Come on, Cullen, we'll go to the bank!" Robert Stone called for him. "I know they've surely got the money to cover that check."

"Right," Murphy said. "I've gotta go out the side door to get my horses."

"You've got your horses out there?" Stone asked. "You really are in a hurry to leave us."

"I got a long trail to travel to get back to Newtown," Murphy said. "So I wanted to get started as soon as I could. I 'preciate you going to the bank with me. I doubt they would cash it, if it was just me, not for that amount of money, anyway."

# CHAPTER 21

"Did you see the size of that stack of bills?" Virgil Price exclaimed. "How much you reckon was in that stack, two or three hundred?"

"Shoot, there was a helluva lot more than that," Harvey Coon replied. "That teller just kept countin'. Wonder what that feller's gonna do with all that money?" They casually walked away from the table, where they were pretending to look at the forms to open new banking accounts, and sidled over closer to the front window. They watched the two men who had made the huge withdrawal as they talked by the hitching rail. "Looks like they're splittin' up," Coon said when the big fellow climbed up on his horse.

"That damn bank guard is watchin' us again," Price complained. "We didn't figure on this bank havin' a full-time guard and he's eyeballin' us pretty close. Maybe we need to ask him what his problem is. We ain't doin' nothin' but thinkin' about openin' a new account."

More interested in the man with the large envelope of cash in his saddlebag, Coon said, "He's fixin' to head out somewhere. He's leadin' a packhorse and that ain't a bad-lookin' bay he's ridin'." He turned to look at Price, who wasn't responding to his comments. When he saw that Price was still fretting over the bank guard's apparent interest in the two of them, he said, "Forget about the blamed guard, we've got a safer bet that's fixin' to ride right out from under us."

"What about our plan?" Price said. They had decided to rob the bank, thinking that the bank would be far more casual about protection against holdups. It was actually Coon's reasoning that a bank in the state capital with a county sheriff, as well as a company of US Deputy Marshals, would be the least likely target for a robbery. Consequently, the bank would not likely think they were in danger and wouldn't be as prepared to deal with a holdup.

"Forget our plan," Coon answered him. "I've got a better plan right now. We can come back to the bank for a bigger score. But there's no sense in lettin' a pretty good payday just ride away from us. And this one don't run as big a risk of gettin' shot as the bank would. So come on before we lose sight of this feller."

They walked back to the table and put the forms down and hurried toward the door. When they passed by the bank guard, Price said, "We'll have to think about it before we give you our business."

Outside, Coon said, "Yonder he is! He's headin' outta town! Wonder where he's headin' goin' that way?"

"Maybe one of them cotton farms on the other side of the river," Price said.

"He didn't look like no cotton farmer to me," Coon said. "Besides that, he's leadin' a packhorse. He's on his way somewhere off from here."

"Well, I don't know where it could be, goin' that way," Price said. "Let's see if he crosses the river. We'd best not get too close up on him. Be bad if he knew we was followin' him."

After Robert Stone had accompanied him to the bank and assured the teller it was okay to cash his check, they walked outside to the hitching rail. Stone wanted to shake his hand and thank him again for going after Hatcher and Foley when he knew what was happening. "I'll admit, I had my doubts about your story, and it was because of my insistence that we had that hearing. And I insisted that Sheriff Hazzard and Deputy Marshal Sawyer should be there. Because if my suspicions turned out to be right about you, I could see you blowing your cork and trying to shoot your way out of there."

"Oh, there wasn't any danger of that," Murphy said, thinking Stone didn't know how close their expectant possibilities were. "First impressions can really fool you sometimes." *Like the pompous ass I thought you were,* he thought.

They shook hands and Murphy climbed up into the saddle and rode out the south end of town to cross over to the west bank of the Colorado River. Once across, he rode a short distance to pick up the Llano Trail to the northeast, a trail that he would follow to the San Saba River. It would take him about three days to reach Newtown, if there were no problems along the way. He was getting a late start, but he still hoped to make about forty miles before camping for the night. It was not a trail that he had traveled very often. In fact, there had been no occasion when he had used it since before the war. But he remembered it as a trail well marked with adequate water stops. From Austin, the trail led virtually to nowhere until Newtown was born. Before that time, it was simply a useable trail to take you through the rugged Texas Hill Country to destinations beyond that.

As he rode along, his thoughts were naturally on the peaceful ending of his adventure to deliver Wells Fargo's money. It had developed into an unbelievable nightmare that took him farther and farther away from the town he was sworn to protect. There was a bright spot at the end, however, in the form of one thousand dollars cash to help pay for some of the trouble. He wondered how long he might have to live on that thousand, if this trip had been the straw that broke the camel's back. What if he was no longer the marshal of Newtown? Baxter could pout and threaten, but he could surely not be so insane that he would make Will Pickens the marshal. The thought of it brought a feeling of outright panic and he prayed that Will would not be placed in a dangerous situation before he could get back. "Well, Nosy, there ain't nothing we can do about it but try to get back as soon as we can."

"I don't know where in the world this feller is goin'," Price said. "There ain't a blamed thing up this trail." He and Coon sat on their horses just shy of a sharp bend in the trail. They had started around the curve, but caught sight of the man they followed and had to pull back out of sight until he reached the end of a long straight stretch in the trail. "Are we gonna follow him all day today and wait until he makes a camp tonight?"

"Heck no," Coon decided, "I'm already tired of followin' him. He's gonna have to stop to rest his horses before too much longer. And I reckon he'll cook himself something to eat. We'll just make a neighborly call on him then. I hope he's got something good to eat in them packs. I'm 'bout to starve already, too."

Up ahead of the two riders, Murphy was approaching a line of trees that indicated a stream or creek crossing coming up. "I expect we'd best stop and rest up there, if it looks decent," he told Nosy. "I hope it's sizable, because I think we'll be gettin' some visitors." He'd had a feeling he was being followed ever since he struck the Llano Trail after crossing the river. But he didn't see proof of it for all this time until he looked back after coming to the end of a long stretch of straight trail when he got a quick glimpse of a horse behind him at the other end. To confirm what he suspected, the horse backed out of sight immediately.

*Ain't that a kick in the head?* he thought. *Ain't been rich but a few hours and already the robbers are out to rob me.* He figured he might as well unload his horses and let them go to water. Whatever mischief the men following him had in mind would have to be played out right where he was. The horses were too tired to run for it. When he reached the crossing, it turned out to be a sizable creek, so he decided how to set up his camp quickly to his best defensive advantage. Hurrying as best he could, he picked a spot for his campfire, then pulled the saddle and packsaddle off the horses. He placed the packsaddle on the ground in front of the fire with his saddle on top of it, hoping they would provide some protection. Next he gathered enough limbs and sticks to get a fire started. Once it was showing signs of life, he hurried to set up his defenses. At this point, he began to wonder what was keeping his guests.

When certain their victim was stopping at the creek, Coon and Price decided their surprise assault would have a better chance of success if their target met them coming from the opposite direction. "He ain't as apt to think we're out to get him if he just meets us comin' in the opposite direction, instead of sneakin' up on him from behind," Coon said. So they left the trail and made a wide circle, striking the trail beyond the creek, giving Murphy extra time to prepare his camp.

With his horses watering and grazing near the creek and his fire burning smartly, he cranked a round into the cylinder of his rifle and propped it against a tree behind his fire. Then he loaded a bullet in the one empty chamber of his six-gun, cocked it, and placed it just beneath the cantle of his saddle, which was sitting on top of the packsaddle. Lastly, he pulled his spare pistol out of one of his packs, inserted a live round in the empty chamber, cocked it, and laid it on the ground close to the fire. He covered the pistol with a rag. Since there was still no sign of his stalkers, he took the time to slice some bacon and put it in his frying pan. Watching the trail he had just traveled, he was surprised when suddenly two riders appeared on the trail on the other side of the creek, coming from the opposite direction. Thinking at first that he might have more trouble than he could handle, it occurred to him then that they had to be the pair who had followed him all the way from Austin. They had circled around to keep him from thinking they had trailed him. It was too much of a coincidence, especially when none of the four would have a packhorse.

"Howdy," Harvey Coon called out. "Couldn't help smellin' your bacon fryin' over there and wondered if you could spare a slice or two. Our packhorse stepped in a crevice comin' over a ridge back there. Killed the horse and jammed him upside down so we couldn't get to our packs."

"I swear, if that ain't the damnedest story I've ever heard," Murphy said. "Upside down in a crevice. I've gotta see that." He looked at Virgil Price. "Did you help him make up that story?"

"It ain't no story," Price protested.

"No kiddin'," Murphy said. "Where did you two start out from back that way?"

"Back there a ways," Coon said. "It don't matter where we started out from. What matters is what you're totin' in them saddlebags. You just hand that over and we'll let you live to eat that bacon." He pulled his six-gun and leveled it at Murphy. Seeing this, Price pulled his gun as well.

"I don't have anything in my saddlebags but some dirty clothes and my razor and such as that," Murphy said, fully aware that he was working with a couple of brain-damaged outlaws.

"That's a lie," Price exclaimed. "We saw you put an envelope full of money in your saddlebag."

"I can't give you that money," Murphy said.

"Why not?" Price asked.

"Because it's not yours," Murphy said. "What the hell is wrong with you two? You can't go around takin' other people's money."

"Man, you're crazy as a bedbug," Coon said. "You think I won't shoot you down? I'm tired of foolin' with you. You get that money outta that saddlebag or I'll shoot you down."

"All right, I believe you," Murphy said. "Can I just turn my bacon over before it burns up?"

Coon planned on eating that bacon right after he shot Murphy. "Yeah," he said, "you can turn the bacon, but hurry up."

"That pan's hot," Murphy said, and reached for the rag lying on the ground beside the fire with one hand, while the other hand grasped his spare pistol that was under the rag, coming up with it at the same time he reached for the hot frying pan. Caught by surprise, Coon was struck in the chest, causing him to pull the trigger. But the bullet from his gun went into the trees over their heads. Price's natural reaction was to try to bat the hot frying pan thrown at him, while Murphy pulled his already-cocked six-gun from under the cantle of his saddle. Price was not quick enough to recover before Murphy's second shot struck him in his shoulder, causing him to drop his six-gun. He sat down on the ground, waiting for the shot that was going to end his life.

Murphy looked at Coon, who was bleeding from the wound in his chest. He had intended to shoot him in the shoulder, just as he had with Price. But Coon lunged just as Murphy pulled the trigger. He was badly injured, but it was hard to say if it was a fatal wound or not. He picked up their pistols and tossed them out of reach.

Then he turned his attention to Price, who was in pain, but not seriously wounded. "You're not in bad shape," he told Price. "I'll bandage that up so the bleeding will stop. Your partner's in bad shape. I'll put him on his horse and tie him so he won't fall off. The only chance he's got is if you can get him back to Austin to the doctor. The sooner you get started, the better his chances. I'm gonna have to keep your guns, though."

"You ain't gonna kill us?"

"No, I think you got punishment enough for what you planned to do," Murphy said. "I was just plannin' to put a bullet in his shoulder, too, but he moved just as I pulled the trigger."

"We was plannin' to kill you," Price confessed.

Murphy shook his head, thinking what a stupid confession to make to someone who might take offense enough to kill him for it. "You better get going. Your horses are tired, but they'll make it if you hold 'em to a slow walk. Your horse would appreciate it if you walked part of the way, too. All right?"

"All right," Price answered. "Thank you for not killin' us," he said as Murphy bandaged him with a fairly clean rag he found in his saddlebags.

Coon cried in pain when Murphy picked him up off the ground and hoisted him up into the saddle. "Just hug that horse's neck," he told him. Then he cut some short pieces of rope and tied Coon's legs in the stirrups. Satisfied that he wouldn't fall off the horse, he tied Coon's reins to Price's saddle.

"You got any money?" he asked Price.

"I've got a few dollars," Coon answered.

Murphy reached into his pocket and took out a small roll of bills. He peeled off four bills and said, "Here's twenty dollars to pay the doctor. Now get goin'."

He stepped back from the horse and watched as the horses walked slowly back to the trail. He continued to watch until they were out of his sight when the trail made a turn. Then he jumped up on the bay's back and rode him to that point where they first disappeared. Then he watched from there until they disappeared again. Assuming they would continue on, he went back and started to cook his dinner again, hoping the incident was not indicative of how the entire trip was going to be.

He remained there by the creek, fairly confident that he had seen the last of the would-be robbers, but not to the point where he would grab a short nap. The one with the shoulder wound had a simple mind, one that could be easily influenced.

So he didn't rule out the possibility that his partner, in seeking revenge, might persuade him to try to do it for him. In spite of that risk, he would wait until his horses were rested enough before moving on.

When it was time, he saddled his horses again, hung the confiscated weapons on his packhorse, put out his fire, and started out again. As it had been during the first segment of his day, he met no one on the trail. It truly was a deserted trail, and because of that, he watched for sign of deer. And while he found sign when he crossed the streams, he never actually saw any deer. *Oh, well,* he thought, *while the thought of fresh venison is appealing, if I flush a deer somewhere along the way, I would have to shoot it, and then I would have to stop and butcher it.* And he was anxious to get back to Newtown as soon as he could. He had been gone for so many days, he could not imagine what the people thought might have happened to him.

It struck him at that point that he missed the people of Newtown. He wasn't sure he even wanted to admit it. The question now more important to have an answer for was, did the people of Newtown miss him? Or was he going to be relieved of his position as town marshal for desertion? A lot, he supposed, was going to depend on what had happened in town while he was gone.

His encounter with Virgil Price and Harvey Coon turned out to be the only meeting with other travelers on the Llano Trail. It took him a little longer to cover the distance than he had estimated, for he struck the San Saba River at the end of the third day and made his camp there. That left him approximately sixteen miles from the point where Brady Creek emptied into the San Saba, the place his cabin once stood.

After another peaceful night, he was back in the saddle early the next morning, riding the sixteen miles to Brady Creek, where he stopped to rest his horses and cook something to eat.

He was only three miles from Newtown, but by the time the horses were rested, he would be too late to get to Irene's Café for breakfast. So he made a fire, made some coffee, fried some bacon, and cooked some hardtack in the grease. He sighed and confessed that he was never coming back to live there. He wasn't going to raise horses as he had planned when he built the cabin, a time that seemed a hundred years ago now. His time as town marshal might be over, so he would be moving on from Newtown. *Maybe,* he thought, *I might take Henry Stephens's offer to ride with the US Marshal Service.*

# Chapter 22

It was late in the morning when he rode into Newtown, after being gone for how many days he couldn't say for sure. Nine or ten he thought, well over a week, but he hadn't really tried to keep an accounting of the passing of each day. The town seemed quiet enough as he rode up from the river road past the saddle shop, where Vince Towns, the proprietor, was out front sweeping off the boardwalk.

"Mornin', Vince," Murphy greeted him.

Vince looked up and, seeing who it was, looked as if he'd seen a ghost before managing a weak, "Mornin', Marshal."

"What happened to your window?" Murphy asked, and nodded toward a window where Vince used to have a fancy engraved saddle on display. The window was now boarded up.

"Somebody shot the glass out and took the saddle," Vince replied.

"Do you know who did it?" Murphy asked.

"No, it was after I was closed and gone to the house," Vince said. He hesitated, then said, "But I know where it is."

"Where's that?" Murphy asked.

"It's on a white horse one of the members of a gang of ranch hands rides. They started comin' into town about a week ago and they're a pretty wild bunch."

"This saddle you've seen on a white horse, are you sure it's your saddle? Have you got some way to identify it?"

"*Vince Towns* engraved under the back jockey on the left side of the saddle," Vince said.

"Oughta be easy enough to spot if it shows up in town again," Murphy said. "I'll keep an eye out for it and you come tell me if you see it in town."

"Yessir, I will," he replied halfheartedly. He stood there, staring at Murphy long after he rode away.

Murphy wanted to stop at the jail first to let Will know he was back, as well as to drop his dirty clothes off, along with his other personal objects. So he pulled Nosy up at the hitching rail in front of the jail, pulled his rifle out of the saddle scabbard, took his saddlebags off, and walked up to the door, but the door was locked. He had his key in his pocket, so he dropped his saddlebags, got his key out, and unlocked the door. He pushed the door open, picked up his saddlebags, and walked in, to find himself looking at the business end of a double-barrel shotgun.

"Murphy?" Will Pickens asked almost in disbelief. He was standing behind the desk, the shotgun aimed directly at him.

"Yes," Murphy answered, "it's me. Take it easy, Will. You wanna put that shotgun down now and tell me what's wrong?"

Will relaxed and shook his head as if just awakening from a nightmare. He put the shotgun down on the desk. "I'm sorry, Cullen. I tried to take over for you till you came back. A wild bunch hit town two days after you left and they just do whatever they want, no matter what I tell them. They come to town and raise hell and I tell them it's against the law and they don't pay any attention to what I say. They told me that if I didn't keep out of their way, they would come and string me up. That's who I thought you were when you came in the door just now. I thought they'd come to get me, and I wasn't gonna go peacefully."

"Do they usually hit town this early?" Murphy asked.

"Not usually," Will replied, "but I always keep the office door locked now, and when I heard somebody unlockin' the door and comin' in, I reckon I panicked."

"I'm sorry that I had to leave you for so long, but I'm back now and we'll just have to come to an understandin' with this new gang. I passed Vince Towns coming up here. He told me somebody broke his window and stole a saddle that was in it. He said they fired a shot through the glass to break the window. You think that's one of the wild gang you're talking about?"

"I know it is," Will replied. "I told them they couldn't fire their guns inside the town, but they still do."

"You pretty sure one of them is the one who stole Vince's saddle?"

"I'm sure he is," Will said. "He even has the nerve to have the saddle on his horse. He rides a white horse and it's easy to spot that brand-new saddle. I asked him where he got the saddle, and he said he bought it in San Antonio."

"Well, don't worry about it," Murphy told him. "I'm back now and we'll have a little talk with these boys. I'm sorry you caught such a bad lot of luck while I was gone."

Will hesitated to say what he knew he had to, but he came out with it. "Eliot Baxter told me, if you came back, to tell you that you're no longer the town marshal."

"Is that a fact?" Murphy responded. "I'm not surprised. I kinda expected it. But that don't make any difference with what we're gonna do about this trouble the town's havin' with this wild gang." Then it occurred to him to ask, "Did the mayor appoint a new marshal?"

"No, not yet," Will answered. "He said that I was temporarily in charge."

*In other words, he's trying to get you killed,* Murphy thought. To Will, he said, "Well, in that case, you're the acting town marshal, so you're authorized to appoint me as your deputy. That is, if you'll have me."

"You're hired!" Will responded thankfully. "I thought maybe you had decided not to come back to Newtown."

"I never had any intention of not coming back to Newtown. When I left here that day, I thought I might be gone overnight. That's why I took my packhorse. But I rode into one helluva surprise." He went on to tell Will where he had been and what he had been doing the whole time he was gone.

Will was properly shocked to hear what the two deputy marshals had done to the four prisoners and how ultimately evil Ward Hatcher turned out to be. "Maybe Eliot Baxter will change his mind when he finds out what you were doing," he said.

"I'm not countin' on it," Murphy told him. "Baxter's more like a king than he is a mayor, and you have to be punished for disobeying the king. But don't you worry, I'm not gonna leave you with all this mess that's goin' on here now." He didn't divulge his more recent thoughts about the town, but the fact of the matter was that there were too many good people in Newtown to simply let it be taken over by the worthless drifters and the lawless breed. "I'm gonna put my things in my room now; then I'll take my horses up to the stable. Then I'll report my return to King Eliot of Baxter. After that, whaddaya say we go to Irene's for dinner. I've been looking forward to that for days. Say, have you ever ate any wolf meat? No? Well, I'll have to tell you about that." He picked up his saddlebags and went back to his room.

Will watched him as he entered the narrow hallway leading to the kitchen and their private rooms, a ton of weight lifted from his shoulders. He knew for sure that he was going to be all right now. The town would revert back to Murphy's Law.

Murphy removed the one flat ceiling board that slid into place, instead of being nailed in his room over his bed. Then he added the envelope, with a thousand dollars, to the rest of the cash he had managed to save, hidden between the ceiling joists. With that taken care of, he went back to his horses and rode up Front Street to the stable, leaving some of the people on the street to stare and wonder.

"Cullen Murphy!" Paul Mathers exclaimed, genuinely surprised to see him. "They said you were gone for good."

"They?" Murphy responded. "Who are they? You mean Baxter, don't you? Well, I'll tell you the truth, Paul. I was gone for good and then I remembered I had this sack of coffee I bought in Austin that I owed you. So doggoned if I didn't have to come back to keep you from tellin' everyone in the county that I don't pay my debts."

Mathers threw his head back for a loud guffaw. "You didn't have to pay that back," he managed to say. "If you don't mind me askin', where in hell have you been?"

"Hell's the proper word for where I've been," he said as he started pulling his saddle off the bay. "I guarantee you, I'll tell you a story you're gonna find hard to believe. It'll make you believe you can't trust anybody." He proceeded to tell Mathers the whole story that ended up in Austin with the burial of a highly respected deputy marshal.

"I swear," Mathers remarked, "that's hard to believe. Ward Hatcher impressed me as a true-blue officer of the law."

"I expect that he was just that for all but the last job he was sent on," Murphy said. "But I reckon he had just gotten too old for the business he was in. And the opportunity to get some reward for your long years of service lands in your lap, it makes you think up different definitions for *right* and *wrong.*"

"I expect that's one excuse for it," Mathers said. "But the same opportunity landed in your lap when you caught up with Hatcher. You took the money back to Wells Fargo. Why didn't you take the money and run with it?"

"I would have," Murphy said, having never given it a thought, "but I ain't as old as Hatcher was."

Murphy left his horses in Paul's care and walked back to the Newtown General Store. When he walked in, Jeff Baxter was at the front counter. When he saw Murphy, he simply turned toward the back counter and said, "Pop."

When Eliot turned and saw Murphy standing at the front of the store, his face drained of all color, and he hesitated a moment before coming forward to meet him. "Cullen," he said simply.

"Mr. Baxter," Murphy returned. "I just got back in town, and I expect I owe you an explanation. If you've got a couple of minutes, I think you'll be surprised by what I found out after I left to try to help save the lives of two US Deputy Marshals."

"Of course, I'll hear your report, but it can't possibly justify your absence from your sworn duty to protect the people of this town. And that was the basis for my decision to terminate your position as town marshal."

"Understood," Murphy said, "so now I'll tell you what it took to keep me from coming back immediately." Once again, he told the story, leaving out no sickening details, from the city limits of Newtown to Austin and back to Newtown. Baxter was shocked to hear of the callous executions of the four prisoners at the hands of the law officers, and was visibly disgusted when told of Foley's execution by his trusting partner.

"And the money?" Baxter asked. "The twenty-five thousand dollars, was it recovered?"

"It was, and it was turned over to Wells Fargo attorney Robert Stone in Austin, and Ward Hatcher's body was delivered to the undertaker there. So that's the reason it took me until today to return to Newtown, but in my defense, I came back as soon as I completed the job. It was my misfortune to have been the only person who was in a position to discover the terrible crime that was being committed. So that's it. I just thought I owed you a report."

"I told you he was right to go after them, Pop," Jeff blurted, and received a stern look from his father.

"I appreciate your coming to tell me all this, Murphy. I'll call a meeting of the town council to discuss the situation," Baxter said.

"No problem, sir," Murphy said. "I'm not here to ask you to reconsider your order to fire me as town marshal. I came back primarily to report this affair to the town council. I'm gonna stick around for a few days because I've got a lot of friends in Newtown. And I'm interested in the development of the town. That's why I donated a city jail to the town. I've got a standing invitation from US Marshal Henry Stephens to join his company as a US Deputy Marshal, so I'm not worried about being out of work for very long. So have a good day." He nodded to Baxter's son and acknowledged him with a "Jeff," then walked out the door.

"If you let that man get away from Newtown, you're crazy," Jeff said when the door closed behind Murphy.

"I'm not just your father," Baxter reminded him, "I'm your employer, too. So you watch how you talk to me."

Murphy walked back toward the jail, but when he walked past the tailor shop, Elmo Dillon, who was sitting next to the window, rushed out the door to call after him. "Cullen! Where'd you come from?"

"I swear, Elmo, am I gonna have to give you a talk about the birds and the bees? At your age?"

"Very funny," Elmo said. "Where the hell have you been? We thought you were dead. When did you get back?"

"Just this mornin'," Murphy said. "I just came from Baxter's store and let him know where I've been."

"He fired you. Did he tell you that?"

"Yeah, he told me, but I already knew it," Murphy said. "Will told me when I stopped to drop off some personal things before reporting to the mayor."

"He's gonna hire you back, right?"

"Well, he didn't say he was," Murphy said. "He said he was gonna call a meeting of the council and they would discuss it."

"He damn sure better hire you back," Elmo exclaimed. "We've got trouble, man, real trouble. We've got a gang of hell-raisers who have discovered there ain't nobody in the marshal's office but Will Pickens. I ain't sayin' Will ain't doing the best he can. He tells 'em when they're breaking the law, but he's kinda helpless to do anything about it, if they do. And they usually do."

"I'm gonna stay on for a while to see if I can give Will some help," Murphy told him.

"Baxter's made Will the acting town marshal," Elmo said.

"I know," Murphy said, "but I'm signin' on as Will's deputy. Maybe we can take care of some of the town's problems."

"His deputy, huh?" Elmo replied skeptically. "You know they're paying Will thirty dollars, the same as you were paying him to take care of the jailhouse for you? How much you reckon they'll authorize him to pay his deputy?"

Murphy smiled and said, "It's a good thing I'm not in it for the money, ain't it?"

Elmo shook his head, exasperated, thinking Murphy wasn't taking the problem seriously. "Cullen, listen to me, you'd best not take this situation too lightly. This latest gang of drifters is set on taking over the whole town."

"Right, Elmo, you know I always listen to you on anything important. But right now, Marshal Pickens is waitin' for me at the jail, so I'd best hurry along." He turned away and started walking toward the jail.

"Dad gum it, Cullen! You be careful!" Elmo exclaimed to his back. Murphy kept walking, but acknowledged Elmo's warning with a wave of his hand.

* * *

When he got back to the jail, he found Will sitting beside the desk in the side chair Murphy had put in the office for him. Murphy laughed when he walked in. "What are you sittin' in that chair for? The marshal is supposed to sit at his desk."

"I ain't the marshal," Will said at once. "That's your chair. Did Baxter give you your job back?"

"No, but he said the council would discuss my return to Newtown. Hard to say what they'll decide to do. They might order me to get back outta town."

"They better not," Will said. "If they do, I'm goin' with you."

"Maybe they won't go that far after we put a few troublemakers in jail. So, why don't we lock the door and go get some dinner?"

"See," Will replied, "you're back and right away you make the right decision. It's still a little too early for Bonnie to open the door. But if they see you, I'll bet they'll let us in early." They locked the office door and walked up the street to Bradshaw's Saloon. "You want to go in the back way to Irene's or go through the saloon?" Will asked.

"We'll just go in the outside entrance in the back," Murphy said. "If we go through the saloon, I'm gonna have to tell Pete and whoever's in there where I've been and the story takes too long to tell."

"Just as well," Will said. "The drifters have started a little early today. I recognize one of their horses at the rail in front."

Murphy looked toward the hitching rail and stopped in his tracks when he saw the three horses at the rail, one of which was a solid white. "Well, I'll be . . ." he started. *Will's right,* he thought. *He is that stupid or that brazen.* "You recognize that white horse as one of those drifters' horses?"

"Yeah," Will said.

Murphy headed directly toward the horses. "That looks like a brand-new saddle on that white horse," he commented as he approached it. "And look at the fancy designs engraved on it." He walked between the white horse and a sorrel next to it to get to the left back jockey of the saddle. He lifted the jockey and discovered the engraving on the underside of it: *Vince Towns, Newtown, TX.* He looked at Will, who was standing there looking confused. "Looks like we're gettin' started right away," Murphy said. He backed the saddlebags off the saddle, then freed the cinch and pulled the saddle off the horse. "I'm gonna ask you to carry this saddle for me," he said to Will, who was now far past confused and well toward flabbergasted. But he accepted the saddle and followed Murphy to the door of the saloon.

Murphy pushed through the batwings and looked the saloon over. Spotting two men seated at one of the tables with a bottle in front of them, he directed his loud inquiry in their direction. "Who in here was ridin' a white horse?" he thundered.

All conversation in the saloon stopped until one of the two men at the table answered, "I was," almost equally loud. "And whaddaya mean, *was*?"

It became so quiet then that those standing at the bar could almost hear the whispered word dropped from the bartender's mouth, "Murphy!"

"Because you won't be ridin' it outta town tonight," Murphy answered the question, and walked over to the table to confront him.

"Who the hell are you?" Jace Blackwell demanded.

"I'm the man who's tellin' you you're under arrest," Murphy said.

"For what?" Blackwell asked.

"For breakin' in the saddle shop and stealin' a saddle," Murphy told him, with one eye on the man seated at the table with him.

"The hell you say," Blackwell responded. "I bought that saddle in San Antonio."

"You ain't just a thief. You're a liar, too. Get on your feet," Murphy ordered. "You're wastin' my time."

A beefy-looking man with a snarl for a smile, Jace Blackwell enjoyed a brawl as well as any whiskey drinker. "Well, I don't never wanna waste no important man's time. Do I, Shorty?" he asked his friend.

"No, sir, Jace," Shorty answered with a smile for what he knew was coming. "That ain't like you a'tall."

Making slow and deliberate motions, Jace slid his chair back from the table and got to his feet. "What if I decide I don't wanna go with you, Sheriff, or whatever you call yourself. What then?"

"You go with me, anyway, only it ain't as pleasant as if you just go peacefully," Murphy said, and prepared himself to meet what was bound to come.

Jace's snarl widened into a broad smile, which Murphy read as a warning signal. In the next instant, Jace suddenly reacted, charging like an angry bull, only to encounter Murphy's right fist, which landed squarely on the top of his nose and eyebrows, dropping him like an ox shot in the head. Murphy looked immediately at Shorty, who held up his hands, wanting no part in it. Murphy reached down and took Jace's gun out of his holster and stuck it in his own belt. He looked at Jace, who was out, cold, then back at Shorty. "Are you gonna give me any trouble?"

"No, sir," Shorty responded. "I just came in for a drink. No trouble from me."

"All right. Will, put the saddle down and give me a hand here."

Will acted at once.

"Grab his feet and we'll pick him up and lay him across his horse. Then you can pick up the saddle and we'll take Jace, here, to jail." Murphy looked at Shorty again and asked, "What's Jace's last name? And yours?"

"He's Blackwell," Shorty answered at once. "And I'm Shorty Boone."

They carried Jace out and laid him across the back of his

horse; Murphy led the horse to the jail, while Will carried the fancy saddle. When they got to the jail, Jace was just coming out of his concussion, but he was still too shaky to protest. So Murphy slid him off his horse to let him fall across his shoulder and he carried him in, while Will opened the doors for him. While Murphy emptied Jace's pockets of all possessions, Will filled his water bucket and made sure his thunder mug was where he could find it. They laid him out on his bunk, then locked him in his cell. "We're still in plenty of time to make dinner," Murphy said. "So you go ahead if you want to and I'll take Jace's horse to the stable."

"It oughta be the other way around," Will said. "You go ahead to the dinin' room and I'll take the horse to the stable."

Murphy laughed. "You're the marshal, you do what you want to do."

"All right, then," Will said. "I'll take the horse to the stable. You go to the dinin' room."

Murphy chuckled. "Whatever you say, Marshal."

Will jumped on the white horse's back and rode him up the street to the stable. When he went by Bradshaw's, he noticed that there was only one horse tied at the rail now. The horse that was beside the white one was gone.

# CHAPTER 23

Still anxious to put off the visit to the saloon, Murphy went down the side of the building to the outside entrance. When he walked into the dining room, he was met by all three of the Floyd women. They came to meet him with hugs. Murphy was astonished to think they were so happy to see him. He told them as much and apologized for returning before he had an opportunity to clean himself up after the long trip in the wilderness. "I was so starved for one of your meals, I couldn't put it off till after I cleaned up."

"Nonsense," Irene told him. "We're just so happy to see you back home safe and sound. When you rode away from here and didn't come back for so many days, we were afraid that something bad had happened at the hands of those four horrible outlaws."

Murphy shook his head and smiled. "You're gonna find it hard to believe who turned out to be the most horrible. It's a heck of a story and I know you wanna hear the whole thing, but it'll take some time, so how about if I sit down at a table and get some coffee. And I'll tell you the whole story when you get a little slack time. Will oughta be here in a minute or two and we're gonna need a plate for a prisoner."

Like everyone else, they wanted to know where he had been

for so many days, but the first question was, did Eliot Baxter rescind his firing order? So Murphy answered that for them before Will joined him. And they had the same reaction that Will had. They thought it was ridiculous to think Baxter was not immediately welcoming Murphy back. Of course, the news from the saloon was in circulation without delay. Murphy was back and immediately made an arrest of one of the trouble-makers that had plagued the town while he was away. While many in the town were happy to see Murphy's return, there were also those who were afraid that his insistence to maintain a strict law-and-order policy would only cause the outlaw breed to react more strongly to his pressure. And there was always the one statistic that was so critical: The outlaws were many; Murphy was only one man.

Murphy and Will were still eating when Tyson Bradshaw came into the dining room, looking for Murphy. He walked directly over to their table. "I heard you were back," Bradshaw said. "I don't mean to interrupt your dinner. Would you mind if I sit down with you?"

"No, we don't mind," Murphy said. "I expect you'd like to hear why I was so long away from Newtown."

"I'd appreciate hearing the story directly from you, if you wouldn't mind," Bradshaw said. "Eliot told me you came to see him this morning and told him what caused you to be gone so long. But to tell you the truth, I'm not sure he remembered everything correctly. I find it hard to believe some of the things he claimed, especially what he claimed those two deputy marshals did."

"He probably remembered what I told him correctly," Murphy said. "It was hard for me to believe it when I found out what they had done."

He went through the story once more for Bradshaw's sake. And although Bradshaw accepted Murphy's version of the cruel events, it appeared he had something else that worried him. He brought it up after Ginger interrupted to ask if he wanted to eat.

"Ah, no, thank you, Ginger," he said. "Just bring me a cup of coffee." When she left to get it, he brought up another subject. "I understand you've already made an arrest right after you got back in town." Murphy nodded, wondering where Bradshaw was going with this. "Was it necessary to put the man in jail?" The question caused Murphy to raise his eyebrows, but he didn't reply. So Bradshaw continued. "I know some of the new customers we've had this past week have gotten loud and rowdy at times. But the fellow you put in jail and his friend were just in to have a drink of whiskey and they weren't bothering anybody, according to Pete Brice. So it seems a little harsh to put that fellow in jail."

Murphy couldn't believe what he was hearing. "Mr. Bradshaw, he shot Vince Towns's front window and stole an expensive saddle out of the window he had just shot out. And after that, he had the nerve to slap it on his horse and ride into town with it. Parked it out in front of your saloon on a white horse, like he was daring us to do something about it. So I accepted his dare. I can't abide men who don't think they're subject to the laws that everybody else is. I always figured you felt the same way."

"Oh, I do feel the same way," Bradshaw hastily claimed. "It's just that there are two different ways to look at things, I guess. Being a businessman and a saloon operator, I suppose I look at things a little different than a lawman would. While you were gone chasing those rogue deputy marshals, we may have had some loud celebrating or some drunken behavior. But during that time you were gone, my business went up almost thirty-three percent. And I can't really complain about this new group of customers. There haven't been a great number of altercations that have resulted in actual violence."

"So you actually keep figures on your business?" Murphy

asked. "I mean, like you said your business went up thirty-three percent, right?"

"That's a fact," Bradshaw answered, "thirty-three percent."

"I wonder," Murphy said, "during that same period, how much did your regular business go down? The local customers who have been buying likker and food in your saloon before the new crowd came to town—how much has their business gone down?"

"I don't keep track of that," Bradshaw sputtered. "I mean during that same period I didn't do their figures."

"I reckon you'll find out when this new crowd gets done with us and moves on to a bigger town, don't you reckon?" He paused to take a long sip of the hot coffee Bonnie had heated his cup with. "You know, Mr. Bradshaw, I reckon when a gang of drifters lights on a town, it don't seem like much more than a bunch of young fellows just havin' a little fun. One of 'em shoots a pistol through a window and takes a fancy saddle. Then maybe one of 'em shows his ropin' skills and lassos the manikin from in front of the dress shop and drags it through the streets behind his horse. How long before one of the cowboys lassos a young woman and drags her through the streets?"

"Well, that's an extreme example of what could happen, I would think," Bradshaw replied. "I think we would all rise up to put an end to that kind of behavior."

"Right," Murphy agreed, "but my way of thinkin' is, why let it get started in the first place? Why not make it plain to anyone who comes to our town, for whatever reason, that they have to obey the laws of the town?"

Bradshaw just sat there, silent for a moment, while he tried to think of a sensible response. Finally he took another couple of swallows from his cup, then got to his feet and said, "Good, I think we all want the same thing for our town." Then he went back to the saloon.

"I don't think he's thinkin' the same thing you're thinkin' at all." Will couldn't help but comment.

"I reckon not," Murphy said, "and you might be the town marshal longer than you thought."

They finished their dinner and Ginger handed Will a plate of food for their prisoner. When they got back to the jail, Jace was fully awake and ready to express his displeasure. "You made one helluva mistake when you put me in here," he informed Murphy.

"I don't think so, Jace. When you steal someone else's property, you go to jail and you stay there until a judge says how long your sentence is. We're kinda isolated over here in San Saba County with no telegraph, so it might take some time before we'll get a trial scheduled for you. Those circuit judges ain't too anxious to make the trip all the way to Newtown just to try a common thief. But we'll try to make your stay as pleasant as we can while you're with us. Will's got a fine dinner plate for you and we'll show you how you can get it."

Murphy told Jace what the routine was for him or Will to pass anything into the cell, and when Jace refused to cooperate, they left the plate of food on the floor outside the door. They went out of the cell room and closed the door, thinking it wouldn't be long before he began yelling for his dinner. While they waited for his surrender to his appetite, Will asked Murphy if he was going to write a letter requesting Jace's trial. "Hell no," Murphy replied. "It might take a month for a judge to get over here, if he came at all. He had enough money in his pockets to pay for his meals for a good while with some left over. So we'll keep him in jail for three or four days and give him a fine for the cost of his food—plus the cost to fix a window."

Although it was a much longer time than he expected, Murphy waited until Jace finally decided he might as well eat the food getting cold outside his cell. He went into the cell room with Will, since it was the first time Jace went through the procedure. When the prisoner was finally eating, Murphy left Will to watch the office and he picked up the saddle and walked down the street to Vince Town's shop.

"Is that my saddle?" Vince asked, surprised, when Murphy walked in.

"It's got your name on it," Murphy answered. "And it's a mighty fine piece of work, I don't mind sayin'. Don't look like there was any damage to it, and here's a little money to help pay for the repair of your window. The thief who stole it is in the jail for a few days, but I ain't sure that's gonna change his lawless ways. So don't stick that saddle in the window for a while. All right?"

"All right," Vince said. "I appreciate it, Marshal Murphy. I was just sick about losing that saddle. I didn't think I'd ever get it back. I'm sure glad to see you back in town."

"I'm glad to be back," Murphy said. "It wasn't a pleasure trip." Vince didn't ask where he'd been, so he didn't volunteer to go into the episode again. He turned and headed for the door and Vince followed him out.

"They're gettin' an early start today," Vince commented when a threesome of riders passed by just as he and Murphy stepped outside.

Murphy turned to look. "Is that some of the wild bunch that's been raisin' hell in town?"

"Yes. I've seen that one, wearing the derby hat, riding on the black horse," Vince said.

"Well, they seem peaceful enough," Murphy remarked.

"They're not likkered up yet," Vince declared.

"You've got a point there," Murphy admitted. "And today ain't Sunday, so they probably ain't goin' to church. Well, have a good afternoon," he said, and walked back up the street.

*I reckon they're going to Bradshaw's to get likkered up, like Vince said,* he thought when the three riders passed by Pratt's Saloon. But before they reached Bradshaw's Saloon, they pulled over when they came to the jail and dismounted. "Uh-oh," Murphy muttered, some distance behind them now. He thought he recognized the one he'd seen in the saloon, now that they were out of the saddle. Shorty, he recalled. He increased his pace when they stepped up to the door and went into the office.

Will came from the kitchen when he heard someone come in the front door. He was startled to see the three men, all too familiar, and one of whom he recognized as the man with Jace Blackwell in Bradshaw's Saloon earlier. In an attempt to disguise his sudden panic, he strained to speak with a steady voice of authority. "Something I can help you with?"

"Yeah, there's something you can help me with," a tall, rawboned man, wearing a derby hat and a brace of shoulder holsters, answered. "I've come to get my brother out of this dump you call a jail."

"Your brother's waitin' to go to trial for stealin' a saddle," Will managed. "He can't get out of jail before his trial."

"My brother ain't a thief," the man in the derby said. "You got no right to hold him in jail. He bought that saddle. You need to get busy findin' the man he bought it from. You're courtin' a whole lot of trouble if you don't turn him loose. He's got a lot of friends that ain't gonna like it when they find out he's in jail. I ain't sure I can keep 'em from comin' to get him outta here."

"Then I reckon I'm the man you wanna see," Murphy said. The man in the derby stiffened suddenly when he felt the cold steel barrel of the Colt .44 against the base of his skull. Neither he nor his two companions had heard the silent opening of the door behind them as the three of them were threatening Will. They had mistook the sudden widening of Will's eyes as a sign of fear.

"That's him, Jesse! The one that hit Jace!" Shorty Boone blurted.

"Will," Murphy calmly said, "reach behind you and get that shotgun out of the rack. Make sure both barrels are loaded. I believe these boys came in here to make trouble, so I wanna make sure they get their money's worth." He cocked the hammer back on his .44.

Hearing it, Jesse exclaimed, "Hold on! We didn't come in here to make trouble! I just wanted to see my brother! Make sure he's all right."

"Well, you coulda fooled me," Murphy said. "What I heard sounded more like Jace has some friends who might try to break him outta here."

"Jace has got friends who wanna make sure he's gittin' treated all right," Jesse said. "That's all I meant—and if you let me see him, I can tell them he's all right."

"If you had come in here and asked if you could visit him, then we woulda said, sure. We don't mistreat our prisoners. There are rules, however. Visits last for fifteen minutes and that's all. All weapons are left out here on the desk and that includes pocket pistols. There ain't no place big enough to stick a pocket pistol into one of the cells. But we still insist you leave them on the desk because a bullet will pass through the screen and we don't know how well you and the prisoner get along."

"Well, how 'bout it then?" Jesse asked, impatient now. "Can I go talk to my brother?"

"Yeah, maybe that'll cheer him up," Murphy said. "I don't think he likes being in jail. Just put your weapons on the desk. Do it carefully. Will, there, has touchy fingers whenever he uses that shotgun and I don't wanna have to clean up a mess in this office. You just hold still. We'll disarm you last."

"How 'bout takin' that gun barrel off the back of my head," Jesse requested. "We're takin' our guns off."

"Pretty soon now," Murphy said. "I bet you're fast as greased lightning when you draw down on somebody, those two handles facin' out like that. I'd like to see you shoot sometime."

"Maybe you will." Jesse couldn't resist the comeback.

"But for today, I'll just have Will reach up and draw them outta their holsters. Go ahead, Will, and be careful you don't pull those triggers before you get 'em out of the holster. You'd have Jace's brother doing a lively dance."

When all the weapons had been collected, Murphy told them they could go in and see Jace. "I'll keep the cell room door open so we can keep an eye on you while you're in there." Jesse told the third member of his party, a man he called Clem, to stay by the desk to make sure their weapons were not touched. Then he and Shorty went into the cell room.

"Jesse!" Jace exclaimed when they came into the cell room. "Get me outta here! I can't stay in this damn jail."

"What kinda jail is this?" Jesse wondered as he looked at the solid wooden walls. "This ain't a jail. It's a dungeon. No wonder he ain't all that worried about sneakin' a knife or a razor through the bars."

"There ain't no bars, except between the cells," Jace said. "Are you gonna get me outta here?"

"I planned to, but he got the jump on us; and before I knew it, he had a gun against the back of my head. He ain't gonna be as easy as I thought. What the hell did you steal that saddle for, anyway?"

"It was a good-lookin' saddle and I was drunk," Jace said in his defense.

Jesse peered through the small steel-screened opening. "What happened to your face? It's swollen all up, over your eyes and your nose."

"That's where that moose hit me," Jace said. "Shorty, you were there. What did he hit me with?"

"His fist," Shorty replied.

"Hell, he did," Jace said. "He couldn'ta done that with nothin' but his fist. He had a club or a gun butt, somethin' heavy."

"His fist," Shorty repeated. "You looked like a dead man when they carried you outta that saloon." He took another hard look at Jace's face. "Your face is all swoll up. Does it hurt?"

"Like I butted heads with a freight train," Jace complained.

"He had something in his hand, a club or something," he insisted.

"His fist," Shorty said, "he weren't holdin' nothin' in his hand." Recalling the incident then, he said, "When you went after him, it was like you rode under a bridge at a gallop, but your head was stickin' up too high to clear the crossbeam."

"Never mind that," Jesse snapped. "Who the hell is he? Where'd he come from?"

"I don't know," Jace answered. "But he's some kind of lawman, 'cause when he came up to me in the saloon, he said I was under arrest. Didn't he, Shorty?"

"That's a fact," Shorty replied. "He sure did. He said, 'You're under arrest,' and then you said, 'For what?' He's some kinda lawman, all right."

"That's kind of obvious, ain't it, since he put you in jail," Jesse remarked impatiently. "What I wanna know is, where did he come from? I thought the young feller was the marshal."

"He is," Jace said, "or he was. I don't know. But the big cat is the one who gives the orders. That's for sure. So, what are you gonna do to get me outta here?"

"I don't know yet," Jesse said. "I was planning to take you outta here today, but he showed up and it's a different story than dealin' with the fellow we've been dealin' with all week. You just set tight for a while until I see what we're gonna have to do with this fellow."

"Ah, come on, Jesse, I can't stay in this damn jail."

"Well, you're just gonna have to till I figure out the best way to take care of it. You oughta sit here and think about how dumb it was to steal that fancy saddle, then show it off all over town." He turned away from the door. "Come on, Shorty. Let's get outta here." He walked out of the cell room and Shorty followed.

"Don't leave me in here," Jace called after him. "I'm your brother! Don't leave me, Jesse!"

When they came back into the office, they found Clem standing nervously by their weapons on the desk, and Murphy and Will standing on one side of the room, both holding double-barrel shotguns. "Since you and your party are new to town, there are some local laws I should probably remind you of. There's no law against wearing firearms inside the city limits, but there is a law against firing them for any reason. And that includes in celebration of holidays or drunkenness. It might be of interest to you to know of another policy the town has adopted in regard to the city jail. To prevent any threat of breaking a prisoner out of jail, the prisoner is shot upon the first sign of any attempt. We've only had to use that policy once, but it did successfully prevent the escape of the prisoner. I don't know of any more specific rules you might be interested in, just generally behave yourselves like civilized people and save your animal instincts for the prairie and the mountains beyond."

"That was all very interesting," Jesse said. "But what do you plan to do with my brother? I understand he got a little drunk and snatched a saddle. He said he never intended to keep it. He thought it would be good advertisin' for the man who made it. I agree, he deserves some punishment for what he thought was just a prank and would do no harm. Where do you plan on sending him to be tried?"

"Let me rest your mind on that score," Murphy said. "We only request jury trials with a circuit judge for the more serious crimes, like murder, rape, and so on, crimes that are going to call for a death penalty. For minor crimes like your brother's, they are heard by city court and are usually sentenced to a small fine and three or four days in jail. Sometimes less than that with time off for good behavior."

"So you think Jace just might be sentenced to three or four days in jail," Jesse said, thinking it might be a good way to teach him to think before he went off half-cocked.

"Or less," Murphy said, "if he behaves himself while he's in jail. And, of course, that would be my call."

"Right," Jesse replied. "That makes a lot more sense. Thank you for your information. Come on, boys, let's go get a drink." He walked out, and Shorty and Clem followed.

Will went to the window and watched them until they got on their horses and rode up the street before he turned around and said, "You made up every bit of that, didn't you?"

"Just as fast as I could," Murphy said. "By the way, did you notice how much respect they had while we were standin' here holdin' shotguns? Be a good idea if you started carryin' one all the time you're walkin' the town. It can do a lot of damage at close range. By the way, is his brother's name Jesse? He never said, but it sounded like what the little fellow, Shorty, called him."

"His name's Jesse," Will said.

# Chapter 24

After leaving the jail, Jesse Blackwell, Shorty Boone, and Clem Baine rode up the street to Bradshaw's Saloon, where several horses were tied. They dismounted and tied up at the hardware store next door to the saloon. "Looks like it's pretty busy for this early in the day," Clem said. "Even if a lot of it is from our boys."

Inside, they spotted a table with three men they were there to join, so they walked over to the table. Shorty and Clem grabbed chairs from other tables along the way. Then they sat down at the table. "Where you been?" Whitey Gribble asked. "We thought you was right behind us."

"We stopped at the jailhouse to see if we could spring Jace," Jesse said.

"And?" Whitey asked. "I don't see him nowhere. Don't tell me that little marshal backed you down."

"There's a new marshal in town," Jesse told him, "and he could be trouble."

"He ain't kiddin', Whitey," Shorty said. "I was in here when he arrested Jace for stealin' that saddle. Jace jumped up and came after that feller and he knocked Jace out cold with one punch with his fist. I swear I could almost feel it!"

"Well, what are we gonna do about Jace?" LeRoy Ellis asked.

"We've been around this town too long already. And we was talking about hittin' this place tomorrow night, or the night after that, and headin' on down to San Antonio."

"If you hit this place before they let Jace outta jail, you're goin' without me," Jesse said. "I ain't goin' without Jace."

"I swear, Jesse, how long are you gonna alibi for Jace?" Whitey pressed. "It might be a good lesson for him to learn if we was to leave him in that damn jail while we're on our way outta here."

"What me and my brother do ain't none of your business," Jesse warned. "We've been leadin' this gang long before you decided you wanted to join up. And we've been doin' all right, ain't we?" He looked around the table for support. All the others gave him affirmative nods and grunts of approval.

"Tell him what that big cat said about the city court, Jesse," Shorty said.

Jessie nodded. "That's right. He said for a minor crime like Jace done, they wouldn't hold him till they got a circuit judge to come try his case. They got a city court to try the minor crimes. He said Jace would get two or three days in jail at the most—and most likely less for good behavior 'cause the city don't wanna pay the costs of holding a prisoner."

"That's right," Shorty said. "And we was talking about pullin' that holdup day after tomorrow or the next day, anyway."

"I swear, Shorty," Clem Baine said, shushing and looking all around him. "Watch what you're sayin'."

"Oh, there ain't nobody payin' attention to what we're talkin' about," Shorty insisted. "The point is, we ought not be gettin' our knickers in a tangle just because we have to wait for Jace to get out."

"I reckon you're right, Shorty," Whitey said. "Won't hurt to hang around here for a couple more days. I wanna take another ride with that gal down at Pratt's Saloon, anyway. Jesse, I never meant no offense in what I said about Jace."

"No offense taken," Jesse replied. "Jace can be tryin' sometimes, but he's my brother." He slapped his hand on the table and ordered, "Let's get some glasses over here and another bottle. I need a drink of likker." Shorty was the closest to the bar, so he jumped up and got three glasses and a bottle of whiskey from Pete. "Thank you, Shorty," Jesse said. Then in a whisper, he said, "I hope you paid him well, because we'll get every bit of it back when we open that safe of his upstairs."

"I took care of him," Shorty said, and chortled.

"Why don't they have no women in here to entertain ya?" Whitey wondered aloud.

" 'Cause this is supposed to be the saloon for the high-class gents in town, and their wives won't let 'em go anywhere there's women to set on their husbands' knees."

"I swear," Whitey remarked, "it must be awful to be married, jumpin' in the bed with the same woman every night. I'd last about one month of that before I jumped off a cliff somewhere."

"As mangy as you are," Clem declared, "any woman married to you would most likely jump off that cliff before the first week was up."

"Now that's where you're wrong, Clem," Whitey came back at him. "That little woman down the street at Pratt's asked me why I don't take her away from there."

"Quit payin' her and see what she says," LeRoy suggested.

The truth of the matter was, the gang had grown tired of hanging around the little town of Newtown. It had provided enough amusement to satisfy them for a week while they decided where they would score their holdup. When scouting the isolated town so convenient to a hideout in the Texas Hill Country, they were disappointed to find there was no bank. And bank holdups were their specialty. So they decided to move on from the hideout on Owl Branch and head down toward San Antonio. It was a decision that took a long time to make because of the lack of real law enforcement in Newtown. It was hard to leave a town that was incapable of controlling your wildest behavior. But they had reached the point when they realized their money was running out, so it was time to go to work. Since there was no bank, they had been trying to decide which business might be making the most money. It came down to two places that were the busiest in the town, Newtown General Store and Bradshaw's Saloon.

Jesse made the final decision, based on an argument by LeRoy Ellis. LeRoy reasoned that Eliot Baxter's general store sold a lot of merchandise, but a great deal of it was on a credit basis to farmers and ranchers who had to wait to pay their bills when the crops came in, or the cattle were sold. And this wasn't the right time of year for either. On the other hand, Bradshaw's was a cash business. You want a drink of whiskey, you put your money down. There was no slack season. Plus the café in the back of the saloon was supposedly owned by Irene Floyd, also a cash business. Possibly Bradshaw had a piece of that business as well. So Jesse decided their target would be Bradshaw's.

Most of the time when Tyson Bradshaw came into the saloon, he came from upstairs, so it was logical to assume he had his living quarters up there. There was no Mrs. Bradshaw, so Jesse figured there was probably an office up there as well. Shorty volunteered to find out. He had been blessed, or cursed, depending on the job, with the face of innocence. So Jesse and Shorty came up with a plan to get a look in Bradshaw's quarters. All they needed was for Bradshaw to be downstairs in the saloon—and he was—while the six men were sitting around the table drinking. Bradshaw spent some time talking to some of his regular customers; then he suddenly went upstairs after talking to his bartender about something. Shorty signaled Jesse at once and Jesse nodded. Shorty grabbed a whiskey bottle off the table and hurried up the stairs after Bradshaw.

Walking as quietly as his boots would permit, Shorty sneaked up behind Bradshaw, who remained unaware, due to the noise from the busy saloon below. Shorty waited until Bradshaw went down to the last door at the end of the long hallway before he went into his drunken routine. When Bradshaw opened the door, Shorty pushed in behind him and staggered into the middle of the room. "Where're the women?" he slurred in his best impression of a drunk. He spun around drunkenly, waving the empty whiskey bottle around, making a mental note of everything he saw, and repeated, "Where're the women?"

"There ain't no women!" Bradshaw replied angrily. "You ain't supposed to be up here. The saloon's downstairs. This is my private quarters. If you're lookin' for women, you need to go to Pratt's down the street. We don't do that kinda business here."

"You don't?" Shorty replied, still in his drunken routine. "Then I reckon the boys was playin' tricks on me. They told me all the sportin' women was up here."

"I expect they were japing you," Bradshaw said, "but no harm done. You go on back downstairs and tell Pete I said to give you a drink on the house."

"I swear, partner, you're all right," Shorty said, then turned around and staggered back toward the stairs. Once he was halfway down the steps, and sure he was out of sight, if Bradshaw was still watching from his office door, his stagger disappeared and he hurried back to the table. He saw Jesse watching him anxiously, so he responded with a wide smile and a nod of his head.

Shorty went back to his chair and sat down. Jesse swapped chairs with Clem so he could sit next to Shorty. "Did you get inside his room?" he asked.

"I sure did," Shorty replied. "He's in one big room up there. His office is the front part of the room and his bed's in the back part."

"Did you see a safe?"

Shorty grinned. "Yes, I did. He's got one of them big old safes with a key lock."

"Good, I 'preciate it when they show you where the money is," Jesse said.

The usual senseless conversation at the table continued on until the subject of supper came up and those who had been more conservative with their intake of alcohol became more interested in adjourning to the café behind the saloon to put something in their stomachs to absorb some of the whiskey.

"I drink much more of this whiskey on an empty stomach and I'm gonna have to stretch out on top of this table and go to sleep," Whitey Gribble declared.

"Me too," Jesse said. "Let's go to supper. That little gal's already turned the sign over."

"I'll go with you," LeRoy Ellis said, and got to his feet. "Anybody else?" Nobody else showed any interest.

"Me and Clem didn't get here before you were half-drunk," Shorty said. "We'll get there before they close the door. Right, Clem?"

"What about you, Alvin? You about ready to eat? You were here when we got here." Jesse asked the silent observant man because Alvin was like his brother, Jace. A little too much whiskey and the quiet fellow had a tendency to go bronco.

"I ain't quite ready to eat yet," Alvin Pope answered. "I'll be in directly."

"Be on your toes, Bonnie," Ginger commented. "Here comes three of our seven favorite customers. So watch your fanny when you're pouring their coffee."

"You don't have to tell me that," Bonnie responded, "especially that one they call Whitey. But I'm not worried about him since supper last night when his hand went roaming. I guess he thought I'd make myself hold still to keep from spilling the coffee. He found out how jumpy I am. I started filling his cup and his hand got out of the corral, and when I jumped, I poured hot coffee all over that wandering hand."

"You be careful, baby sister," Ginger warned her. "Men like that have no sense of respect for anything wearing a dress. You got stuck with Whitey last time. Let me wait on him this time."

"I'm not afraid of him," Bonnie said. "He found out it'll cost him if he doesn't behave himself with me. Besides, Will and Cullen will be coming in here any minute."

"Let me take him," Ginger said. "I want him to know he has to respect the whole family."

"Be my guest," Bonnie said, "if you enjoy dueling with a pig."

The three men sat down at a table that was a little apart from the others. And because of that, several parties already eating showed expressions of relief. When Ginger walked from the kitchen to greet the threesome, she was aware of Whitey's gaze at her every step. She felt as if she was being graded like a show pony.

"Good evening, gentlemen. What can I get you to drink?"

"Coffee," Jesse said, and was echoed by LeRoy with the same choice.

Whitey didn't answer right away, but just continued to grin at her, so she asked, "Do you want coffee, too?"

"There's a lot of things I want—" he began, but she interrupted.

"I'll give you more time to decide," she said, and abruptly walked away. In a few seconds, she was back with three cups and filled two of them. "I brought another cup, in case you decided on coffee, too," she said to Whitey.

"Yes, ma'am," Whitey said, "I'll take coffee, too. I like a woman who knows what I need. What is your name?"

She ignored the question. "Tonight we're offering a choice between roast beef and ham steak. Mashed potatoes and gravy and red beans comes with both of them."

"I'll take the roast beef," Jesse said, and once again LeRoy made the same choice. As he had done with the coffee, Whitey didn't answer right away, but continued to grin at her.

After a long void with no response other than his lecherous grin, she said, "I'll give you some time to make up your mind." To Jesse and LeRoy, she said, "While he's trying to make up his mind, I'll get your plates for you." She turned away quickly without giving anyone time to comment.

"What the hell's the matter with you, Whitey?" Jesse blurted. "Are you too drunk to make up your mind?"

LeRoy laughed and said, "He's just got his eye on that gal. Ain't that right, Whitey? He's using his deadly charm on her."

"Well, it ain't workin' too good, is it?" Jesse declared.

"She knows what I want," Whitey insisted. "She's just playin' hard to get, just like most women do. But they all come around after they play their little hard-to-get game."

"Maybe you oughta use that same deadly charm you used on that big ol' gal at Pratt's when you laid that two dollars down on top of your smooth talk," LeRoy japed.

In a couple of minutes, Ginger came back out of the kitchen carrying a big tray with three plates, all three with roast beef. She placed them on the table. "I'll bring you some biscuits. They're just coming out of the oven."

"She didn't wait for you to make up your mind," LeRoy said, pointing to the roast beef on his plate. "She made it up for you."

"See there, I told you she knows what I want," Whitey declared smugly. "And I know what she wants. She just don't wanna admit it yet."

"You mind you don't do nothin' to cause any trouble," Jesse warned him. "This is the only place to get food this good in the whole town. And I'd like to eat here as long as we're still in town."

"Hell, Jesse," Whitey responded, "we own this town."

"We did," Jesse agreed, "but I ain't so sure we do anymore."

"Why not?" LeRoy asked, genuinely surprised.

"Because of that," Jesse said, and nodded toward the back entrance. LeRoy and Whitey both turned to see Murphy, carrying a Henry rifle, and Will, carrying a double-barrel shotgun, walk in the door. "I don't care what everybody's told us, that's the *real* town marshal. I don't know where he's been, but I'm pretty sure he's a handful."

"He is a big'un, ain't he?" LeRoy remarked. "No wonder he put Jace's lights out." They watched as Murphy and Will walked through the dining room on their way to a table near the kitchen.

Seeing Jesse sitting at a table, Murphy paused to speak to him as he and Will walked past. "Blackwell," he acknowledged. "How's the grub?"

"Mighty fine," Jesse answered. "I recommend it."

"That's the same thing your brother's gettin' for supper, in case you might be wonderin'," Murphy said. "And it's one of our biggest problems with prisoners in the jail. They don't wanna go home when their time is up."

"I can understand that, Marshal," Jesse replied, calling him by the title he felt was appropriate. "It's good eatin'."

"By the way," Murphy said, "we never got around to it when you came by the jail to see Jace. But I'm sorry I wasn't in town to welcome you when you first got here. I had some business to attend to in Austin. Will tells me you've been here over a week, so it sounds like you might have some future plans for Newtown."

"Oh, no real plans," Jesse replied. "We're just passin' through on our way to San Antonio and the boys were ready for a little time off the trail. And your little town here is a nice little town to kick back in. We ended up stayin' longer than we intended and we found a nice little campsite not too far from town."

"About three miles, I'd guess," Murphy said, "with a nice cabin and a little barn, on a strong stream."

Jesse cracked a knowing smile. "Well, there was no sign that anybody lived there. So we thought there was no harm in taking advantage of it."

"No harm at all," Murphy said. "I don't blame you."

"I expect we're about ready to get back on the trail to San Antonio," Jesse said. "Ain't that right, boys?" Whitey and LeRoy both coughed up affirmative answers. "About the only thing we're waitin' on is for Jace to get outta jail."

"I might be able to help you with that, if you're wanting to get started right away," Murphy said. "I've got a little pull with the city court, and the fact of the matter is that your boys just raised a little too much hell while I was gone. So they'd just like to see you go—and good luck to ya."

"I'll tell you this," Jesse said at once, "the day you release Jace, you can count on not seein' us again the next mornin'. We'll be on our way to San Antonio."

"If I thought I could count on it, I'd release him tonight," Murphy said. "But if I did that, and one of your men caused some trouble tonight, I'll throw his butt in jail tonight. I don't tolerate no hell-raisin' like I was told happened while I was gone. How 'bout it? Are you a man of your word?"

"If I say we'll leave tonight, then we'll leave tonight," Jesse said. "Just turn my brother loose. I can't go to San Antonio without him."

"All right," Murphy said. "We've got a deal. I'll even take him some supper and tell him to meet you at Bradshaw's so you can celebrate his freedom with a drink before you leave Newtown for good."

"You're a reasonable man, Murphy, and I appreciate what a big chance you're taking. I know the mayor and the town council wouldn't be willing to go along with this deal, if they knew you're making a deal with the devil. I'd like to shake your hand." He extended his hand and Murphy shook it.

"I'll let you eat your supper now and wish you a good trip tomorrow," Murphy said. "I'll have Jace's horse down at the jail for him when I let him go." He looked at Will, who was apparently in complete shock over the conversation he just witnessed. "Come on, Will, I see Ginger standin' by our table, tappin' her foot impatiently."

"I thought maybe you wanted to sit down at that table and eat with them," Ginger said when they came to the table. "I'll get your coffee now. Roast beef or ham?"

"Ham," Murphy said, "and we'll need a plate of roast beef for a prisoner."

She looked at Will then.

"Roast beef," he said. Then as soon as she left to get the coffee, he looked at Murphy and asked, "Are you really gonna turn Jace Blackwell free tonight?"

"Right after he eats his supper," Murphy answered.

"Are you sure you wanna do that?" Will asked, still finding it hard to believe. "Do you honestly trust Jesse Blackwell to keep his word?"

"No, I can't say as I do," Murphy answered honestly. "I think he's plannin' something, but he can't do it until he's got his brother back. So we're just gonna turn him loose and try to be ready for whatever he's got in mind."

"I swear, Cullen, I don't know," Will declared.

"I don't, either," Murphy said, "but whatever he's plannin', I wanna find out sooner."

# CHAPTER 25

"Do you think Mr. Baxter or Mr. Bradshaw, or anybody on the town council, will get upset when they find out we let Jace Blackwell out of jail?" Will asked.

Murphy took a moment to finish chewing up a bigger bite of ham than normal. "I don't think Baxter or Bradshaw have any idea what we're doin' at the jail most of the time, and I think they don't really care as long as it's not interfering with their business. I doubt if Baxter even knows we put Jace in jail. Bradshaw knows, since we made the arrest in his saloon."

"Is something wrong with your supper, Will?" Ginger walked over and asked.

"No," Will said, "nothin' wrong with it. It's just fine."

"Do you feel all right? It looks like you're just picking at it," she insisted. "Because if there's something wrong with it, just tell me and I'll fix you another plate."

"There's nothing wrong with his supper," Murphy told her. "He's just got his mind workin' on something else. When he thinks hard like that, the rest of his body shuts down. He'll be all right directly. Won't you, Will?" Will looked at Ginger and nodded. "See," Murphy said, "he's all right, but I'm in desperate need of another biscuit."

She turned and went to the kitchen to fetch a couple of biscuits.

Murphy looked at Will and the image of his face when he surprised him that morning in the office returned to him. Standing behind the desk with the shotgun aimed at him, Will looked terrified at that moment. And he had to wonder now if he was doing him a grave injustice by trying to make a deputy out of him. He was never able to completely forget that he was responsible for the death of Bert Walker, the young blacksmith that he trained to be a deputy marshal. He taught him to the point where he was appointed to the position of town marshal. Will was even less qualified to take on a deputy's job than Bert had been. So Murphy was more intent on teaching Will how to keep himself alive. That was why he was encouraging him to become intimate with that double-barrel shotgun. When outnumbered in a tight space, one can do a helluva lot of damage with a shotgun.

The other three members of Jesse Blackwell's gang came into the dining room and sat down at a table next to the one where Jesse, LeRoy, and Whitey were just finishing up. Jesse waited until they had ordered their food before sitting down at their table with them. "We're goin' back into the saloon," he said. "But I'm tellin' you, we ain't gonna be doin' no heavy drinkin'. You boys come back as soon as you're finished eatin'. And I don't want you to do no heavy drinkin', either. We're gonna hit that target tonight and I don't want to be slowed down by no half-drunk clowns. Get yourselves ready for a long night of work. When we leave here tonight, we're going back to Owl Branch and pack everything up to ride. When we leave there, we ain't comin' back."

"No kiddin'?" Shorty asked. "We're leavin' here tonight?"

"Are we leavin' Jace?" Clem asked.

Jesse smiled. "Wait and see," he said, preferring to surprise them all with Jace's sudden appearance at the saloon. "I'm just telling you we've got a job tonight and I expect all hands on deck."

"Aye, aye, Captain," Shorty responded.

"So eat a good supper, 'cause breakfast is gonna be on the trail. We'll wait for you in the saloon." He left the money on the table for his, Whitey, and LeRoy's supper.

"I'll be along in a minute," Whitey said. "I wanna give the money to that gal."

"The hell you are!" Jesse fumed. "Didn't you hear a word I said? Get your mind back between your ears!"

"All right! All right!" Whitey exclaimed. "I was just gonna give her a chance to say she was sorry for bein' so rude."

The three of them went back to the saloon through the inside entrance. While Whitey and LeRoy claimed a table, Jesse went to the bar and bought a bottle of whiskey. "Just one bottle?" Pete asked, knowing they usually bought two.

"Yeah, one'll do till the rest of the boys come outta the dinin' room." He paid Pete for the bottle. "You know, Pete, I'm gonna miss that food at Irene's, but we're gonna have to be leavin' here in the next day or so."

"Is that a fact?" Pete responded, not really interested.

"Yeah, we've stayed here longer than we intended to. Time for some long hours in the saddle." Pete answered with a bored nod of his head, but Jesse continued. "I don't have to tell you about long hours, do I? You know about long hours. This place stays open just about all night, I bet."

"No, not really that bad," Pete replied. "We usually wind down soon after midnight."

"Well, that's not as bad as I thought," Jesse said. "Then I reckon it's home to the little woman and the kids."

"Shoot, no," Pete responded to that. "There ain't no little woman. Home for me is right up those stairs over there."

"Well, I'll be . . ." Jesse started. "So you spend your whole life here in the saloon. I expect you eat at Irene's Café in the back, so you don't ever leave the buildin'."

"Sure, I do," Pete said. "I go to the outhouse three or four times a day."

They both enjoyed a chuckle over that remark. "I hope you got a big room," Jesse said.

"Nope," Pete said, caught up in the conversation now that it was all about him. "I like a small room. All I need room for is my bed and a washstand. I get all the room I need behind this bar. I got the smallest room upstairs, first one at the top of the steps, so I'm not ever very far from this bar."

"No, you ain't," Jesse agreed. "Anybody else stay in them rooms up there?"

"Not right now, there ain't. Sometimes somebody will rent a room when they're gonna be here for a couple of days. Right now, it's nice and quiet up there."

"I reckon I'd better take this bottle over to the table," Jesse said, "or they'll be comin' after it."

"Here, don't forget these," Pete said, and put three glasses on the bar. Jesse stacked them so he could carry them in one hand while he carried the bottle in his other hand. Pete watched him walk away. Then he shrugged his shoulders and thought, *Maybe he ain't such a big horse's butt as I thought he was.*

"Here you are," Bonnie announced as she placed a covered plate down on the table, "one delicious supper for your hungry prisoner. You know, I'd give you coffee, too."

"I know," Murphy said, "but by the time we get it into the prisoner, it's gettin' pretty cold, so we just make a pot and Will and I have a cup, too."

"I declare," Bonnie remarked, "it's a wonder you and Will don't just float away on all the coffee you drink. I told Mama we oughta up the price on your coffee a nickel a cup and we could retire in a couple of years."

"Yeah, but then what would you do to entertain yourself, if you didn't have us to serve coffee every day?" Will asked.

"I can think of a lot of things," she replied.

"Do you need us to hang around a little longer?" Murphy asked, then nodded in the direction of the table where the three drifters were eating.

"I don't think so," Bonnie said. "Those three aren't usually any trouble. The worst one, the one they call Whitey, has already had supper and gone." She could have told him that all of the saddle tramps were better behaved in the short time since he returned and arrested one of them. But she didn't want to make Will feel bad.

"Okay, then," Murphy said, and they got up from the table and went out the back entrance. When they got back to the jail, Will put the coffeepot he had already set up on the stove to boil, while Murphy passed Jace's supper inside the cell. When the coffee was ready, Will put a cup in Jace's cell. Once the prisoner was taken care of, Murphy walked up to the stable to get Jace's horse.

"Here he is," Paul Mathers said when he led the white gelding out of the stable. "I put his saddlebags back on him, but he still ain't got a saddle. I've got an old saddle that I've been trying to sell for ten dollars. It ain't much, but it'll hold a fanny on a horse, if you wanna ask your prisoner if he wants to buy it. I'll throw the blanket in with it."

Murphy looked at the tired old saddle and said, "He'll take it." Then he reached in his pocket and pulled out a roll of bills and peeled off ten dollars.

Paul put the saddle on the horse and said, "You're gonna have to adjust the stirrups. The feller that owned it before didn't have legs as long as yours."

"We'll just leave 'em where they are. I'm afraid if I go to yankin' on those straps, they'll come off in my hand," Murphy said. "I'll just lead him back to the jail."

By the time he returned and tied the horse at the rail, Jace had finished his supper and was sitting on his bunk when Murphy walked into the cell room. He unlocked Jace's cell and left the cell door wide open. Then he backed up to the office door and said, "You can come on outta there now." Will, still not ready to believe Murphy was going to let Jace go, picked up his shotgun and held it, ready to fire.

Jace, confused, got up from his bunk, but did not move toward the open cell door. "What's goin' on?" he asked.

"You're free," Murphy answered. "Come on out of the cell."

Immediately suspicious, he replied, "The hell I am. Shot while attemptin' to escape, right? No, thanks." He sat back down on his bunk. "You might as well lock that door. I ain't goin' nowhere."

"You're free," Murphy said. "I'm releasin' you to your brother's care. Your possessions are on the office desk and your horse is tied out front."

"Oh, yeah? Then where's my brother? Why don't he come tell me to come on outta here?"

"He's waitin' for you, along with the rest of your saddle tramp friends, at Bradshaw's Saloon," Murphy said. "You're wastin' my time now. So if you don't come outta that cell right now, I'm gonna lock the door and it's gonna stay locked." Still, Jace did not move off the bunk. "All right," Murphy said. "You had your chance. Will, lock the door. He's too stupid to know he's been released."

Will started toward the cell door. "No! Wait!" Jace blurted, and ran to the open cell door. Holding on to the steel frame of the heavy oak door as if it was his refuge. "You said my horse was outside. Let me see my horse!"

"You're gonna have to come into the office to look out the window," Murphy told him. "I'm not gonna bring the damn horse in here." He turned around and walked into the office. After a long minute of indecision, Jace walked into the office, where he found Murphy sitting on the corner of his desk, and Jace's six-gun, his money, and personal possessions were in the middle of the desk. He stopped when he saw Murphy watching his reactions. "Go on and take a look out the door," Murphy said.

Jace moved slowly toward the door and looked outside. When he saw his horse standing at the hitching rail, he turned to look back at Murphy, still not certain he was not about to be executed.

"Come over to the desk and get your personal stuff," Murphy told him. "When you count your money, you're gonna come up twenty dollars short. Consider that a fine instead of a night in jail, but it ain't a loss. It bought you that fine saddle out there on your horse."

Jace walked over to the desk, giving a cautious look to Will, who was standing near the cell room door with his shotgun in hand. Then Jace switched his gaze quickly back to Murphy, who had now gotten up from the desk to give him room to reclaim his belongings. He didn't bother to count his money, but picked it up quickly, along with his pocketknife, his tobacco, and his tobacco papers and matches. Last of all, he strapped on his gun belt, then drew his Colt .45. When there was no reaction from Murphy, he smiled and broke the cylinder and spun it.

"They're in your gun belt," Murphy said. "I use .44s."

Regaining much of his cockiness when it finally occurred to him that it was a legitimate release from jail, he japed, "It'll look better if I'm shot in the back while I'm gallopin' away on my horse, right?"

"It would look good seein' you get shot in any circumstance," Murphy answered. He walked to the door and held it open for him. "Tell your brother I kept my part of the deal, so I expect him to keep his. I don't wanna see any trace of the seven of you in this town after tonight." He followed him out the door and watched as he untied his horse.

When he started to climb up on his horse, Jace paused and asked, "What kind of chicken house did you find this saddle in?" He held the stirrup up and asked, "Who the hell was ridin' it, a monkey?"

"That was what inspired me to buy it for you," Murphy answered. "Too bad the saddle shop is already closed or you could have bought yourself a saddle more suited to your taste. That reminds me. I was able to get that saddle for ten dollars. The other ten was to help repair that window you tore up."

Jace didn't say anything else while he lengthened his stirrups under the watchful eyes of Murphy and Will. When he was finished, he climbed up into the weathered old saddle and started backing his horse away. "You never know, Murphy, me and you might meet up again somewhere down the trail."

Clem, Shorty, and Alvin left the dining room and went into the saloon to join the others. They were surprised to find the other three men drinking shots from a single bottle. "Has there been a change of plan?" Clem asked.

"Yeah," Shorty commented, "I thought you said no drinkin' tonight."

"I said no heavy drinkin'," Jesse said. "You know what I mean. A couple of drinks ain't gonna hurt any of us. But like I said, if you want a couple of drinks, go ahead and do it, because we're leavin' town early tonight. We've got work to do."

"What are we waitin' for?" Clem asked. "If we ain't gonna do no drinkin', I ain't interested in sittin' around this table and talkin' about the weather. Let's go now and get started with this work we gotta do."

"We'll go pretty soon or we won't go at all," Jesse answered him, which left them all looking at each other wondering what that was supposed to mean. "All right," he said after a few minutes passed. "We'll get outta here right after Jace has a couple of shots of whiskey. I know he's gonna want 'em."

LeRoy and Alvin both realized Jesse was watching the front door of the saloon. When they followed his gaze, they saw Jace standing in the doorway, looking over the crowded room. "Jace!" Alvin exclaimed, and he and LeRoy waved their arms up in the air to attract his attention. He soon spotted the whole table waving and made his way through the after-supper crowd.

"How did you get outta jail?" Shorty wanted to know.

"Yeah," Whitey said, "they said you was gonna be in jail two or three days."

"My brother made a deal with that big-cat lawman," Jace replied. He looked at Jesse, who was smiling confidently. "Didn't you tell them about the deal you made to get me out of that jail?" When Jesse didn't answer, Jace went on explaining. "He agreed to get outta town tonight, to be gone tomorrow mornin'. Ain't that right, Jesse?"

"Yep, that's right, Jace," Jesse said. "But we have already planned to be gone tomorrow mornin', because we're gonna hit a big target tonight. When the sun comes up in the mornin', we're gonna be a long way from Newtown."

"No foolin'?" Jace asked. "What's the target?"

Jesse leaned over closer to him and whispered, "You're sittin' in it."

"Hot damn! I'll drink to that!" He grabbed Jesse's glass, poured himself a shot, and tossed it back. Jesse poured him another one and told him to take that one a little slower.

"The rest of the boys and I have made a pact to hold off on the heavy drinkin' tonight, since we've got a lot of work to do to be ready to move outta here way before sunrise." He went over the preparation already accomplished to get into the saloon's safe. He told him about Shorty's scouting mission to find the location of the saloon's money and what kind of safe it was kept in. There couldn't be a better time to hit the saloon, he emphasized, for there was no one on the second floor at the present time but Bradshaw and Pete, the bartender. And he already had a plan for the bartender. "So, whaddaya say? Have another drink, because I think you need it; then we're pullin' outta here."

Jace said he was ready to get started, so Jesse made the announcement to the rest of the gang. “All right, boys, let’s ride. There’s a lot of work to be done.”

“They’re cuttin’ out kinda early tonight,” Elmo Dillon commented to Pete when all seven of Jesse Blackwell’s gang got up from the table and walked out the front door.

“Blackwell said they was leavin’ town in the mornin’,” Pete responded.

“I can’t say I’m sorry to see ’em go, but they’ve been a lot better behaved ever since Murphy got back.”

“Don’t tell anybody I said this, but Bradshaw would like it if they stayed longer,” Pete said. “They’ve been really good for business.”

# CHAPTER 26

Another person surprised by Jesse Blackwell and his gang's early exit from town was Murphy. He expressed as much to Pete Brice when he stopped by on his early-evening walk around town.

"Yep, they left here right after they ate supper," Pete said. "They didn't buy but one more bottle of whiskey, even when the one you arrested came in. The one that acts like the leader, Jesse, he told me they was leavin' in the mornin'. So I thought they might be raisin' hell like they used to do when you was outta town."

"Yeah, I thought the same thing," Murphy said. "I told Will it might be a good idea to go ahead and put fresh water in all of the cells, just to save a little time later. I let Jesse's brother out of jail so they could go ahead and leave town. But I didn't expect them to leave this early. I just told him I didn't wanna see him in town in the mornin'."

"I was wonderin' why you let that feller outta jail so quick," Pete said. "He didn't even stay one night."

Murphy chuckled and commented, "Will thinks I'm crazy to let Jace out. Figures he's liable to be right back in his cell tonight, along with some of his friends. I thought he might be right, until I walked in here and they're already gone. I reckon

I just oughta be glad they're not gonna be in town. I'll walk the rest of the town to make sure they ain't just moved down to Pratt's or someplace else to raise hell tonight."

He walked down the street to Pratt's and stopped in to talk to Albert, even though there were no horses tied at the rail in front. "I ain't seen any of them boys this evenin'," Albert said. "Bradshaw got all their business, anyway. We'd get one or two of 'em come in here to see the women. Most of the time, it'd be that one they called Whitey. He used to come right regular to see Hazel. And that's about all we've seen of 'em since you got back."

"So you're tellin' me I'm bad for business?" Murphy japed.

"Sorta looks that way," Albert declared, then chuckled.

Back out on the street, Murphy continued his walk around the town. The only description he could think of was *peaceful.* But instead of comforting him, it gave him a feeling of uneasiness and he couldn't understand why. When he got back from Austin, he had been met with tales of wild behavior and hell-raising by Jesse Blackwell's gang. But he had seen no such signs of ill behavior since his return and the arrest of Jace Blackwell. Everyone seemed to be of the opinion that it was his return that stopped the misbehavior. But he knew that could not be the reason. They were seven hard-living drifters who showed no signs of fear or respect for law and order. And they had money to spend. That was the thing that made them different from other drifters. *Maybe,* he thought then, *it's time to replenish the money they've spent.* The notion hit him like a right-hand punch. *They're preparing to make their final visit to the town, the one that replenishes their money supply!*

*Not likely,* his common sense told him; *but highly possible,* his warrior instinct cautioned. So he decided to think it through from that perspective.

The first thing to determine would be the target for the robbery. Since there was no bank in Newtown, where would the biggest accumulation of cash be? He didn't have to think twice before answering his question. Bradshaw's Saloon would be his opinion by far. They had probably guessed the money was kept upstairs in Bradshaw's office, in a safe. And they would prefer to make the attack in the middle of the night, instead of in the daylight with people in the streets and a rifle or shotgun in every other window. They would strike at night, when the town was asleep, breaking into a nearly deserted building. Murphy knew that there was usually no one in the building at night but Bradshaw and Pete. So the most important thing to consider would be the safety of those two individuals. In that case, he knew what he had to do. But his next step at this point would be to find someplace quiet to think through it again to make sure his imagination had not taken over his common sense. He went to the only close friend he could claim.

"Howdy, Cullen. What can I do for you?" Paul Mathers greeted him. "You need your horse saddled?"

"No, thanks, Paul, I just wanted to check on him a minute. Is he in the stall? I don't see him in the corral."

"He's in the stall. I just put him in there about ten minutes ago. Anything you're worried about?" Paul asked.

"No, nothin' wrong a'tall," Murphy insisted. "It ain't been too long since I put new shoes on him and I just wanna take a look at his hooves." He went into the stall and Nosy gave him a little whinny and stuck his nose against his chest. He stroked the big bay gelding's face and ears while he tried to think like Jesse Blackwell would. He took all his men out of town early, right after they all ate a good supper. So they went back to that hideout on Owl Branch and, most likely, packed everything up in their saddlebags and their packsaddles, ready to load on their horses. Maybe they'd eat something later on and take some time to catch an hour or two of sleep before they started back to town. They'd plan to get back to town after midnight, two or three o'clock maybe. Nosy nudged him when he forgot to keep petting, so he resumed the scratching of the horse's ears. He continued until he decided there was enough of a possibility that this was actually what Jesse had in mind to do. The next step was to go to Tyson Bradshaw and convince him of the possibility and persuade him to go along with a plan to prevent the robbery.

"All right, Nosy, good talk. I needed a quiet place where I could concentrate and it was either here or the outhouse. Whaddaya think?" The bay nodded his head and whinnied.

"Everything all right, Cullen?" Paul called out when he saw him walk out of the stable.

"Yep," Murphy responded, "everything looks good."

He walked back down the street to Bradshaw's Saloon and went inside. "Is Bradshaw upstairs?" he asked Pete. When Pete said he was, Murphy asked, "Is anyone with him?" Pete said there wasn't, so Murphy headed for the stairs. When he got upstairs, he walked down to the end of the hall and knocked on the last door.

"Who is it?"

"Cullen Murphy."

There was a long moment of silence and Murphy figured Bradshaw was wondering if he was there to seek his reinstatement as the town marshal. Finally Murphy heard the lock turn and Bradshaw opened the door.

"What can I do for you, Cullen? You know that I don't have any final decision on matters the council votes on, don't you? And even if the council has voted on it, it's Eliot Baxter who announces the final decision."

"I'd be happy to discuss that with you at some other time," Murphy said. "Right now, I wanna talk to you about a possible attempt to rob your safe tonight and what we can do to prevent it."

"What are you talking about?" Bradshaw blurted in response. "Who wants to rob my safe?"

"Seven fine young men who have been takin' a holiday week or more in our fair city. In fact, they've probably outspent all your other customers combined. Now, before you get too worked up about it, I'll confess that it's all speculation at this point, but it makes so much sense that I feel some action must be taken to prevent it. And I will be taking that action whether you think it's a real threat or not. It's just that I know it will be a lot easier to accomplish my goals—which are the prevention of your robbery and the loss of your life—if you're working with me."

"Come in, Cullen, and tell me why you think all that's true." Bradshaw backed up, pulling the door open wide. Murphy came inside the office and laid out all the things that were going on that pointed toward a farewell robbery of the saloon. He started with the fact that he had released Jace Blackwell from jail early, and Jesse agreed to be gone from Newtown tomorrow morning. "It is my belief that he intends to be far away from Newtown when the sun comes up in the morning, and he intends to have the contents of your safe with him.

"So, like I said," Murphy continued, "this is all speculation, and I could be dead wrong. And if I'm wrong, you're gonna be out a little comfort tonight and some loss of sleep. But if I'm right and we don't do anything to prevent it, you're gonna be out a helluva lot of money and possibly your life."

"I'm gonna trust your judgment," Bradshaw said immediately. "We'll do whatever you say is best."

"Fine," Murphy said. "We'll start by keeping as few people as possible from knowing anything about what's going to happen here tonight. If we're lucky, it'll be over before the town finds out."

Bradshaw went over to a table behind his desk, where a bottle and some glasses sat on a tray. "I'm going to be honest with you," he confessed. "I need a drink." He poured one, then looked at Murphy and paused.

Murphy waved him off and said, "Thanks just the same, but I wanna keep my head clear tonight, all night."

Bradshaw tossed his drink back and said, "I want you to know I appreciate your attitude about this. I should have been suspicious about this myself. Earlier when I came upstairs to my office, one of them followed me up here, and I didn't even know he was behind me till I opened the door. He was drunk. Well, at least I thought he was, but he just pushed his way on inside and looked the room over. I know he stared at the safe. Said he was told there were women up here."

That incident fit right in with Murphy's idea of what Jesse Blackwell and his men were planning. "You say he stared at the safe?" Bradshaw said that was a fact, so Murphy turned to take a good look at it as well. "Most likely checkin' to see what kind of lock it has and whether they might need black powder to blow it. Of course, my guess is that they're hoping to capture you and force you to open it. For that reason, I want you out of here tonight. Take your money and any valuables you keep in that safe and put them in a suitcase or something we can carry. And leave the safe open. No need in lettin' them damage it when there ain't nothin' in it."

"I don't know where I could take it, where it would be safe," Bradshaw complained.

"Take it to the jailhouse and you spend the night in there with it," Murphy said. "Now that we let Jace Blackwell out, there ain't anybody in the cells. We can lock you in one of the cells and give you the key, and Will Pickens will be on guard duty with his shotgun. Hell, you can even have a shotgun in the cell with you, if you want one."

"That sounds pretty safe to me," Bradshaw said, "even though I'd rather have you guarding me."

"I'm gonna be busy back at the saloon, tryin' to keep your office from gettin' shot up and keepin' Pete from wakin' up and walkin' into a hailstorm of bullets. Where does he sleep?"

"He's upstairs, too," Bradshaw said, "first room at the top of the stairs."

"Maybe we oughta put him in jail, too," Murphy said. "I wanna look this building over real good to try to guess where they might try to break in. Of course, the best place to wait for 'em might be right here behind this safe. We know they'll be comin' here."

"Should I be packing up the stuff in the safe and getting out of here?" Bradshaw wondered.

"No, there's no big hurry," Murphy assured him. "They're not gonna be hittin' this place until two or three in the mornin', I reckon. So you and Pete can just close up as usual, then go to the jail instead of your rooms."

Murphy went over a few more things he wanted to check on and answered a dozen questions from Bradshaw, who was all in for whatever Murphy said by that time. When he figured he had covered everything he could think of, he told Bradshaw that he was sorry for interrupting his evening. And Bradshaw said he would have never forgiven him had he not. "I'll be back to check on the building later on," Murphy said. "I've gotta go tell Will about the exciting night he's gonna have. I haven't had a chance to tell him about what we've got planned."

"He might resign his position," Bradshaw joshed. "I know I would."

"He might," Murphy allowed. "Well, I'll check with you later." He went to the door and stopped when he thought of something else. "You know, I told you at the first that I had no real proof that this robbery attempt is even gonna happen. If that's the case, I apologize in advance for the inconvenience."

"Whaddaya mean?" Will exclaimed. "Put him in jail for what!"

"For his own protection," Murphy answered. "I ain't certain, but I'm pretty sure Jesse Blackwell and his gang are plannin' on robbin' Bradshaw's tonight. So just in case, Bradshaw and Pete are gonna come here after closin' and bring the contents of the safe with 'em."

"And they're gonna stay all night?" Will asked, finding it hard to believe.

"That's the plan. It'll give 'em a chance to see how clean you keep the prisoners' cells," Murphy joked.

"I better go check 'em over again," Will said, "in case I missed something."

"I wouldn't worry about it," Murphy said, "that ain't gonna be the biggest thing on his mind." He went on then to fill Will in on what he suspected was Jesse Blackwell's plan.

Will listened with wide-eyed interest. When Murphy was finished, Will's first question was: "Are you trying to commit suicide? You're plannin' to wait there, by yourself, to arrest seven gunslinger outlaws?"

"I never said anything about arrestin' them," Murphy replied. "And besides, I don't expect all seven of them will come upstairs into the office. Somebody will have to watch the horses. They'll have packhorses, as well as the ones they're ridin', so maybe two of them will watch the horses. Maybe a couple to watch the front and back of the saloon. If so, there would only be three that came inside to take care of Bradshaw and rob the safe. Since I'll be the one who really has the element of surprise, I figure that's like havin' an extra man with me." He didn't know who would actually break into the office, but he was betting it would be Jesse and Jace and one other.

He didn't tell Will, or Bradshaw for that matter, but his mind was operating as if at war. So his objective would be to destroy the enemy, more so than to arrest them. If they tried to surrender, he would accept it and arrest them, but they would have to act fast, because he did not intend to waste time and the advantage of surprise by demanding their surrender.

"I think you'll need me in that saloon with you," Will volunteered.

"I appreciate your offer, but I need someone I can depend on to guard Bradshaw and Pete Brice here in the jail. Bradshaw will have the contents of his safe with him, so I'd feel better with you and your shotgun to take care of them. The one thing I don't know is how the four men left watchin' the horses and the break-in entrance are gonna react when they hear the gunfire—and whoever went up there to get Bradshaw don't come back down. When they see it was an ambush, will they run? Especially if I show up downstairs? Or will they make a try for the money? We'll just have to wait and see. But if one of 'em is smart enough to think we mighta put Bradshaw and his money in the jail, then I know that you're here to protect him."

His remarks were primarily to boost Will's self-confidence and his ego; this way, he wouldn't feel he was not trusted to take an active role in the anticipated shoot-out. Murphy couldn't guess how the outlaws waiting outside would react when the planned robbery went sour. If he was forced to bet on it, he would probably bet that they would just run. And that would be a win for the town because they would not likely return.

"Which cells are you gonna put Bradshaw and Pete in?" Will asked.

"Doesn't make much difference," Murphy answered, "one and two, I reckon."

"Right," Will replied, and went back to the cell room to take another inspection of those two cells.

Murphy had to smile when he thought, *You'd think we're getting an inspection by the state prison commission.* "I'm gonna go take a walk around the outside of the saloon again," he called through the open cell room door. "I'll be right back."

He went back around the back of the saloon and walked around the dining-room addition. He figured they would leave their horses there while the robbery team went inside the saloon. It would be too much trouble to break in the café addition, because they'd still have to break in the door between the dining room and the saloon. That would also make a more difficult exit in the event a quick escape was called for. So the logical entrance would be from the alley between the saloon and the hardware store. There was only one window on the first floor on that side of the saloon and it was high up the wall. Standing beneath it, he could not quite reach the windowsill, but he knew he could reach it if he was on his horse. So he went inside to take a look at it.

Inside, he looked along the wall on that side and saw that there were no windows at all. So he walked by the bar and told Pete he wanted to check something in the back room for Mr. Bradshaw, but didn't stop long enough for any more explanation than that. He went through the door in the back of the room and found himself in a large storage room with extra tables and chairs and various other items. The thing that caught his attention, however, was the small window high up the wall, so he went to stand under it. *I could get through that window,* he thought. He envisioned the bulky torso of Jace Blackwell and decided he could, too. The window was obviously for ventilation only. He was surprised when he reached up and found that it was unlocked. *That's careless.* Then he took notice of a metal frame around the window with brackets to hold two metal pins, and it occurred to him that the frame was designed to hold a heavy grill. The unlocked window was not an act of carelessness; somewhere in all this jumble of furniture and boxes, there had to be a heavy grill of some kind. Whoever removed it didn't go far to hide it. He found it under a table about ten feet from the window.

So this was the entry point for that night's raid on the safe. The robbery was definitely on—and not the product of an overworked imagination.

# Chapter 27

When it was time, Murphy made his late walk around the town to check on all the businesses and make sure that the town was buttoned up good for the night. As usual, the saloons were the only sign of any activity, and that was winding down as well. Since there had been no official reinstatement of his status, he was merely keeping Town Marshal Will Pickens company.

When they had completed their rounds and everything was peaceful, they returned to the jail and Murphy took one of the double-barrel shotguns out of the rack behind the desk and filled the pockets of his coat with shells for the gun. As always, when not sure what kind of shots he would be required to make, he took the Henry rifle as well. With a full cartridge belt, he had ammunition for both his Henry and his Colt, since they both fired a .44 cartridge.

"You ready?" he asked Will, and Will said he was.

So they walked back to Bradshaw's Saloon, where Pete was cleaning up the bar and some of the tables. "Ready to close up?" Murphy asked.

"Yep," Pete answered, now aware of the situation. "That's about all I plan to do tonight. I was gettin' ready to go upstairs and see if Mr. Bradshaw needs any help with his bags."

"We'll go with you," Murphy said.

So the three of them went upstairs to the office, where they found Bradshaw closing up a large trunk.

"I got everything in the one trunk," Bradshaw said, "but I'm afraid it's gonna be a little bit heavy."

"That's all right," Murphy retorted, "we've got Will and Pete here to walk that trunk down to the jail. How 'bout you, are you ready to go to jail?"

"I never thought I'd ever hear anybody ask me that," Bradshaw responded. He looked at Murphy with a look of concern and motioned toward his desk with his hand. "I took everything off my desk that might break easily. I left the safe door open, like you suggested. I didn't know if I should take those pictures off the wall or not. Where are you going to place yourself? Behind the desk? Or maybe behind the safe?"

"I'm not gonna be in here," Murphy answered. "I decided I'm gonna be downstairs in that supply room, or whatever it is, behind the barroom. That's where they're plannin' on comin' into the saloon. There's a little ventilation window in the wall big enough to crawl through, and they musta got in that room and unlocked the window and took the steel grill off. That's their way in and I wanna be there to greet 'em."

When Bradshaw just stared at him, wide-eyed, and mouth open, Murphy added, "I thought about sitting up here in your office and waiting for them to come upstairs for a shoot-out, but that woulda shot your office to pieces."

Finally finding his voice, Bradshaw insisted, "But you told me to empty the safe and leave the door on it open, so they wouldn't try to open it with black powder; to pack anything valuable in the trunk and take it to the jail."

"Right! That's in case they get by me and get up here to your office. Hopefully, they won't make a mess lookin' for something that's obviously not here."

"Should I lock the door?" Bradshaw asked then.

"I wouldn't bother," Murphy replied. "Matter of fact, you might even leave it partially open. Because, like I said, if they get by me, they'll know you were expectin' 'em. If the door is closed, they'd probably just kick it open."

Bradshaw finally saw a clear picture of what Murphy was going to do and realized the risk he was taking. "I know the little window you're talking about in the storeroom," he said. "And you intend to shoot one of them when he tries to come in through that window. If you shoot one when he comes in the window, no one else will try to crawl in the window. And there'll still be six of them to go and break in somewhere else."

"That's a fact," Murphy said. "That's why it would be a mistake to shoot the first one to come through the window. Ideally, I'd like to let three or four crawl through the window before I start shootin'."

"I swear, Cullen," Will commented, "that sounds like a dangerous way to try to stop 'em." Like Bradshaw, he was also under the impression that Murphy was going to wait for them in the office. "Don't you think you'd have more cover behind the desk with your shotgun when they came in the door?"

"Maybe so," Murphy replied, "but you'd have to shoot the first one to come in the door and then nobody else would come in. It's better to have a little room for more than one person to come in, and there ain't enough room in here to do that. We might end up in a game of hide-and-seek all over the saloon. You ready to go?"

Bradshaw answered that he was.

Then Murphy said, "All right, Mr. Bradshaw, you're under arrest." He picked up the trunk to test its weight. "I believe you boys can handle that all right." So he set it down and picked up his rifle and shotgun while Bradshaw held the door for Will and Pete to carry the trunk. When they got out in the hall, Bradshaw closed the door; then remembering, he opened it slightly.

When they got downstairs, Murphy let them out the front door and stood on the boardwalk and watched them walk the trunk down the deserted street. He remained there until he saw them go inside the jail; then he closed the doors and put the heavy beam in place across them. "Well, I've got a little work to do," he announced, and went back to pick up the lamp that Pete left burning on the end of the bar. Then he went into the storeroom behind the barroom to arrange a "corral" to hold his expected guests. The room was filled with tables and chairs and odd pieces of furniture, as well as boxes of several different sizes.

By dragging the different objects around, he made a small enclosure under the window that extended about halfway to the door into the saloon, before he blocked it off with a stack of boxes. Once he had his corral fixed to his satisfaction, he cleared a path behind one side of it so that he could move quickly back and forth. He brought four sets of handcuffs, all that he had, and placed them where he could get to them quickly.

When he had done all he could think to do, he went back into the saloon to the little iron stove near the bar, where Pete made his coffee. There were enough dying embers to quickly bring the stove back to life, so he went to the pump and put some water in the coffeepot and made a small pot. Figuring that he was about as ready as he could be, he waited for it to boil. When it was ready, he poured a cup, pulled the pot off the stove, and returned to the storeroom.

A glance at his watch told him it was about a quarter after one, so he loaded two shells in his shotgun and stood it up against one of the tables that formed his corral. Then he cranked a cartridge into the chamber of his rifle and laid it on a flat box, where it could be quickly reached. Loaded for whatever, he sat down in one of the chairs next to his corral, turned the lamp out, and drank his coffee.

His intention was to stay awake, but he realized that he must have dozed off when he was suddenly jolted alert by a sound outside the window. The storeroom was totally dark except for a path of faint light from the window. The sound he had heard was the raising of the window, and now he could hear whispered exchanges between several voices below the window. Then he heard a closer voice: "Ain't no problem. Hold the horse still till I get my feet on the windowsill. Let me get down and tell Jesse to come on and I'll guide him down to the floor."

Murphy lifted himself up slowly from the chair and took the shotgun in hand. Remaining in a crouch, he could see Clem Baine through the cracks in the side of his corral. With his back toward him, Clem was reaching up to the window to assist Jesse. "I gotcha," Clem said softly. "We got a nice little landin' spot. Who's behind you?"

Once on the floor, Jesse answered, "Jace. I told him he was too big, but he wanted to be in on the stickup, in case we have to persuade Bradshaw to open that safe."

"Well, we better get ready to give him a hand—so he don't fall on us," Clem said, and they both turned toward the window. "I thought LeRoy was gonna come with us. He's the one who knows how to use the black powder."

"He's comin'," Jesse said, "right after Jace."

With nothing between them but a stack of chairs and tables, Murphy listened intensely while holding his shotgun in a ready position. He heard Jace when he dropped to the floor. *That's three,* he thought. *I ain't sure I can handle four.* But at this point, he knew there was no other choice.

A few moments later, LeRoy Ellis joined them. "I swear," he commented, "it's dark as unwashed sin in here. Which way's the door?"

"It's that way, where the light from the window is leadin'," Clem said. "At least that's where the door's supposed to be."

"There ain't nothin' that way but a pile of junk," Jace said. "You musta been drunk when you came in here to fix that window."

"Doggone it," Clem insisted, "it *is* in that direction." He went to the end of the light path on the floor and peered through the junk. "I see it. They just piled all this stuff up in front of it."

The other three moved up behind him. "I told you," Clem said.

"Just unbuckle those gun belts and let 'em drop on the floor, if you want to walk outta here alive," the calm, steady voice advised.

Jace Blackwell recognized the voice immediately and didn't hesitate. "Murphy!" he uttered, and spun around, drawing his .45 and firing blindly in the direction he thought the voice came from. Clem drew his weapon as well and followed Jace's line of fire, blindly shooting through an old chair. For their indiscretion, they each got blown over backward by barrel one and barrel two of Murphy's shotgun.

"Murphy," Jesse said, now that he could see where Murphy was standing. "You've killed my brother, but you've shot both barrels of that shotgun. Can you reload faster than I can draw my Colt?"

"Unbuckle the gun belts, both of you, if you want to live," Murphy said, and dropped the shotgun.

"I don't think so," Jesse said, and reached for his revolver, only to stagger backward and fall when Murphy grasped the Henry rifle on the table beside him and fired the round already loaded in the chamber. LeRoy, forced to jump out of Jesse's way, got off a shot that was wide of the mark before Murphy put a round in the middle of his chest.

With four of the gang of seven lying dead on the storeroom floor, Murphy was immediately concerned about the three outside the saloon. And when he heard several rifle shots fired, he rushed to open the door in time to see two of the outlaws galloping down the middle of Front Street, leading a string of horses. When he saw a man running toward him from the other side of the hardware store, he cranked another round into the Henry and prepared to shoot.

"Cullen! Hold your fire! It's me!"

"Will? What are you doin' out here?"

"Tryin' to help you," Will answered. "It didn't make any sense, you goin' up against seven of them."

"Well, I didn't see but two riders ridin' away with their horses," Murphy said. "So there's one more around here somewhere."

"He's over there under the window," Will said. "He was trying to go in that window after he heard the shootin' goin' on inside."

"Well, I'll be . . ." Murphy started, ". . . and with a rifle, too."

"I didn't shoot him, Joel did." He turned and motioned toward the back corner of the hardware store. "They're all down, Joel, come on in," he called out, and Joel Trout, the blacksmith, trotted out from behind the building. Turning back to Murphy, Will said, "When you left the jail this evenin' to take another look around the saloon, I went to tell Joel what you were plannin' to do and you might need help. He volunteered, and said to come wake him up if I needed him."

"Well, I'll be . . ." Murphy started again. "I 'preciate the help from both of you."

They walked over to the window to make sure the man Joel shot was dead. He was, and Will said, "He's the one they called Whitey. We're gonna need a wagon to carry the bodies to Doc's funeral parlor. There's four inside, right?"

"That's right," Murphy said, "both of the Blackwells and I don't know the names of the other two."

"So two of them got away," Will said. "What are we gonna do about them?"

"I don't know, Marshal," Murphy answered. "Whaddaya wanna do about 'em? We got the leaders, and I don't expect we'll ever see the two that got away again. That's pretty much what we were after, wasn't it, to get rid of them?"

"Yes, sir, Deputy," Will replied in kind, "I reckon we got the job done."

"I expect it would be a good idea to carry those four out of the saloon," Murphy said. "They're probably messin' up the floor in that storeroom pretty bad already."

“We could use my wagon to put ’em in,” Joel offered, “but my horse is in Paul’s stable.”

“Let’s tote ’em outside, then decide what to do with ’em,” Murphy said. So they followed him back into the front door of the saloon and into the storeroom. The two Blackwell brothers were the biggest mess, one having had a close encounter with a shotgun blast, the other a Henry rifle. There was no necessity to check for signs of life. When Murphy checked Clem and LeRoy, he found no pulse in either of them. So all four bodies were carried out to join Whitey in front of the saloon.

It had been some time since the eruption of gunfire had awakened the town. So here and there, lights appeared in the windows of some of the buildings. And before long, a few brave souls were attracted to the repulsive scene in front of Bradshaw’s Saloon. Two of the first to appear were Tyson Bradshaw and Pete Brice. Bradshaw was still in possession of Will’s key to the jailhouse office, which he said he would return when he went back for his trunk.

To Murphy’s surprise, Eliot Baxter showed up, with his nightshirt tucked into his trousers and bedroom slippers on his feet. After Bradshaw told him the whole story of Blackwell’s planned robbery, and Murphy’s role in the prevention of it, Baxter felt obliged to congratulate Murphy on a job well done. Unable to forget the Ward Hatcher affair, however, he said, “I suppose you’ll be leaving town again to track down the two that escaped.”

“No, I hadn’t planned to,” Murphy replied. “I figured what we wanted was to get the Blackwell gang out of town. Looks to me like we pretty much accomplished that. I don’t expect we’ll ever see those two that got away back in this county again.” He paused to watch Baxter’s expression. “Why? Do you want me to track those two?”

“No,” Baxter responded at once. “No, you’re absolutely right, they won’t be back. Good job.”

By the time Irene Floyd and her daughters came to the café

to start breakfast, Doc Ennis had arrived with his wagon, so they were brought up-to-date by the earlier spectators. Bonnie couldn't resist informing her sister that if she wanted to say goodbye to Whitey Gribble, he was waiting in the wagon for her. Seeing Murphy and Will carrying Bradshaw's trunk back to the saloon, Irene told them not to wait for the dining room's usual opening time. She told them to come in as soon as they were ready, and if the pancakes weren't ready, they could at least have some coffee until they were.

The sun was barely visible over the tops of the buildings on Front Street in Newtown when Cullen Murphy and Will Pickens started the new day at Irene's Café. This morning, they were joined by Joel Trout, since Irene made sure that he was invited to a free pancake breakfast in appreciation for his contribution to the defense of Bradshaw's safe.

"Tyson was keeping my savings in that safe, too," she informed them.

"She might have more money in my safe than I do," Bradshaw said, walking up in time to hear her remark. "Mind if I join you?"

"Please sit down, Mr. Bradshaw," Will spoke up right away. "I would like to resign from my position as acting town marshal and recommend that you reinstate Cullen Murphy as town marshal in my place. And I request that you urge Mr. Baxter to call for a meeting of the town council to discuss it right away."

"As vice president of the town council, I must call this an emergency meeting of the council, and in the absence of the president, I hereby rule that Cullen Murphy shall be reinstated as the Newtown town marshal, effective immediately. All in favor, say *aye.*"

Everybody in the dining room, including Irene and her daughters, shouted, "Aye!"

**TURN THE PAGE FOR AN EXCITING PREVIEW!**

**JOHNSTONE COUNTRY. WHERE YOU CAN'T KEEP TROUBLE FROM VISITING, BUT YOU DON'T HAVE TO OFFER IT A CHAIR.**

Fate—and a couple of murders—in Three Forks, Idaho, lead one innocent man on a quest for justice, redemption—and revenge—in this blazing new series from the bestselling Johnstones . . .

Once, Logan Trent was a well-respected man. A decent and hard-working deputy sheriff in the town of Three Forks, Idaho, his life changed forever when his rival for the affections of a beautiful saloon owner was found murdered in cold blood. And Logan was the obvious suspect. Despite no evidence—no arrest, no conviction—everyone believed he did it. So, Logan quit his job and left. Bought a saloon in Montana. Tried to forget the past . . .

But the past never forgets. And neither do Logan's enemies.

When Logan learns that his brother's been murdered, the nightmare comes rushing back. After all these years, Logan must return to Three Forks to console his grieving father—and find his brother's killer. But on the way, he's ambushed and forced into a deadly gunfight. One of the attackers is a Donovan, the family of the man Logan was accused of killing. Seems the whole clan is waiting for his return—and want him deader than dead.

Now, Logan has one last chance to clear his name. And no way out—without spilling more blood.

# Chapter 1

Logan Trent poured whiskey for a prospector named Wiley Phillip, then corked the bottle and reached under the bar for his sawed-off twelve gauge, or his "Peacekeeper" as he called the old stagecoach gun, which had been used by many shotgun messengers here in Big Rock in the shadow of the Absaroka Mountains, Montana Territory.

It had cut many a man in two and in even smaller pieces. Amazing how much damage a seasoned shotgun messenger could inflict with such a weapon when the chips were down, and it was his job to keep "his" strongboxes out of the hands of trail scum.

Wiley Phillip saw the move and grinned, showing a mouthful of whiskey- and tobacco-stained teeth. He'd seen the move before and knew that trouble was on the horizon. Logan owned the Stray Dog here in Big Rock, having purchased the saloon nearly five years ago, and he was known to cut trouble off at the pass, so to speak.

Or nearly cut it in two with a double load of double-aught buckshot to the belly.

Wiley glanced over his shoulder. Trouble was indeed on the horizon, for a big Swedish woodcutter, Lars Holstrum, had nabbed one of Logan's bar girls, pulled her onto his lap, and was nuzzling her neck against Miss Clara's ever-loudening protestations. She struggled to free herself from the woodcutter's brawny arms, but Holstrum was a big, powerful man. He was also drunk, as he usually was, and wasn't of a mind to let the girl go.

Wiley returned his gaze to Trent and saw rage building in the saloon owner's eyes. Logan Trent was a big man, too, nearly six and a half feet tall, none of it tallow, and he ruled the Stray Dog with an iron fist . . . er, with the iron Peacemaker, which still had old bloodstains on it from past altercations. Truly, the twelve-gauge had known violence in its day. Wiley Phillip had a feeling, judging by the ever-building darkness in Logan's eyes, that it was going to get another round of it soon.

Sure enough, when Clara squealed, "Oh, won't you please leave me alone—you're *hurting* me!" out came the Peacemaker from under the bar, and the apron-clad Logan, dark-haired and dark-eyed, with a severely chiseled, handsome face, pushed through a swing door to Wiley's left, and marched over the table where the big Swede was molesting Logan's eighteen-year-old serving girl. He held the savage popper straight down along his right leg.

He stopped six feet from the Swede's table and said quietly but tightly, "All right, Holstrum, you've had your fun—let her up."

The Swede pulled his bearded face out from the girl's neck, where he'd been nibbling the girl's right ear, and said with casual defiance and a jeering grin, "Nah. I don't want to." He laughed and went back to chewing the horrified and repulsed girl's ear.

"I don't care what you want," Logan said with quiet menace. "You either do it, or I'll smash your face in. If that doesn't work, you'll get buckshot to the belly, and you will not be walking out of here."

The smile left the Swede's bearded face. There were maybe a dozen other drinkers in the rough-hewn place. Now they all went quiet, swiveling their heads toward the scene of the trouble, until there were only the sounds of Clara's protestations.

The Swede glared up at Logan.

Logan glared down at the Swede.

Holstrum flared his nostrils, face reddening with rage. He said in his thick Swedish accent, "Who in the hell are you, Trent? No one knows a damn thing about you. You show up five years ago on that big roan of yours and you don't say a damn thing about yourself!"

"If I wanted you to know, you'd know. Now, let her go."

"You know what I think?" Holstrom said. "I think you're *hunted*! I think you're a *wanted man* hiding out in Montana!"

"You think what you want, but if you don't let that girl off your lap, you're going to get your face caved in."

The Swede's lips quivered as he hardened his jaws.

He threw the girl off his lap and straight into Logan, who dropped his shogun as he caught her. The Swede leaped out of his own chair, charging like a bull buffalo at Logan. Logan threw the girl into a chair an eye blink before the Swede, who was two inches taller than Logan, barreled into the saloon owner, knocking him flat on his back onto a table that was vacated quickly by the two miners who'd been sitting there, playing poker.

Holstrum slammed a ham-sized fist into Logan's face, scrambling the saloon owner's brains. The Swede pulled his fist back and slammed it forward once more, but it got only halfway to its target before Logan, suppressing his aching head and blurred vision, reached up and wrapped both hands around the miner's big fist, stopping it. The Swede's gray eyes widened in renewed rage, but he yelled out in pain when Logan head-butted him twice and slammed a knee into the man's groin—maybe not a sporting move, but then this was no sport.

It was survival.

The Swede groaned and rolled off the table to the floor.

Trent bounded off the table and picked the Peacekeeper off

the floor. He turned to see Holstrom bounding toward him once more, roaring like a gut-shot griz. Logan flipped the shotgun around and slammed the butt into his opponent's face. The man's nose and mouth exploded like a ripe tomato.

The Swede staggered backward, clutching his nose in both big paws. As he did, Logan slammed the shotgun's butt against the man's forehead. That dropped Holstrom like a poleaxed bull. He lay groaning, writhing, glaring up at the saloon owner.

Logan flipped the Peacemaker again, drew back both rabbit-ear hammers, and aimed down the side-by-side barrels at Holstrom, the barrels a foot from the man's face.

"*No!*" the Swede begged, turning his head to one side, stealing himself for two rounds of double-aught buck.

Logan started to draw both triggers back.

"*Logan!*" a man shouted.

The saloon owner looked up to see the Lonely Bear town marshal standing between the saloon's batwing doors, gazing warningly at Logan.

The lawman, Lou Gentry—tall, gray-mustached, gray-headed under his high-crowned black Stetson—gave his head a single, admonishing wag.

"Turn around, Lou," Logan said. "You don't want to see this. Not gonna be *pretty*!"

Gentry released the batwings and walked into the saloon.

He stopped several feet from where Logan stood still holding the shotgun's barrels three feet from the terrified Swede's bearded, bloody face. He looked at Logan. He didn't say anything, didn't even shake his head again. He just stared at the saloon owner, who after several seconds gave a frustrated chuff, depressed the shotgun's hammers, and raised the gun until its barrels were aimed at the ceiling.

He kept his eyes on the Swede, whose nose was turned sideways on his face, and said through gritted teeth, "Get the hell out of here. You ever come back, not even Gentry will be able to save you."

Gentry said to Holstrom, "I won't even try."

The big Swede gained his feet heavily, miserably, and grabbed his whiskey shot off the table, threw it back, and slammed the glass back down hard. Glaring at Logan and Gentry, he set his feathered canvas hat on his head, then stomped across the still silent saloon and through the batwings.

Immediately, a low roar of conversation rose from the other drinkers.

Gentry looked at Trent and jerked his head toward the bar. "Buy ya a drink, Logan?"

"I'll buy."

Logan pushed through the swing door, set the shotgun on a shelf behind the bar, and, as Gentry leaned over the bar and entwined his hands on top of the scarred mahogany, filled two shot glasses, and slid one to the aging lawman he considered a friend. Gentry lifted the glass, said, "That was close," and threw back the entire shot."

Clara came to the bar, set her tray on it, and said, "Thanks, Logan."

"Why don't you take the rest of the night off? I can handle it to closing."

"Thanks."

When she was climbing the stairs, Gentry glanced at her clad in her corset and bustier, and said to Logan, "Pretty girl. Ever seen others of that cut . . . from where you came from?"

"Oh, sure, sure." Logan smiled, knowing the lawman was probing him for secrets.

"Where is that, Logan?"

Logan shrugged and refilled the lawman's shot glass. "Here an' there."

"You sure keep your cards close to your chest, Logan."

"Never thought of it that way." Logan threw back his whiskey.

"Oh, I think you have, Logan. And it's not just because you're a man of few words."

"Why, then?"

Gentry grimaced, deeply curious. "Can't figure it out."

Logan left the lawman to pour drinks. When he returned, he finished his shot and refilled both their glasses.

"I'll figure it out," Gentry said.

"It's not worth it, Lou."

"I got me a feelin' it is. Just to satisfy my curiosity, of course." The marshal raised his shot glass in salute and threw back the shot.

Steeling his voice a little, Logan said, "Let it go, Lou. You'd just be bored."

"Ah, another clue." Gentry sipped his whiskey. "When a man rides to town on a fine horse, buys a saloon, and doesn't seem to have a story—at least, none he wants to talk about—it makes people curious. Makes people think he's got a past he's runnin' from."

"People should mind their own business." Logan threw back his shot to try to temper his annoyance. He didn't like sharing much about himself with anyone—not even with his only friend in town. Gentry was a former cowboy and shotgun rider before age caught up to him and he became the lawman of a small, mostly peaceful town in the Montana mountains.

Logan knew Gentry's story, but that didn't mean Gentry needed to know his.

Gentry refilled his glass from the bottle on the bar, removed his hat, and set it on the bar beside him. He winced and scratched the back of his head. "Seems to me, if I remember right—I've had the memory of an old man for years—when I was trailing owlhoots over in Idaho, I heard a story about some trouble down in the Valley of the Three Forks of the Wolf River."

Logan just stared at the man, squeezing his empty shot glass. Warm blood rose in his face.

"What was it now?" Gentry said, scratching the back of his head. "I don't think I got the whole story, just that some deputy sheriff was accused of killin' some young man from a wealthy ranching family over a woman in a town called Three Forks. He went to trial, but the jury said they couldn't convict him because they didn't have enough evidence. I guess everyone in the county figured he did it because this deputy and the dead man were blood enemies. Feelin' disgraced and wantin' to spare his family further scandal, this deputy fled town soon after the trial."

The lawman shook his head as if he didn't know what to make of the tale.

"Crazy story," Logan said.

"A sad one, too. Especially if he was innocent with everyone believing him guilty."

Logan sighed fatefully and set his empty glass on the bar. He set his Stetson on his head. "Reckon I best get back to my evening rounds. Have a good night, Logan."

He tapped his knuckles on the bar and headed for the batwings.

"You, too, Lou."

The lawman had taken only two steps when he stopped, turned back around, and pulled a small leaf of yellow paper out of his suit pocket. "Almost forgot—you got a telegram earlier. Ain't it a coincidence? It came from a place called Three Forks in the Idaho Territory. Imagine that!"

He laughed as he set the note on the bar, then started once more for the swing doors.

Trent stared down at the penciled telegram addressed to Logan D. Trent of Big Rock, Montana Terr.

LOGAN, YOU'RE NEEDED AT HOME. TROUBLE—DAD.

# CHAPTER 2

Three days later, in Hell's Canyon in southwestern Montana Territory, Logan sat astride his big roan, Wolf, so named because the horse had been born on Logan's family ranch in the Wolf Mountains near Three Forks. He stared down into the muddy offshoot of the Jefferson River, which he and Wolf had traversed minutes ago. He and the horse were soaked, but despite the river's strong current Wolf had gotten them across safely.

As soon as they'd gained the opposite bank, Wolf lifted his head high and whinnied. Logan knew from experience of fording previous waters with the roan what was about to happen. He leaped off the horse quick as lightning, landing flat-footed, just before the big stallion shook himself so violently, ridding himself of the river water, that he shook off his saddle as well as his bridle. Logan's saddle scabbard in which lay his Winchester "Yellowboy" repeater went flying with the saddle, saddlebags, and bedroll wrapped in his rain slicker.

Logan turned to the horse, the light of mischief in the mount's eyes, and said, "Doggone it, Wolf—why do you always have to do that?" The horse took one step forward, whinnied shrilly, and did it again, showering Logan with water from his soaked roan hide.

Logan swabbed his big, chiseled face spiked with a three-day growth of dark-brown beard stubble with his sleeve. He knew how the horse felt, however. His own denims, a good strip of his shirt, and his vest were soaked from just above his cartridge belt. His pants hung heavy on him, clinging uncomfortably. The Jefferson was deep, and it flowed rapidly, violently in places, so when horse and rider had plunged into it from the bank on the opposite side, the current had swept them downstream as the roan had fought his way to freedom. They'd been in the river for several long minutes, however—always a bit of a harrowing maneuver. Logan wouldn't have tried it with any other mount, but only with a tall, tough, determined stallion like Wolf.

The horse turned to him now, craning his neck, and that devilish glint remained in his eyes. There was pride there, too—oh, make no mistake! He was a ham, Wolf was, and he enjoyed showing off for his beloved rider, who loved him back in every way.

"You suppose I can put your saddle back on now, ya ornery cayuse?" Logan said with fake frustration. "We best keep movin'." He glanced at the sky in which clouds were building. "I think we're gonna get rain in a coupla—"

Logan cut himself off. Just then he spied a foreboding glint from atop a low rise maybe a hundred yards to the north. He cast his gaze to the ridge crest just as the crown of a hat dropped down behind the ridge. He'd been watched, surveyed through a spyglass or field glasses. He'd be damned if he hadn't been. He was a veteran of the long coulees, having been an outlaw of petty sorts as a much younger man before his father, owner and operator of the Wolf Ranch in the foothills of the Wolf Mountains, had put the kibosh on that, threatening his youngest son with a bullwhipping and being stripped of his considerable inheritance. Ben Trent had taken the hangdog, humiliated Logan to the town of Three Forks and had coaxed the sheriff, Dan True, into giving his firebrand son a job as deputy sheriff.

He cast his cautious gaze again to the top of the ridge.

Who'd been eyeing him?

Could just be range riders wanting to know who was crossing their range. On the other hand, many men salivated at the sight of the handsome roan. Whoever is up there might be following him and Wolf, hoping to get their hands on the handsome horse. Many men were killed for their horses and long rifles, whatever coin or greenbacks they had in their pockets. The west was largely still a wild, untamed frontier.

Logan quickly resaddled and bridled the roan, getting everything strapped back into place. As he did, he kept a watchful eye on the crest of low ridge to the north, not wanting to get dry gulched. He stepped up into the saddle, loosed his Winchester in its sheath, and cast another cautious glance at the ridge, relieved not to see any more hatted heads and, best of all, no rifles trained on him.

When he was a good mile away from the crossing, threading his way between long, sloping rises, spiked with sage and pines that made you know you were in Montana, he began to let his guard down a bit.

"Prob'ly just a cattle puncher keeping an eye on his boss's range." Rustlers were a dime a dozen out here.

After he and Wolf had ridden another quarter mile, thundered rumbled throatily. Logan looked up. The sky was completely gray with the purple of thunderheads building and spreading. Lightning flashed in those purple clouds and a coolness touched the building breeze. The smell of rain grew stronger.

Time to seek shelter.

He surveyed a pair of high, stony dikes rising around him. On the one on his left, sitting atop a grassy apron slope peppered with pines, he thought he spied a notch cave beneath a stone overhang. Perfect . . . if the cave wasn't already occupied by some mountain lion or some other wild beast that wasn't looking for company. He swung Wolf off the trail and heeled the mount into a gallop.

Wolf took the slope easily, weaving around the pines and occasional aspens. They wound their way through the forest in about three minutes. When they came out on the other side, the sandstone dike rose before them, its face sheer. The cave was near the bottom, at the top of a low, gravelly rise sheathed by two large boulders sitting about fifteen feet out from the dike's wall. They too were shielded from above by a stone overhang.

Perfect place to shelter Wolf.

Now, if only the cave itself was unoccupied.

Logan slid his Yellowboy from its sheath, swung his right leg over the saddle horn, and slid smoothly down from the saddle. He racked a round into the Winchester's action, then moved to the cave, crouching, peering inside, which was nearly all shadow. With his gloved right index finger snugged against the cocked rifle's trigger, he stepped up to the entrance and crouched even lower, poking his head inside to give the place a thorough scrutiny.

Empty.

There was the sweet, wild smell of some animal of the forest that had recently occupied the cavern, with bits of rabbit fur and broken bones scattered here and there, but it was empty, all right.

Quickly, Logan leaned his rifle against the face of the dike and went to work, unsaddling Wolf and laying out his gear in front of the cavern entrance, under the stone overhang, which would be a good place to build a fire, if he could find dry wood before the storm hit. When he'd secured Wolf between the boulder to the left of the cavern and the dike's front wall, ground-reining the well-trained horse, he hurried off on foot back down the slope, gathering two good armloads of fallen pine and aspen branches. He'd just returned to the cavern's entrance when he felt the first drop of cold rain.

He built a fire ring from surrounding stones, beside the pile of branches, and had a smoking fire going just as the rain began to fall in earnest, the thunder building now to the tone and volume of kettle drums. Logan hauled his speckled tin coffeepot out of his burlap possibles bag, filled it from his canteen, set it on an iron claw in the fire, then sat back, enjoying the soothing warmth of the crackling flames, as the water began to sigh and gurgle.

When it came to a boil, Logan pulled a handful of ground Arbuckles from a small burlap sack, Logan pulled the pot out of the fire and dropped the coffee into the water. He set the pot back on the claw. and when it came to a boil again, the bubbling dark-brown brew gurgling out of the spout and steaming in the fire, he pulled it off the claw with a worn leather swatch, lifted the lid, added cool water from his canteen to settle the grounds, then filled one of his two white-speckled black tin cups, which he'd also pulled from his possibles sack, and sat back with the smoking cup in both hands.

A contented man.

He looked over the fire at the rain curtaining down off the overhang six feet away from him. It smelled like minerals, forest, and mountain rain. Rain smelled different in the mountains. In his thirty-four years, he had spent time in both the mountains and plains, and he knew the difference.

It was good to be back in the country. Mountain country.

He'd grown up on a mountain ranch, as beautiful a place as a man could ever see, and he'd preferred it to town. He'd punched cattle from dawn to midnight, and he'd broken horses for his father. But, to no one else's fault but his own, he'd spent a good many years working as a deputy sheriff in Three Forks and then as a saloon owner in Big Rock. He yearned for the wide-open spaces again. Running a saloon entailed a lot of responsibility, but he thought it would help him blend in with the rest of humanity. He supposed he could have lived like a mountain man, but that was a lonely life. In that life, he'd have bitten off more than he could chew. He could no longer break horses because he'd been nearly stomped and thrown to death more times than his body could tolerate. He may have been only thirty-four, but he often felt ten years older than that. When he'd come to Big Rock and bought the saloon, he'd wanted to hide from his past.

But now with one thin yellow scrap of paper with six simple words scribbled on it, he was about to ride back into the past he'd tried so many times to forget.

He may have been a grown man, but he could not defy his father.

He could not defy Ben Trent.

His aging, crippled, leonine-headed father, shorter by several inches than Logan and stove up from tangles with wild horses and dangerous and mercurial bulls and heifers—he'd even been attacked by a grizzly once and been near death for two months—still made him feel like that eighteen-year-old firebrand his father had hauled out of bed by his ear.

He wondered what the trouble was.

But for his father, the only one who knew of Logan's whereabouts, to have summoned him home it had to be for a good reason. Probably not one that Logan even wanted to hear about, but hear about it he would.

Dread touched him, tempering his enjoyment of the coffee, the fire, the rain . . .

He was glad for the storm, though. It slowed his progress along the trail back to Three Forks. He was in no hurry to arrive in that cauldron of ancient trouble, even though he knew his father was waiting for him and he'd had a damn good reason for calling his boy back to where he'd endured so much strife and scandal, dodging the bullets of the many men who'd been out to kill him and even kill the woman he'd loved.

Still loved.

*Clarita Ortiz . . .*

The sound of her name, the image of the beautiful Mexican saloon owner in his head bit him deep.

He sipped his coffee, lowered the cup, and shook his head, staring through the curtain of rain once more that acted like a very thin curtain on his past. "Damn, Pa," he said, his voice nearly drowned by the thunder and the rain, witches' fingers of lightning forking nearly right above his head. "Why . . . why . . . why? Liable to get me killed. Liable to get others killed, as well. You have to know that."

Still, Logan, whose past was a yoke on his shoulders, was on his way home . . .

"Hello, the camp!" a man's deep rose distantly, muffled by the storm.

Instantly, one of Logan's two Russian forty-fours was in his hand, his coffee cup lying on the ground between him and the fire.

His heart was a war drum in his chest.